To Liesl —

Enjoy!

HUNGER HILL

A NOVEL

Op C B

PHILIP C. BAKER

Hunger Hill
Copyright © 2023 Philip C. Baker

ISBN: 978-1-63381-361-8

The cover art was done by Elise Bolduc in 2022. Each scene was conceived as a 9x12 original done in oil pastel.

Designed and produced by:
Maine Authors Publishing
12 High Street, Thomaston, Maine
www.maineauthorspublishing.com

Printed in the United States of America

To Mom for your love of books and reading.
To Dad for your mastery of storytelling.

"Some animals are
more equal than others"

—George Orwell

CHAPTER
1

Silakha Rhenko splashed her face with water from the tap. It was three years since the smell of burning hair first insinuated itself into her memory as the real stink of follicles on fire. Her black hair had since returned, covering the only outward signs of burns on her body. The inner scars persisted. The rhythmic scraping of the motel fan got into her head, driving the twenty-year-old Russian from the bathroom. She wiped the doorknob down with her microfiber cloth.

At seventeen, Silakha had found sport in skinny-dipping. One night, she swam naked in the lake to escape the Ukrainian heat. She had suggested to a young man that he join her ten minutes after she left the compound. Her friend was named Arkady, a recent addition to her father's payroll. Moments before the tryst was to be consummated, the frustrated lovers saw the fire. They watched flames leap up, red and orange dancing like the Firebird in the Tsar's garden. Her life changed from indescribable comfort to ash and dying sparks in a matter of minutes.

Now, three years later, the wrinkled carpet in the hallway had a slight smell of mildew that irritated her. She'd checked into the cheap motel, taking a room one door from the exit, knowing she might need to escape for fresh air. Or to escape for her life, a reasonable concern given her new occupation.

She knocked on the neighboring door, which opened to the end of the chain.

"Silk?"

She said nothing. Who else would it be?

Her new partner was handsome in a big-lug kind of way. She wanted to work alone, but her Russian boss, Fyodor Umarov, had made the decision. She would work with Nurzhan Iskakov, also from Russia. Nurzhan was Umarov's electronics man. He would assist her in ways she couldn't imagine. She was skeptical. This man had shortened her name, calling her

1

Silk. Liking the economy of it and the degree of anonymity, she allowed it. Her name might as well be short, pleasant, and associated with her former wealth. Silk: fine to the hand.

"I'll unlock," the voice said. The door eased closed. When he swung it open, he turned his back to her. Rookie mistake. She was a rookie, too, but would never make such a mistake.

The walls were a textured tan. A window on the far wall was slightly eccentric, which offended her sense of symmetry. The dark-brown rug was coarse like indoor-outdoor carpet. Hers was the same. It would be rough to sleep on tonight, but Arkady, her former tutor, had said that motel beds harvested DNA the way flypaper gathered insects. A Specialist should sleep on the floor. The smell in Nurzhan's room was powerful: his aftershave. Her room smelled like Silakha Rhenko, a scent Arkady had known but no one else.

The primary egress, the door, was three strides behind her. Her secondary egress, the window, was across the room. Desk to the left. Lamp and cord, useful as a weapon. Alarm clock and cord could also be used as a weapon. Mirror. A potential weapon, a source of broken shards of glass. There was a gun on the bed. Smith & Wesson, M&P Shield. She knew the gun. Two seconds in and she knew the room and the many tools she might use to defend herself.

Now she could think about her partner. Nurzhan stood to her left, a meter beyond reach. Her body against his would be a mismatch; he doubled her weight. She worked herself between him and the gun. She focused on every twitch of muscle in his body, every slide of his eyes.

Nurzhan took in an eyeful of her. Unauthorized but understandable. She was exposed; she might as well have been wearing paint. She ignored Nurzhan's attention. The hugging fabric was far better than the bunching of cotton or wool or rayon binding and pinching into her skin.

"This kind of work we do tonight," Nurzhan said, "is new to me, Silk."

The AC unit, mounted on the wall eight strides in front of her, droned like distant thunder. Despite herself, she focused on the noise and it intensified to the rumble of a city bus or the roar of an airliner. She wanted to squeeze it from her skull. With her hands pressing at her temples, she strode to it and snapped it off.

"It's too hot, Silk. Leave it on."

He was right; it was hot. If Silakha Rhenko knew anything, it was heat. Nonetheless, her first three words to her partner were, "I hate AC." She walked away from the dormant appliance and focused on quiet and why she preferred working alone. Silk Rhenko was not at the normal end of any kind of spectrum and she knew it. Welcome to my world, whoever you are. Deal with it.

CHAPTER
2

At six-foot-two, Detective Basil Keene used all the legroom in his 1968 Dodge Charger. He glanced into the rearview and ran his hand over the graying stubble of his head then returned his gaze to the door they'd been watching.

Keene's partner, Dennis Hurley, said from the robin's-egg-blue vinyl passenger seat, "You sure he keeps a regular schedule?" He questioned Keene about Steve Falstaff, the object of their scrutiny. Then, "What time did your guy say Falstaff leaves the office?"

Keene had a guy. A confidential informant. A guy who knew Falstaff.

Keene said, "Six o'clock. As I said, Dennis, should be any time now." Keene wasn't a patient man, and his little patience with Hurley was waning. The partners had covered this subject. "The fundamental truth, Dennis, is that Falstaff tends—the operative word—*tends* to leave the building around six. Okay?"

Hurley grunted. Keene's partner was ten years younger than he. He was an enthusiastic weekend athlete who ran 5K's and 10K's every Saturday. Had to, he said—he liked booze, food, and women too much. The truth was, as Keene knew, he liked a little whiskey and good food but who doesn't? And Hurley seemed to have fallen hard for one woman, Michaela Mack. It seemed that womanizing was a thing of the past.

Cars passed. The migration home had started an hour ago but intensified with the six o'clock quitting time.

"He's late," Hurley observed.

Keene sat still as a fox fastened on a scent and said, "He'll be out."

Another couple of minutes.

"He's more late," Hurley said.

Hurley was right, Falstaff was later than Keene's informant had said.

Five minutes had stretched to ten, and Keene was devising ways to get revenge with his so-called informant.

The detectives were surveilling an antiques and jewelry establishment, Nelson and Falstaff. Steve Falstaff, a nobody in life or the world of crime, was the proprietor, and Keene hadn't found any kind of Nelson. The down-market establishment was substantially a pawnshop. If the informant was correct, Falstaff was no more than a minor fence.

Hurley said, "I got eleven past already."

Keene said, "Keep your shorts on." The exactitude of digitalism was a chafing annoyance at any time, but when Keene was in a state of high agitation because an informant's intelligence appeared to be anything but, the specificity of time somehow infuriated him.

To fill the silence Hurley said, "Sucks about the City Council."

"Yeah." Keene snapped his gum and ground his teeth, not wanting to discuss the second "non-recommend for promotion" from the City Council. "To paraphrase Plato, it is what it is."

"Plato said that?" Hurley paused, trying to decide whether to go on. Then he said, "Did the shooting come up?"

"Hey," Keene said, saved by Falstaff from having to tell Hurley that this was none of his business. "There he is."

They watched as Falstaff started down the steps. He was dressed like a tourist, a guy going out for a cocktail. He was a small man whose triangular face made the standard weasel look cultured and trustworthy. A brown mustache dripped into a goatee.

Hurley swung his door open and lifted himself from the Charger as though the core of his body was on a spring. He called Falstaff's name and approached him. Keene couldn't hear the conversation. Hurley, naturally affable, smiled openly. Falstaff spoke with his arms folded over his chest. Hurley's demeanor changed. He folded his arms as well and closed in. The two men jawed face to face.

Keene got out of the car. No spring in his core.

Falstaff ran into the lengthening shadows.

Hurley chased and Falstaff saw Keene and picked up speed.

Falstaff ran like a halfback toward Trader Joe's grocery. Hurley stopped to avoid being mown down by a pickup truck towing a trailer, then ran down the street parallel to the store. He applied the logic that if a fugitive runs in the front door, he's likely to find an alternative exit, for example, the back door.

Keene followed Falstaff into the grocery, running hard. He quickly had a stitch in his side but ignored it. He ran past a clerk with a snaking collection of grocery carts and a woman with a cart large enough to carry a head of lettuce and an onion. He nearly plowed into a ponytailed man who was headed for the salad bar.

Falstaff went down the frozen foods aisle. Keene was still at the Chicken Kiev when Falstaff skidded past the Tater Tots. He broke around the endcap; Keene was losing ground. The fugitive dealer of antiques darted into the wine section, slowed, and swept armloads of French reds off the shelves resulting in a slickened floor and a treacherous minefield of broken glass. He turned for the emergency exit and crashed through the door.

The French reds maneuver was effective. Keene was forced to hopscotch his way through the carnage. Trader Joe's helpless sommelier looked on and wiped his face with both hands, frustration and possibly tears behind his corkscrewing fingers.

Outside the back door was a smokers' pen enclosed with a chain-link fence with green bands woven through the links. Falstaff sprang to the fence and was climbing when Keene came through the door. Keene demanded his quarry stop, his effort about as effective as a hound barking up a tree at a squirrel.

Falstaff glanced over his shoulder from the top of the fence and dropped out of sight. Keene assessed his options and broke to the left, where it seemed he could run around the barrier rather than scale it. The fence had slowed Falstaff considerably.

When Keene rounded the fence, he discovered that Falstaff had stumbled upon a junkyard of castaway iron and steel. Falstaff had stopped short and found himself at an impasse, Keene to his left and Hurley having appeared on his right. A yard of immovable junk was arrayed before him.

"Freeze!" Hurley said from the street side of the junkyard, his gun trained on the antiques dealer.

Keene bent at the waist and sucked in oxygen.

Hurley said, "Hold it right there, Falstaff."

Breathlessly, Keene stepped over a rusting transmission. His foot landed on an unseen pipe, which rolled out from under him, and he dropped with a hyperextended knee and a stretched gluteus maximus. Which was, techni-cally, literally, and in the vernacular, a pain in the ass.

———————◆◆◆———————

The Charger rumbled to a stop, and Keene crutched his way past the recycling and trash containers and slipped in the back door, painfully happy to be home. He tossed his grease-smeared jacket to the refurbished church pew in the entryway. He leaned the crutches against the wall as he flipped his cap on top of the jacket. Doctor Flint, Keene's humorless dermatologist, had urged the detective to wear a hat. Mowing the lawn. Meeting a confidential informant on the docks. "Playing golf," he had said. "Do your fifteen-years-down-the-road self a favor; wear a hat now." Keene had winkingly called the dermatologist Dr. Skin Flint, but the doc hadn't acknowledged the joke. The doc was a dick; the joke was funny. Screw the doc. Still, Keene wore the hat. Now, he wore an ace bandage wrapped tightly around his knee and thigh.

He stopped in the kitchen and poured some Jim Beam. The bourbon warmed his throat. He hobbled into the bedroom and listened to Melena's soft snore. Her breathing was regular and deep. She slept on her side, her back to his side of the bed. The bathroom door was ajar and he pushed through it quietly, the only light a green afterglow from the digital clock. He snugged the door closed and washed his face, brushed his teeth, never turning the light on. He used the john and slid into bed caring for his left side. He drifted off, Falstaff not far from his mind. Falstaff, the Council, and the shooting that the Councilors couldn't seem to get beyond crowded his mind.

———————◆◆◆———————

Keene woke to the alarm and the ache in his ass. He remembered Falstaff, Trader Joe's, wine, and junk. And an unseen pipe. He flailed at the alarm clock and welcomed the sight of Melena putting a stop to all the nonsense.

"I don't know why," she said in her husky morning voice, not sharp enough to be resentful. Then she stopped because it was the same thing every morning. He didn't have to hear her grievances again. She walked to the alarm clock, which was closer to him, and turned it off. It was the routine of a married couple and it didn't make sense, but it made Keene happy and he welcomed the sight of Melena because she was nice to look at.

"You got home late?" Melena asked as she wrapped herself in a satin robe. She was used to the unpredictable hours of a policeman and accustomed to Keene's occasional non-life-threatening injuries.

He got up and brushed his teeth. She did too. He splashed water on his face. She, hers. Her dark skin, flawless. Her face was framed by black hair, cut so it fell in waves short of her shoulders. Her eyes were the color of a moonless night sky.

She and Keene had met twenty-one years earlier when she was seventeen. Twenty years of marriage and zero kids later—sixteen years of trying to not have kids, four years of serious effort toward the affirmative—Melena ambled into their kitchen and started her daily cup of Cuban coffee. She wandered to the deck where Keene was reading his habitual paper and drinking his daily cup of Keurig coffee. She took a deck chair next to him.

"Lawn looks good," Keene said. It smelled freshly mown. Usually, late in the summer, Melena ran the mower over baked brown grass bent in the sun. There was that relentless drive that he loved about her. Dead brown grass be damned, she was going to mow. It's what she did. But that summer, her lawn was green as Ireland. The late summer flowers—summersweets, daylilies, and petunias—thrived in the humidity and added their singular fragrances to the perfume of Melena's yard.

He sipped his coffee and told Melena about the previous night.

After hearing the full story with only a minor comment or two, she changed the subject. "They didn't take the broken recycling container." She added, "Again."

"Yeah," Keene said. "I almost took a header over it last night."

The recycling container, deployed every Thursday evening for years, hadn't survived the Thursday night two weeks earlier, at least not in a functional condition. An elderly neighbor had experienced a self-diagnosed senior moment and ran over the container when returning from a Shriner's meeting. Melena suspected the neighbor's affliction had been early-onset drunkenness, nothing more, but Keene reminded her about the fundamental legal principle of presumption of innocence. The container broke nearly in two and its identity as an acceptable recycling vehicle was damaged beyond repair.

Keene opened his laptop.

"That damn recycling container," he muttered. "Try throwing away a recycling container. I talked to a guy at Public Works. He said it *is* recyclable. I don't know why they won't take it. Its essential nature, its containerness, has been altered..."

Keene had learned about the essential nature of things while studying the Greek philosophers during an irrationally exuberant first year of college, determined to philosophize his way into the beds of coeds. When the strategy proved to be an ill-conceived notion, and the subject matter became too dense for Keene's rational mind, he declared his major to be Criminal Justice and hadn't looked back. Then he met and fell in love with Melena Ramos.

Having spent her first seventeen years in a village outside Havana, Melena was an expert on many things: Cuban coffee and heat and becoming an enthusiastic American girl chief among them.

Melena and her father, Eduardo Ramos, had emigrated from Cuba a year before she met Keene. Eduardo was an MIT-trained chemist who worked in the hydrocarbon industry, a low-pressure position in Cuba, whose oil reserves were in quart containers in petrol stations. His skills, however, were valued by his comrades in Russia, and he was welcome to visit Moscow anytime. Eduardo wanted to defect to America so he devised a plan. He had carte blanche to travel to Moscow (which was the one place he *didn't* want to visit), but Moscow it was.

He arranged for airline tickets for himself and his oldest daughter, Melena, ostensibly on an educational trip to the capital city of Russia, the land of onion domes, borscht, and frustrated KGB assassins. On the tarmac in Frankfurt, at a scheduled refueling stop, a garment bag in the hold caught fire, an unfortunate mixture of chemicals igniting at just the wrong time. Think liquid accelerant, a glass pipette, and a powdered combustible with a sudden influx of oxygen that occurs upon landing. The plane, with an unexplained fire in the luggage compartment, was evacuated. The chemical genius and his daughter made a full-out run to the terminal, found a customs and border protection officer, and demanded political asylum.

Ramos went to work retrieving the rest of the family while Melena went to work becoming an American girl. Her English was excellent and her cultural adaptability, acute. At seventeen, she met Basil Keene, a new officer of the Fort Lauderdale Police Department. Her father had a healthy respect for everything American, and the law was no different. He was happy his daughter wanted to marry a police officer when she turned eighteen, not considered young for a Cuban *chica* to marry.

━━━━•••━━━━

Keene's leg ached. A malevolent deerfly buzzed his head.

Melena said from amid some Cuban steam, "I take it the Council recommended against." She reclaimed her deck chair.

"Uh, yeah."

"When were you going to tell me?"

He closed the laptop. "I didn't want to talk about it."

"Basil, we have to talk about it," Melena said.

Promotions to higher office in the Portland Police Department, sergeant and higher, were considered by the City Council and given a "recommend" or "recommend against" vote. Either recommendation carried a lot of weight.

Keene said, "Once again, they recommended against."

This was Keene's second bite at the apple. The first, six months ago, had resulted in the same judgment, and the previous Chief had accepted the advice.

"The Chief can override the recommendation, right?"

"That's true, but an Interim Chief can't. Charlie's the Interim Chief right now. It's up to the Commissioner, and he'll never override the Council. He's afraid of them."

"He's an ass," she said.

"He's the ass who signs my paycheck."

"Well, we'll put it aside for a week, right?"

Keene and Melena looked forward to their annual end-of-summer cruise this year maybe more than usual. Last year's cruise on their sailboat, the *Ventosa*, had been canceled. When you're considered a possible murderer, you don't cruise on your 38-foot yacht. This year was different. For one, he was no longer suspected of murder. Now that yesterday's injury had added to the Council's insult, he and Melena were ready to go. The City Council's decision had forced him to wonder if he'd ever be out from under the dark cloud of the incident of a year ago. Keene had shot and killed the Eastern Prom Sniper while on duty. But could an unarmed man be the EPS, as the press had come to call him? Keene had shot and killed an unarmed black man. Why would a sniper be without a gun?

When he was a recruit in Florida, Keene had ridden with an older colleague who served as a mentor, a man named Bert. Bert had been a cop philosopher who spoke freely about his theories of policing. He had told Keene once that they must treat the lowest criminal as if he was their boss, and that fact should always be remembered. He had said, "When you are arresting an individual, you are arresting the Chief. Don't ever forget that." It was a question of respect, and respect was due to all human beings; Keene knew that and had never forgotten it. The fact remained, however: He had shot an unarmed man.

CHAPTER
3

The office was a small room behind the kitchen that was the beating heart of Sully's Tap, hot as freakin' Hades. Eileen Mack opened Twitter on her phone. She tapped in "Job Interviews" hoping to find advice. All she got was one successful interviewee after another crowing about their brilliance but no guidance, no tips, no tutorial on technique. In the column to the right, she touched on "Jobseekers" and was plunged further into the unhelpful world of others' successes. She rolled her eyes as she scrolled lower and lower to the purgatorial depths of useless suggestions from the Twitter world.

The framed victualer's license on a wall in the office of Sully's Tap appeared in good order, she guessed. Up-to-date, anyway. Eileen glanced back at the phone. Somehow the Twitter subject matter had morphed into a tweet about psychokinesis. If nothing else, she liked the word. The Tweeter was named Babylon Psycho, which made the whole thing worth coming back to.

A further glance around the office revealed a laptop, open on a small desk with some kind of business software, all green and tan lines with numbers and letters sprayed across them. It appeared Mr. Sullivan paid attention to business, a good trait in a prospective employer.

"Sorry to hold you up," Gary Sullivan, owner of Sully's Tap, said as he moved through the door. If Eileen was honest, the sudden entrance of the owner spooked her a little. He was tall and skinny. ~~The mustache made him look a little pervy, a little child molester-y.~~ "Three amigos just showed up. Gotta keep them happy. Three of my most loyal customers." He held her application in his hand. The bar owner looked at the application for a while and, in the end, said, "Which Mack is your dad?"

Eileen's hand went to her cotton-candy-pink hair and moved a swatch of it behind her ear. All by itself. The hand's owner wasn't aware of the movement because the question—the very first question of the interview—

presented a minefield to navigate. She wanted to tell him Mike, Michaela's dad, her uncle. Or make up a name. But she couldn't do it. She couldn't disown her father. She'd been sure about renouncing Satan upon her confirmation. That was a no-brainer. But abandoning her dad? Though there seemed a potential upside to the renunciation, it was just wrong. "Francis," she said with a sigh of resignation. She could only hope the answer didn't disqualify her out of hand.

"How *is* Franny?" Sullivan asked.

You mean, she thought, since you banned him from this establishment for being drunk, disorderly, and exceptionally unappealing? "Um...he's okay...I guess."

Mr. Sullivan's smile was meant to be comforting but still had a little pervy-ness to it. "Tell me about yourself. How old're you? Says here..."

She clasped her slick hands in her lap. "Twenty-three," she lied, just the way she'd practiced.

The Greek expert on age misrepresentation had suggested this age. "You see, when you turn twenty-three you get a different license." He fished one out of his wallet. "For example, like this. What they call landscape," he explained. "Show me yours." Eileen had pulled her legitimate, brand-new driver's license—the ink only recently dried—and showed it to the Greek. The man pointed out in a professorial manner that the one the State of Maine had issued was printed in the portrait attitude. Eileen, sixteen years old at the time, had only had the genuine license for a couple of months. The Greek had said she looked older than her sixteen years. "Like," he said, "goddamned close to seventeen. So, we make you twenty-three? Don't have to remake it in a couple of years. Right? It's a win-win." His enthusiasm might have been worth twice the money. If she'd had it. They agreed, if you're going to lie, lie big. A hundred and thirty dollars for his services was an equitable exchange in Eileen's assessment. Francis, who held lawful title to the cash, wasn't consulted on the squareness of the deal.

"I didn't realize Franny had a daughter...so old," Mr. Sullivan said.

"Yup," she said. "Twenty-three."

"Huh," he said. He changed the subject: "You like people? You a people person?"

She was interviewing for a bartender's job. Of course, he wanted to know if she got along with your average Joe.

"People?" she said. "I love people. I often think, 'where would we be without people?' Y'know?"

Jesus, why couldn't she keep her mouth shut? *Where would we be without people?* How stupid is that? Bafflingly stupid.

"Yeah," Mr. Sullivan said. "Um. You got any experience, Eileen?"

She hadn't thought about this one either. Why had she gone into this interview so poorly prepared? Twitter had failed her. Always did. Stupid social media. Typical, she thought, typical of me. Cripe sake. He thinks I'm twenty-three. He supposes I must have experience. Think, think, think. "Uh, I've been making drinks for my dad since I was seven... if that counts. Like, ten years...or...more, I guess, like, fif–, like, whatever twenty-three minus seven is, I mean." She laughed like a seventeen-year-old trying to pass herself off as a twenty-three-year-old. How can I be so stupid? Ten years? I'm an idiot.

"But you haven't worked in a bar?" The owner of Sully's Tap seemed to ignore the faux pas, the tremendous, towering, Eileen-toppling fuck-up.

"Not yet. But you gotta start somewhere, right, Mr. Sullivan?"

"Can I reach you at this number?"

❧

Damn, she thought as she scuffed along the sidewalk. Experience? How was she supposed to have experience? She was seventeen years old, cripe sake. She was seventeen years old and she needed money. She couldn't live with Francis much longer. She had to get out. Her father wasn't bad to her. He wasn't violent. He wasn't an abusive reprobate. Dad was merely a reprobate. He slept on the couch a lot. Francis Mack wasn't passive-aggressive; he was aggressively passive. Eileen was more responsible for him than the other way around. So, it was time to leave, and force him to grow up. She wanted to find an apartment of her own. Like Michaela, her glamorous cousin. Michaela was a bartender at the Cougar Club, an upscale gentlemen's club, and made good money. Eileen wanted to start making her way. On her own. Francis didn't even know she'd graduated from high school a year early. Didn't care. Didn't know she'd gotten damned good grades. She thought she'd go to college if she could make some money first. Before that, it would be first and last month's rent for a place of her own. Like Michaela.

As she scuffed along, she retrieved her phone from the back pocket of her skinny jeans. She was horrified that mom jeans were taking over the fashion world. She liked them; they were cool, the thing. But she was horrified because she'd spent the last purloined hundred bucks from Francis on skinny jeans. One of these days he was going to catch her. After the hundred for the jeans, the one-thirty for the ID... She checked Twitter to help keep her mind busy. Babylon Psycho was a cool name. Psychokinesis, he explained as a preamble, was the ability to move things with your mind. In her advanced physics class, she'd learned about creating movement with sound waves. That seemed more likely, as sound waves were made evident in certain media... Her phone rang. She didn't recognize the number.

When she'd first gotten the phone, she'd considered a salutation of "Yeah" like they do on TV. "Yeah," like, let's get on with this. Kind of like saying "What?" like, what do you want? Do you know that Eileen Mack is crazy-busy? But that was sort of unkind and clearly on the south end of the northbound truth train. She decided on:

"Eileen Mack, ready when you are."

Mr. Sullivan said, "Just what I wanted to hear; when can you start?"

———•••———

Eileen raced up the back stairs of 6 Romasco Lane making more noise than, by all the laws of nature, she should. As she pounded the stairs, the picture of the Last Supper rattled on the wall. She thought about vibrations and waves and radio waves, and sound waves in particular. If Eileen Mack could transfer soundwaves through the air to liquid media and mix a whiskey sour, for example, she'd be a highly sought-after celebrity bartender. Kind of like Michaela at the Cougar. It was no secret that Micky had a devoted clientele at the Club. The bartender who can figure out this remote mixing thing will never be fired. Not even for being underage and having pink hair.

The beige carpet had been worn to burlap where Eileen pivoted at the top of the stairs. This brought her to Number 4, and she fumbled with the key in one hand and held the grocery bags in the other. Wait, she thought, remote openers for apartment doors; cripe sake, the possibilities are endless. The door crept ajar and she kicked it the rest of the way and wondered about humming a note, a particular tone, that would make the liquid in a drink start swimming on its own.

A year ago, she had changed her hair color from mousy Mack-brown to cotton-candy pink. She'd taken a selfie and paid the hundred and thirty bucks she'd stolen from her father's booze fund for a fake ID. This was soon after Kaye had left. Eileen missed her mother. Kaye was pretty and voluptuous and fetching. Eileen was plain and slight and easily overlooked. Kaye had finally taken a better offer. Eileen wasn't sure where Kaye had gone, but she guessed Boston. Kaye would call eventually. Eileen was sure.

Dark wood, carved with initials and a penis, trimmed the walls of the hallway. This hallway led her to the kitchen, and she wondered why, given the opportunity, her brothers inevitably drew a penis.

Eileen had slept in a bureau drawer when she was a baby. No room for a crib. Kaye and Francis's only daughter had waited for hours while the three boys used the bathroom and used up the hot water. In the department of lovely memories, Eileen clung to the one of brushing Kaye's hair while Kaye sat on her bed in a satiny robe and counted to a hundred and Eileen ran her hands through the silky and fragrant auburn cascade and breathed deeply because somehow, she'd known the moment would end with a finality that she couldn't control. *Ninety-eight, ninety-nine—*

"Make me a drink," Francis called from the living room.

"A drink? It's eleven in the a.m. Are you already drunk?" Eileen hated to sound like a nag, but she felt she should press the point.

"Drunk?" he slurred. "I'm as straight as a rattlesnake with his dick in an outlet." He raised himself from the couch. He continued, "You're good at that, Ei, making drinks. Be good at something and you'll be okay in life. That's my motto."

Interesting, she thought. Aren't mottos meant to be expressed as an organizing tenet of one's life? Or can they be marooned in a mental malaise and still serve as philosophy? The list of Francis's life accomplishments was short. He was a horrible dad, a horrible husband, not even a good drunk despite his dedication to the craft. But he was right; if she managed to do something that nobody else could, she'd be well above okay.

He watched her drop the second emptied bag to the ground.

"What's new?" Francis asked.

"I have an idea, Francis. I think I can mix a drink, like, remotely," she said.

"What does that mean?"

"I think I can mix a drink with soundwaves."

He said, "What in the actual fuck are you talking about?" There it was, Francis's undiscovered talent—he was gifted as an active listener.

"I think I can hum a note, for example," Eileen said, "and the contents of the glass will automatically turn into a, like, a whirlpool of liquids mixing themselves. You know?"

"Jesus, Ei. Get a life."

"Right," she said. "Descartes has spoken."

"You can't even sing. Mix me a drink."

She spoke from the kitchen, "Like the note that opera singers sing, you know? That shatters glass. Like that."

Eileen took his drink to him. "I think if I can figure it out, I'll be able to mix a drink without a swizzle stick or spoon or even a shaker glass." She held the glass before him, hummed a middle C, and twisted the glass so the gin and tonic turned into a swirling mixture. "See?" she said.

"Jesus, Ei, sometimes you need a shaker glass. You know? How ya gonna make a vodka gimlet, Chrissake?"

"You have a valid point there, Francis."

"Gimme that. Why don't you call me Dad anymore?"

It was nearing noon. She grabbed her bag and raced out the door without saying goodbye. She was a busy working girl now.

Maybe it's not soundwaves; maybe it's brain waves as Babylon Psycho purports. Mind over matter. If she could pull that one off, she could tend bar wherever she wanted. Eileen had a vision: a job in Boston; she, walking down Newbury Street, shopping bags crooked over her arm, sniffing the air and seeing her mother: *Kaye! So nice to see you. How have you been?* Kaye, loaded down with packages as well, looking a tiny bit tired. Eileen would flip her cotton-candy-pink hair, and Kaye would say: *Oh, Eileen, I love what you've done with your hair!*

CHAPTER
4

Silk Rhenko's dark eyes, donated by her Philippine mother, were drawn to Nurzhan's face and his blue eyes and flashing white smile that balanced out his heavy features. Despite herself, she found him attractive.

The big Russian motioned to his bed, on which he had arrayed some equipment: two transmitters, two cameras, and two wads of putty. The transmitters and cameras were manufactured by a company called Micronics which made miniature electronic components. Each minuscule transmitter would receive and send signals from the two Micronics cameras, each no bigger than a coin. The two wads of putty, the size, and color of a pencil eraser, were wrapped in cellophane.

Arkady had first suggested her ultimate career choice. He had been a Specialist. He was invited to her father's compound when an individual threatened the organization and required cancellation. He had stayed, befriended his new boss's daughter, and convinced Silakha that she could provide these services as well. Under certain circumstances, a female assassin could prove to be valuable to the organization, and Silakha was ultimately trustworthy. But then the fire. Arkady would take care of her, he had promised.

"Putty." Nurzhan lifted the wrapped wads as if she hadn't guessed what the material was. "Place camera, okay?"

She didn't answer. The purpose was self-evident.

"Camera, of course; transmitter sends signal to cloud so we can receive from a distance." She remained aware of her surroundings and kept the door within a couple of steps. As he named them, he lifted each device. His English wasn't bad but not as good as Silk's. He continued, "I hooked up these devices. Doubled."

"*Paired* them," she corrected.

"Yes, of course. Paired them," he said. Then, "Blue tooth." He put the items back on the bed. "Okay, Silk. Your mobile, please."

She slipped the phone from the waistband of her pants. He waited while she performed the security protocol.

"Open app store," he said. She did and he read a complicated series of numbers and letters to her. She entered the code, clicked download, and opened the app. A window showed a close-up video of the firearm on the bed. He picked up a tiny camera and pointed it at Silk's face. "Is good, okay?" he said. "I program these things."

Now her phone showed a high-resolution video of her face and the bags under her eyes like ash stains.

She asked, "How close?"

"The camera can be, so, maybe twenty meters from transmitter. Is far, yes? Even around the corner. Through buildings." He fussed with the equipment, then said, "So you use camera to look at my brother, Yakov, at the corner. Is strip club called Cougar? You know this?"

"Yes, of course," she said. Silk knew of Yakov. He was the perfect specimen to be a strip club bouncer, big and mean. He would provide a valuable service as a lookout for the job.

"You will cover the back as I go through the front door," Silk said. She would surprise the butcher. He would wonder who she was and how she had arrived through a locked front door. "You will be at the back door, ready if he runs." But Silk knew the butcher wouldn't run from a small woman.

Nurzhan asked, "You got the thing...is called what? The *prezervativ*?"

"Condom. Yes, I have it."

He looked her up and down and reached out as if to touch her. She whirled away from him, grabbed the 9mm from the bed, and trained the gun on his face in a single motion.

"Don't," she growled from a fight-or-flight crouch, the M&P Shield tracking on his forehead. "Never, without permission."

Three years earlier, the night of the fire, her nudity had saved her life. In hysteria, she had charged toward the out-of-control blaze. Clothing would have ignited and burned her alive. Only her hair flamed up. Arkady caught her. But the searing heat had caused damage to her peripheral neuropathic system. Arkady had taken her into his home, and when merely wearing clothes ignited pain and discomfort, he brought her to specialists who pronounced that she would be hypersensitive to touch for the rest of her life.

Nurzhan put his hands up and begged her forgiveness. "Only want to know where you put these things. I am sorry. I don't see no pocket or something like that."

"Don't ever touch," she said rising from her crouch. She looked across the iron sights at his face. He was four strides away. She relaxed the gun.

He made a good point, but the cameras, transmitters, and wads of putty fit in her small fist. The condom fit in her cheek like a wad of gum. She jacked the rack of the Shield and a bullet ejected onto the bed. She dropped the mag, confirmed it was fully loaded, and jammed it back in. The gun, tucked into the waistband of her tight lycra pants in the middle of her lower back, wasn't comfortable but it would do. "I'll take the gun," she said.

• • •

The chore of driving fell to Nurzhan. He drove to the commuter lot at the base of Hunger Hill. At nine p.m., most of the slots were open. He backed into one near the bridge abutment that was decorated with boxcar graffiti.

Nerves pinpricked Silk's neck. Her hands were bloodlessly cold. She was about to kill a man. Tonight, she would sleep as a newly coronated assassin and tomorrow drink the coffee of an experienced man-killer. The work she had started with Arkady would finally pay off. They had fired endless rounds at the range. He'd taught her breaking-and-entering techniques and the management of the kill scene afterward. But the one skill he'd identified as preeminent was her desensitized moral perspective and, as he well knew, you can't teach crazy. Arkady had recognized her reckless social conscience as much like his own, and he knew he could train her to kill. Even with all these skills, her blood still ran chill through her veins and, like a glass of cold water, her skin beaded with sweat.

Slipping unnoticed along Washington Avenue, Nurzhan said to Silk, "I'll be behind store in five minutes."

The street was empty, deserted in the humid weather.

The store, she thought. Dropping articles was a nasty habit derived from Eastern European languages. *I'll be behind store* sounds unintelligent. *I'll be behind* the *store*. When she was in school, while her father was still alive, the girls had to be drilled day after day with article quizlets. For instance, *The boy went to the store to buy milk* was confusing for the girls. *The boy*, and *the store*, but not *the milk*? It was more efficient to say *Boy went to store to buy milk* but so goddamned Russian. Silk had worked on her English by watching YouTube. She still practiced. *The girl went to the store to kill butcher.* No. *The butcher, the butcher, the butcher. The girl went to the store to kill the butcher.*

Nurzhan's devices were crucial, but he himself was not. She had discovered a trick to subdue a man twice her size. Tonight, she would demonstrate to Fyodor Umarov that she could be his exclusive weapon; no need for a supporting team. Silk Rhenko could perform as a lone snow leopard prowling the streets of Portland, Maine.

She pinched a piece of putty and pressed it to one of the cameras, which she placed underneath the brick windowsill. *Girl went to market to kill butcher.* She adjusted the camera to pick up the door of the Cougar Club. *The girl went to the market to kill the butcher.* She opted not to place the second camera. Retrieval of the second camera was a step she could avoid. The bar, Sully's Tap, was easily visible over her shoulder. Adrenaline charged her heart. Her blood had finally heated up, and her fingers shook as they had on the night of the fire.

If Yakov made a signal—hands up for wait, thumbs up for okay, a throat slash for abort—she would catch it in her phone screen. Arkady had said to use all the resources at her disposal. Always. Silk pushed the impromptu notion away. She had many tasks to perform. Camera retrieval was one extra step she didn't have time for. Go away, Arkady.

The tight waistband of her pants held the transmitter firmly. She worked the door lock. Use all available resources. Arkady, she thought, second-guessing is no good to an assassin. She worked the card in the lock.

Yakov had said the Cougar Club was slow on Sunday nights. She eyed her phone. She worked the lock.

Silk checked Sully's over her shoulder. Then the phone screen. Then the bar again. No one. The card was slippery in her sweaty grip. The strip club's music thumped, still muted by the closed door. The butcher blared music from the rear of the market. She could break in with a sledgehammer. She slid the card up and down. The lock didn't click open. The lycra was soaked through at her armpits. She looked over her shoulder. The bar, nothing. Strip club, no activity, but then Yakov threw his hands into the air.

Silk turned her back to the market door and flattened against it, invisible in the dark, her black clothing a perfect camouflage. Her eyes stung with sweat. Her body responded aggressively to the ancient fight-or-flight conditions. Sweat-soaked, she watched Yakov drop his hands when two guys came out and staggered away. Yakov appeared to glance into the club. A minute passed. No signal from Yakov. She waited, her back pressed against the door. Her hair was wet and ropy. The music still boomed from the back of the market. She wouldn't see the butcher coming if he'd heard anything, but how could he? Still no signal. The butcher would have his gun if he was coming, and she'd never see it. The gun was in the register. The plan would fail if...if he had the gun; if he shot her as a common burglar. She was holding her breath. She released it slowly into the mist of the night. If he killed her, she would die anonymously. Acceptable for her employer, of course, but did she want to leave without a trace? The job, yes. The world?

CHAPTER
5

Keene was at the controls of an airplane and didn't know why. He had inadvertently put the plane in a steep dive. He'd meant to do the opposite, but he'd struggled with the controls. He thought he should pull on the stick to increase altitude but stupidly pushed it away. Keene realized that he was seconds from driving the nose of the plane into the earth. Into Wheeler, because Wheeler stood directly in front of Keene with his hands up. With a lucidity reserved for such things, Keene recognized that he was seconds away from dying. He said out loud, "I'm about to die. This is what it feels like." The death sensation buzzed in his nerves, his body preparing for disintegration, the final assignment entrusted to the mortal vessel. He and Larry Wheeler would do it together this time.

Like a bystander, he watched the plane crash, watched himself and Wheeler, the Eastern Prom Sniper, die.

He sensed motion—Melena to his right. He was awake, and this awareness replaced his hallucinatory anxiety. Melena repositioned herself in the bed next to him, and snuggled down into her Sunday morning sleep.

Enough light invaded the bedroom to illuminate Melena's shape and reassure Keene he'd been dreaming. He pushed the sheet away and dropped his legs from the bed. Soreness crept from his thigh into his butt. He turned and touched Melena because this morning he needed the connection with her and with his world like an electrical charge seeks ground. He'd not had a dream this disturbing in a long time. Wheeler had kept to himself, nocturnally anyway, for months.

Keene lifted himself from the bed with a combined groan and yawn and limped into the bathroom, where he sleepily and with intent, pushed Wheeler out of his mind. He thought if he'd stuck with philosophy in college, he might get out of bed on Sunday mornings without a pain in the ass. But he'd made his decision: He was a cop and must live with the aches and pains and nighttime horrors. The mirror showed a guy in the process of aging. Not possible—he was only forty-nine. Fifty this fall. The sore leg was making him feel older. There was no denying the wrinkles around the eyes, lines like high-tension wires on the forehead, graying stubble. But seriously, he was only forty-nine. He had twenty years on the force, twenty-four in law enforcement. Half his life. Retirement? He'd get another shot at the sergeant's exam and the promotion. He wanted the advancement badly if for no other reason than self-affirmation.

His career had run a smooth course, as smooth as a cop's career could. Until a year ago. Many—most—officers go twenty years without shooting a suspect. Most go twenty without discharging their service weapons at all other than on the range. The killing of a suspect was reserved for a very few officers across the country. A small club of men in blue. Keene was in the club. The City Council found this to be a problem. Keene did too. That's not why he had signed up.

He was a peace officer, a keeper of the peace. Or was he kidding himself? The night he killed the man officially changed things. He was a brute, a violent beast, an executioner. He must admit it.

The demographics of Portland had changed over the twenty years Keene had been on the force. He knew as well as anybody that a cop's ethnicity was critical vis-à-vis the race of a suspect. One incident had proved this, and the incident, the shooting, had put his career path in jeopardy. One comment—one stupid comment—and he was nearly fired. He thought maybe he should have been. Now he worked, not for a paycheck, not for self-satisfaction, not to serve and protect, but for redemption. Perhaps if Charlie was the Chief, he'd be an advocate, a tie-breaker, or a workaround. Regardless, Charlie's promotion seemed the only way for Keene to put this incident behind him.

Keene lathered up and began to shave. Melena wants to move the clock. Which would require moving the bedside table to Melena's turf. Which would require moving the bed to allow the closet door to open. Which would make his side of the bed too close to the bathroom resulting in injury or death when he simply wanted to take a middle-of-the-night piss. Why don't we just switch sides of the bed?

The overhead fan, lacking spirit or ambition, pushed hot air around with a shameful indifference to Keene's suffering. Melena insisted that

Keene didn't know what *hot* was. The AC didn't come on until a third figure of Fahrenheit was achieved. Therefore, the air in which they lived and slept and attempted to procreate remained hot.

He put a K-cup in the coffeemaker and filled the carafe. The Keurig burbled, groaned, and finally sighed, indicating his coffee was ready.

He looked at his phone. A new message. Hurley. His fellow detective, colleague, and coconspirator in the recent Falstaff imbroglio had texted.

"hope not too late. switch shifts today? need to be someplace eight p.m. text me."

Keene thought, why not? He could sleep in and have the rare opportunity to make his partner's day. This would allow him to adjust the timing on the Charger. Or putter on the boat. The *Ventosa* was a 38-foot sloop built by Sabre Yachts in Casco, Maine, in 1986. She had classic lines, pleasing to mariners and lubbers alike.

"No prob. Got a date?"

The return was immediate: "thanks, man. yeah, date. M and me dinner. her night off."

Hurley's texts always had a breathless quality like telegrams from European war correspondents in the forties. Warsaw falls, stop. Paris under siege, stop. Venice streets underwater, stop.

Hurley's girlfriend Michaela, M in text shorthand, worked nights tending bar at the Cougar Club. She didn't get many nights off. Keene was happy to do his friend a solid. Hurley was one of those guys who hadn't found his Melena, his soul mate in his first marriage. Maybe Michaela Mack was the one who would make Dennis Hurley happy. She was pretty and had a sweet disposition, kind of Zen-like, Keene had often thought.

Keene dumped his coffee and went back to bed. Retirement was an idea. Disabuse himself of this redemption bullshit and move on. After all, the evidence had proved him right in the end. Keene had known they had the right guy, but until the man's weapon was found, Keene had buried his face in a sweaty pillowcase without sleep for many nights. The actual proof, the real weapon, was found in a false bottom contraption in the floor of the van. It was beautifully engineered, precisely cut, successfully hidden for weeks from the best investigators in the state., Keene had killed a man in the conduct of his job. Guilty or not, the fact made Keene a brute. He was a violent beast. He was an executioner.

Retirement wasn't the answer, though, not for him. Keene had to work. It was the way he was made. Freud said the two great life motivators are love and work. The two things that make you human. Keene's life was working for the department and loving Melena. The only missing element, which Freud either didn't know about or had intentionally ignored, was being a dad.

Well, Jesus, Keene thought, that's my deep reflection for the day. That was deep enough to last a week. A good way to start a vacation. He got into bed and spooned with his wife. Two things came to Keene's attention with blazing and profound acuity. One: Melena was naked. Two: Keene had the immediate opportunity to exercise one of Freud's two great life motivators, and it wasn't work. He decided to affirm his humanness if he could just get his little Chiquita going... He caressed her beautiful curves and she turned to him, dark and gorgeous. This was a time he could share his side of the bed; his turf was hers, and three figures of Fahrenheit was okay by him.

Several unhurried hours after the humanness in the Keene household had been reaffirmed, the detective pulled the Charger into the garage under the Bricks, a nickname the employees gave the PPD building. The smell of gasoline that, real or not, accompanied all muscle cars in Keene's mind, invaded every corner of the garage. Melena's Camry simply didn't exhibit such panache and swagger. The Charger shouldered its way into a parking spot, elbowing any competitor away. The Camry would, with its eyes cast down and arms folded, slip into a slot.

Toyota relied on computers and individual ignition coils to start the Camry, but as far back as 1968, Keene's Charger had been equipped with a set of points and a condenser, and human interaction was required to set and maintain the ignition timing. Keene was ready to make adjustments, an old but serviceable timing light at the ready. But until he could get to it, the throatiness of the engine was a welcome distraction.

He parked the Charger next to Hurley's Toyota Supra, a vehicle whose registered owner didn't need it for five to ten years. The red car suited Hurley. A little flashy. Similarly, the Dodge Charger suited Keene. Not because it was old, but because this particular '68 Charger R/T with a 440 Magnum had a lot of Keene in it. After Keene acquired the broken-down, beat-up project car, he rejuvenated it and made it his and part of him.

He walked to the door, the Aleve starting to kick in or the exercise loosening up the muscles. In either case, his ass was feeling better. He held the door for a new receptionist, Lara or Laura, who was leaving her shift.

"Thank you, Detective Keene," she said politely.

This was a crisis. Whether Laura or Lara, he didn't know, but she had called him out, and used his name confidently. He must respond in kind. Keene couldn't say *Ma'am*—she was younger than him by twenty years. He'd completed the Respectful Workplace Starts With You course, so he knew he couldn't call her *Babe*, *Sweetheart*, or *Honey*. At a loss, all Keene could do was step out on the ledge.

"You're welcome, Laura," he said.

"It's Lara. I get that...all...the...time," she said, weary of the world, her round face split into a fearsome grin.

Detective Dennis Hurley held a ball cap while he spoke with a reporter from the *Portland Press Herald*, Leo Venti. Leo didn't use his full name, Leonardo Della'Ventimiglia, because, he said, there wasn't a newspaper out there that could afford that much ink for a byline. Leo Venti it was, and simply Leo would do. He'd been simply Leo since he was a small boy; the inky byline had nothing to do with it.

Trust between Leo and the Department had once existed, having developed as Leo started covering the beat ten years earlier. That changed after the shooting a year ago. The thin blue line had consolidated around one of their own, unifying against Leo's violation of their confidence. The press is a vital part of law enforcement, a fact acknowledged—and held dear—by both parties. Each feels a heavy responsibility to the public, sometimes shared, often at odds with one another. Citizens need to know that the police are protecting them to the extent the law allows but not overstepping the restraints implicit and explicit in the Constitution. The police can and do use the press to appeal to the public and, occasionally, directly to a suspect for cooperation and information. Leo, however, had overstepped a boundary in the eyes of the Department. The Portland Police Department had watched him systematically dismember one of their own. Unjustly and unfairly and for his own personal gain. The Bricks was his beat but, a year later, his welcome was tentative.

"Sorry, Leo," Hurley was saying as Keene joined the two men. "We got nothin'. Keene, got anything for Leo? Any naked man stories or lost dogs?" He said to Leo, "Readers love lost dog stories."

"Only ones that end well for the dog," Leo said. "Naked man stories are better. Always ends badly for the naked guy. Readers love that shit. Keene, how's your ass?" Leo had only recently been communicating directly with Keene. Man to man. The once friendly relationship was tepid, barely warmed from a deep freeze.

"Fine, and I got nothing for you," Keene said. "And I hope it stays that way. I'm on vacation tomorrow."

"There you go, Leo," Hurley said. "Twenty-year veteran cop takes vacation with beautiful wife. Video at eleven."

"It's Sunday, why you working?" Keene asked.

"I could ask you the same," Leo said hefting a shoulder bag.

"We're cops. Cops work all the time," Keene said.

"Except this week? That's why it's a story?" the reporter said. "Old Cop Goes on Vacation with Young," he stressed the word *young*, "Young Beautiful Wife."

"Screw you, Leo," Keene said. "Try this one: Confidential Sources Dry Up for Stupid Reporter."

Leo said, "The love is overwhelming. You guys have a good rest of the day, okay? Call me if you apprehend a naked man. Call Vicki with the dog story."

Keene said as he watched the reporter go, "The son of a bitch should be taking the stairs. Starting to get a paunch." Venti had been the lead reporter on the shooting. He had cast Keene as an out-of-control cop and had heedlessly implied that he carried racism in his heart. The two suggestions had stuck in the collective minds of Leo's readers. Keene had liked the guy until his personal ambition had rolled over him, leaving him and the truth flattened in the mud, both mortally wounded. Keene hadn't helped the racism charge with his unforgivable comment, but he would always feel Leo had pushed him into it.

"Not healthy for a young guy," Hurley said. "Appreciate you filling in. Micky's got the night."

"Going out to eat?"

"Taking her to Three Guesses," Hurley said.

"Goofy name," Keene said. "I mean everybody had fun with the name twice. 'Where ya goin'?' 'Three guesses, ha-ha-ha.' You know? A who's on first kinda thing. The second time, okay. But now?"

"Yeah, I know. But the food's great."

"Yeah, sure. Tell Michaela I said hi."

"You bet. Thanks again, man." Hurley slapped Keene on the arm. "Hope you guys have a great vacation. I'll see you in a couple weeks, right?"

"Ten days."

Hurley left the Bricks. The building was called the Bricks because it looked like a huge pile of bricks. Yes, there was a roof and a sidewalk and doors and windows. A little glass here and some concrete there. Mortar, glazing compound, and caulking held it all together. But when Keene looked at the building, he saw course upon course of the kiln-fired red building blocks. Bricks.

The Sunday evening shift was typically a lonely time at the Bricks. Keene could use some downtime to catch up on the cases he had going. He would hand over the ongoing stuff to Riordan via detailed reports of his open cases. Hurley had volunteered to write up the Falstaff report and would handle all the other bullshit. The report had to be filed the next day. Keene, the better writer, would write up the addenda to help out his partner.

Keene would ask the new detective, Diane Peterson, to interview the cashier in a 7-Eleven robbery. She'd have the robber and the complicit manager in custody before the end of the day tomorrow. The Indianapolis Police Department hadn't taught the redhead to be a pushover.

The only murder case of the quiet summer had been a tough one for everyone involved. Man murders wife. Nothing out of the ordinary in the realm of murder. Money, love, and power, the golden triad of motive. It seemed to be a slam dunk. The husband did it and admitted it at the crime scene with tears flowing down his cheeks. His wife of forty-five years had been struck with dementia. Husband couldn't care for her. It was a different generation; she'd always cared for him. He was a problem-solver, not a caregiver. Disabled wife, foam pillow, problem solved. Except for the law and the all-encompassing misery of the rest of his life. Keene would testify in a month or two. It had been an easy solve but a terrifying case to be part of.

June, July, and August had been slow, and Keene was ready to wrap things up the way he and Melena always brought the summer to a close—

with their vacation cruise. Keene's phone signaled a text. Alfred Hitchcock once said a story consists of life with the dull interludes removed, and in the same sense, Melena believed a man's job is how he spends his time between vacations. Keene wished he could believe that, and he wished there wasn't another dull interlude he had to contend with before he and Melena continued their story. But the text he had just received was convincing him otherwise. He looked at his phone and read how he would spend his time until his next bit of relaxation.

CHAPTER
6

Yakov raised his thumbs. Silk relaxed, looked at the app on her phone, and shook perspiration from her forehead. Twenty seconds had elapsed. It had seemed like twenty minutes. Too much time had elapsed. They had discussed aborting if they hadn't reached the butcher in thirty seconds. The time window was closing and she'd been ignoring Sully's.

This was a test to prove her value to Umarov. She slid the card up and down. She had less than ten seconds to enter and retrieve the gun. Umarov liked the idea of a female assassin but wasn't yet convinced she was the one. Up again. Nothing. She'd worked locks like this many times, and some locks were stubborn. Fact of life. Up. This is a test. She worked more deliberately. Down. Slowly. A test. Sweat soaked through her lycra. A glance over her shoulder: Bar still quiet. Sweat on her forehead. Six seconds. Glance at her phone: Club's door still closed. The second camera might have been a useful resource after all. The sweat stung her eyes. She soaked it away with her forearm. Work the lock. Work it. This is a test, this is a test, this is a goddamned test. Was she good enough for Umarov's needs? A peek over her shoulder. The lock. A glimpse at the phone. The stubborn, goddamned lock.

A noise...

She nicked a look at the bar. A man walked out into the heavy mist. This goddamn lock. You must not be seen. The sweat on her face, in her hair. You must abort the mission. Arkady had said: *To be successful, you must have complete confidence in yourself.* Nurzhan had said: *We will abort after thirty seconds.* The phone screen showed nothing at the door of the club. She turned from the lock, the stubborn, unopened lock. She knew they must abort but she couldn't.

At the bar, a man wearing a tweed fisherman's cap walked up the street, toward her, slowly. You must not be seen. You must abort the mission. Self-confidence, self-confidence. She flattened her back against the glass of the door again and snitched a look at the phone. There was activity at the club. This was it. She must abort. Witnesses at both ends of the block.

Nurzhan's brother, Yakov, peered down the road. Thumbs up. It was okay. Did he not see the guy with the tweed cap? Yakov signaled it was okay at his end of the street. The job had become survival. You must abort. Self-confidence. Abort the mission. Total self-confidence. She could not abort. A weakness of hers?

The man with the tweed cap seemed unsure of the sidewalk then found reliable turf. He looked up as she worked the lock behind her, her back pressed against the window. Did he see her? Abort? She fumbled the card up and down again, her arm at an awkward angle. Silk twisted the lockset at the curve of her figure. Seen? The door behind her jerked ajar, she snapped up the camera and slipped into the store. Self-confidence. God, it felt good. Jesus Christ, it felt good. Everything was all right. It was all good. Except for the guy with the fisherman's cap. He had seen her. She was sure. There must be no witness. Too late for that.

A Russian girl in Yakov's stable worked for the butcher, the owner of DeLuca's Variety Store. Patrick Grogan paid the girl illegally low wages as the status of her work visa seemed in question. The butcher didn't trust a soul, but he never suspected Lena of providing all the intel Silk and Nurzhan needed: the layout of the store, the habits of the owner, and the location of the firearm and keys. Silk slipped on latex gloves. She searched under the cash in the bill organizer.

Umarov gave Yakov the girls. Many employees of the Cougar Club spoke with Russian, Croat, and Bulgarian accents. Up and down the coast of Maine, service was provided, attractions were attended, kiosks were manned by young men and women with similar accents. Lena had told Silk she would find an extra key under the bills. Silk, her size sixes squishing slightly, slipped the key into the arch of her left sneaker. She fit the condom over her tongue with well-practiced dexterity.

Startled, Grogan peered at her face, his mind working. Suddenly he was not alone. A woman in wet clothing stood before him. Silk didn't doubt his immediate assessment was something about a girl in distress. The certain assumption of gender inequality was already working in her favor. Exactly as predicted.

Girl went to store to kill butcher. No! *The* girl, *the* store, *the* butcher. *The, the, the.* Silk invaded his space and pulled his face to hers. She planted her mouth over his, both hands on his neck. He opened his mouth reflexively. Carotid arteries are an Achilles heel, and Silk applied enough pressure to prevent blood from getting to Grogan's brain. In less than ten seconds, he was woozy, and Nurzhan was there to keep him from dropping. There it was, she thought, a reason for Nurzhan. If she was to work alone, she must come up with a work-around for this problem. With a twist of her tongue and a deep breath, she filled the condom in Grogan's mouth. With the initial lack of blood to the brain and now the deprivation of air to his lungs, he was unable to resist. The Medical Examiner would discover hypoxia in the tissues of the corpse. The doctor would claim this to be consistent with the bullet found lodged in his brain. Arkady, a student of the science of killing a man, had explained this: The damaged brain will not allow the lungs to deliver oxygen to the cells in the body. Hypoxia. Grogan was alive but unconscious in Nurzhan's arms. Silk allowed the condom to deflate.

She increased the volume of the music playing in the store. There were no open windows. She pulled the door to the back room closed. They had created an eight-by-eight-foot cell. The report of the gun would present itself as a thump outside the market. Inside their small cell, the report would ring in their ears for an hour.

She pulled the gun.

The muzzle of Grogan's Beretta APX jumped from his slick temple when she pulled the trigger. The report of the gunshot in the limited space was a massive crack followed immediately by temporary deafness. The butcher slumped forward in Nurzhan's grasp. Silk wrapped Grogan's warm and pliable hand around the grip of the gun, his index finger in the trigger cage. Her hearing returned. Nurzhan allowed the body to slump backward. The body didn't look quite right. Silk pulled Grogan's shoulders to the left. Her hands were twitchy, full of adrenaline. Blood pounded through her veins. She wasted no movement as she wiped the scene down. The acid aroma of cleaning fluids melded with the sulfurous smoke of gunfire. The mist had become rain and it drummed against the metal door, blending with the music. They slipped through the back door, snugged it closed, and locked it with the extra key. Silk smelled the rain, the mud, her musky scent. Her skin twitched sensually below the lycra. Her skin felt good for the first time in years.

Careless footsteps to the right.

Who else would be out on a night like this? First, a drunk, now someone else?

Nurzhan bolted to the left in the direction of the path. A tall figure was silhouetted by light. Silk crouched at the door then slipped behind a trash compactor. Her petite body, enveloped in black, was nearly invisible. Ironically, the last thing she wanted was to be separated from Nurzhan.

She heard pounding, a fist on a door, then: "Dad?"

———•••———

Eileen worked when interstate traffic was scarce. At night. Graffiti was illegal, but she was gaining a certain infamy. She was Portland's "Tagger," in the words of the *Portland Press Herald*, a term of respect the paper had coined for the anonymous artist. Her work became newsworthy when the city pressure-washed a piece she'd created from the side of the fire station on the Hill. There'd been an uproar; the city would not make this mistake again. The current piece—a fierce lobster presenting the unseen cook with some crustacean push-back—welcomed drivers entering Portland from the north.

The mist was turning to rain. The pleasant rhythm of high water licking the base of the bridge abutment was now drowned out by the spattering of rain against the sidewalk. She wasn't done, but the work could be finished tomorrow night. She pulled her hoodie up and tucked her hair inside, then dropped the can of paint into her camo backpack. Roots and rocks created an irregular pattern of steps up the side of the hill and the improvised path led to her street. A big man in black skidded from her path and paid no attention to her. He walked out onto the bike trail and took a left, past her work of art.

The roots were rain-slick and only luck could account for the big man's successful navigation of the path. Eileen made it without falling but nearly ran into a small woman also dressed in black at the top. She was attempting to find her way to the bike trail, too, via Eileen's personal root-bound trail. If this wasn't a WTF moment, nothing was. Two people, both in black, scampering down the hidden pathway from Romasco to the bikeway below. Unlike the man, the woman looked directly at Eileen. The woman was dressed in black, the clothing as tight as paint. She was wet as a haddock. After a moment, she looked away as if she were involved in something illicit. An affair, Eileen thought.

She quick-walked along Romasco Lane in the rain. She made up a story: They were lovers, illicit lovers. Lovers: an antiquated term, a term Eileen liked. Sometime, she wanted to call someone Lover. Hey Lover. Come to me, Lover. Kiss me, Lover. These two were stealing time for themselves, time for their love affair, which is why they looked away. They wanted to remain anonymous, too. Why else were they walking among the shadows, in the rain, wearing black? Just now they were finding each other on the bike trail and laughing that they'd each seen the girl. Cripe sake, what was she thinking? They were people taking a walk. In this weather?

Francis was passed out on the couch when Eileen entered the apartment a couple of minutes later. Sirens pierced the saturated silence and engines roared; another Hunger Hill ruckus. Cripe sake, what this time? She peeled off her wet hoodie and thunked her sneakers into the corner of her room. She didn't attempt to be quiet; Francis was out cold, numb as a hake.

The Hill had always been a challenge to outsiders. Romasco was dark and was among the lanes where a vehicle should not be left. Not if you were an outsider. A woman should never walk alone on the Hill. There was a protected class, though, the Hill Girl. Eileen could go anywhere, anytime. Until recently. The balance was changing. Her oldest brother, Frank, told her she must take a self-defense class. He would pay for it. She refused until she could pay her way. With the sirens still wailing, she googled "self-defense - women - Portland, Maine." The words *Krav Maga* came up. She googled it and read that it was a type of self-defense devised by the Israelis. It taught weapons takeaway, grappling techniques, and karate-like kicks and punches. It taught a smaller person how to deal with a larger foe. She found the Star Martial Arts Studio promoting the art as the perfect discipline for self-protection. Man or woman. She signed up for a class that started at the end of the week. Eileen took care of herself. She always had. She opened a can of root beer and took a deep swig.

CHAPTER
7

Detective Basil Keene and Melena scratched vacation dates into their calendars using a No. 2 pencil. In Keene's experience, such plans were merely theory until the *Ventosa*'s engine fired to life. At nine fifteen Sunday night, two hours and forty-five minutes before theory was to become fact, a call came in from Dispatch: suspicious death. The butcher at DeLuca's Variety Store on Hunger Hill had been shot. Probably dead. Keene's vacation plans were thrust into aspirational limbo.

"Evening," Keene said to Terry Arnaud, the responding officer, when they met at the scene. Keene fished out a pack of gum.

"Evening," the cop in blue said. Officer Terry Arnaud wasn't heavy, but she might be called rugged, like a barrel of chain. She was young; she was the Department's newest recruit at twenty-six. A no-nonsense haircut, under the unisex hat of the uniform, allowed her to fade from notability as a woman in a male-dominated field. Her voice had a certain timbre as if it came from a bubble near the back of her throat.

"This your first?" he asked, wondering how his responding officer was going to take the death scene. Some were better than others. To some officers, it was just another day on the job. Others internalized the sight of a dead body, often their first, and had difficulty dealing with it.

"My first?" Arnaud said as if she wanted to be sure before she reacted.

"What else?" he asked.

"Oh, um, yes. My first death scene." She'd felt a detachment as she might feel for a dead squirrel. A sociopath understands human death by reducing it to the death of a squirrel or a rat or a mosquito. Of course, Terry Arnaud wasn't a sociopath. She was merely detached from others. This helped her through some of the challenges of social interactions she found heavy and onerous. Showering after gym class, for example. Showing her body to others.

The grind of tires on macadam was followed by the slam of a car door.

"Evening, Chief," Arnaud and Keene said in unison as the heavy man entered. *Tough* heavy. Nothing flabby about Interim Chief Charlie Riordan's extra weight.

"Yeah. Great evening," Riordan replied. "Where's Hurley?"

"I'm on the clock," Keene said. "It's my case." When a case came in, it became the case of the detective on duty. A self-defining element of Keene's nature was professional pride. He accepted his responsibilities regardless of outside circumstances. If it was Keene's case, it was Keene's case.

"Sorry," Riordan said. "Thought Hurley was on."

"We swapped. He had another engagement."

"And I didn't know this, *why*?" Riordan raised an eyebrow. He had risen through the ranks and had retained some aspects of every level he'd achieved. The Interim Chief had been an excellent lieutenant, and an excellent lieutenant knows where his people are. Keene should have let Riordan know.

"It just came up." He nodded at Riordan and said, "Gum?"

"Nah. M&Ms?" Each man—tall, lanky Keene and stout Charlie—held a pack of their preferred candy out to the other.

"Nah. Gum?" Keene said to Arnaud.

She said, "No, thank you."

"M&Ms?" Charlie offered Arnaud.

"No, thank you."

Riordan said, "You were saying...?"

Arnaud said, "Dead vic. Called in by his son, a Professor Thomas Grogan." She nodded toward the back of the store where another officer was speaking with a tall man. "Upstairs tenants didn't hear anything. Grogan's music was too loud. Apparent suicide by gunshot," Arnaud said.

"Where'd the gun come from?" Riordan asked.

"Sir?"

"Where did he keep it?" Keene asked. "Safe? Drawer? Did he carry? This information could help determine if it was suicide or murder."

"I'll ask. Um..." She paused. "Tough to fingerprint a store. Lotta prints." Arnaud's face was broad and fleshy, her tone monotonous. She had few features that might be considered attractive.

Keene said, "Murray will do a survey." Under such conditions, all the evidence tech could do was collect the prints and form a database for future reference. The survey would become courtroom evidence indicating a suspect had been in the store—for the little that was worth.

Keene and Riordan turned from Arnaud. Keene said quietly, "Don't worry, Chief, I'm on it."

"Yeah, yeah," Riordan muttered. "Just that Hurley knows the Hill. Y'know?"

"We'll work together on it."

"Depends on what else is going on." Then, "He knew Grogan." He looked around the busy scene as if everything being done was meant to make his headache worse. He said, "Suicide, cut and dried, right?"

"It all seems consistent with suicide. The front and rear doors were locked."

"Just give me a short and to-the-point plan. I got meetings and conference calls and Zooms and Skypes and...Jesus Christ." The Interim Chief sounded like he'd been told to carry a hundred pounds of shit in a fifty-pound shit bag.

"This about the Senator?" Keene asked.

"Why she can't just come to Portland, get a room at the Hilton, give a speech...Biggest fuckin' cluster I've ever seen." Riordan took a breath and said, "'Scuse the language, Officer."

Arnaud nodded.

Riordan continued, "You're on vacation if it turns out to be nothing, right?" It sounded like a suggestion to Keene. "And, seriously, you want to give this to Hurley, I'm okay with that."

"Not how I roll, Charlie. We were planning to head out on the boat tomorrow. We can leave on Tuesday just as easily."

Riordan said, "Melena deserves some time off." He stomped out the door of DeLuca's Variety Store.

Keene nodded and said to Arnaud, "Let's get to work."

CHAPTER

8

Keene tapped Melena's number. She claimed the late-night ring was baked into the cake of being a cop's wife for twenty years.

"Everything's fine," Keene stated. That two-word announcement meant he was not hurt, not shot, and not hospital-bound.

"But?" Melena said, knowing another shoe dangled, suspended somewhere between *everything's fine* and *but*.

"But...I won't be home until late tonight." More likely early morning, he thought as he gazed around the crime scene. They would not be on the boat tomorrow, and he knew she knew it.

"What about our vacation, Basil? You caught one, didn't you? The weather is supposed to be beautiful. Sailing weather this week."

"I'm sorry, Babe. Maybe we can take the Whaler out for a cocktail on Little Chebeague." Keene continued, "The good news, in a way, is it looks like the guy took his own life. We can still get our vacation in. Just a day or two late as I clear this one." It felt like lying.

"You promise?" she asked, knowing he couldn't. "What happened?"

"As I say, looks like suicide."

"And, if it is, you'll be off the hook?"

"Something like that. I'll see you soon. I love you, Babe."

"Love you, too," she said. Then she added, "How's your ass?"

Keene found himself standing over the body with the Evidence Tech, Sanblasio, predictably nicknamed Sandblaster. The transplanted Bostonian was a young guy with a neat black goatee and a shaved head. Keene and the tech squatted above the remains of Patrick Grogan.

Never the husband of the year, Grogan had taken out his considerable anger on his pretty wife, Annabella. The abuse was widely known at the Bricks. Even so, Keene owed it to the butcher to determine how he died and who was responsible, the man himself or someone else. Keene wondered if he'd ever answer one question: Why does a woman stay with an abusive man?

The dead man wore a white T-shirt with the name of the market arched over the left breast. He wore cargo shorts and sneakers with ankle-length dark socks. His gray hair was parted on the right side of his head, and there was a small, almost neat bullet hole at the right temple. Thick hair for a man in his sixties. The left side of his head was blown out, missing from the jaw to below his left ear.

The butcher had spent most of his time at the store, often in the back, carving; sometimes at the register, smirking at his customers contemptuously. Hurley, who knew the man, had said he was only happy when he was unhappy. In death, he looked angry. He glared at Keene with the opaque eyes of the dead like white disks, and his bloodless skin made him look evil.

Sandblaster said, "The cause of death is evidenced by a GSW by vic's gun." Sandblaster's shorthand referred to a gunshot wound, evidently inflicted by the victim's weapon.

Keene asked, "Sure it's his gun?"

"His gun. His son—" Sandblaster motioned with his head toward the finding witness, "confirmed this."

"Where'd the vic keep it? Back here, or did he carry?"

"Don't know yet." The ET gestured to the body. "Entry wound at right temple, exit wound is found below the left ear."

"What does that tell you?" Keene asked.

"If there was a shooter, he was taller than the vic."

Like his son, Keene thought. Thomas Grogan had to be three or four inches taller than his deceased father.

"Let's look at the eyes." Keene shifted his attention. "Usually, Officer Arnaud," Keene started, "we look for petechiae in the eyes to indicate hypoxia—lack of oxygen to the brain caused by strangulation."

Sandblaster said, "There is definite petechiae present." The ET pointed to the tiny red pinpricks in the whites of the butcher's eyes.

"Goddamn," Keene said. "Interesting."

"Does this mean he was strangled first?" Arnaud asked tentatively.

"Not necessarily," Keene said. "The phenomenon is caused by a sudden lack of oxygen to the brain. It can sometimes be caused by death itself. Kinda rare, though. See, Arnaud, if we focus on one thing like suicide, we might miss something else. So, we record all observations and start putting a puzzle together with no preconceived notion of what happened. That's a perfect world. In this case, it will be hard to look at the evidence without prejudice. It seems so cut and dried, right?"

The man identified as the victim's son stood alone a few feet away. Keene introduced himself and said, "I need to ask you some questions."

"Sure."

"Where did you come in, Professor Grogan?"

"The back door."

"It was open?" Keene asked.

"It was locked. I have a key."

Both doors locked. The locked door was consistent with suicide. Everything was consistent with suicide. Too consistent? An Agatha Christie locked-room mystery? That doesn't happen, of course. Keene had an inkling, a hunch. He started to feel the presence of a stage manager. "And you found your father just like this?"

"Yes," Grogan said. "And by the way, the back door isn't normally locked."

"When did you last see your father? Alive, that is?"

"This afternoon. I came in around three," Tom Grogan said.

The door isn't normally locked. Stage management. To do this, one needs a key. Tom Grogan has a key.

"Why did you see him around three?"

"I came to help in the store. There's a bit of a rush at three-thirty or four. My mom hasn't been able to help out as much. I'm getting ready for classes and have an overload on my plate right now. But still, I came in to help."

But still, I came in to help. Was the professor resentful of his father's demands on his time?

"The store has been busy, then?" Keene asked.

"No, the store has been slow. Losing business to the big stores and..."

"And what?"

"It's not a secret. My father was," he searched for the word. "Disliked. Unlikeable, to be frank with you. He was nasty to his customers and the tenants upstairs. Most didn't understand this. I did. He was simply mean. A lot of people were choosing to shop elsewhere."

"What was his state of mind as far as you could tell?"

"My father was never cheerful, but he was not suicidal, either," Grogan said.

Keene thought about that. "Yet you called this in as a suicide. Have you changed your mind?"

"Looked like a suicide. Doesn't mean it was," the professor said.

"Okay," Keene said. "Let me ask you this: You say people are choosing to shop elsewhere because he was nasty to them. Anybody make another choice, you think? Do you think anybody might have chosen to kill him because he was nasty to them? The tenants?"

"Pretty drastic option. The tenants are simple, nice people. Immigrants. No-waves kind of people." Tom Grogan scratched his head in a classic thoughtful gesture. "I've known this neighborhood since I was a kid. Some folks may be ornery. May be nasty themselves, but murderous? I can't imagine it." He paused. "There's Vito, I suppose. Troiano... No. He was a blowhard but he wouldn't do anything."

Keene wrote the name down. "Troiano? Can you tell me more about that?"

"Just a feud. A stupid pissing contest. You might talk to him, but I doubt it's anything."

"Who else was here?" Keene asked. "At three."

Tom said, "The girl who works the register."

"What's her name?"

"Um. Lena; I don't know her last name. My father has been employing some...guest workers, I guess, over the last couple of months. She's Russian. He didn't pay her a lot, but he hired her. It was kind of a win-win thing. My mother hasn't been well. Dad needed the help. The girls need cash."

"Girls, plural?"

"Been a couple, I guess."

Keene waited for him to say more. When he didn't, Keene said, "I'll need to see Lena. Do you know how I can find her?"

"I think she'll make herself hard to find, her immigration status being... ambiguous," Grogan said. "My mother might know her full name."

"I'd appreciate it if you'd get that name and an address."

"I'll ask my mother. Look, can I get back to her now? I think she needs me."

Keene said, "You're not going anywhere, right? You have classes to prepare for?"

"Yup," Grogan said.

"Thank you. Go take care of your mom. Oh," Keene thought of a question. "You said the back door was locked?"

"Yes. I have a key."

"In heat like this? There's no air conditioning. Do you know why he might keep the door closed?"

Grogan looked a question at Keene like he hadn't considered it. Then he said, "No, like I said, he usually keeps it open."

"Thank you," Keene said.

He scanned the store. He noted an industrial push broom standing in the corner, leaning against a shelf. The butcher had closed for business. Locked the door and started cleaning up. But he usually keeps it open.

"Oh, Professor Grogan," Keene lifted his voice; Grogan was on his way out the door. "Do you know where he kept his gun? For instance, did he carry?"

"Sorry, I have no idea," the professor replied as he left the crime scene.

"Arnaud, start a neighborhood canvass with the tenants upstairs. Sandblaster," Keene said, "lemme see the gun."

Sandblaster said, "It's bagged." He presented the handgun in a transparent evidence bag and yawned. He apologized and scratched his goatee the way all men with goatees do.

Keene took the gun, and looked at it from all sides. It was a Beretta APX 9-mil, semiautomatic pistol. Not the most popular gun; that honor fell to Glock, probably. The 19 or the 43. The APX was a reliable 9-mil that sold for around $400, a natural price point for the home-defense crowd, a growing demographic in the arms business. As he turned it over, he thought there was something wrong; well, maybe not *wrong*, merely inconsistent with something he'd seen on or about the victim, but he wasn't sure what. The mag-release? The takedown lever? Something bothered him. The gun and the scene. The victim. Something was wrong. Bert, Keene's Fort Lauderdale mentor, had said a scene was never what it seemed and way more than it didn't seem. Keene had taken that to mean you had to take what you see with a grain of salt and see clearly what you don't see. At this crime scene, Keene was as clear as day that he was missing something important.

CHAPTER
9

Melena carried her coffee to the deck where Keene was reading the paper. She drank her coffee from a cup not much bigger than a baby's fist. Keene's cup was a full-sized mug. Melena made her coffee in an hourglass-shaped "Italian" coffeemaker. Her Cuban coffee—two brands called Pilon and Café Serrano; no others would do—was sweet. To Keene, Cuban coffee and American coffee were two different drinks with only ground coffee beans in common. The way Guinness Stout and Bud Light shared nothing more than a wide classification.

She said, "Are you feeling better?"

Melena, still wearing the slinky little satiny green slip that favored the caramel color of her skin, fanned herself with a leaflet from the newspaper. The sun was already hot, and the Portland newspaper and Leo Venti were turning up the heat on the suspicious death on Hunger Hill.

Keene said, "Much better. Took a couple of Aleve anyway, but I'm on the mend."

Melena sat in a deck chair and said, "We should be motoring out through Hussey's Sound right now." She sipped her coffee.

Keene said nothing.

"We gonna keep trying to get rid of the recycling bin?" she asked.

"I'll make another call. I'll get rid of that thing if it kills me."

Melena said nothing as she crooked her hair behind an ear. Everything was beautiful about his wife. Her ear, for God's sake.

"Riordan wants a quick end to this case. Needs it," Keene said. "Meaning the less press, the better."

"Is the story in the paper?"

Keene nodded.

"Is it Leo's story?"

"Yeah, it is."

"He's a prick," she said simply and as a matter of irrefutable fact. You don't piss off a hot-blooded Latina and return to her good graces anytime soon. Not this Latina, anyway.

The headline read, "Suicide or Murder?" and the teaser line read, "Unnamed sources claim there is a difference of opinion at the highest level of the Portland PD."

Keene said, "If it's suicide, Charlie can focus his attention on the Senator's visit."

She asked, "What makes it look like suicide?"

"Oh, you know, the normal signs. Like holding his gun to his temple and pulling the trigger. Unhappy guy; unsuccessful business. Just that kind of stuff."

Keene opened his laptop and typed into the search engine: 1967 Dodge Coronet R/T Magnum 440. The vehicle was the father of his Charger. He would take any year in the mid-'60s, but '67 would be sweet.

Melena fanned herself with the entire paper and said, "I feel a *but* coming on."

Keene said, "But the scene had a staged feel to it." He absently clicked on one entry Google suggested. "It has the Hercule Poirot 'locked-room' feel to it."

"What do you mean?"

"An Agatha Christie device was to start a story with a murder in a locked room. It's impossible, but it happened. This feels like that. The only explanation is suicide. I think that may be what we're meant to believe. It's an idea."

Keene's phone rang, he looked at the caller ID, answered, and said, "I'm not the unnamed source, Charlie." He held the phone away from his ear. "...I don't know. Yeah, yeah, I'll call Leo."

Riordan said, "Do you think it's Arnaud? Should we take her off this?"

"First of all: No, I don't think it's Arnaud. Why commit career kamikaze when you're still a rookie? But secondly, what's the big deal? So, we have a disagreement."

"See, Keene, that's the other element here: Do we? Do we disagree? It's too early to have a disagreement."

"I agree." Keene thought about it, then said, "Why don't *you* call Leo? Tell him that. Nobody has *any* opinion, let alone conflicting ones."

"Okay, but that doesn't address this unnamed-sources thing."

"Yeah, I'll ask around."

Keene canceled the call and reread the piece. Later in the article, the unnamed source was referred to as someone "close to the investigation." *Close to the investigation.* Unnamed source inferred PPD. Close to the investigation inferred otherwise.

Back to the results of the search for his 1967 Dodge Coronet. All the available vehicles, at least on the first few pages, were restored. The work, the fun part, is already done.

"They're beautiful," he said about the cars. "Look." He turned the laptop to Melena. "Look at that one, Babe. That guy's got quite a collection of muscle cars. I think I've seen this one on a calendar."

"Most men have bikini calendars, don't they?" Melena sipped her coffee.

Keene had never been one to hang his desire on the wall. He was a healthily lustful man, a man who loved his wife in a holy matrimonial way and equally in a libidinous sexual way. He leaned and kissed Melena and said, "We'll be on the boat soon, I promise. By the way, I don't need a bikini calendar to brighten my day. You take care of that."

CHAPTER
10

Keene settled into the Charger and turned the key. The 440 V-8, four-barrel power plant came to life like a growling dog. No purring under the Charger's hood. The day was off to a steamy start. Sailing weather.

The detective had a hunch. He also had good instincts, but hunches were just hunches and had no standing in court. The butcher had likely killed himself, and tomorrow, Melena would be at the helm while he hoisted the mainsail. But still, he had an intuition as he wheeled into the parking garage of the Bricks.

He climbed the stairs to the first floor, and a small man wearing a tie-dye T-shirt and khaki shorts that reached to his knees nodded to him.

"Morning," Keene said.

The black man was bald and had a close-cropped graying beard. He had hiking calves and a flat stomach and appeared to try to gain one more inch of height by pitching his head back and up. His ears stuck out like anemometer cups. But he ignored Keene's greeting, and that didn't sit well with the PPD detective.

Cali Wordsworth, on the other hand, said, "Morning, Detective." She had a cup of coffee in a paper tray with mounds of sugar packets and a tumbler full of plastic creamers. Cali was a blast of sunshine, the little guy, a passing cloud.

"Hey, Cali. Who was that guy?"

"Some kind of Fed," she said. "Nobody bothered to introduce him. Something to do with the Senator, I guess."

"Seems like a dick. I thought the Feds dressed GQ."

Cali, blonde and blue-eyed like an ad for Swedish tourism, said, "I have to get this coffee to the Chief." They walked together. "The Feds think they're on vacation. Maine in the summer. Beach this afternoon."

"Yeah. Go to the floating restaurant for lobsters." Keene hurried his long strides to keep up with Cali. She was five-eight and had long legs, and damned if she didn't smell like cucumbers. Or melon, maybe. Something juicy. Perhaps we should skip the sailing cruise next year, and go to Sweden, he thought.

Cali said, "Maybe they'll go fishing. You ever go deep-sea fishing on one of those charter boats?"

"Nah. If I want to fish, I'll go out on my boat. Have you?"

"I'd like to. Sometime," Cali said.

"Sometime Melena and I'll take you." He realized he'd never asked her to sail with them. Probably ten years, he'd known her.

"Yeah," she said, "I'd like that."

They reached the Chief's office and Keene opened the door for Cali.

The Chief was on the phone and held a just-a-moment finger up. Then waved Keene in, and pointed to a seat.

He covered the phone and said to Keene, "I'm on hold." Then he barked into the phone, "Hello?" Then, "Yeah, sure. Have her call me." He dropped the old-fashioned receiver into its cradle.

To Keene: "They had me on hold while they determined the Police Chief of South Portland is not available to talk. What the Christ?"

"Yeah. I know."

Riordan said, "South Portland takes the Senator and the Secret Service ghosts from the airport to the city line. Then we take the bunch of 'em from there."

"You can't simply meet the candidate at the airport and take her to the hotel?"

"The Service is talking about a decoy motorcade."

"What the...?" Keene said. "You gotta be kidding. So, they'll have *two* motorcades?"

"It'll double the personnel. Double the plans. Maybe triple. I don't know yet if we'll now need a third redundant route to the hospital. We won't know until four hours before touchdown, so we have to be ready for a decoy. And she's only a VP candidate." Riordan wiped a hand across his brow. Then he said, "Who's talking to Leo?"

"I don't think it was a cop. I'm going to ask but..."

"What makes you think it's not a cop?" Charlie asked.

Keene said, "If Leo's anything, it's precise. He means exactly what he writes."

"Except when he doesn't," Riordan said.

Keene understood Riordan's shot at Leo. The entire Department still held the grudge against the journalist. When Leo began tearing Keene a rhetorical new one, it all went to hell for the reporter at the Bricks. But it was admirable that the man hadn't asked for a new beat even after the fallout from his inaccuracies rained down on him. Keene was a big boy and could handle the kind of scrutiny a shooting was bound to bring. It wasn't easy, and every cop wants to avoid discharging his weapon. But it happens. The unforgivable element of the event was Keene's quote. There was no denying he said it. He could never take it back, but he would only have said it under extreme pressure, and Leo had brought that pressure to bear when he knew he had Keene down on the canvas.

Keene continued to Riordan, "He doesn't write the headlines or the teasers. The teaser said 'unnamed sources claim,' implying someone who's part of the investigation. Unnamed sources. Later, in the body of the story, he wrote 'sources close to the investigation.' You get the difference, *part of* versus *close to*? That says to me that Leo didn't talk to a cop."

"Not sure I buy that. What about the scene, Basil?"

"The place was clean, Charlie. Spotless. The scene was, like, staged. Like it had been made to look like suicide. Both doors locked. Do you do that if you're killing yourself? Lock the doors? And he was doing his chores."

"You're trying to tell me something."

Keene said nothing but lifted his eyebrow.

"Yeah, yeah. Jesus Christ. I knew you were going to say that. Now we got a hired gun running around Portland."

"Technically, I didn't say anything."

Riordan stirred in more sugar and cream. He said, "Yeah. What else we got?"

Keene presented the facts like a grocery list. "Gunshot wound at the temple. Egress at the lower mandible. The gun in the vic's hand. We'll have a luminol report tomorrow morning. Opinion: Scene looks manipulated to look like suicide."

"Will the test be admissible in court?"

Keene admired Charlie's instincts. "Nah. The guy was a butcher. There's blood everywhere. What I want to see is if there's a drag pattern. Was the body moved? That kind of stuff. That will be apparent to us, but the report would be all about reasonable doubt to a good defense attorney."

"Got it. What else?" The Chief took a handful of candy from the jar on his desk.

Keene slapped his thighs and said, "That's all I got right now. I'll fill you in with more when I get it." He stood, and before he turned to leave, said, "You getting enough sugar?"

"What? Oh, I quit drinking. Gotta get sugar somehow."

Keene said. "I got a call to make."

"Hey, before you go," Charlie said. "After this case, take that vacation, okay? And remember, I want you on my team. I hope you stick around." He looked at Keene with a you-know-what-I'm-saying look as he popped a couple of green M&Ms into his mouth.

Keene wondered if he was interpreting his old friend correctly. If I get the job, you get a job? As in a big job?

"Yeah, Charlie. Thanks."

Was Riordan telling Keene if he stuck around, he'd be rewarded? Or was he simply saying that despite not being promoted, Keene was still needed? Keene was eager to find out. He wouldn't mind getting that promotion despite the City Council.

———— •••• ————

Keene asked Arnaud to revisit the scene with him while things were still fresh in their minds. She drove a black-and-white Explorer while he rode shotgun. Over the noise of the AC, he said, "He was sweeping." He remembered the broom, next to a small pile of dust and debris. "If you were going to commit suicide, would you sweep first?"

Arnaud didn't answer immediately. She pulled the Explorer to the curb, and they walked into the market without speaking. They walked to the end of the store and scanned the scene as they'd done many times over the last twelve hours.

She said, "Maybe he was sweeping up the way you clean up for your host after you spent the night...I guess."

"Huh. That's an interesting point. Like thanking the world for having you over as you're getting ready to leave." Keene found the observation uniquely compelling. An idea that wouldn't have occurred to him. A creative idea. He believed creativity to be an important tool for an investigator to possess. He thought creativity was *as* important if not *more* important than knowledge of the penal code in the approach to a detective's work. Einstein had said that imagination is more important than knowledge, and Keene adopted the idea as an organizing principle in his life. Imagine. Imagine all the possibilities or you miss the one you need.

CHAPTER
11

Detective Basil Keene had before him what had once been a neat stack of photos and a composed list of notes and was now a scatter of information. Tom Grogan had confirmed that his father typically locked the front door at closing. A killer coming through the front door would have picked the lock and he would have picked it well. It had not been compromised as far as Keene could tell. Can you tell if a lock has been picked? He'd call a locksmith. Having relocked the door, the killer would have retrieved the gun. But from where? He needed to talk to the Russian girl, Lena.

The location of the gun was crucial information for Keene to continue the line of questioning. The logic map relied on this minor but critical piece.

"What've you got?" Hurley, Keene's partner, asked from the other desk.

"Questions," Keene answered. "Let's go down the murder rabbit hole for a minute. Two ways in. Front door. Guy comes in. Gets the gun. From where? Kills Grogan. Leaves through the back door."

Hurley said, "It's locked. How'd he lock it?"

"Another key." Keene wrote, *Prof: Second key?* "Easier to come through the rear door. But, no struggle. Somebody he knows?"

"Even so," Hurley said, "there'd be a struggle. You can't place a gun to a dude's forehead without resistance."

"There was no sign of a struggle. If Grogan had resisted, there would have been evidence. So, if it is someone he knows and he resists, clean-up becomes a complex matter. But if the killer comes through the back door, he still has to get the gun. From where?"

Hurley said, "If Grogan carries, there'd be evidence of a massive struggle. Then the guy kills the butcher and cleans up the mess."

"Someone he knows?"

"There's still a fight."

"Hurley," Cali interrupted. "Call for you."

Keene made notes on a yellow pad.

1: Known assailant. Son had a key. Who else might have an extra key? The widow, brother-in-law, Dominic DeLuca? The Russian girl?

2: Unknown assailant. Botched robbery?

He crossed out number 2 immediately. This was not some crime gone wrong.

What else?

3: Suicide. Cleaned up to leave the world a tidy place. Like he'd never been there at all. Arnaud. Interesting. Suicide? But something's wrong.

There wasn't much evidence *against* suicide. Many arguments *for*. The butcher seemed to be unsuccessful and maybe depressed, but clinically? Maybe. Suicidally? The firearm did belong to the victim. Seemed to have been fired by the victim. There was something about that firearm, though. Something had caught Keene's attention. He couldn't retrieve the image. But the clue was right downstairs, right now with the gun.

He picked up the phone.

"It's Keene. You wanna pull the gun from the Hunger Hill suicide?" He told the clerk he'd be down.

At the evidence locker, the clerk retrieved the gun and displayed a chain of custody form on a clipboard for Keene to sign.

Keene waved it away. "Don't need to sign it," he said. He didn't even handle the gun because he remembered. "I'm all set. I got what I wanted."

And the location of the gun just before the murder became all the more important. Because now he knew it had been murder. He didn't have evidence that rose to prosecutorial value, but he believed he had evidence enough to begin the game. To Keene, this was the most exciting moment in the investigation, the kickoff, the time when his teammates began running the ball and he, Keene, was responsible for the game plan.

CHAPTER

12

Keene needed more evidence to convince a jury. More than the sketchy, circumstantial stuff in the evidence locker. The firearm evidence all but confirmed his hunch that Grogan was murdered. Someone had killed the butcher, and it had been someone who didn't know the man well. Randomness replaced motive in a statistically meaningless percentage of cases. So, it stood to reason that if an unknown assailant had killed Grogan, there was a motive.

Wait. Unknown, or not well known. Who owed Grogan money and vice versa?

"Keene," Hurley interrupted Keene's thoughts. "Tom Grogan just called with the girl's address. Coming with me?"

"Hell yeah. I got a couple of questions for her."

The Supra, unlike the Charger, purred after roaring to life. Hurley chirped the tires in the garage and headed for the street.

"She's up on Vesper—72 Vesper, Apartment 3. Had some complaints centered around that house this summer." Hurley provided a running commentary of the history, recent and from his childhood, regarding 72 Vesper Street. Recent complaints: partying, drugs, public nudity. As for ancient history: "My mother grew up across the street. Used to be a nice neighborhood."

"Bull*shit*!" Keene said as the Supra hugged a corner Hurley took too fast. Hurley sped by the back of the grammar school he'd attended.

"No, I'm serious. Nice family neighborhood."

"Sorry, Dude," Keene said. "I just don't believe it."

Hurley wheeled the Supra onto Vesper and found the four-car mini lot of the apartment house empty of vehicles—which had been replaced with four plastic chairs, four unfinished drinks, and a bong cooling its heels among the chairs. "Feel like we're crashing the party?"

"Yeah, but where are the guests?"

Hurley pulled his sidearm and pounded on the front door. "Police!

Open the door." He said to Keene, "Go around back; there's a fire escape."

Keene circled the building and saw two girls in bikinis hopping off the wrought-iron ladder.

"Stop! Hands where I can see them!" He eyed the terrified girls, who were, by substantial evidence, unarmed. Keene saw Hurley round the building and called to him to get back to the front. "There are more girls than just these two."

Realizing his mistake, Hurley ran back to the front entrance in time to see the back end of a retreating Nissan Sentra. He jumped into the Supra, switched on the blue bubble, and started the chase.

At the back of the house, Keene confronted the two girls but had no interest in cuffing them. The accepted method was to pull a suspect's hands to the small of his or her back and wrap the cuffs or zip ties. As Keene considered the abbreviated thongs the girls wore and the intimacy of the cuffing process, he chose to merely ask their names. They weren't running, neither was named Lena, and Keene chose not to intervene further.

"Where is she? Is she in the car?"

Both questions were met with *No speak English* shrugs.

"Go," he said to them. "Go back to your party." He walked to the parking lot with them, and the girls plopped back into their chairs, watching the detective questioningly. Another girl, wearing cutoff jeans and a tank top, bolted from the apartment house and ran when she saw Keene.

He followed her to the Eastern Prom and was on her until she made a quick right-hand turn between a sausage vendor and a pretzel van. He overran the turn; beyond the pretzels, he turned right and saw her running down the hill toward the bike trail. He angled toward her and the pounding of the downhill run shot pain up his thigh and into his ass, and the girl was laboring, too. They leveled out on the bike trail and she turned right. She was small and her strides were short. His were longer and he caught up with her. She tried one last evasive maneuver, turning right, where the hill stopped her dead. She finally fell and cried. Fortunately, she wore more clothing than her colleagues, and Keene was able to cuff her without feeling obscene. She had, however, succeeded in making him feel old.

He sucked in his breath and wiped sweat from his forehead. His charge did the same. She looked at her hands, which he'd zip-tied at her stomach, and wept quietly. The law did not require him to ask for her paperwork if he didn't have a reason. His purpose was exclusively to ask questions about her place of employment. But she didn't know that.

"What's your name?"

She said nothing.

"Lena, I know your name."

"Then why you ask?" she said.

Despite her fear, her logic was sound. Keene said, "I am Detective Keene of the Portland Police Department and I have some questions for you."

"I done nothing. Always wear something of clothing. Those girls lie around naked." She wagged her head in the direction of the apartment house, her chin trembling.

"What?" Keene was perplexed until he remembered the litany of complaints against the residents of her apartment house. Chief among them had been public indecency. "Never mind that, though it is commendable to clothe yourself." He continued, "Did you work at DeLuca's Variety Store this summer?"

She said nothing, and it appeared she had no intention of giving anything up.

"I'm not ICE. I'm not interested in your documents, okay?"

She said nothing. She had stopped talking entirely the moment he had mentioned work. "All I want you to tell me is where Patrick Grogan kept his gun. Do you know?"

She remained quiet.

"Come on," he said. "I'm gonna book you for disorderly conduct, illegal interruption of commercial activity, and obstructing an officer of the law. As I book you, Lena, it might get out to ICE that I have an undocumented worker in custody."

"No," she said. "What if I answer questions?"

"Lena, if you answer my questions, you would not be obstructing an officer." He didn't tell her the other items were bullshit. "Where did he keep the gun?"

She told him. Under the register. Right where an intruder could lift it on the way in from the front door.

"Who else knew this?"

She didn't know. Nobody.

"Did other girls work there? Other Russian girls?"

"I don't know."

Beyond now knowing where the weapon was, this line of questioning was going nowhere. He had what he needed anyway.

"Had any customers threatened him recently, that you know of?" he asked while snipping the zip-ties.

"No. Well...maybe one guy very angry."

"Who? Do you know a name?"

"I don't know name. He's drunk, I think, when he says these things."

"Can you tell me what he looks like?"

"Very skinny and wears a hat; not like ball hat. Not like that. Like a flat hat like in my country, they wear these kind of thing. Is fisherman hat in my country."

"What kinds of things did this man say to Grogan? Did he threaten him?"

"Threaten?"

"Did he say something like—" Keene stopped himself. He couldn't put words in the witness's mouth. How could he define threaten without an example? "Threaten means to say you will do something to someone that will be bad for that person."

"Like *kill*?"

"Did he say that?"

"No, no. I just say that to know the *threaten*."

"Oh," Keene said, deflated, having thought they were getting somewhere. "But did he say something like that?"

"The drunk with the hat, he say maybe something like 'up yours, mister.' Or maybe 'fuck you.' Or something else like that."

"Huh," Keene said. "But you don't know the guy's name?"

"Is some kind of name I never hear. Not too much, no."

"Lena," he said and gave her a business card. "Thank you. Call me if you think of anything. Please tell your friends to keep their clothes on like you. In America, we do this."

"But I think the topless is okay, no?"

She smiled fetchingly at him, and he knew she was right. Portland had passed such an ordinance. Keene wondered who benefited from the relaxation of social restraints. Was it the socially restrained who found themselves with newfound freedoms? Or was it the person who was uninterested in restraint—or perhaps *unable* to restrain him or herself? Keene couldn't be sure of anything but the consistency of change and the universality of corruption. It was hard to imagine who truly benefited from bare breasts. He supposed testosterone-ridden teenage boys profited in a sense.

CHAPTER
13

Bud Cushing was a friend and a fellow muscle car enthusiast, and he owned a beer distributorship. If Grogan was stiffing anyone, or the other way around, Bud would know.

Keene keyed the number for Casco Bay Beverage Distributors. The receptionist put Keene through and his friend picked up the phone.

"I thought you and Melena were on vaca, right? Sailing?" Bud said.

"S'posed to be. But...you heard the owner of DeLuca's died last night?"

There was a pause on the line.

Then, "Who died?"

"Patrick Grogan. Owner of DeLuca's Variety Store on the Hill. Did you know him?"

"Oh, Jesus," Bud said with an audible sigh. "This is not good. This is gonna mess things up, bad."

"What do you mean by that?" Keene noted that Bud didn't ask how the man died.

Bud said, "The deal. He just sold the business."

"Huh," Keene said, trying to square Bud's unexpected reaction. "Can you explain that?"

"Well, Patrick dies, there's no deal. But that's not uncommon, you know."

Keene said, "No. I don't know."

"Any transaction. The principals' gotta be at the table. Patrick can't be if he's dead."

Keene said, "There's no doubt he's dead."

"This is gonna screw up a lot of people. Grogan was insolvent, see? Broke. He owed us money but I've known the family."

"The Grogans?" Keene asked for clarification.

"No, the DeLucas. We've known each other for a long time. Dom contacted me. Said he knew Grogan owed me money. Asked how much—agreed to pay it off at the closing. I still had to shut Grogan off. Made him

COD. Cash only. His checks were bouncing around like four-year-olds at a chocolate factory. There's been more than one weekend this summer when you couldn't get a cold Bud at the Variety."

That explained the "cash only" sign posted on Grogan's wall. He was capitalizing the requirements of his suppliers.

"Jesus, that had to hurt. So, if the family paid everybody off, the store was sold, and Grogan's liquidity problems were solved, nobody would want him dead, right?"

"Wait," Bud said. "He was murdered?"

"No, no, I'm not saying that," Keene said, having just said that. "I take it you don't get the paper. We have to look at all possibilities. We think he killed himself, Bud."

"Why would he do that? The sale solved all his problems. He owed people money. The deal got him out from under all that. He was looking at a somewhat well-funded retirement. Doesn't make any sense."

"Would any supplier want him dead?"

"Hmm, I guess that's just it," Bud said and stopped.

"That's just what?"

"Some suppliers were gonna get screwed, I suppose. The family is going to take care of me, but I have no idea how the rest of the deal was structured. You better call Dominic DeLuca."

"Was the deal brokered by somebody?"

Bud said it was and gave Keene the name of the agent who'd handled the deal.

"Hey, Basil," Bud said as they were winding up the conversation.

"Yeah, Bud?"

"Talk to the broker about what happens to the deal with Grogan's death. I'd be surprised if it isn't squashed and back to the negotiating table."

"What would that mean?"

"I'll get hosed. Or at least until Dom restructures a deal."

"What about the other creditors?" Keene asked.

"They might be back in the game. They get another opportunity to try to get their money."

"Thanks," Keene said and underlined the broker's name three times with dark slashes. He clicked off and thought: Creditors. Got to get a list started.

Keene tapped on the door. Looked in. Charlie Riordan was rubbing his forehead. About the same thing he was doing when Keene left him that morning.

"Charlie, I've done some digging. Grogan wasn't in great financial shape," Keene said. "But his death screws things up for a lot of people. I can tell you this: Bud Cushing, owner of Casco Bay Beverage?"

"I know him. Good guy. What's he got to do with it?"

"Bud's suddenly mourning the loss of his customer. A dead-beat customer; Grogan owed him. But if the sale went through, DeLuca was going to take care of Bud. However, now that Grogan is dead? Who knows?"

"Grogan hated the DeLucas," Riordan said. "Maybe he shot himself just to piss them off."

"He didn't."

"He didn't what?"

"Shoot himself, Charlie. He didn't shoot himself."

"Good. You got proof?"

Good? Keene thought. Not long ago, Charlie had wanted this to be suicide. Keene decided to keep his logic to himself for the moment. "Circumstantial. The long and the short of it is if he was murdered, there are a lot of new, motivated suspects. Guys who weren't on the table this morning. I'm going to need some help."

Riordan said, "Have a seat," and he made a call. Put on hold, he rested the phone on his shoulder. "I'm in a bad position, Basil. I trust you, but I don't know how to substantiate the requests for man-hours unless you got evidence. More than circumstantial. The Council is up my ass on every-thing I try to do." Riordan tentatively put the phone to his ear.

There was a light rap on the door. Cali opened it and Riordan waved the phone like he was guiding a plane on the tarmac. Hurley, compact and muscular, moved in. "You wanted to see me?"

Riordan slapped the phone against his ear and said, "Hello? Hello?" Then, not into the receiver: "Shut the door."

Hurley did and settled into the other chair in the office and said, "How's the security plan for the Senator coming?"

Riordan held the phone out demonstratively and then said, "Fuck it." And hung up. "Sonsabitches," he muttered to himself.

Riordan updated Hurley on the Grogan case. "Keene thinks this is more than Grogan eating his gun. You hear anything on the Hill?"

"Nobody's talking about it yet."

"What about the upstairs tenants?"

"Arnaud has good alibis for both of the families," Keene said. "They're okay." Then he said, "DeLuca is the biggest loser as a result of Grogan's death."

"But," Riordan said, "shouldn't we focus on the guys who *win* because of his death? Follow the money?"

"Yeah," Keene said and explained to Hurley what Cushing had told him.

"What if you're a supplier and you got nothing promised to you? What happens then?" Hurley asked.

Keene said, "Those are called unsecured creditors, according to Bud. I want Peterson to talk to the broker about how the deal was structured. Bud expected a payday, but did anybody else?"

Riordan looked at Keene. "Peterson had some financial crimes experience in Indy. Fuck the budget. She and Hurley are yours. We gotta make some headway on this."

"I want Officer Arnaud, too. I need a sit. room." A situation room was a war room with desks with phone chargers and chairs, a conference table, and whiteboards.

"You think these unsecured creditors stood to lose if the closing happened as scheduled?" Hurley said, getting back to motive. He took his cup from Cali.

"That's what I want Peterson to find out," Keene said. "If anybody didn't want that deal signed."

After a pause, Riordan said, "You sure you want Arnaud? You really want a rookie on this?"

"Chief, she's a good officer. Smart, observant...teachable."

"I don't want her on the case if she's going to mess you up," Riordan said. Then to Hurley, he said, "You got anything else going on?" Hurley shook his head no.

"Okay, I can make a case for three detectives if I'm not taking you away from anything else. But if something comes up..." Riordan said and left it at that. "I'll get back to you on a room. Hurley, let me ask you something else. If Keene's right and this isn't suicide, I want you to find out if something's going down on the Hill. Quiet-like."

Hurley said, "You know all this secured and unsecured creditor bullshit? That's all it is. Bullshit. Grogan and his debt and creditors and all are very small potatoes. You know Granda Mack is dying, right? Granda Mack is very *big* potatoes. I'm as sure as Charlie likes green M&Ms that the Macks are involved."

Keene was leaning back in his chair when his phone rang. He was ready to leave for the day and considered not taking the call. He looked at the caller ID and saw the name, Venti. Shit. He'd had to work up to giving the reporter the time of day, let alone working with the guy.

"Keene," the detective barked into the phone.

"Detective Keene," Leo said.

"Leo, what do you want?"

"I'd-a thought that was self-evident, Detective. You're sitting on a juicy unattended death, and I need some info from you."

"I'm not saying a word until you tell me who's talking from my staff."

"You know I can't give that info up," Leo said. "What makes you think my source is from your staff?"

"Your words: 'unnamed sources' gives the clear impression that your sources are in the Department and you know that."

"You need to reread my article. I used the phrase 'sources close to the investigation.' There's a difference."

"Yeah, yeah," Keene admitted. "I pointed that out to Charlie. You don't write the teaser, do you? That's some editor. But your average reader doesn't know that."

Leo said nothing for a few seconds, then, "I'll tell you this much: Your staff is not talking. End of story. But enough semantics. What do you have for me?"

Keene thought for a minute. What could Leo do for him? "As you said, Leo, we have an unattended death. Possible suicide. No disagreements here. You can take that salacious tidbit off the table. I also can tell you this." Keene paused to craft his words. He didn't want to say it was a professional hit. He didn't want to say that it was not a suicide. But he wanted to plant the doubt a little more firmly. He thought the killer should know the Department wasn't completely in the dark, and Leo could tell the killer so. "There is some evidence that casts a shadow of ambiguity over the assumption of suicide."

"Did you read my article? That's a rehash of what I've already written."

"I know that. I want you to send a message to the killer. Write that the PPD is..." Keene paused again. "Look, Leo, if you don't use the words, or infer the idea, that the Department is at odds over this case, I'll owe you." Then he said, "I take that back; you'll owe me less. Write that the Department is dealing with an ambiguous case at this point..." He thought again. He wanted Leo to convey the idea that the earlier inference of a Department at odds was incorrect. "With a businesslike..." he paused. "Resolutely, Leo. Use the word *resolutely.*"

"You can't write my article for me, Keene. Despite what you think of me."

"I know, Leo. Just help me here. Maybe we can get back to working together. I'll get you the leads on this thing. I'll put you ahead of the TV nerds. If I'm right."

"Okay," the reporter said. "Look, I got a call coming in from...the Interim Chief. No shit. Wonder what he has to tell me. That the Department has a *resolutely ambiguous* case? Let's talk later." Leo ended the call.

Keene clicked off the cell, mildly detesting the reporter and wondering about the seeds he was planting. Was it ethical to use the press to help a guy get a job? Probably not, but why not? Was it ethical for the press to run an innocent officer through the mill and not apologize? Apparently. Nobody had expressed remorse or written a retraction. Journalism is never having to say you're sorry. Keene was a little tired of the one-sided stories.

CHAPTER
14

Sully's Tap sported six pulls at the center of the bar. Gary taught Eileen to pour a Guinness with a spoon. He taught her a couple of exotic drinks, and she'd come to the job with a wealth of experience. Francis, her dad, had seen to that.

A guy with a squirrel's-nest beard arrived and sat in front of Eileen.

"Christ, it's hot," he said through the squirrel's nest. "Bud."

She drew his beer. "Keep a tab?"

"You new?" he asked.

"Fairly," Eileen said brightly. "Keep a tab?"

"Pete," he said and stuck out his hand.

She said to call her Eileen and asked if he was from around here because he seemed to have a southern accent. Then she said, "I'll start you a tab."

"Nope. New to Maine. I'm from Florida," which he pronounced Flaw-da. "Thought it was supposed to be cool up here."

A second guy came in. He was called Paul. He said, "Bud. You new?"

She said, "Eileen," and started pouring Paul's beer.

A third guy joined the first two. He loosened his tie, a striped number, an ugly navy and brown. "Bud, please. I'm John. You new here?"

Jesus, Eileen thought. These frigging guys.

"Eileen," she said and went to work pouring a beer for John. Peter, Paul and John, like the apostles, she thought.

John said, "Did you hear? Someone killed the butcher."

Pete said, "Guys at work said he killed himself."

"The butcher at DeLuca's?" Paul asked.

"Yeah. Pretty sure he committed suicide," Pete said, wiping foam from the squirrel's nest.

"When did this happen?" Paul asked.

"Last night," John said.

Last night, Eileen thought. All those sirens and speeding cops and ambulances. "What time?" she asked.

Nobody knew.

John nodded at the TV that was on a news channel. "Guess you're happy you're not in Florida now, Pete."

Eileen said, "Yeah. Hurricane Liam's gonna nail the panhandle, I guess."

"You talk to the wife and kids?" John asked. Then, to Eileen, he said, "Pete's ex and kids live in, where, Pete?"

"Panama City. Right in the bullseye."

"Jeez," Eileen said.

Then Paul said, "They don't own the store anymore, do they?"

"Who? Pete's ex and kids? What are you talking about?" John said.

"Who owns the damned store, douchebag?" Pete said.

"Oh. Not Dom DeLuca, right, Eileen?" John said.

"I d k," she said.

The three guys looked at her like she'd answered in, well, merely letters, which she had.

"Sorry," she said. "I don't know."

"Grogan, the butcher, owned it," Sullivan said helpfully from the other end of the bar. "Bought it a while ago. Wife's DeLuca's sister."

The three regulars nodded and said, "Huh," and settled in, their energy having established itself.

Pete said, "So, Eileen, you from around here?"

• • •

After her shift, she sat at the bar with a glass of beer and a glass of water. A TV blonde with glossy lips explained the dynamics of the storm in Florida. The formation of a hurricane is dependent on… Is dependent on what? Gary hit the remote button to change the channel to the Sox game. Cripe sake, she'd have to Google the dynamics of a hurricane. Pressure. Swirling motions. Vectors. Is it possible to apply pressure merely by thinking?

"Hey," Jamie Mack surprised her.

"Oh," she said.

"What are you doing?" Jamie asked Eileen. "Guinness," Jamie said to Gary.

"J-chilling," she said.

"Cheers," he said and held his glass up briefly.

She sipped her beer. "Well," she ventured. He'll think I'm nuts, she thought, but why not. "I'm concentrating. A lot."

"On what?"

"Don't make fun of me?"

He took a drink and said, "No, 'course not."

"I have a project. I'm concentrating on this glass."

"Why?" he asked, elongating the word the way people do when challenging someone to explain what the heck they're talking about.

"Actually, concentrating on the water in it." Oh boy, certifiable, she thought.

"What about the water?"

"You're going to think I'm crazy."

"Maybe, but so what if I do, right?"

She looked at him as he spoke. He seemed sincere. Cousin Jamie had always treated her nicely.

"I think I can exercise mind over matter. I think I can make this water move if I think hard enough." There. She said it. Nutso! Flipso! Calypso! Out to lunch in a bucket.

"How ya think you can do that?"

He thinks I'm soft, she thought. "That's the problem. I don't know," she said. Soft as a grape, she thought.

"Cool," he said and took a long gulp of Guinness and clunked the glass down. "When you figure it out, let me know. I heard you're workin' here now."

"Correct," she said.

"Let me see your ID."

"Cripe sake, Jamie," she whispered urgently looking left and right. "Jeez."

"You're a Mack, kid. Nothin' to worry about." He held his hand low, below the bar. She handed it to him and he looked her over carefully. "Not bad. I was going to say I could get you a pretty good one, but this is good. The pink hair was genius. That's all you look at in the pic. Who'd you get the ID from?"

"The Greek, why?"

"What did he charge you?" She told him and he called the Greek some names and said he'd get her money back. "He can't charge a Mack that kind of money. Sonofabitch."

His attitude mercurially changing, he said, "Kevin and I come in here after work a lot. Be seeing more of you."

"Where is Kevin?" Eileen asked.

"He's tied up. With some family business. Kevin's got himself in a little hot water with Granda. No big deal. Just gotta tie up some loose ends. You seen Granda?"

She said, "No. I gotta get over there."

"He's been seeing everybody lately. He ain't gonna last much longer, Ei. Go see him. Tomorra."

He touched her face with an unexpectedly gentle hand like the stroke of a lover's cheek and left without paying for his drink.

Gary finished getting a beer for Squirrel's Nest Pete and wandered over to Eileen. "Your cousins, Jamie and Kevin, drink on the house. They pay in kind with other services."

"Oh. Okay." She stared at the glass of water. She realized no matter how hard she looked at it or thought about it, the water was not going to swirl at her command. Not tonight, anyway.

CHAPTER
15

A professional killer, like any professional, must review his or her work. A pro identifies his or her strengths and weaknesses. A pro examines the execution of her practices to diagnose the mistakes made and surgically remove them before they become a fatal affliction. Silk Rhenko's first professional job could have gone more smoothly, meaning she had some diagnosing to do. But her strengths were noteworthy as well. Silk had passed the test; the subject was dead; the scene was clean. Silk was the killer Umarov needed. A man can't see the danger a woman can pose, notably a small woman, and, having predicted so, Silk was the newest member of the hitman guild, had there been one. Using her gender, she could and would disarm and disable targets of the opposite sex. These were her strengths, and she would hone them and go into battle with the sharpest knife she could.

The mistakes were few but dangerous. Summed up in one word: witnesses. There should have been none, but there'd been more than one. Silk's fumbling with the lock had nearly been fatal. If she had better lock-picking skills, the drunk wouldn't have stumbled upon her messing with the front door. Solution number one had two parts: Hone her skills and kill the drunk.

The guy pounding on the back door and calling the butcher Dad was problem number two. This occurred for the same reason: Silk screwed around with the key card for too long. Picks. Lock picks. She would find them. If the butcher's son had seen her, she would kill him. But she was sure he hadn't, and she'd rather not kill more people than necessary. Live and let live wasn't exactly the motto of the hitman guild, had there been one, but in this case, Silk thought it prudent inaction. Which led her to the girl on the bike trail. She had seen them. She was a threat. That girl must die. But how could they have avoided this? Pre-placement of cameras along the escape route?

Killing a man wasn't the terrible thing she'd thought it might be. Thrilling, even. Two witnesses might be twice as thrilling. The drunk and the girl must be hushed. The questions were how and how soon. The final goal, the confrontation with Umarov, must happen before the *Ice Cold* sailed at the end of the summer. There wasn't a lot of time.

Who slips into a motel room late in the evening dressed in a black, skin-tight outfit that is soaked through to the skin? Only the quirkiest; and Nurzhan and Silk were these guests. A fellow late-night guest stared at her as though she was in a wet T-shirt contest, and he missed the firearm jammed at her hip. From the trigger cage down, the gun was covered by her pants; the grip was covered by the top she wore. Her carry gun was concealed, but only technically. If the guest hadn't been looking at her nipples, he would have seen the perfect imprint of a Smith, M&P Shield on her hip.

She threw her bag on the carpet, piled her wet clothes on the shower floor, and stood in the cool water. This sensation was all she wanted to feel. The crack of the pistol was a distant memory. Water splashed over her, enlivening her from the nuclei of her cells out to the tips of her nails. She was a Specialist. Arkady, if he'd lived, would have been proud.

Silk tucked her chin and thought about the job. Her black hair curtained her face. The drunk. People had habits. Particularly drunks. The guy with the fisherman's cap was a problem with a simple solution.

Silk's skin was blue goose-flesh. She turned off the water, toweled her hair in a turban, and stood naked with her arms out like an A for thirty minutes. She allowed the heat to dry her; a towel would be too rough. Tonight, she would sleep on the bed. She lay on the bath towel, coarse as it was, and prepared to battle for sleep. She allowed the warm air to settle on her. The heat of the day had left the room almost sauna-like.

There was a light knuckle rap on the door. She wrapped herself in the towel and retrieved the pistol. She looked through the peephole and saw Nurzhan. She cracked the door.

"What?"

"We need to talk."

She thought he was right but didn't want him in her room. However, after pulling on a soft scoop-neck T-shirt, she allowed him in. At gunpoint.

"Do you have to hold that gun on me?" Nurzhan asked.

"Yes," Silk said.

She watched every move he made.

"Are these witnesses a problem?" he asked.

"Of course," Silk said.

"All three?"

She thought for a minute. "The drunk is. Yes. I will take care of that."

"Okay. What about the man; did he see you? The butcher's son?"

Silk thought. She didn't want the body count to mount. Drunks met with unfortunate accidents. But the grown son?

"I don't think so," she said.

"I talk to Yakov."

She said, "No, don't. Let it go. What do you think about the girl?" Silk knew she must find her and eliminate her. The butcher's apparent suicide would be examined. Silk and Nurzhan had done the setup and cleanup well, but the death would be investigated. The girl had seen two suspicious people near the time of death. She would tell this to the police. The girl must be disposed of in a manner that was inconsistent with the other deaths. Nothing can tie them together.

"I don't think she is problem. But—" Nurzhan started.

"But maybe we should be sure?"

"No," Nurzhan said. "Not necessary."

"But if it becomes necessary, her death must be unlike the others. Deaths can be tied together. They must be inconsistent."

Nurzhan said, "Butcher commits suicide. Son is killed in drive-by."

"No. Don't be stupid. Father and the son? In a couple of days? No."

"Is drive-by. Happens all the time."

"No. Let me think." Silk recalled the dumpster she had hidden behind. She was small and in black—the son did not see her. "No. We won't kill him. Can't afford to. Girl, though, if we can find her, drowns...somehow. This does happen all the time, yes?"

CHAPTER
16

The *Dominator* turned a graceful curve, slowed, and sidled to the boarding float at the stern of the much larger *Ice Cold*. Dom DeLuca, the operator of the smaller boat, throttled back expertly and brought the *Dominator* to a stop. Nurzhan stepped over the rail and held a hand for Silk. He carried the suitcase full of currency. A week's work.

Fyodor Umarov's yacht, with its two lounges and two pools, made DeLuca's 24-foot Grady-White look insignificant. Umarov had renamed his ship *Ice Cold*. The vessel had begun her career as a small yet luxurious cruise ship, the *Aegean Princess*. She soared to a full five decks in height and had a high prow. In every respect, the ship filled a wealthy man's imagination as a presentable yacht.

The hydraulic platform rose two meters and put the two visitors on the first deck. When the *Ice Cold* was a working cruise ship, she had been deployed to exotic ports of call around the world in small-ship luxury. She was now owned by Umarov, one of the fabulously wealthy Russian oligarchs who had asexually propagated in post-USSR Russia like mushrooms spreading on shit. If asked about the boat, Umarov would say that very little sucks about owning a nearly two-hundred-foot yacht. Umarov would say that the *Ice Cold* would do as a stand-in while the 280-foot super-yacht was being built.

Silk and Nurzhan climbed to the third staircase, which was grand, and it brought them to the last deck that passengers were privileged to visit. The top deck, the one above the bridge, was for Umarov alone. For him and his special guests. Silk had a standing invitation, but she remained in her cabin on the first deck, one of the cabins with many beds. Nurzhan stayed in another cabin; she didn't care where it was.

An attractive waitress offered them drinks speaking her native Russian. She was tall and slim and wore a simple peach-colored mini-dress. Silk watched the *Dominator* disappear behind the island on its way back to

Yarmouth. As large as it was, this ship made her feel claustrophobic. She pushed a chair under the umbrella and sat on the edge of it, staying close to the cash-laden suitcase.

Silk felt Umarov watching her. Comfort was something she'd never felt in the oligarch's presence. He seemed covetous and patronizing toward her.

The concept of the oligarchy is not uniquely Russian. However, the vast Eurasian nation has existed with the system since the 1400s, and the modern idea of the oligarch is widely understood to be Russian. Fyodor Umarov owned an enterprise of many businesses, small and large, legitimate and not. He was one of the biggest private owners of business in Russia. By definition, oligarchs are close to the governing class and rule their smaller empires by power and intimidation. He fit the definition. The man was rumored to be on the list of the top fifty richest men in the world. He wasn't comfortable with the fiftieth-largest bank account, however. The man with ice-blue eyes wanted top-ten status. Umarov wore stylishly thick-rimmed glasses, blue frames around blue-tinted lenses. He was short, big-boned, and thick. His stature had been given him by the peasant stock from which he was descended. His wide face looked like it had been molded by the constant easterly winds of the steppes of the Caucasus. He claimed—without genetic evidence—that his heart pumped the blood of Genghis Khan. Umarov's guiding construction of life was derived from a quote from the dreaded Mongol: "The greatest happiness is to vanquish your enemies, to chase them before you, to rob them of their wealth." Umarov had the bloodthirsty warrior's words memorized. "To see those dear to them bathed in tears, to clasp to your bosom their wives and daughters." The last element of his happiness, the ownership of Rhenko's sole surviving woman, was within his grasp. Umarov's interpretation of this element had been to reduce the girl to her lowest level, then raise her to his. Total and complete ownership. She had finally made her way to him. She was about to be his. It was something that transcended ownership. He was about to manage her from astride his horse with a bullwhip and satin sheets.

"Da," he said with a wave at the suitcase. "Good. We have enough now to ship out." He screwed up an avuncular smile for Silk and said, "Drop it in Suite Four, please."

Nurzhan said nothing.

"Okay," Silk said and stood and thought that some people shouldn't even try to smile. Umarov looked like a trained porpoise, only far uglier.

She took the private stairs to the bridge level and then the wide staircase leading below to the third deck. The doorknob of the suite was solid brass in which she saw her reflection ballooned in the spherical knob. Open, the door revealed a room the size of a large hotel suite. Cardboard crates occupied the room, reaching to each corner, stacked six high to the ceiling. An arrow indicated the side that should remain upright next to a printed warning to stack no more than three high. The brand name of an American clothing manufacturer identified the contents. She set the suitcase of currency on the floor.

Suite Four was only the second stateroom she'd been allowed to see. On the occasion of her weekend visits, she'd been given a suite of her own on the first deck. She stuck her head into another suite. She saw even more crates, these marked with a broken wine glass icon and the brand name of one or, another American distiller of bourbon and rye, rum, gin, and tequila. Opening the door of another, she saw more crates and boxes of contraband. Another door, more of the same. She noted the egresses; all the suites had an entry door and a door to a balcony. She navigated a path through the wooden crates of one room. The liquor and clothing must be contraband, but what about all the cash? And where would Umarov go with the contents of the ship? Back to the Black Sea? It was as if he intended to offload the cash and then sell the goods to whoever now had the cash. Why didn't he just keep the money? She couldn't wrap her head around what the transaction could be. Or two different transactions, one for the cash and a separate deal for the goods?

The stateroom was as breathtaking as Suite Four. The first-deck berths were simple compared to these upper cabins. The entire wall opposite the entry, the ocean side, was glass. She slid the full-length door open and stepped onto the balcony, also completely constructed of molded glass. The architecture was ingenious. The space was angled and cantilevered over the ocean, which was slapping against the hull and visible through the glass floor. Silk felt like she was suspended in the air as though she'd run from the suite and jumped overboard and been arrested in time and space.

Back in the hall, she tried some doors to other suites, all were locked. Umarov would notice if she was gone much longer. She rejoined the cocktail party on the top deck. The captain had joined Umarov and Nurzhan. The waitress served drinks. Nurzhan didn't take his eyes off Silk. She surveyed the entire deck for escape if necessary. Sun glinted from polished brass surfaces and angled into her eyes. She put her hand to her forehead as a visor and walked to the table.

"No sunglasses?" Umarov asked her.

"In my bag downstairs."

He said to the waitress, "Go to Silk's quarters and get her glasses."

Silk said, "It's not necessary."

Umarov waved his hand. "It's not a problem."

He continued his discussion with Nurzhan. "I think I need to teach him a lesson." He didn't need to tell Silk he was talking about DeLuca. "In a day or two. The market and the apartments had their purposes, you see. While Silk and I are gone, we still need to generate cash, and those two are money machines."

Nurzhan asked a perfectly reasonable question: "Where do you and Silk go?"

"That's not your business, is it?" Umarov snapped.

After listening to this exchange and Umarov talk about himself further, the captain begged his leave. The waitress asked if the boss needed anything else and then she left. At times, Silk felt a twinge of jealousy. Sex was something others enjoyed, but Silk hadn't and wouldn't since Arkady was gone and any further personal relationship seemed a waste of time. Sadness was in her life, but without sadness, Silk was afraid she wouldn't feel anything at all. She heard a giggle from the unseen waitress and thought happiness was for others.

CHAPTER
17

Diane Peterson's path to Portland had taken her through Indianapolis, a larger city, a larger department, and a more compartmentalized organization with too many glass ceilings. When Diane found herself crowded up against one of these glazed impediments she ran out of oxygen. She found this position in Portland and was able to breathe again. The position with the department in the port city of Maine gave her more responsibility immediately and more promise of advancement. As a female detective in the larger midwestern city, she investigated vice; drugs, the sex trade, and their quaint cousin, gambling. In Portland, she was hired as a detective with duties ranging from computer crime to arson. She solved cases of white-collar theft, fraud, and technology crime. She wouldn't have seen the inside of a homicide investigation in Indianapolis for years, if ever. Homicide was for the good old boys. But Portland raised her to homicide quickly, purely based on merit. The way life should be.

On this day, the tall detective wore pressed jeans and a white long-sleeved oxford with the sleeves rolled to her elbows. The shared desk she used was cluttered with Hurley's stuff, paperwork, reports, and the previous day's newspaper. In a digital world, he and Keene still retained the habit of reading the paper. She was an online consumer of the daily news.

She called the broker, whose name she'd gotten from Keene, with questions about the specifics of the transfer of assets and liabilities in the Grogan deal.

"I arranged the transaction on behalf of the buyer. It was an asset purchase."

"Which means?" Peterson said.

The broker said, "Just what it sounds like. The buyer purchases the assets alone. In this case, the DeLuca family owned the building and Mr. Grogan owned the inventory and capital equipment. My buyer purchased all these assets at a theoretically elevated price. Which is conventional." The broker's voice sounded dry like she needed water. Nerves? It happens when a detective calls.

"But what happens to the liabilities?"

"The seller remains liable for all debts and obligations. Much of the inventory was subject to this sort of liability, I suppose. Theoretically, the price will be enough to satisfy the creditors. Assuming there are no liens on the property. In this case, there were none."

"So, Grogan and DeLuca would pay off Grogan's debts with the inflated proceeds, correct?"

"The primary lender gets paid first in a case like this. The primary lender on the business loan was the family. From the proceeds of the real estate deal, Dom DeLuca made sure the family was paid in full. And he made sure that's all there was."

This ran contrary to Bud Cushing's assertion to Keene that Grogan would be okay after the deal.

"But I thought the sale was for a lot of money."

The broker hesitated.

"The DeLucas ... I don't know how much I can tell you. Um, legally."

"I'm the cops," Peterson said. "You will tell me everything if I get a warrant. Or you can give it to me now and save us both time."

"Okay, I guess. He, Dom, structured the deal so that the real estate was paid out first. After the real estate was taken care of, the business loan was dealt with, and there were just enough funds to cover Grogan's obligation to the family. They left him swinging in the wind with other creditors."

"Ouch," Peterson said. "What about the wife? She was family, right? Dom's sister?"

"Dom's a smart guy. There's a family trust. With certain restrictions. I think you might want to talk to his attorney for details. But the sister couldn't pay any business debts. Grogan got hosed and he didn't know it. He would have found out at the closing."

Peterson drummed her fingers. What is going on here? She penned: Find Dom's attorney and speak with Dom. Somebody didn't want this deal to happen.

"So, what about the vendors?"

"Therein lies the problem. If there is no money and no guarantor behind the obligation, then Grogan is an empty piñata. No matter how many times you hit him, there's nothing there. Bankruptcy is not a zero-sum system."

Peterson realized that was how the beverage distributor was being paid. The family could pick and choose the suppliers who got satisfied and those who didn't. "And these folks might very well be angry with Grogan for a perceived hosing? And not with the family."

"Yes. I guess that would be very possible. They'd be wrong. They should be upset with DeLuca. Dom's the bad guy here."

"One other thing," Peterson said. "Detective Keene spoke to Bud Cushing at Casco Bay Beverage. When he was informed of Grogan's death, his immediate response was that things might get screwed up. Why would he say that?"

"The closing was scheduled for tomorrow at noon. It won't happen now. You need all principals of the deal to be present. There is no dead-or-alive provision."

The broker wasn't going to get paid. Cushing wasn't going to get paid. They didn't want Grogan dead—just the opposite. The suspects were falling away like icebergs from a calving glacier. Take them and DeLuca off the suspect list. DeLuca may have wanted to screw his brother-in-law, but he couldn't finish the job without him alive.

"Thank you for your help."

She clicked off. The relevance of the closing threw a different light on Grogan's death. She made a note to investigate the books for the last few years. Had anyone suffered enough to eliminate Patrick Grogan? Seemed unlikely to her but she didn't have skin in the game.

The unlikeable butcher of Hunger Hill was bankrupt, and his brother-in-law had seen to it. It seemed to Peterson that Patrick Grogan and Dom DeLuca might share culpability in the eyes of an unsecured creditor. Kill Grogan for revenge? Was DeLuca in danger?

———◆◆◆———

Keene had written, *One: The immediate family.* Tom and Annabella. He was cold on both. The professor had too much to lose and had sidetracked his career to protect his mother. The butcher and his family seemed to have reached a stasis, a cease-fire. They weren't off the list, but in Keene's judgment, they weren't hot.

Two: Neighbors and customers. These were people who might have a particular dislike of the butcher. The team would conduct interviews to narrow it down. It would require time and patience. Keene was short on the former, and he was afraid Riordan was short on the latter. The results of the canvass would help, Keene knew.

Category *Three: The DeLuca family.* He only had gossip to go on, but he knew the family had not gotten along with the butcher even though they were in business with him and he had married one of them. It wasn't a small family. He hoped Peterson's interview with the broker would shed some light on this category.

Number four was the intriguing one: *The Mack family.* There was a history there; it was weird, but it was a history. Keene knew there was bad blood between the Macks and the Grogans. He was confident Hurley could drill down into the dynamics of that one. His relationship with Michaela could help. Or hinder significantly.

One through four, a short list constituted of long sub-lists. The victim was an unpopular man. The community might be full of enemies. Nearly any member of the neighborhood known as Hunger Hill could reasonably be considered a suspect in the murder of the butcher.

Then it came to him. Vito Troiano. A blowhard, but...? Keene filled in the name under *Neighbors and customers.* Keene tapped his pen. He wasn't happy with any of this. When he stepped back from these lists, he realized just how much he depended on Hurley. The neighborhood, the DeLucas, the Macks. It seemed to Keene that the neighborhood either contained the answer or was the answer.

CHAPTER

18

Pete with the squirrel's-nest beard arrived first among the three regulars.
Eileen said, "How are the kids, Pete?" She surprised herself with the
sincerity of her concern for Pete's kids. Only a couple of days ago she hadn't
even met the dude with the facial rodent breeding ground.

"I haven't gotten through yet, Ei. I think they got out, but I don't know.
I'm worried about them. I'm worried about my ex, too."

"Oh, cripe sake, Pete," Eileen put down the dried glass she'd been polishing. She reached for his hand and said, "They probably got out of there,
right? It wasn't a surprise or anything. Your ex had warning, right?"

The all-news channel showed Panama City, flood waters filling the
downtown streets, the hurricane smashing into the panhandle at that very
moment. The storm surge was carrying yachts and fishing boats into the
streets hundreds of yards from the beach like a giant bathtub ring. The
TV showed images of boats tilted and jammed into the lobbies of hotels,
marooned in parking lots, and, conversely, cars and trucks being carried
back by the floodwaters into the sea.

A customer ordered a Bud, and Eileen started pulling it as several other
people wandered in, then more. Busy night. The guy down the bar hollered
at Eileen for another Smithwick's.

"Lighten up, you ass-hat!" she yelled back. "Cripe sake," she said to herself.

John, wearing a floral tie, arrived and said to Pete, "How ya doing,
buddy? You get through to them?" He looked at Eileen. She was looking
away but he called out to her, "Get me a Bud when you get a chance, Ei.
No hurry."

"I don't mind if you grab it yourself," she whispered to him while she
attended to the Smithwick's customer.

Pete answered John with a head shake and, "Not yet."

The phone rang and Eileen didn't hear the rest of Pete's answer.

"Sully's Tap, Eileen Mack, ready if you are," she said and pushed the Bud to John, who hadn't heard her whisper, and she thought that was probably for the better. A guy asked for a Jameson neat, and she poured one-handed while shouldering the cordless phone.

"Ei? It's Jamie. How ya doing?"

She totaled the tab for a couple who were leaving, took their credit card, and swiped it still cradling the phone.

"Up to my ass in elbows," she said.

"That hurricane is something else, right? You busy?" he asked.

She poured another Jameson neat and the guy claimed he had said bourbon neat. She said, "Well, what kinda bourbon?" and poured a Makers for him.

She said to Jamie, "Yeah. No. Not particularly; the bar that is," she lied for no good reason. "But I'm busy. I'm working...you know?"

"Yeah. I do know. That's why I called you at the bar. Because I know you're working, right?"

"Oh. Right," she said and saw a customer waving her to his table. She said to Jamie, "What's up?"

"When do you get off?" Jamie asked.

"Six. Why?"

"'Cause you and me, we're gonna go see Granda. I'll pick you up at six."

She hung up the phone and, by now, the customer was waving his hand frantically as if he had a front-row seat on the bow of the *Titanic*. She hurried over, apologized and asked what all the fuss was about, and reminded him that she didn't do table service, that if he wanted table service, he could go to any number of other establishments in the city, but since he was here and she was here what could she get him?

By quarter of six, the rush had slowed considerably. Cousins Jamie and Kevin walked into the bar and nodded at the guys sitting there. The three amigos, or biblical prophets, wouldn't break until after seven unless hell had frozen over while Eileen had taken her eye off it.

"Ei-Mack!" Kevin said loudly. "How ya been, sweetheart?" He leaned over the bar and kissed her on the cheek. Kevin, family, could call her Ei-Mack and live to talk about it.

"Hey, Kevin," she smiled. "Good, 'n' you?"

"I'm great. You look great. Ready to go see Granda?"

"Well," she said, "I gotta finish my shift."

"Yeah, yeah. Get us a couple of Smithwick's," Kevin said.

"Hey, Cuz. How's the mind-over-matter thing going?" Jamie asked.

The twins quaffed their beers, and Jamie explained Eileen's remote drink-mixing to Kevin, who asked Eileen about it and she told him.

Kevin was entertained by the idea despite the undeniable fact that he didn't know what the heck she was talking about. He was captivated by his little cousin and always had been. Gary arrived and let Eileen go ten minutes early. She thought about asking Jamie if he had any apartments available, and tell him she wanted to have an apartment of her own like their cousin Michaela, but she was nervous about asking. What if they mentioned it in passing to their cousin Franny? In the end, she didn't ask.

An impossibly large dark-blue pickup truck was parked in front of Sully's. A cop car waited for a vehicle coming the other way before he swung around Jamie's illegally parked truck. The friendly cop waved to the three cousins as they got into the giant vehicle.

Jesus, Eileen thought, friends in high places.

They drove to the intersection and turned up the Hill. Granda lived in the street-level apartment in the building he owned on Montreal Street, where he'd lived as long as Eileen could remember. The building was sheathed in asbestos siding, yellow at birth, presently a sickly brown. Like all the three-story apartment houses on the Hill, it had been used hard and, if not neglected, at least treated with a generationally cloned indifference.

The apartment door stood open and they entered. Jamie said, "Granda, how ya doin'?" He leaned down to the once big man and kissed him on the cheek. The last time Eileen had seen the old man was before the stroke. He'd lost a lot of weight since then; he looked bony under a colorful blanket that wrapped his legs.

A skinny woman with graying dark hair backed away from the patient and busied herself with flower arrangements near the window.

Jamie said, "Hi, Connie, lots of flowers, huh?"

She said hello and continued puttering with the flowers.

Kevin said, "Granda, we brought you somebody. You remember Eileen, Francis's youngest?"

Eileen stepped forward, her hands clasped behind her back, a flush warming her face. "Hi, Granda," she said, her voice small. She struggled to think of something to say to the old man. "You look good," she lied.

After some lighthearted banter, salted with empathy for the dying, Jamie indicated that Eileen and Connie should leave and they did, leaving behind an old man whom Eileen suspected she wouldn't see alive again. Jamie could make people do things with a look. He'd always been kind to Eileen, but she'd seen the devil's look in him.

Connie and Eileen went to the concrete stoop and sat. Connie lit a cigarette and offered one to Eileen. She shook her head no, and her pink hair flew statically around her face.

"I don't know what those two are up to, Eileen. They've gotten into something for your Great Granda," Connie said, smoke climbing like a cobra rising from a basket.

Eileen said, "What do you mean?"

"The boys have been up to no good. I think they're settling some old scores. I think Granda wants to go out knowing that he's still on top."

Eileen said, "Like what scores? And with who?"

"I don't know, Eileen. I don't know who or what. I just know there's some bad business about and some bad things happening around the neighborhood."

Kevin stepped onto the stoop. "Ei, can you get home? I'll get you an Uber. We're gonna be a while. Granda wants to see you before you leave."

She went back into the room, and Granda fussed about her hair and thanked her for coming, and she said she loved him and he said he loved her, too, and he held her in a fierce hug, his grip surprisingly strong, and she turned to leave and was unaccountably gloomy.

"I don't need an Uber, Kevin. Just going down the street," she said and told Connie goodbye.

She walked home thinking about Granda and his wrinkles and his scores that needed settling. Does it ever stop? She thought about Francis and wondered if anybody would show up to see him when he was wasting away. Probably not. But maybe he had time to change that. Nobody caring for you was the definition of lonely. Nobody deserved that. Francis wasn't a bad man; he just wasn't attached to anything, like a lobster buoy broken free from its ropes. He floated around with only Eileen to keep him from going out to sea.

She couldn't go home now, though, and she had time to kill before her Krav Maga lesson. She didn't want to go back to the Tap. She wondered if Michaela was working. Go see Michaela at the bar? Eileen enjoyed the strip joint. It was fun and lively. It was an entertaining place to be, and she liked seeing her cousin Michaela.

CHAPTER
19

Yakov the Russian was collecting an exorbitant cover when Eileen arrived at the door. Yakov, who had appeared at the beginning of the summer, was big and aloof and had a thick Russian accent. He was called Yakov the Russian by everyone in the neighborhood.

"Ten bucks?" she asked considering the fee little more than extortion.

"Girls is free," Yakov drawled, presenting a far more reasonable position in the argument.

"Is my cousin working?" Eileen asked.

"And how I know this? Go and see for self, cutie."

She peeked in and didn't see Michaela.

She left the club and walked several blocks to Michaela's place, pushed the button, and Michaela's disembodied voice said, "Who is it?"

"Hey, Michaela, it's me, Eileen."

The buzzer sounded and Eileen pushed the heavy door open. She took the stairs two at a time. Michaela lived in a classy building that had been built in the heyday of downtown banks. Nothing had changed. Portland was still populated by bankers and attorneys. The difference was the current professionals worked in ever-expanding sky scratchers, and nonprofessional people like strip-joint bartenders leased repurposed spaces in the converted bank buildings.

The staircase was trimmed with narrow white spindles topped with an oak banister buffed to within inches of its life by years of hands like Eileen's thoughtlessly oiling and waxing and polishing as they navigated the stairs.

Michaela welcomed her with a hug and a kiss on the cheek—she did that glamorous double air-kiss thing that Europeans do—and a bong hit.

"Gary Sullivan gave me a job tending bar at the Tap," she said and stroked Cat, the cat. Her fur was soft and smooth and felt like Michaela looked. Her cousin was beautiful, Eileen thought. She wore short shorts and a cut-off T-shirt and looked cool even though it was hot and muggy. Michaela sprawled like a cat herself.

"I heard. Dennis told me."

"Who's Dennis?" Then Eileen realized who Dennis was and she felt stupid and a little embarrassed, a little anxious. "Oh. I'm dumb. Is that Detective Hurley's name?"

"Yeah," she said. "He's coming over later."

"Does he smoke pot?" Eileen asked, scandalized.

"No. Of course not. I have to hide all this shit. He hasn't caught me. Yet."

"Would he arrest you?" The idea seemed reasonable in a pot-fueled fold of reality.

"Probably not, but he might put me in handcuffs." This was over-the-top funny to the weed-whacked girls.

Not to be out-scandalized Eileen said, "I'm just coming from Granda's. Have you seen him lately?"

"He's gotten pretty small, hasn't he?" Michaela took a sip from a can of beer. "Do you want a beer? There's one in the fridge."

Eileen went for one and came back and cracked it open and said, "I was there with the twins." Within the family, that could only mean their cousins, the Mack brothers. She moved closer to Michaela and the couch caved. They rolled toward each other, and Eileen lowered her voice. "Something's going on, Michaela. I don't know what, but the boys are up to something. Yesterday, Jamie came to the bar. I said, 'where's Kevin?' He said, 'Kevin's in hot water.' Like he did something. Fuckin' A, Michaela, like he did something, like, the day before? The butcher was killed, Michaela. You heard. The butcher, Mr. Grogan? He was murdered…" Eileen whispered the word. "And you know how Granda hated him, right? Do you think Kevin could have killed Mr. Grogan?"

"Oh, my god, Ei. Oh, my god," Michaela said. She rolled her head toward her cousin. "Do you think? Oh, my god." She took another bong hit and packed the bowl for Eileen.

Eileen's head was already reeling, and the pot made her mind run at an even higher speed after she sucked on the bong and coughed and let the smoke out after allowing it to bugger around in her lungs, and she thought about trying to explain her vortex theories but realized she and Michaela were too high for explanation and understanding. Instead, she said, "Connie—you know, the caregiver—said she thinks Granda is evening some scores. But he can't get out of bed and go and shoot Mr. Grogan himself. But that's what he'd want to do, isn't it, Michaela? Cripe sake, Michaela, what have the twins done?"

"Do you think they're murderers? Do you think they could have done this, Ei? What are you gonna do?"

"I don't know," she slurred all one word. Her head was spinning the way it had when she turned around a hundred times on the playground when she was a kid. "Cripe sake, Michaela. It's eight o'clock; I got a Krav Maga class."

"That's what I like about you, Ei. Always doing cool stuff. Who's your teacher?"

"Professor Grogan. Speaking of the Grogans..."

"Wait, what? Did you say it's eight? Dennis'll be here soon." She pulled herself into a sitting position; her arms hung between her legs and she groaned. "I gotta hide all this stuff. Damn. I'm fucked-up."

"It's my fault. I'm sorry," Eileen said.

"No, it's okay. But you better get going."

Eileen said, "Yeah. I gotta go." She kissed her cousin and left and thought she might have said too much. More than she should have. *Dennis'll be here soon.* Who's Dennis? Detective Hurley? Detective Hurley. Is that Detective Hurley's name? Oh, my god, cripe sake; had she just screwed up?

CHAPTER
20

Two years earlier, Dom DeLuca had hired a local contractor named Wally Wallace to renovate his oceanside home in Yarmouth. DeLuca drove his 2019 Carpathian Gray Jag through the gate Wally had built of steel and wood and had installed with concrete and fanfare. The locals had collected to watch Wally put the final touches on the gate, which was constitutionally unwelcoming but incontrovertibly prestigious, lending a certain standing to the neighborhood, which had become of a higher grade if not quite first-class. The locals cheered when Wally swung the gate closed. They sneered when they realized that it would never again open for the likes of them. They went home and drank Budweiser and crumpled the cans in their fists, and some folks even crushed them on their foreheads.

Now, two years after the celebration turned sour, a container of fresh pesto accompanied a loaf of Italian bread in Dom's reusable grocery bag. Pasta abounded in the pantry, while hundreds of bottles of wine lay cheek by jowl in the cellar. The custom-made racks fairly sagged under the weight, and the labels were of such high quality that his lawyer had recommended he line-item this asset in his will.

He rolled to a stop on the pea-gravel drive and slung his legs from the low car, lifted himself out—which, if he was honest, was more challenging now that he was sixty—and walked straight for the kitchen. He snagged a bottle of Côtes du Rhône, uncorked it, poured it, and headed for the deck. He was reading a novel by James Lee Burke and sipping wine. His legs were up as he listened to the cry of gulls and the rhythm of the water, which was calm but always at work, and saw other seabirds carving wheels backlit by purple. It was six o'clock, stacking up to be a perfect evening. Nothing other than solitude sounded like this. He thought he might even doze.

Possibly the greatest of frights is when you are so sure of your privacy that you would fart out loud. But then you hear a chair scrape across the hardwood floor directly above you. Or your name is spoken from only feet away while you relax on the deck you had convinced yourself was deserted. Adrenaline surged to his heart and DeLuca snapped alert. Bloodless tingling iced his fingers when he heard the feral woman's voice. He whipped around as the ancient part of his brain prepared for fight or flight and his eyesight was acute, and it was her.

She was not an unknown figure to him. Standing, framed by the patio door in the glare of the sun, she was small and pretty but dangerous, too. Silk. The fear was not merely that she was dangerous. He knew she was soulless. This unannounced visit was proof that he had seriously messed up. There was an eight-hundred-pound gorilla anchored in the middle of Casco Bay waiting for Dom to drop in with a real estate contract, and Dom had pretended that Fyodor Umarov, the Russian oligarch, wasn't there at all. Dom had made a lucrative deal and sold the property piecemeal to another, and now he was going to pay for it. Hopefully, not in the same way Patrick Grogan had.

Silk emerged from the backlight of the glass-glare wearing a loosely pleated lemon-yellow skirt and scoop-neck top of the same color. Not especially intimidating. At least she shouldn't have been. She took a teak chair and pulled it in front of him. Silk sat, staring at him. Her skin was unmarked and darkly tanned. The color of pine wood seasoned in the sun.

"How did you get in?" DeLuca asked as alarm and adrenaline simmered down.

She didn't answer.

Instead, she said, "We go, DeLuca."

"Yeah? Where?"

She said nothing. It was maddening.

Then she asked, "You know Keene?"

Keene? The detective? Of course, the detective. He was on the case, but it seemed the Department was treating Dom's brother-in-law's death as a suicide. Just as she had engineered it, no doubt. "Depends what you mean. I know of him. I've met him. He's good at what he does. He solves his cases." He said this last to get under her skin for a change.

Silk stood and said, "Let's go." She gathered her hair with an elastic band and said, "It is hot."

"You just saw Umarov." His voice faltered. "Is he expecting us?"

The distinctive sound of a slide jacking a shell into the chamber of a semiautomatic handgun inspired him to stand.

Silk said, "Now."

"Okay," he said uncertainly.

"*Ice Cold* by eight."

"Is beautiful day for boat ride," Nurzhan said in his delightfully idiosyncratic way as he suddenly appeared from the invisibility of the glare. He was sighting the barrel of his P229 at the wine bottle four inches from DeLuca's left hand. His finger was recklessly on the trigger. Inside the trigger guard. Locked, loaded, and ready to dance. The wine bottle exploded.

Silk's hands flew to cover her ears.

"Oops," Nurzhan said, grinning.

Silk reprimanded him for the noise, and DeLuca tried to shake the cottony deafness from his ears.

"Okay. Let's go," DeLuca said warily, still bobbing his head around searching for conventional soundwaves. "You didn't have to shoot the wine."

"Is mistake," Nurzhan said. He shrugged his shoulders with his finger still resting on the trigger. "Pulled trigger, gun went boom." Delightful.

Silk was already halfway down the dock.

The captain was expecting DeLuca's boat. He ordered the crew of two to deploy the boarding deck. The sunning salon on the first deck doubled as the so-called Marina. When hydraulically dropped, it opened into an expansive garage where water toys of all varieties were stored. It also served as a dock that easily accommodated DeLuca's 24-foot Grady-White. DeLuca throttled in reverse, bringing the *Dominator* to a virtual stop. A crew member of the *Ice Cold* met them, and DeLuca tossed him the bowline. They worked well together, having accomplished this task many times before. The *Dominator* was usually packed with crates and boxes of goods that were brought to DeLuca by Yakov, Nurzhan's surly brother, during the week. Usually after dark. Silk, on the other hand, was there with Nurzhan most Friday afternoons, no secrecy or hiding. They were there ostensibly as weekend guests with a few pieces of luggage.

But this day was different.

Dom's brain was working itself into a mania. Trying to escape and failing might be a better way to go than being shot while groveling at the

Russian oligarch's feet. He could dive into the ocean, numbingly cold as it was, and make a swim for it. They were more than a mile from the island, and he was not the swimmer he used to be, but drowning might not be a bad thing. A pleasant way to go, they say. Who are *they*? And in this case, seriously, who are *they*? Why was he thinking such shit? Because he should have brought the real estate deal to Umarov in the first place. He knew it, he knew it, he knew it. Umarov wanted the store, the apartments on the second and third floors, and the buildings next door. Now, because of him, Grogan was dead. The deal was dead. And Dom was about to meet with the killer of both.

He stepped to the boarding deck and the Russian sailor helped Silk. She was a tough little screw and had maintained one of her freaky silences the entire boat ride. She never took her eyes off him as the hydraulic unit rose to Deck One. A sailor fingered a shoulder mic, the kind a cop would wear. DeLuca was sure they were discussing more and more gruesome methods to dispose of him, the businessman who had sold the real estate out from under them. Silk had told DeLuca that Umarov's favorite method of elimination was to remove the skin while the subject was still alive. Two-inch strip by two-inch strip. Longitudinally. Head to toe. It was the longest sentence he'd ever heard her utter. The subject matter amused her.

Silk, Nurzhan, and DeLuca climbed to Umarov's private suite. DeLuca had never been this high in the boat. He had been told that Umarov had a vise on a workbench. It was large enough for a human head, but the lunatic started with fingers and toes, then graduated to the hand and foot. The head was saved for last for obvious reasons. Was this before or after the skinning? DeLuca had dismissed these rumors as scare tactics or urban myths. Or holdovers from KGB torture methods. DeLuca and his boat-mates approached the stateroom where the Russian psychopath spent his seafaring days.

DeLuca thought, Goddammit, I'm dead. Then he thought, Who did I leave the wine cellar to? The damned lawyer. I line-itemed it and left it to the goddamned lawyer. He was depressed.

CHAPTER
21

Silk's eyes darted about. The one way out was the same way they'd entered. Not an ideal situation. She hung back by the door. The only man who made Silk's blood run cold was dwarfed by Nurzhan, who was nearly six-foot-four. Even DeLuca, who was of average height, stood a couple of inches taller than the oligarch. His stature notwithstanding, Silk chose not to underestimate Umarov.

Silk said nothing while Nurzhan and DeLuca murmured some kind of greeting.

"It's too bad your real estate deal fell through," Umarov said to DeLuca as he poured a glass of water and offered the same to Silk. She declined. He continued, "I'm sorry about your brother-in-law, but it had to be done. How is your sister taking this? Annabella is a pretty name. A pretty woman, I think."

"How do you know her name?" DeLuca, perhaps realizing the stupidity of the question, clamped his mouth closed.

"Do you understand what's going on, Dom? I'm teaching you a lesson about how it's done in the real world. I'm a businessman by nature. I'm not risk-averse; that's what business is all about. I am, however, averse to losing. So, I need to be able to rig the game in my favor, and that's what you took away from me, Dom."

"Well—" DeLuca started.

"What makes you think it's time for you to speak?"

DeLuca shut his mouth.

"So, this is how it will go from here on. You and your broker will tell the former buyers that there is no deal. We will come to a deal that will be far less advantageous to you. Should have come to me, Dom. Now you say something."

DeLuca said, "The deal will be a matter of public record. If the numbers are skewed significantly, it will look suspicious."

"And I care about this, why?"

DeLuca said nothing.

Umarov said, "By going to the open market with this real estate deal, you screwed up, dude." Holding his ice-blue eyeglass frames in one hand, he took a small jar from a drawer with the other and said, "We need to be alone, Silk and I." He put his glasses down and daubed out a finger of cream and worked his hands together.

"But Silk and I are..." Nurzhan said with a reedy voice and then stopped.

Silk wondered what it was Nurzhan thought they were. Partners? Colleagues? Pals?

DeLuca said nothing. Silk thought the old man might have been scared silent. Umarov waved the two men away and turned the lid back onto the jar.

Silk knew the two men would be angry with her. The way Nurzhan looked at her left no doubt that she could if needed, use her sex as a way in. Unchecked and unnuanced, her personality was abrasive. She knew that. She hadn't learned the secrets of charm as a hooker in Kharkiv and selling cigarettes in Kiev. But she had had thorough instructions on how to use sex to achieve her goals.

In Kharkiv, she screwed men in simple exchange for money. Not a complicated transaction. When she arrived in Kiev, however, she met a woman. A woman who liked women. This woman had offered to bring her to Odesa, give her a place to stay, and a job selling cigarettes at a casino. Her education in using her gender to achieve her goals resumed at a higher level, at an artistic level.

After the men left, Umarov sighed deeply.

"New enemies, Silk."

"Da," she said shrugging dismissively. So, the two of them thought alike. Good. "The American is like a mosquito. Iskakov is a powerful man but too big, too loud. I don't need him." She rarely used Nurzhan's family name. Call me Nurzhan, he had said.

"What about his technical expertise?" Umarov said, finally off the subject of Silk's comfort level with adversaries.

"The devices are good but not necessary. I can kill without them."

Umarov thought quietly, then said, "We need to wrap things up. I've established bank accounts for all the managers, up and down the coast, to start using legitimately. No more cash drops. Go to York Beach to familiarize yourselves with the system. Then I need you to meet all our people at our restaurant in Old Orchard Beach. All our associates will be there. Get them started with the new processes." He took a drink of water. He continued, "And then, after that, Nurzhan will continue to collect the cash, but I need you here. On board."

"Good," Silk said. "Why on board, though?"

"What I need right now, Silk is a bodyguard. You've made a case for yourself."

She was pretty sure he could take care of himself.

"All summer I've been accumulating liquor, cigarettes, and clothing. Plus, cash. It could be conceived that I might take a fall over the side. It would not be difficult to move this cash-laden boat to an entirely different location. What I'm saying is I need another set of eyes. A set I can trust absolutely."

Silk couldn't have planned it better. She'd been afraid Umarov would expect her and Nurzhan to be a team, but he'd seen to it that she could leave the big man out of her business altogether. Just two more days.

Secondly, he wanted her on board and armed. What good was an unarmed bodyguard? Her quarters were only a few decks down, and she sensed that Umarov wanted her for more than protection. The lesbian had instructed her to trust her senses. If she was correct about his desires, success might look completely different. Before this turn, she had envisioned success as deadly for her as surely as for Umarov. Kill and be killed. Now, she might be able to survive and come out with something of value. The exact suggestion he'd just made.

But something was wrong. He couldn't be unaware of all this. He was setting her up.

He interrupted her thoughts. "Tell me of the butcher."

"Okay." She paused and stared directly into Umarov's eyes.

"For example, how do you plan to dispense with the witness?"

He knows about the witness. The witness. The girl went to the bar to kill the witness. He doesn't know everything, does he?

"The drunk from the bar?" she said to determine just how much he knew.

"Yes, him. Are there others?"

The informant was Yakov, of course. "No. Just him."

"Your plans?"

"Drunks live a dangerous life. On the edge. Portland is surrounded by water. Drunks have accidents."

He continued staring at her and said, "We sail soon. For Caracas. You will come with me. Be my arm candy. Wear expensive dresses, dripping with jewelry, etcetera."

So, it was Venezuela. Silk said, "No."

"I don't negotiate with my people."

She would sail with him. This would give her ample opportunity and cover to get it done. A cruise to Caracas; how long would that be? And why Caracas? She wanted to ask but she had learned from Nurzhan's experience that you don't speak out of turn. It didn't matter; she could still execute the job safely and perhaps survive.

———— ◆◆ ————

The *Dominator* motored away from the *Ice Cold* first thing in the morning. Silk sat in the stern of the boat, rocking lightly with the rhythm of the engine while Nurzhan and DeLuca ignored her. This suited her just fine.

CHAPTER
22

The door cracked open and Sandblaster poked his head in. "Good morning. May I?"

"Of course," Keene said. "I'm the only one here."

"Great. I need a minute to set up."

He dropped a file folder on the table and put a laptop next to it. The evidence tech left the situation room and returned with a projector and connected the two pieces of equipment using a blue cable. He hit a power switch and a photo materialized on the wall.

"Grand Canyon," Sandblaster said for Keene's benefit.

"Yeah," Keene said. "I'd narrowed it down. Are you ready? Let me get Hurley and Peterson." He corralled the two detectives and found Arnaud, too.

"Morning," Hurley said as he and Peterson entered the room together. "That the Grand Canyon?"

Peterson said, "No, Hurley. It's Back Bay. You really gotta get out more."

Detective Diane Peterson wished Keene a good morning and he noted, as always, there was something about Peterson. She was a tall redhead who didn't wear makeup; she didn't wear dresses or skirts. Though she wasn't conventionally beautiful, she made a pair of faded jeans look pretty good. The sleeves of her button-down white shirt were casually rolled to the elbow that day. She smelled clean and fresh... like cucumber. Since Peterson had come to Portland from Indianapolis, the Bricks had been redolent with the aroma of juicy vegetables. But as tender as she may have smelled, the Department had learned she was tougher than a canvas bag of railroad spikes. Peterson. Huh.

Arnaud pulled something out of her pocket as she entered. "Altoids?" she said. "Anyone?" The three detectives said, nearly in unison, "Nah."

Five people can make a lot of noise. When the detectives, the officer, and the Evidence Tech clicked down to quiet like a cooling engine, Sandblaster started, "I want to share the findings of the luminol report. I have some computer models, populated with the luminol evidence." Sandblaster presented copies of a photo showing a spray pattern seen under a black light, and the Portland detectives passed them around. The Evidence Tech advanced the PowerPoint presentation to the first slide.

He walked to the screen. "What we can do is take this spray pattern, you see there enhanced by the luminol, and—" he traced a rough circle around the purple splotches seen on the wall and floor, "and project a cone backward to find a point in space that represents the egress wound in the vic's lower mandible." He clicked the remote. "Second page. This answers questions like was the vic standing? Was the shooter, if there was one, tall or short compared to the vic? How was the vic positioned? You know, turned to the left, turned to the right, straight on, etcetera. You'll see some interesting inconsistencies with suicide."

Sandblaster clicked on another image, a computer-generated projection, and others. His PowerPoint presentation showed projections suggesting another shooter and relative positions and heights.

"It's that exact?" Keene asked when Sandblaster suggested the height of a possible shooter.

"Yes, sir. It's that exact. See, the spatter would have been way up here if the guy shot himself, not even close to the floor. A guy doesn't shoot down to kill himself, he shoots horizontally." He put his hand to his temple, fingers arranged like a gun, and said, "Right?" Then he put his elbow drastically above his hand and said, "Woulda been like this to achieve this spatter. A guy doesn't do that."

He clicked forward. "This, however, is an interesting anomaly to me."

The slide showed the blood pattern up close with arrows imposed on it.

"These arrows," Sandblaster said, "indicate a side slip in the spray pattern."

"I don't understand," Keene said.

"I didn't get it either," Sandblaster said. "The body, having suddenly lost the rigidity that living muscles and ligaments provide should drop directly down, giving in to gravity. Probably slump forward if anything. Do you see?"

Arnaud said, "I'm not sure. No. Can you explain, Murray? I'm sorry."

"What we believe happened, Terry is that the body lost rigidity as expected but was dragged back, in a sense."

Arnaud said, "But you said there was no drag pattern."

"There isn't. Not in the way that we were originally thinking—like, the body was here, then dragged over there. There's no evidence of that. What the luminol is telling us is there was a second man in the room. I believe the vic was being held from behind, and his fall, as he died and gravity took over, was drawn back toward a person who was holding him from behind. The vic's rigid muscles went limp suddenly but the musculature of the man behind him did not. The body was pulled, unintentionally, back toward the man holding him while the spray was hitting the wall. Only slightly, but enough. The spatter should have been here." He pointed to a final representation showing a theoretical spatter array shifted several inches forward from the actual pattern.

"So," Arnaud started, "if the body had started from a vertical point directly above the cone, it would have resulted in a different spatter."

"Exactly!" Sandblaster said, pleased that his audience was getting his presentation.

"And if you're right, we're looking for two perps," Keene said.

"I'd bet the farm on it," Sandblaster said. "The luminol never lies. Any questions?"

Keene's conviction was that luminol *rarely* lies. Nothing in crime-solving is universally true. However, luminol carried significant evidentiary weight in a court of law. Sandblaster's work would present well as a brick in the wall of the so-called preponderance of the evidence. Keene's team was building a decent case against a suspect. Now, all Keene had to do was provide the DA with a suspect.

CHAPTER

23

"Let's go see Big Sis," Keene said to Hurley. The Chief Medical Examiner, Dr. Eugenia Coffin, was covertly called Big Sis by much of the law enforcement community in Maine. As big as a tackling dummy and with less social grace, Dr. Coffin wasn't someone you should openly disrespect.

Hurley groaned but despite his inclination to run the other way he thought he should see the evidence the corpse would supply firsthand with Keene. In gathering cadaver evidence, two heads were better than one. But there was something about the doctor that got under Hurley's skin. Normally unflappable—Hurley had made a career of dealing with violent criminals, sociopaths, and psychopaths, after all—Dr. Coffin's sarcasm pissed him off. Unreasonably. He realized he was squeezing his paper coffee cup dangerously out of shape. Keene went to talk to Riordan while Hurley grabbed his ballcap. Hurley wondered what drove a physician to deal with the dead exclusively. He supposed that there was no pressure with a patient who was already dead. But more than that cynical supposition, it was probably the same puzzle-solving attraction that motivated many cops and evidence techs, and crime scene professionals. This was what kept them in the profession even though they saw the outer limits of man's inhumanity to man and were, for the most part, paid substandard wages to do so. In Dr. Coffin's case, however, it was probably merely because she had the bedside manner of a dog-track vet. The deceased, dog or human, doesn't care.

The detectives got in the car with their coffees. Hurley had a breakfast sandwich from Amato's. Keene drove from the Bricks onto the Arterial Way and pointed the Explorer north on the interstate. He sipped his black coffee and thought about what Dr. Eugenia Coffin might have found to support his theories. Or refute them.

"This is the ballgame here, Dennis. The body's gonna tell us. Murder or self-inflicted."

Off subject, Hurley said, "Bitch." His disputes with the medical examiner were legendary; David and Goliath, Ahab and Moby, Randle McMurphy and Nurse Ratched.

"Good morning, gentlemen," Dr. Coffin said, looking like a specimen in an arboretum, more oak than willow. The air conditioning was on full force, threatening to influence the weather patterns from Alberta to Cape Cod. "I'm happy to see you two. Especially you, little one. How's the traffic cop business?" Eliciting no response from Hurley, she took them from her office to the morgue. It was colder still in the space designed for the disassembly of the human body to its unblended parts. Patrick Grogan lay on a chilly-looking stainless-steel table with a thin white sheet covering him from his chest down; the sheet was the sole element of tenderness in Coffin's hard shiny world. The damage to the victim's head was less bloody now than when Keene had seen him last, partly because the contents had been removed from the cranial cavity through a hole Coffin had cut with a bone saw and partly because Grogan had left a great deal of organic matter back at the shop. Coffin had left the yarmulke-shaped top piece of the skull resting on the table. The face was distorted like a Dali clock. "You two have met Mr. Grogan?"

"We're acquainted," Hurley snapped.

Keene slid a pack of gum from his pocket. "Gum?" He offered a piece to the doctor.

"No, thank you," she said.

"Hurley?"

"You bet," he said. Anything to counter the bubbling bile in the back of his throat.

Keene popped a piece of Orbit Sweet Mint and started chewing, giving him foundational sensory support. Better to focus on the flavor of Sweet Mint than the smell of Coffin's business.

"Well," the doctor said, "I think the cause of death, which is what interests you two, I'm sure, is quite simple. There was no blunt trauma anywhere on the body. Not the head, the kidney, or the heart."

"The heart?" Keene said.

Water buffaloes muck about in mudholes more gracefully than the doctor moved around the stainless-steel table. "Yes," Coffin said as she bumped the table with her hip, which caused Grogan's face to slip and distort further as though winking at Hurley. The detective emitted an involuntary groan. "A blow to the chest can cause sudden cardiac death. Commotio cordis and contusio cordis are the leading causes of cardiac arrest in violent death." She noticed she had her audience right where she wanted them, glassy-eyed. It was her sublime pleasure to place law enforcement officers, particularly big-city dicks like Hurley and Keene, under her spell. Glazed eyes, colorless skin, and even tossing their cookies in particularly gruesome cases were only a few of the goals Coffin set for herself when conducting an autopsy. "But that's neither here nor there," she crooned. "We're all interested in what *did* kill him, not what didn't." She pursed her eyes at Hurley. He didn't respond. She said, "The cause of death was the cranial and occipital lobe damage caused by a through-and-through injury consistent with a gunshot wound. My guess at the caliber is a .357, a .38, or a 9."

"Well," Keene said, "a 9-mil was in the vic's hand."

"Meaning you think it was self-inflicted?" the doctor asked.

"The evidence may point in that direction," Keene said.

"Not all the evidence, Detective," Coffin said with a menacing smile. She drummed her tented fingers like a villain in a silent melodrama.

Hurley said, "You have some that doesn't point that way?"

"Yes, my little friend. Based on the travel of the bullet, the course the bullet took through the head, ingress at the right temple, and egress at the left lower mandible, suggests a shooter stood at the victim's right." Dr. Coffin indicated the two wounds on the corpse with a pencil. "Here and here. A shooter stood here and placed the muzzle of the 9-mil here. His or her hand holding the pistol was high and angled down. A self-inflicted wound will tend to point upward."

"Horizontal," Hurley said, remembering Sandblaster's presentation. He immediately recognized he'd fallen into a trap of Coffin's making. He was too eager to correct her, and she knew this about him and she'd ambushed him knowing he'd never see it coming.

With a sigh that sounded like the release of a truck's air brakes, and the dead eyes of an executioner, she continued, "Having a preponderance of the body of evidence at hand, we know that, in self-inflicted temple shots, the hand holding the weapon is naturally angled up from below the wound." She demonstrated with a finger gun. "Do this quickly."

Both detectives made a gun with their fingers and held it to their temples. The barrel of Hurley's finger gun poked above his red ear angled more up than down. The attitude of Keene's finger gun was the same. "You see, gentlemen? Not horizontal as my little friend has been misinformed. Or perhaps you came to this miserably mistaken position through your dim deductive detecting? In any case, both of you, and I too, placed the gun in such a way that the egress wound would be *above* the ingress at the opposite temple. This was not suicide." She slap-dusted her catcher's mitt hands together. "But it is your job to determine what happened, isn't it? My job is difficult enough. I shouldn't have to do your work as well. But you two bumblers leave me no choice. Unless you have more questions, I have my occupation to attend to."

"Well," Keene said, "thank you."

"Of course," the ME said. "There's one other thing that Mr. Sanblasio seems to have missed: contusions at the wrists. Your victim was held against his wishes. My report will be emailed to you, Mr. Keene, before the end of the day." She turned away and bumped into the table again, which sent the gurney rolling toward the two policemen. Hurley stopped it with his hip and rolled his eyes at Keene. "I saw that little one," the ME said, her back still to the cops. "And that."

Hurley smiled because he had not given her the finger as she had anticipated he would.

CHAPTER
24

"**H**ungry?" Keene asked Hurley as they left the morgue parking lot.
Hurley said, "Jesus, that woman pisses me off... If I kill her one of these days, which I probably will, do you think I could get away with it?"

"I won't tell anyone."

"Hot dog at Sasses'?" Hurley suggested as they neared the tiny restaurant.

"You bet," Keene said. "Best hot dog in central Maine. Nothing makes me hungry like a good medical examiner's report." Keene guided the Explorer into a parking space.

"That bitch," Hurley said. "If she called me 'little one' one more time I woulda slugged her."

"That would have been convenient; there was a stainless-steel gurney right there for your remains."

Neither of them glanced at the menu painted on the wall above the take-out counter while they waited for the ancient waitress to find them a table. They knew what they wanted. Many cops—and neither Keene nor Hurley was an exception—took their lunch at the restaurant when they had business in the state capital. The food was good and cheap and reliable.

They sat opposite each other and Hurley said, "You were right, Keene. How did you know it wasn't suicide? The position of the two wounds?"

"I didn't know for sure. I didn't catch that particular inconsistency originally. Not till Sandblaster coached us. It was the ingress wound that bothered me. Gun was in his right hand. The ingress wound was in the right temple. I was pretty sure he was left-handed. I noticed his hair was parted on the right. A guy usually parts his hair on the opposite side of his dominant hand."

Hurley took his right hand and felt for his part. He said, "That's it?" Then he said, "He held the gun to his temple. It's not like he's going to miss."

Keene knit his brow as he looked at Hurley. Then he said, "Hurley, of course, he's not going to miss. But why would he use his right hand?"

"I was joking," Hurley said with a little *duh* in his voice. He ordered a Chicago Dog and a Mountain Dew from the waitress.

"I'll have a Coney Island and an iced tea," Keene said.

"Just the part of his hair convinced you that he was murdered?" Hurley said.

"Did you take a look at the gun?"

Hurley said he had.

"Check the mag release?"

"Oh, shit," Hurley said, the truth dawning on him. "I missed it. The mag release was configured for a lefty?"

"Yup. Easy to miss. It might be an eighth of an inch difference side to side. Also, I knew the Beretta APX has been popular with lefties because it's ambidextrous. The other thing that's bugged me from the start was how clean the place was. Like a pro."

"You thinking OC?" Shorthand for Organized Crime, the initials meant an entirely different kind of criminal, an entirely different mode of investigation. Keene and Hurley would have to expand their search parameters outside the city and probably into Boston, Providence, or even New York or Montreal. If the thought was OC.

"What about your idea of Mack sending a warning shot?" Keene asked.

"That's not Jamie's style." Hurley paused. Then changing the subject, "Big Sis found contusions at the wrist. I'm surprised Sandblaster missed that."

"Yeah. Coulda been held from behind," Keene suggested.

"Or tied," Hurley suggested keeping the possibility of a second man off the table. A second man presented problems to an investigation. Two people supported the idea of OC. There was nothing compulsive about two men killing a third.

"Who else would contract a hit?" Keene unfurled his utensils as the waitress brought the hot dogs, just in time to hear *contract* and *hit*. Likely a *Soprano's* watcher, her eyebrows popped up.

"Chicago Dog?" she said.

"Here."

She placed the hot dog and soda in front of Hurley. She placed the other food and said, "I've heard just about everything from you cops but...?"

"Detective," Keene said and pushed his badge to peek over his shirt pocket.

"Mafia," Hurley whispered and lifted his windbreaker to show the butt of his gun.

Keene bit down on his hot dog not caring that seasoned ground beef and chopped onions and yellow mustard escaped in a mess on the paper plate. That's why he had a fork and napkin.

"I love kicking off a good murder investigation with Sasses' hot dogs," Hurley said as he corralled the vegetables and pickles arrayed on the steamed hot dog that represented the center of his universe just then. Onion rings and Dew were the other features vying for his attention. He breathed in deeply. "That's the second-best smell in the world." He breathed out, the picture of a satisfied man.

"What's the best?" Keene asked.

"Bourbon."

"Oh yeah, yeah. You're right about that. Nothing like it."

"Well, there is fresh ground coffee," Hurley suggested.

"True. There's that and there's nothing like Cuban coffee, Dennis. Melena makes it in an Italian maker. Sweet as maple syrup but...Jesus. Tastes like angels pissing down your throat."

Hurley paused. Looked at his partner. Shook his head. Then said, "There's pipe tobacco. Fresh-baked bread on a foggy morning on the Hill." Hurley took a bite of the dog after listing his aromatic memories. Then, mouth half-full, "But Maker's Mark poured over ice just under your nose? Whoa."

"Yeah..."

Hurley shot a double take out the window and Keene followed his gaze. An oak tree wearing a helmet rolled by on a straining motorized scooter.

"Jesus," Hurley said.

"I don't think I've ever empathized with a motorized inanimate object before," Keene said.

"It's probably impossible to kill her, now that I think about it."

"Nope. She'll never die. She'll outlast the White Mountains."

Keene tapped Melena's cell number and waited.

"What's up?"

There was a definite chill in that greeting. She knew. Woman's intuition or something, but she knew.

"Hey, Babe. Um..." Should he get right into it? "I have some good news and some bad news. Which do you want first?" This gives the news-giver neutrality; absolves him of fault or responsibility. The receiver knows that the good news is predicated on the bad. Why not give the bad news and roll from there? Cowardice. Keene knew it, and worse, Melena knew it. This realization reached through the cortex of Keene's brain too late; Melena chose her poison.

"I already know the bad news," she said. "No vacation this year."

"No, no, no. Late vacation. Maybe shortened a bit." Keene cursed himself for choosing the cowardly presentation. Melena had seen it coming, turned it around, and cut him off at the pass. "How did you know?" he asked weakly.

"What else could it be? I haven't heard from you all day. I've been expecting some kind of news, and you call and say 'bad news.' How could I not know?"

"Yeah," Keene said. "I'm sorry I didn't call sooner. Things have been kinda hectic."

"Uh-huh. I take it the butcher didn't kill himself?"

"Nope. I gotta go break the news to Charlie."

———•••———

Keene sat in Charlie's office and said, "Much of the evidence points to murder. That should solve our press problem. I'll talk to Leo."

"Make sure he thinks he's getting an exclusive," Charlie said and covered his face with his hands like he was wiping away the truth he didn't want to understand.

"I'll give it to him like we're giving him the story."

Charlie asked, "What *are* we giving him?"

"In a nutshell, the trajectory of the bullet suggests a shooter other than the vic. Coffin found contusions on the wrists. It's possible he was being held. Two guys."

"You're not saying anything about a contract," Charlie said as if telepathically connected to Keene's thought process.

"No, I'm not going there. Not sure I buy it yet."

"Two guys."

"Maybe two guys. The presence of contusions would support that possibility, but he could have been tied, right?"

"One guy. Two fuckin' guys. I don't want an open murder investigation hanging around my neck, Basil. Jesus, I hope you get this done before Thursday. What are the chances?"

"I was up the entire night thinking about that very question, Charlie."

Riordan opened a big plastic container of peanut M&Ms. He dipped in for a few and held the jar toward Keene. While he waved Charlie's offer away, Keene thought about the suggestion of two perps and the implications that possibility raised. A single murderer usually kills in a state of emotion: rage, fear, or passion. When two killers are involved, it means the murder is committed in the opposite frame of mind. It is an activated plan; the killing has been strategized and the plan has been implemented. This sort of crime horrified Keene. Rage and fear and passion are human emotions that we all share and, fortunately, most control these impulses. Keene had taken a life and it had come at an enormous cost, a nearly debilitating cost. The ability to build a plan to end a life is cold and insanity beyond Keene's comprehension.

CHAPTER
25

The following morning Keene held the door open for the young woman. Lara?

"Good morning, Laura."

"Good morning, Detective. It's Lara," the receptionist said, and her round face split into a grin.

Shit.

At the top of the stairs, he ran directly into Leo Venti.

"Where you been?" Leo said.

"Jesus Christ," Keene said. "I can't buy a break."

Leo said in a disbelieving tone, "Nothing's happened?"

One thing about Leo, he knew that there was more there than met the eye. If there wasn't more there, he'd make it up.

"Christ's sake, Leo. I promised you you'd get the real news first, and you will. There just isn't anything yet. Let this thing get on its legs, then you can run with it. Okay? Do that for me?"

"I can't do that, Keene. I either give the story a good leaving alone—which makes me look bad when it does get its legs—or I contradict my previous assertions that you guys are lying to us." Leo hunched his shoulders and turned his hands up in a what're-ya-gonna-do gesture. "Right now, you're telling me I have nothing."

"Yeah." Keene thought he was playing this too close. He should have let the reporter run with it and let the scribe's words drop where they may. Trying to manipulate the story for Charlie's gain could blow up in Keene's face. But Keene had left fate alone to mess him up too often. "Give me till ten this morning. We got a meeting right now. We're gonna figure out our next moves, and I'll call you as soon as we got a plan. Okay? Works for you?"

"Ten doesn't give me much time."

"Leo. Think about it. What's Aneni going to do?" Aneni was a TV reporter of compellingly good looks and one who worked her stories. She was smart, had a large platform with the NBC affiliate, and was a hard worker with exceptional instincts for news. Tough competition for Leo. She trumped Leo in all but the intelligence category, and even that was fifty-fifty. "She's gonna come out here with her gorgeous legs and get some film of her saying, 'We don't know what's going on. Back to you, Jim.' Nah, I don't think so. Leo, this one is yours and it's going to be good. Trust me." Keene hoped he was right.

Keene greeted Diane Peterson and asked about Hurley then smelled something refreshing. Hmm. Peterson.

"He called," Peterson said. "He's picking up donuts and coffee."

"What's wrong with the coffee here?"

"He prefers Dunkin' and assumes everybody else does, too."

Keene said, "Do you? Prefer Dunkin'?"

Peterson said, "I hate Dunkin', but he's going out of his way, you know, spending his own money."

"Yeah," Keene said. "I suppose we should be grateful. I hate Dunkin', too. I wonder why?"

Peterson said, "It tastes like the adhesive on Band-Aids. It's got that flavor, you know? That certain flavor."

Keene did know. Just then the door burst open and Hurley strode in bearing a box of donuts and a bag of cups of coffee, and the Dunkin' odor chased away Peterson's cucumber scent. That's it; cucumber. Like a salad. He ought to eat more cucumbers.

Keene whispered to Peterson, "The donuts are good, though."

"I love the friggin' donuts," she said.

"Good morning," Hurley sang.

Detective Dennis Hurley had once told Keene he knew Hunger Hill like the back of his head. He'd been born there. Gone to school there. Ate, drank, and played there. Keene hadn't bothered to correct the anatomically misaligned simile because behind it was a verifiable truth. Hurley wore a golf shirt, light-blue microfiber with dark-blue vertical pinstripes coordinating nicely with his dark-blue cap with Hunger Hill scrawled in gold. Dennis Hurley had Hunger Hill on his headgear and in his DNA.

He set the Dunkin' bag and the donuts on the conference table and emptied the bag, one cup at a time.

"Peterson," he handed a coffee to her. "You look lovely this morning." He pushed a cup toward Officer Arnaud. "Arnaud, I don't know how you take it but there's cream and sugar." He took another cup and handed it to Keene. "Looking sharp this morning, Basil." He popped the cover off the last cup for himself and dumped a creamer into it.

Keene didn't doctor his coffee; he sipped it black. More pointedly, he allowed the drink to steam his lips. He selected a chocolate donut. A wolverine might bite into a vole with less vigor. Keene devoured the unlucky pastry with unbecoming zeal.

"In case you don't know, or haven't figured out, Hurley didn't spend the night alone," Peterson said. "Is it getting laid or the coffee that brings the whirling dervish out in you?"

"Arnaud, you're not drinking your coffee?" Hurley said, ignoring Peterson.

"Oh," she said with an immediate flush of red. "Um. I drink tea."

"Where was I?" Hurley said, barely disguising his disapproval of Arnaud. Keene had told him he shouldn't judge; everyone has their tastes. This woman, Hurley had countered, has too many of them.

The conference room wasn't huge. It was more like a big residential dining room. Eight chairs surrounded the table, four on each side. The team could squeeze in another chair should it be necessary, but the group wouldn't need it. Three detectives, Keene, Hurley, and Peterson, were there. Arnaud and Sandblaster crowded into the room. The responding ME, Dr. Coffin, had replied that she would not be able to attend. They had everything she had to offer, and she was far too busy to hold their hands through the entire investigation. Hurley had visibly inflated at the news. Was that the reason for Hurley's glee?

"Okay," Keene started. "You all know by now we're shifting our approach to the death of Patrick Grogan. The evidence is suggesting the vic did not take his own life. Seems very likely we have a murder on our hands."

Keene started a timeline on a whiteboard. "Okay. Nine fifteen, Tom Grogan finds Patrick Grogan dead." He entered activities and deeds germane to the investigation up and down the line.

He wrote on another whiteboard: *Family/neighborhood* and then *Gain or lose*

A third board: *Mack family*

The final board: *Real Estate*

He put his hand on the Family/neighborhood board. "We've got a good sense of the neighborhood. Animosity for Grogan. But probably nobody's gonna off him, either. Doesn't rule it out, but we gotta prioritize here. Family on the other hand...Tom Grogan? The finding witness. Always a good place to start." He wrote the name and waved back at the timeline. "Hurley and I have interviewed him. He's got a good story. Not ruled out but pushed down the list.

"Hurley, what do you have on the Macks?"

Hurley explained his theory. Granda was dying. Jamie Mack was about to take over as he'd already been running the show prima facie. Hurley's theory was the possibility that someone—Irish? Italian? outside influence?—was positioned to grab power.

"Now," Hurley said, "I'm talking to my guys up there, on the street, etcetera, and they're tight-lipped about it. Nobody is saying much. Which worries me. Could be a real problem."

"You mean," Peterson said, "More than just the murder of Grogan?"

"Yeah. You've seen how quiet this summer has been. It worries me."

"My first summer here," Peterson said. "Wanna explain that?"

"Portland is a minor playing piece within the Boston and Providence crime organization. The organization is loose, but there being honor among thieves, I believe things have slowed down this summer as they figure out how to handle Granda's eventual demise. Let Jamie handle it for the honorific that the family has always paid. Or maybe someone else is ready to take over. I don't believe Jamie and Kevin would go quietly. That's my worry."

"Keep talking to your people. If we gotta bring Jamie in, we gotta bring him in."

"Keene," Hurley said, "one thing Jamie's gotta show right now is strength. Cooperating with us might give the wrong impression. Just saying."

Peterson said, "Dennis, I hate to ask the question, but will your relationship with Michaela Mack put any pressure on you?"

"Or her?" Keene added.

"I guess it should be part of this conversation. Granda is her great-grandfather and Jamie and Kevin are her cousins. If she needs to give a statement, maybe you, Diane, could do the interview. I can't. Keene knows her socially and you're a babe—"

Diane interrupted, "A *woman*, you mean?"

"Yeah. Like that. I'll talk to her tonight discreetly about the case."

Keene said, "I don't think you should do that right now. Let's see how things shake out. The Mack thing is just a lead. If it heats up, we'll discuss it further."

He asked Peterson for a refresher on her conversation with the broker.

After her interpretations of the broker's conversation, Keene said, "Other suppliers? Track them down. Dom DeLuca's lawyer needs to be contacted." He added, "I'll handle Leo. We need to be together with the press. Now, we've all but ruled out suicide based on three things. One: Forensics. The luminol report and the ME's report strongly suggest an outside shooter. There's an outside chance there were two people in addition to Grogan.

"Two: It is nearly impossible that he shot himself with his right hand. He was left dominant. If he had held the gun in his right, the bullet would have traveled in an upward trajectory due to his weakness in that hand."

He passed photos around. "Three: The scene looked so much like suicide that I took a contrary view of it. I was pretty sure it was staged. The ME called ten minutes before this meeting, and she's got more evidence against suicide. There was acid in the blood. She thinks he was asphyxiated. Not suicide."

CHAPTER
26

The room went quiet with the news. Asphyxiation.

"What?" Peterson broke the silence.

"Could be," Keene said. "There were petechiae in the eyes, and the acidosis suggests the possibility of suffocation."

"Shouldn't we stick with the obvious? Big Sis seemed pretty sure the GSW killed the vic and that two people were on the scene, right?" Hurley asked.

Peterson said, "Was there any sign of a struggle?"

"No," Keene said.

"How do you suffocate with no signs of a struggle?" Peterson asked the obvious.

"I don't know," Keene said. Then, thinking aloud, "Brings us back to the scene. Lack of struggle. Someone he knows, right?"

After a pause amid nodding around the room, Peterson asked, "How else does the blood acidify?"

"Kidney failure and lung failure are the two causes. But Grogan's kidneys were not failing. That would have been in Coffin's pathology report. Lack of oxygen would seem to be the cause in this case."

"The fact of the matter is, somebody shot him, right?" Hurley said. "Seems the acidosis is a medical anomaly. We shouldn't get tripped up on it."

Peterson added, "Hurley's right, Keene. Somebody shot the guy. Suffocation may have been used to subdue him, maybe? But he died of a gunshot wound."

Arnaud said, "You said, um, when we were at the scene—death can be a cause of petechiae."

"True," Keene said. "But the ME thinks it's more. It's most likely asphyxiation."

Arnaud said, "Then, um, about suffocation as a method of overpowering the victim."

"Yeah? What are you thinking?" Keene was growing impatient with Arnaud's tentative shtick.

"Well, I'm thinking that could be important."

"No shit; what about it?" Hurley said.

"I'm thinking it could indicate that the perp is small. Perhaps a woman."

"What's your take on that, Officer?" Peterson asked.

"If the perp," Arnaud started, and if she saw Hurley's eyes roll, she didn't show it, "was small, he or she might have subdued the victim by preventing him from getting air and, ah, maybe he didn't feel threatened by her."

Keene said, "Sandblaster recovered a strand of black hair at the scene."

Sandblaster said, "Long coarse black hair."

Hurley said, "The widow has long black hair. But she's worked at the store her entire life."

Keene said, "Yeah," and he marked Annabella in the *Family/ neighborhood* column. "We need motive. Grogan was allegedly beating Annabella, right?" He addressed Hurley.

"Does the Pope shit in the woods? I mean, we were all called at one time or another on a domestic up there, and he wasn't *father* of the year, either."

"I mean lately. Had he beaten her lately?"

"Beat her once? Belt her harder the next time." Hurley shrugged.

"Has everybody read the transcript of my interview with Tom? I could have liked him for this. When we talk about violence in the home, he gets squirrelly."

"Get a warrant to search the apartment?" Hurley said.

"I don't think we have anything yet," Keene said.

"What about the professor's house?"

"Same thing; we need probable cause. Somebody find it in the transcript." Keene underlined the son and the widow on the whiteboard. "The transcripts will be here before the end of the meeting. We need to get Annabella's DNA."

"Or the professor's," Sandblaster said.

"Yeah?" Hurley said.

"Annabella's would be more conclusive," Sandblaster said. "Somebody want to ask her nicely for a piece of hair?"

"Yeah, we'll get it somehow."

"It's not gonna do shit," Sandblaster said. "If it's hers, well, of course it's hers. If it isn't hers, that's all we'll know: It isn't hers."

Peterson said, "And even if it is hers, no judge will give us a warrant based on that. She works there."

Keene gazed at the board thinking about the breadth of the suspect list and said, "Peterson's right. She practically lives there. It's an exercise in futility." He continued looking. It was critical to have the murderer in the initial pool. The best way to overlook the perpetrator in the end was to overlook him in the beginning.

"Arnaud. What do you have from the canvass?"

Officer Arnaud explained that the results were still incomplete, but so far nobody had seen or heard anything. "We left our cards. By the time we got to most of them, it was the middle of the night. I don't think we got much of anything."

Keene said, "Follow up on that. We got a cluster, folks. Everybody on the Hill disliked Grogan. His customers bought from him grudgingly, right? His in-laws, the DeLucas, resented that he was running the family business into the ground. Immediate family? He ain't the husband or father of the year. The Macks didn't have much love for him. Dennis, can you explain that history?"

Hurley did. Patrick Grogan was left to fend for himself at nine years old; his parents returned to the old country without him. The Mack family took him in. He explained how that relationship turned 180 degrees when Grogan drove the car into a piling on Tukey's Bridge, killing Sean Mack in the accident; Granda lost his favorite son and hated Patrick for it. Hurley said, "A lot of us had thought he might have him killed. Over the years."

"But why now?" Peterson asked.

There was a pause in the room as the information was digested.

"To tidy up before he dies," Officer Arnaud said, breaking the silence.

Keene said, "Hurley, talk to the Macks. We need some alibis from those two. We gotta knock down this list of suspects."

Then Keene said to Peterson, "Diane, talk to Cushing again. Talk to DeLuca. DeLuca's lawyer. Get a list of creditors. Again, I want to knock this list down to a more manageable number."

He said, "Arnaud, re-canvass that neighborhood. Somebody knows something. We gotta know who we missed."

Hurley said, "Something else we might be missing; there were probably some gloves involved. No prints on the gun. Nothing on the body. Where are the gloves?"

"Good question," Keene said.

"I wanna check on the Macks. Check Jamie's place. Check Kevin's."

"How ya gonna get a warrant to do that?" Keene asked. "What do you have on either one of them?"

Hurley said, "Tonight is trash night. The reasonable expectation of privacy ends at the sidewalk. Their trash cans will be on the curb tonight."

Keene thought for a long time before he said anything. "What do you expect to find on the gloves, GSR?" Any fired gun left gunshot residue. A particular gun did not leave a signature residue, however. The evidence would only be significant with other circumstantial evidence building into a case. At this point, they had next to nothing. It probably was a worthy effort to retrieve the gloves. It was tricky, though. The reasonable expectation of privacy's end at the sidewalk had been tested in court. The subsequent question was: Does the evidence harvested from a trash can withstand a custodial challenge? In other words, once the trash can is outside of the house, it's subject to more than merely a search by law enforcement officers but could also be used as a trash container by another party. So, even if they found the gloves, a good lawyer could argue that the provenance of the evidence is unknowable. *They're not my gloves, Judge. Prove that they are.*

"Okay, that gives us something to think about," Keene said. "That wraps it up. Thanks, Sandblaster. See you tomorrow. Peterson, Hurley, and Arnaud, stick around for a second."

Keene closed the door. He voiced his concerns about the trash evidence.

Peterson said, "What if we have eyeballs on the trash from the door to the sidewalk until the trash is harvested?"

Hurley said, "Has that been tested in court?"

Peterson and Keene both said they didn't know.

Keene said to Hurley, "Wanna check with the AG?"

Hurley agreed and left the room to make the call.

Peterson said, "What's up with that? Hurley has a direct line to the AG or something?"

"I've never asked," Keene said. "But he gets through to her every time. They went to high school together, and perhaps there was some kind of youthful indiscretion. As I say, I've never asked, but Hurley has a way with her."

"Jesus," Peterson said. "For the largest city in Maine, this is a small town."

Hurley returned and said, "She said go for it. The eyeballs thing has not been tested in court and she said, 'Why not us?' So, I asked what documentation she'd need, etcetera, and she gave me some guidelines. I made notes." He handed them to Keene, who read them through.

"She wants it done quietly, right?"

Hurley said, "Yeah. We'll be better off if the subject remains unaware of the harvest until deposition."

Keene called Leo and got the reporter's voicemail. He took the time to organize his thoughts. He could tell him he had nothing. True. But Keene didn't want to give up control of the narrative. The reporter would tell all he knew, relate that the police had no better info. They've made no progress in finding the murderer. That was the direction this thing was taking; they were looking for a murderer. Leo knew it. That's what Keene would give him. The Department was unified; the butcher had been murdered.

The phone rang.

"Keene," he said.

"What do you have?"

"Breaking news," Keene said. "Hang on." He wanted to make sure Charlie was on board, or at least on the same page, and he was pissed at himself for not having prepared beforehand. Department unification was the point, and this call was conveying anything but togetherness and kumbaya. "Let me call you back."

He trotted down to Charlie's office. The door was closed. He knuckled it softly.

"Hang on," Charlie barked.

Keene waited a minute then decided to text him. *Telling Leo murder, not suicide. Signs of suffocation. Confirm asap.*

Whomever Charlie was with didn't have his undivided attention because a confirmation came in seconds. *As planned.*

Keene called the reporter, got his voicemail again, and got a call within a minute of leaving another message.

"You can report that the Department is well into an investigation into the murder of the butcher of Hunger Hill, Patrick Grogan."

"The Butcher of Hunger Hill. I like that. You guys finally get it, huh? I've known it all along. What took you so long?"

"Because we don't like making mistakes. Do you, Leo, like making mistakes?"

"No."

"But you can, right?" They both knew he had made a terrible mistake with the reporting of the incident a year ago. "The cops? We can't. The PPD can't survive making mistakes."

"It's eleven," Leo said.

"I'm not done, Leo. There were signs of asphyxiation."

This news sent Leo into a frenzy of questions that were better answered by the ME, but Keene used the old "ongoing investigation" trick to duck out of questions he couldn't and wouldn't answer.

"The Butcher of Hunger Hill," Venti said. "I love it."

The phone went dead, and Keene tucked it in a pocket. He watched the bald guy he'd most recently seen on the docks walk down the hall. He was the guy who'd been in Charlie's office.

CHAPTER
27

The ring of her phone startled Silk out of a reverie brought on by the monotonous drive. Only Umarov and Nurzhan had the phone number, and Nurzhan was next to her. It was the boss.

"Da."

"Have you been to York Beach?" Umarov asked.

"Yes."

"Do you understand the new systems?"

Silk recited, "Business as usual but now make normal deposits. Simple. We understand."

He asked if they were in Old Orchard and if she was alone.

"Nyet," she said.

"Can he hear me?"

Silk glanced to her left. Nurzhan gazed steadily down the highway, engaged in his task.

"Nyet." Nevertheless, she pressed the phone tightly to her ear.

"Did you read the paper this morning?"

"Da," she said. They were claiming the butcher had been suffocated. Shot? Suffocated? Who cares?

"This is good. A little misdirection could come in handy."

Silk said, "I don't understand."

"I will explain." He dropped his voice. "Yakov is skimming. I do not trust Nurzhan, either."

And why would he trust *her*? He didn't. She knew what was coming: A loyalty test. She must succeed. This was one last test to make sure he could trust her set of eyes to see that he wasn't pitched into the sea anytime soon. Perhaps she could carry on long enough to survive. She was falling in love with the idea of killing Umarov and surviving to talk about it.

"Eliminate them, Silk," he said, his voice still low. "Same MO. Acid in the blood. This will confuse them. Get this done, then we sail for Caracas."

"What about last suitcase of cash?"

"Fuck the cash. Get this done."

"Yes." She knew what Umarov was doing now. He was done here. Cut and run was serious business with the oligarch. Now she knew Umarov had killed Arkady. He had finally eliminated the last of the Rhenko compound survivors. Other than her. Was he making her do the final cleanup of this operation in Portland just as Arkady had done with the crew in the Rhenko compound? Had Arkady set the fire? She couldn't believe these things. He had been kind to her, told her he loved her, and it had been a lie. He and Silk had watched the flames consume the compound, the houses, and the bodies of her family. Not to mention the bodies of Umarov's expendable men. Then Arkady, the final expendable man, was gone. What kills a wolf, Arkady? A bigger wolf, he'd told Silakha. Now Umarov needed her to dispose of the supposed untrustworthy—the Iskakov brothers, Yakov and Nurzhan. Nurzhan, the big, stupid, and clumsy Russian. Silk wanted to scream. She knew Nurzhan wanted her. She would kill him. It wasn't fair that she suddenly mistrusted her Arkady as Nurzhan should mistrust her. But it was Fyodor Umarov's will. Nobody else. Silk knew with whom to cut and run and how to do it. She would follow his orders. For now.

So, her plan would come down to sex after all. She had seen how Nurzhan gathered her in with his eyes. When she had worn the black lycra, his eyes had roved over her like ants in a sugar bowl and he'd tried to touch her. Nurzhan probably thought her idiosyncrasies had created barriers. He would have slept with any other woman ten times by now. But she was different and he probably wanted her more because of it. If she was the aggressor, he would fall into line like a lamb. The brother, Yakov, on the other hand, she didn't know well. She would meet him at the Cougar Club but she was no good at small talk. He and Nurzhan were two olives who fell from the same tree, though. She could make Yakov want her, too.

"Yes," she said into the phone again even though Umarov had ended the conversation.

A good test for the new assassin, Umarov thought. Could she kill her partner? She was difficult to read except when the dark cloud of anger covered her face. But he felt kinship; she was detached like he was detached. This would prove his theory about her. Nurzhan, on the other hand, was no poker player. He'd do anything to have her. He wanted her badly; Umarov had seen it.

Silakha Rhenko—adorably calling herself Silk—was tough. She could kill. She had proven herself. But was she tough enough; was she ruthless enough to kill her partner? Umarov knew this assignment required something special. He'd watched over her in Kharkiv and then dug her out of the gutters of Kiev. She was a whore blowing old men for a handful of kopeks at the age of seventeen. But was she sociopathic? He'd had the lesbian pluck her from the cesspool of the Ukrainian city, allowed her to think she'd gotten to Odesa on her own, then employed her as a cigarette girl, a dealer, and a manager. The lesbian had done well. Silk probably thought Umarov didn't know of her connection to the Rhenko family. Poor thing. She knew nothing of Genghis Khan's highest level of happiness and the ownership of the enemy's surviving women yet, she was about to bring this joy to him. This ought to be a pleasant cruise to Caracas.

This assignment, killing the brothers, would help answer the question of her ruthlessness, her cruelty, and her loyalty. Somebody had to take out the trash.

Birches and yellow poplars and the pervasive pine trees that gave Maine its nickname, the Pine Tree State, flew by as one. Silk watched them amalgamate into one stripe of green.

The stores and kiosks and restaurants and take-outs and parking lots continued producing cash. Umarov owned these enterprises and the managers—the "associates," as Umarov called them, were to learn the new processes from Silk and Nurzhan. All summer, the managers of these establishments piled the cash in lock boxes. A Russian, man or woman, emptied them and disappeared with suitcases full. If anyone was looking, it appeared that an attractive woman—or lately a couple, as if she'd hooked up with this big man—joined Umarov on the *Ice Cold* for a social weekend. Their suitcases were filled not with their clothing and personal effects but with cash. What happened to the cash after that? Silk only knew the *Ice Cold* was filling fast. Maybe as full of cash as Suite Four was with jeans and Suite Three with bourbon. But now, she and Nurzhan were to inform the associates of the new plan. She supposed she could do it alone.

Silk said, "Your brother's not dependable."

Silk knew why Umarov had wanted Patrick Grogan dead. DeLuca had put all this in motion. He'd become greedy and decided to sell the property to someone other than Umarov. DeLuca needed Grogan alive to complete the deal. Umarov knew this. DeLuca would learn about Russians. When you give a Russian the option to buy, that means there's only one option: The Russian buys. On his terms.

And now Umarov wants Nurzhan dead. Okay, no problem. Umarov wants to clean things up, she'll do the housework for him.

"Left," Silk said and Nurzhan turned into the trailer park, an array of manufactured homes that stretched away to a vast saltwater marsh.

"Trailer is down here," she said about the fictional manager they were to visit. Silk had manufactured a tale about a kiosk manager skimming Umarov's profit. He lived in a trailer park that Silk had visited before. The last was true. She had scouted the park before, and now she could use this place.

After a few minutes, Nurzhan, happily unaware of Silk's artifice, had driven nearly to the end of the road. Silk had given him sexual signals in the universal language of the hormone-driven. A stray touch, a revealing slip of the cotton scoop neck. Eye contact. Lingering eye contact. Wholly revealing slip of the cotton blouse.

When she had taken this road before, she had driven to the marsh before she turned around. This afternoon, Silk and Nurzhan drove to the marsh, too. He pulled over where the road turned.

"You want to...?" Nurzhan asked, unsure of Silk's rituals involving sex. When she removed her blouse and reached for his hand, even though she felt awkward, she sensed he had a firm grasp on her intentions.

"Okay, Silk. Let's get out."

She stepped out of the car and looked at the muddy roadside. She needed to see her feet on the ground when she was uncertain of herself. She leaned forward and took her shoes off. Slowly, one by one. Her bare feet anchored her to the earth, the soles of her feet giving and stretching to accommodate the uneven gravel surface. The skin at her waist twitched at his touch. She pushed his hands from her.

Silk slipped out of her skirt and left it on the seat of the car. A second later, she twirled her thong playfully around her thumb. Finally, she turned to see him staring at her, as naked as a zoo animal.

He reached and held her breast and said, "Okay, yeah, baby." He hopped on one foot, his jeans around his ankles.

She bent at the waist and reached into her bag. She stood abruptly. In one quick and silent motion, she leveled her Polish-made Tokarev 33 at him, his hands poised to grope her body. She said, "Don't ever touch me."

A shocked egret, white as a bride, took wing and lifted from the marsh at the sound of hot gases mixing with relatively cooler ambient air as the 7.62mm shell broke from the muzzle of the naked assassin's gun. The bird didn't see a big man stumble forward and the assassin's silky hair swirl as she twisted to sidestep the falling body. The big Russian pitched into the marsh as planned. His body rolled shoulder over shoulder. His legs, free of his jeans, flopped over his head, and he came to rest in the swallowing muck like he was sitting on the beach. She dressed, then watched for almost ten minutes. She collected his jeans and her brass. The body refused to disappear, unlike the way a certain Volkswagen had many years ago. The article she'd read said that when the car was found, the driver was remarkably well-preserved after thirty years in saltwater muck. But by then, Nurzhan would be an unknown, and she would be forgotten. But the big man, sitting like a toddler on the beach, refused to sink. It might take some time, this kind of thing.

She tucked the Tokarev into her bag. Her father had given her the firearm when she turned sixteen. It was Soviet vintage, his from his days in the KGB. It was then she remembered the acid in the blood. The newspaper reporter had written that acidosis indicated suffocation. But Nurzhan wouldn't have fallen for her trick. This would have to do.

CHAPTER
28

Dennis Hurley's car was parked illegally in front of Sully's Tap. Keene peered inside the vehicle. Hurley had placed a hand-lettered card that read "Official Police Business" on the dash.

Keene laughed.

"You got one?" Hurley had once asked. Keene shook his head. Hurley had produced a duplicate from the console of his Supra. Keene was busted by a rookie the one time he used it.

He walked into Sully's and found Hurley and Peterson at the bar, front and center.

"Ginger ale," Hurley said to a slender girl with pink hair behind the bar. Keene ordered nothing. Peterson was drinking a Poland Spring sparkling water.

"You're a Mack, right?" Hurley asked the girl with pink hair.

"Uh-huh," she said as she shook Hurley's hand.

"What's your name, honey?" Hurley asked.

Peterson rolled her eyes and said, "Probably not *Honey*."

"Eileen. Michaela's my cousin."

Keene said, "Who's your dad?"

She scrunched up her forehead as if deciding whether the question was worthy of an answer. "Francis. Why?" She added, "The crazy one if you're wondering."

Keene said, "Kevin and Jamie are your cousins, right?"

"Yeah," Eileen said tentatively.

"They wouldn't happen to be here?"

"They're in the back," Hurley said.

Keene ducked his head to Hurley and asked, "Do a drive-by yet?"

"Yeah. No trash at Jamie's house," Hurley whispered.

Keene whispered, "Same at Kevin's."

The trash would be picked up the following morning in the Deering neighborhood where the twins lived. That evening was the night to put out the trash containers and, in the sort of heat the city was experiencing, you didn't miss trash collection.

Keene was startled when Eileen whispered, "They haven't been home yet."

"You listening to us?" Keene snapped at her.

"News flash, Detective. When two grown men whisper in each other's ears, it's hard not to eavesdrop if you're three feet away." Eileen dropped the glass she was cleaning into the sink full of water.

Hurley said, "They call you Ei-mack, right?"

"Those that did, sleep with the fishes, Detective," Eileen said.

Peterson snorted a laugh and said, "She got you there, Hurley. I think I'm going to like you, Eileen." She held out her hand and said, "Detective Peterson. Call me Diane. Those that call you Honey might sleep with the fishes, too." Then she turned to Keene and said, "Arnaud coming?"

Keene said, "She doesn't drink. I probably should have insisted she come. None of us know her well."

"And none of us are drinking," Peterson said in a self-evident way.

"I don't see she has that much to offer," Hurley said.

Keene said, "She was the responding officer. She's smart. A little cool."

"Unsociable," Peterson chimed in.

Keene found himself defending the young officer. "No, Diane, I wouldn't use the word *unsociable*."

"What word would you use?"

"I would say *socially awkward*," he said, choosing the term on the fly.

Diane sputtered and said, "Okay, Detective, whatever you say."

Hurley changed the subject. "You ever meet Tom Grogan before this?"

"Seen him around," Keene said.

Hurley said, "He was a tough kid. The neighborhood tough guy."

Keene knew this by reputation, but he also knew Grogan was smart, smart enough to pull himself from the embrace of the Hill.

"You grew up around here; you know him?"

"Younger than me. Michaela knew him," Hurley said.

"What else do you know about him?"

"Told you he was the tough guy. Had to be," Hurley said indifferently. "He would have gotten eaten alive if he hadn't been."

"What do you mean?" Keene asked.

"Grogan's father, Patrick, was as Irish as me. Ma and Da come from the old country. As I said, they packed up and went back to the Emerald Isle without him. Imagine that."

"Yeah, I know, right?" Peterson said, pushing her empty glass forward for another Poland Spring. "No wonder the butcher was a cranky bastard."

Keene said, "Nine years old?"

"How callous is that?" Peterson said. She leaned an elbow against the bar. "To leave a nine-year-old boy to fend for himself."

Hurley said, "So, Tom's got a cranky Irish bastard for a father and a hot Italian babe for a mother. Tommy-boy learns to fight the Irish because they say he's a Dago and the Italians because they say he's a Mick."

Diane said, "Became a helluva good fighter. I've taken lessons down at Star Martial Arts from him."

"Yeah? You do karate?" Hurley said.

"Krav Maga," she said.

Hurley said, "Krav Maga, huh? How 'bout you and me, grappling match, when and where?"

Keene said, "She'd beat the crap out of you."

Diane said, "Not tonight, I got a date."

Hurley wished he'd never said it. The thought might have come but should never have been spoken. But, despite himself, he'd said it and, as a result, he took an open-palmed smack to the back of his head when he said, "Man or woman?"

"See you in the morning," Diane said to Keene after clobbering Hurley. "Thanks for the drinks." Peterson waggled her fingers at Eileen and left.

"Hey, Detectives," Leo said, his hand wrapped around a Bud.

Keene and Hurley turned and looked Leo up and down. They turned away from him in unison without a word.

Hurley said, "Eileen, what's the cover charge for reporters? One snuck in without paying."

She said, "Fifty bucks. Where's the scofflaw?"

"There goes your tip, Pink," Leo said. "So, Detective Keene, a word?" The reporter motioned with a wag of his big head that looked like a pumpkin on a fence post.

"You have to work for it, man," Keene said.

Leo reasserted, "Come with me, Detective." He walked to a table in the back, looking over his shoulder to monitor the cop. Keene didn't leave his seat at the bar. The reporter returned, tail between his legs.

"Tell me, Keene, what's the story on the asphyxiation angle? You working on any leads on that aspect?"

"Look, Leo, as I said, you gotta work harder than this."

"Cut the shit, man. Give me something. What's your angle on this?"

"Okay," Keene said after a moment. "Follow me."

They took a table by the bowling machine. Keene could see the Mack twins. They were still playing pool in the back room. In his mind, Leo owed him, and he had used the reporter's help in the past. He would use him this time with no regrets. If he *felt* used, that would be because it was what Keene was about to do. Getting the word to the murderer that they had the suffocation info had been easy through the print media. Print had a shelf-life, and Leo had performed well. Television was good, but the killer had to be tuned in. "What I can give you right now is that our team—use the word *team*. Sorry, don't mean to write the story."

"Bullshit. I think that's exactly what you want to do. You should have been a reporter."

Keene looked at Leo wondering if the guy had a conscience. "Nah, I have a soul," he said without the least hint of humor. "Okay, but it's not a task force. Please. That is inaccurate. I got three people on it. That's all there is to it."

Leo asked, "Did I just see two of them?"

"Maybe. Look, it'd be helpful if you didn't identify them."

"Naming them wouldn't move the story forward in an appreciable sense so I won't. But give me something substantial, dude."

"Well, dude, what we have now isn't much more than what you have now," Keene lied. He continued, "We have no more potential suspects than we had yesterday. Huge list. We're developing timelines, canvassing the neighborhood."

"I have a source," Leo interrupted. "He tells me you already canvassed the neighborhood. Don't try to feed me bullshit."

"No, no, Leo. What your source *doesn't* know is we're *re*canvassing. Now I know your source isn't police or he'd know this shit happens all the time. You do, too, for Christ's sake. When the cops change the fundamental outlook on a case, they do the survey all over again. Right? Asking more appropriate questions."

"You guys aren't sitting on your thumbs. You have more than you're telling me. If not a suspect, you gotta have a motive or something you're chasing. An angle." Leo was starting to sound desperate.

Hurley interrupted them. He wagged his head toward the twins.

Keene looked up to the pool table and the Mack brothers were moving to the door. "Okay. Let's go"

"You take Jamie," Keene said as he and Hurley stepped out of Sully's. Jamie Mack drove a big blue Ram pickup. Kevin Mack drove the same rig but the color of a fine red wine.

"You're gonna need these." Hurley handed Keene a roll of purple Portland trash bags Keene had asked him to buy.

They took off, not wanting to follow too closely but close enough to assure they witnessed the twins curb-siding their respective trash receptacles. From inside the house to the sidewalk. Missing nothing. Jamie's home was in Deering, Kevin's, off of Ocean Avenue, almost in Falmouth, in a quiet neighborhood whose houses sat on an acre to acre-and-a-half parcels of land. The development had been built fifteen years ago, and the homes were owned by people with money. Each house had been placed carefully on its lot and, with the aid of extensive landscaping, remained largely invisible from most of the others.

Keene drove the Explorer because it was quieter than the Charger. He rolled to a stop one curvy block from the end of Kevin's driveway. With the window down, he heard the garage door grinding open, though he could not see the house behind some ornamental shrubs. A vehicle door closed with a thud, and Keene imagined he heard Vibram soles grinding on the hard surface of the garage floor. The back door, into the house, slammed. Keene waited.

He waited until he heard the back door that led to the garage open and the unmistakable thump of a heavy trash bag dumped into a plastic trash can. Then another one. Then a third. How much trash did one man generate? Keene knew Kevin Mack lived alone. The door into the house closed. Kevin had left it open while he brought all three bags out, but now it was closed. Keene eased his car door closed and in the gathering dark, moved forward in the direction of Kevin's driveway. Then he heard the grinding roll of trash can wheels on asphalt. Keene dropped to the ground. He peered through the shrubs and saw Kevin Mack wheeling the trash to the end of the drive. The only time Keene didn't have his eyes on the trash was while it was inside Kevin's house and subsequently inside his garage. Kevin walked back to the garage and rolled another receptacle out to the curbside. The recycling bin. He placed this bin next to the trash can and manipulated it until it was lined up in some specific way that was apparent to Kevin alone. He turned. Stopped. Shifted the receptacles to perfection. At last, he returned to the garage and the overhead door came down behind him with a final clunk.

Keene slipped forward to the plastic trash can. He blew noiselessly into a latex glove and then another. He pushed his hands into them. One handle resisted the push and then folded down easily. The other, the same. Keene lifted the lid off and placed it on the ground. He quietly lifted the top bag out and tore it open. The guy drank a lot of coffee and not K-cups. There were grounds liberally dispersed throughout the bags; all three bags were contaminated with wet, garbagy-smelling coffee grounds. It was slow going. He didn't want to make a mess because the AG had insisted the operation remain discreet. Keene discovered how one man could produce this much trash: He ate take-out every night. Spaghetti from the Italian place at Allen's corner. Chinese, Thai, and Vietnamese from local restaurants. Mexican. Pizza. Sandwiches. McDonald's, Wendy's. The network of aromas resulted in an amalgamated smell that qualified as a stink that nearly gagged Keene, who was relatively immune to odor-induced barfing, but this job pushed the limits.

He sifted through each of the three bags. Every examined element of Kevin Mack's trash was placed in a new purple bag. At the end of it all, he'd found nothing of interest. No gloves. No receipts for gloves. It seemed the man hadn't disposed of any receipts for the last week. Though he was eager to hear of Hurley's results, Keene was getting closer to taking Kevin and Jamie Mack off the suspect list. He wasn't there yet, but he was close.

CHAPTER
29

Keene pulled his to-go cup from under the mechanism that sucked and slurped and sounded like a scuba diver having an underwater medical emergency. He returned to the bedroom and whispered to Melena, "Bye-bye, Love. I'll see you tonight." He expected a mumble of unintelligible gibberish but she surprised him.

"Lunch? If we can't vacation, at least we can have lunch." She said she had something she wanted to tell him. Something she'd wanted to cover while on vacation, but lunch would have to do.

"One o'clock? Suki's?"

"One o'clock," she said and reached and kissed him.

"Morning, Chief," Keene said.

"Morning," Charlie Riordan grumbled. "Sit down. Coffee?" Riordan said as Cali placed the paper cup in front of him.

"Sure, thanks."

"There you go," Cali said. Then, to Keene: "Black, right?"

"Yeah, thanks, Cali."

She said, "No problem." Then, not quite under her breath, "I feel like a goddamned waitress." Cali smiled and left.

Keene said to Charlie, "How's the Senator's trip detail coming?"

"Ach, fuck me. So, where are we on Grogan?"

"Hurley and I were looking at Tom Grogan, the professor. The butcher's son. Big and physically fit."

"But who do you see as our second guy?" Riordan said.

"Yeah, well, if there *is* a second guy. We talked with the son." Keene explained that the butcher was left-hand dominant, and the professor knew this and wouldn't make the mistake of placing the gun in the right hand. "The killer didn't know this. I don't like the son for it anymore."

Cali rapped the office door and entered.

"Here you go, Detective. Hot and fresh. Anything else? Did I tell you the specials?" She smiled again and left.

Keene didn't have the chance to thank her so he continued to Riordan, "When I met with the professor, I gave him every opportunity to cop to it and he didn't. The finding story makes sense and holds up," Keene said.

"No love lost, though, as I understand it," Riordan suggested.

"Right. But why now? If Professor Grogan was going to kill his father, why did he wait twenty years?"

"Yeah." Riordan reached for his jar of peanut M&Ms. "What's Hurley's take? Anything on the Hill?"

"He's looking at Granda Mike."

"He's a hundred years old or something," Riordan said.

"Right. Hurley's looking at the Macks," Keene said. "Focusing on the twins. Jamie's probably going to take over when his grandfather dies."

"Why would he kill Grogan?" Riordan asked.

"Hurley's theory is Granda wants to settle the score."

"What score? That Patrick killed Sean in a car accident thirty, forty years ago?"

Keene said, "Seems unlikely to me, too, but I'm letting Hurley run with it. You don't know what he might come up with."

"Watch him," Riordan said. "I don't need him sending something to the DA that won't pass the smell test."

"I got another name. Tom Grogan said Vito Troiano had a thing about his father."

"Vito Troiano. The guy is wrapped a bit tight."

"Or loose. Sounds like the wrapping might be coming off the package." Keene pulled out a pack of gum.

Riordan said, "I don't know anything about that guy."

"I'm going to see him today. He self-medicates at Sully's regularly." Keene paused while he unwrapped the gum. He carefully slipped the wrapper into his jacket pocket.

Riordan said, "What are you doing? You can toss that in the trash right here." Riordan motioned toward a trash can.

"Nah, I save the wrapper so I can re-wrap the chewed gum and... never mind."

"You're not telling me you rechew, are you? Do you need a raise or what? Tell me you're not a rechewer."

"No. I...Melena saw me spitting it out once, and she said the birds were all going to fill up with xanthium gum or some shit and die because I spit it out. So... What are you laughing at?"

Charlie Riordan, red-in-the-face laughing, said, "You save the wrapper so you can put it in your pocket and throw it away later." He continued to laugh and said, "Grow a pair, Keene, and spit your damn gum out. You ever see a seagull choking on gum? I've seen them swallow a whole lobster claw sideways. Killing the birds...you gotta be shitting me."

Keene tried to ignore the Interim Chief but couldn't. Instead, he said, "You've never seen a seagull swallow a lobster claw sideways. That's a goddamned lie." Keene chewed on his gum intensely and, intentionally changing the subject, he said, "Peterson is looking at the financial stuff and unsecured creditors. The broker of the sale of the market told Peterson that Grogan wouldn't benefit from the sale but his wife would. However, the funds were to be put in trust. Not available to his creditors. Some guys were going to take a financial loss even though Grogan's wife had the means to pay them."

Riordan's phone rang. He picked the old-fashioned receiver from the cradle and said, "Hang on."

He held his hand over the mouthpiece and said, "After you meet with the team, let me know the plan."

Keene stood to leave and turned toward the door.

Riordan said, "Get me this guy. At least before—" Riordan looked at his desk blotter, "—my meeting with the Service: Thursday at four, Detective."

"Yeah, sure." Keene looked at his phone. "No problem. We'll wrap it up around three. Work for you?"

"Basil, I'm serious. The Secret Service guys are all over me." He held the phone up as evidence. "Like we got nothing else to do in Portland, Maine."

Charlie Riordan was a guy sitting in a seat that was getting too hot for comfort. His problem was, immovable forces were sitting on his lap. The predictable result was that Charlie's ass was going to get burned.

CHAPTER
30

Eileen was washing a shaker glass when Detective Keene entered Sully's Tap. She wondered about telekinesis as she plunged the grimy glass into soapy water, and when the glass resurfaced, she admired the rainbow-hued bubble over the top of the glass. It quivered like an oyster with the chills. With mental energy alone she attempted to pop the bubble. She exuded popping energy. Exuded telepathic waves of energy. Pop! She jumped. Jesus, God, it popped. Hallelujah!

"Ahem," Keene said, un-self-consciously verbalizing the throat-clearing syllables.

She was dropping the glass into rinse water, having dispensed with the shivery bubble when she looked up at Keene. He made her nervous. He must know how old she is. The other cops didn't look at her the way he did like he knew her ID was as fake as the hundreds the Greek passed last summer just for fun.

"Afternoon, Detective Keene. What can I do you for?"

"How's Eileen?" Keene asked.

What did he mean by that? She didn't trust this line of questioning. Like he was asking: Are you some kind of little seventeen-year-old, illegal, pink-headed bartender?

Eileen, not able to think of a more appropriate response, said, "Jesus."

Keene said, "Eileen, can I say something?" Before she could give him permission, he said, "You look very young to me."

She thought maybe it was Sun Tzu—or was it General Tso?—who said the best defense is a good offense. Go right after him. She leaned on the bar directly in front of the detective. Challenging squinted eyes like a rattlesnake. A muscle twitched below her left eye. The bartender with pink hair set her jaw and said in measured tones, "Most young people do."

Keene laughed and said, "Yeah, I guess they do."

A sliding noise was followed by a thump followed by an electronically generated facsimile of crowd noise.

Keene asked Eileen, "Know where I can find Vito Troiano?"

She nodded toward the source of the noise with a sneer.

He said, "Thank you."

Eileen said, "Cheerio."

Keene walked past the smoky kitchen entrance and found himself in the back section of the bar. The place was quiet. It was one o'clock in the afternoon. There were no couples seated in booths in the dark or even singles hovering over tankards of beer. There was just Vito Troiano, short and wiry, shaking a can of alley wax along the lane of the Shuffle-Bowl game. He deposited a quarter and leaned along the narrow table and let the puck go. He split the pins.

"Suck me," Vito groaned.

"Vito Troiano?" Keene asked and displayed his badge.

Troiano peered from under the brim of his tweed fisherman's cap. "Yeah?"

"Got a minute?"

"Yeah. Let me make this shot." With that, he angled the puck with an exaggerated spin. Only the pins on one side jerked up. "Fuckin' suck me."

"I guess spinning the puck doesn't work," Keene said.

Vito glared at the detective. "Not that time. Everybody's got an opinion," Vito said.

"Day off, Vito?" Keene asked.

"Got laid off," he said. "Might get some union work soon."

"Huh. Makes it tough. You been out of work a lot?"

"Yeah, so? This about Grogan? Figured somebody'd be looking for me."

"Yeah?" Keene asked.

"Everybody knows I didn't like the asshole." Vito poured a glass for himself.

"Yeah, I heard you two didn't get along," Keene said.

"Mind if I play?" Vito nodded at the bowling machine. "Don't wanna lose the table."

"Go ahead." Keene looked around at nobody waiting for the table.

Vito pushed a button and the pins dropped. He made a strike and threw his fist in triumph.

"Good bowl." Keene paused a tick then said, "Would you say you had... unfinished business with the butcher?"

Vito laughed. He drank his glass and refilled it.

"What do you think, I did it? Like I finished my unfinished business?"

"Well...where were you August fifteenth around nine o'clock?"

Vito said, "I didn't kill him. I was relaxing with my wife."

Keene said, "She'll corroborate that?"

Vito said, "He was an asshole, Detective. Plenty would have liked to kill him, but I heard he killed himself." He retrieved the puck and sprinkled wax on the lane.

"You mind if I take a whirl at that?" Keene asked.

Vito handed the puck to Keene, who leaned into the game and let the puck go with a flourish.

He said, "Why'd you dislike the butcher so much?"

"Everyone disliked him." Vito looked at the remaining pins and told the detective to aim to the left.

Keene did as he was told, and the rest of the pins folded up with a slam.

"Nice bowling." Vito air-fist-bumped the detective.

"Thanks." Keene held the puck when Vito tried to take it away. "Why did you have a grudge, Vito?"

Vito held his hand out for the puck.

"You mind?" Keene said. "One more."

Vito nodded reluctantly and said, "It was Easter. Sharon went to DeLuca's for a lamb."

"Sharon's your wife?" Keene asked. He leaned over the alley and let the puck go. Ten pins jumped up. The crowd noise exploded from the game.

Vito nodded and shook his head, conceding Keene's well-placed shot. He said, "Grogan told her to thank him. Can I have the puck?"

"Thank him? What did he mean by that? Let me take just one more shot."

Vito said, "She used food stamps. He dissed her and made her say thank you because, according to him, he paid for food stamps with his taxes or whatever."

Keene leaned and let the puck go. Another strike. "Yes!" he cried and pumped his fist.

Vito scooped the puck from the table. Threw a split.

"Is lamb expensive?" Keene asked. "I never buy it."

Vito poured another glass of beer and watched Keene chalk up another strike.

"When did this happen?" Keene asked after pumping his fist again.

After a gulp of beer, Vito said, "Last...Easter."

"And that's it?"

"Go ahead. Take another shot if you want," Vito said in a defeated voice. "He disrespected my wife. What do you want?" He poured the last of the beer into his glass and yelled, "Gary, another pitcher." He placed the puck on the machine and circled back to his seat.

Keene left the puck on the machine.

"Here you go, Vito," Eileen said. "But Gary says that's it." She set the smaller pitcher on the table.

"That's a half pitcher. What the hell, Ei?" Vito topped off his glass.

Eileen said, "Gary wants you to pay this." She dropped the check on the table, "Plus twenty tonight."

"Ei-mack," Vito whined. "I ain't got it. You guys know that."

"Drink up," she said. "Then go home." Then she said with a different tone, "Detective? Can I get you something?" She was cold, like she was pissed off at him. Keene wondered if he'd said something at the bar. The thing about age?

"No, thank you. I'm leaving," he said. He turned his attention back to Troiano.

Vito said while watching Eileen walk back to the bar, "She's got a nice ass, don't ya think?"

Keene ignored the comment. "Would it be fair to say you were still angry with Patrick Grogan on Sunday night, August fifteenth?"

"I got an alibi, Detective," Vito drawled.

"Pay your bill and go home, Vito, or I'll charge you with theft of goods and services." Keene smoothed his tie and walked into the main part of the Tap. He would need to see Mrs. Troiano. "Evening, Eileen," he said and nodded to her. She nodded back.

"Suck me!" Vito moaned from the game room.

"Must have rolled another split," Keene said to Eileen. He raised his voice and said, "Vito, don't spin the puck." Then to Eileen, "It's an easy game."

He walked into the sunlight and considered Vito an intriguing possibility; someone to look at and Mrs. T as somebody to interview. If she would say they weren't together and Keene could get Vito's prints at the scene, he'd have probable cause to arrest. Sandblaster said there were too many prints to be helpful. But he probably did a survey, and with a warrant, Keene could Blue Check Vito against Sandblaster's database. That put the cart uphill of the horse. What Keene needed was Vito at the scene. The Blue Check was a cell phone-sized blue tooth device used for identity verification through fingerprints. It was used by law enforcement and corporate America. Schools and the military were starting to use the equipment for screening purposes. Originally, the relatively new technology communicated with national databases alone, but recent upgrades allowed police departments to populate local databases and program the Blue Check to use that data as well. Sandblaster should have just such a database from the crime scene.

If they could find a witness to contradict Vito Troiano's alibi, they might have something on him. As Keene considered this, Detective Hurley was talking to just such a witness, but Keene didn't know it.

Keene looked at his watch. A watch tells you the time, but for what purpose? To what end did Keene need to know that it was two o'clock? Only two things: He's either early or late for an appointment. Unfortunately for Keene, a watch doesn't tell you what the appointment is. His cell phone would give him that information, but only if he had originally entered such data. Cell phones are not better than their masters. Only as good. Two o'clock. Two o'clock. Huh.

CHAPTER
31

A striking redhead wandered across the park and stopped next to a towering old elm tree. She stood looking around for a minute. She sniffed the air and squatted and urinated. Detective Hurley spied her from across the street and crossed to talk to her owner, Angus O'Roark. Also known as Reddog. His companion's name was Zinfandel. O'Roark had been a young auto mechanic when he acquired his first Irish setter, whom he had christened Cabernet. He had thought such a beautiful dog required a sophisticated name—a sophisticated name for a sophisticated lady of Irish descent. Red wines; all his Irish setters since Cabernet had been named for red wine. Or at least pink. Zinfandel yawned and sat regally and flamboyantly bored.

"Reddog, how ya doing?" Hurley said to the human, then leaned to the dog and said, "Zinnie," and stroked the Irish setter's head and murmured things like *good dog* and *who's a good girl* and other things found in the human-to-dog lexicon.

"Afternoon, Detective," O'Roark said. "Nice day, isn't it?"

"Corker," Hurley said and straightened from the dog. "Real attention whore, isn't she?" The two men laughed quietly. "Got a couple of questions for you, Reddog. Got a minute?"

"Of course, Detective. I'm an open book."

"Yeah. Right. The night Patrick Grogan died, were you around? Did you hear anything that night?"

"I'm always around. I heard Grogan blasting his music, is what I heard. Which is what I always hear and don't bother to call PPD anymore because you never did anything anyway, be honest with you."

"Don't know what to tell you. Noise ain't high on my priorities list."

Reddog said, "No, of course not. You've got bigger fish to fry, am I right? Speaking of fish, you hear about them pogies stinking up the place?"

"Mackerel. Anyway, anything else? Other than loud music?"

"Pogies."

"What?" Hurley asked.

"Pogies are stinking up the joint."

Hurley thought they were mackerel but wasn't going to get in a pissing contest with the famously stubborn Reddog. "Did ya hear anything else, Reddog?"

"Couldn't hear anything else, be honest with you." Reddog depressed a button on the leash handle. It was a red plastic piece that magically shortened the leash as Zinfandel returned from roaming to the end of the line.

"Okay, fine. Did you see anyone? Did you see, well, anyone from the neighborhood?"

"You know Vito hated Grogan. You think Vito done it?"

"Person of interest maybe," Hurley said. "But I gotta know if anyone seen him or anybody else."

"I thought Grogan killed himself. Now you got Vito doing it?"

"No, Reddog. I don't have Vito doing it, all right?"

The dog turned in a circle, squatted, then thought better of that particular latitude and longitude, and turned the other way, squatted, and released a steaming mound on the grass. Her owner said, "Jesus God," and slipped a plastic bag from his pocket.

Hurley batted at the air as the offensive odor assaulted them.

"Jesus, what do you feed her?"

"The finest food available. Fish guts."

"Jesus," Hurley said again, waving an open hand against the stench.

"Fact of the matter is, for sure, I did see Vito wandering around that night," Reddog said. "He hated that douchebag of a butcher, you know." He glanced over his shoulder as he attended to Zinfandel's big job. "I gotta hang onto this shit until I find a damn trash can, Hurley. Can you get the goddamn city to put some more trash cans over here? It's a crying shame there ain't a shitload more of them."

"I'll get right on it, O'Roark," Hurley said. "You saw Vito at the scene?"

"I said so to that officer was asking me questions himself. Don't know nothing about what Vito was up to, be honest with you."

"Was he alone or with someone?" Hurley asked.

"Alone."

"Are you sure?"

Reddog took an instant, then said, "Of course, I'm sure. Why'd I say a thing like that if I'm not sure, Detective? I'm an open book."

"What time did you see him?"

"Not sure, be honest with you."

Hurley said, "Was it after dark, for example?"

"Oh, of course, it was after dark. Why you asking these questions? You know what time the butcher was killed."

"Was it before all the cop cars showed up? Like, before ten? Let's say between dark and ten p.m.?"

"I'm sure it was." He gave a short, sharp whistle for Zinfandel, as she wandered again. "I'm sure it was," he said. Then he said, "Be honest with you."

"Was Vito carrying anything?"

"Like what?"

"Reddog," Hurley had to count to three before he continued his thought. "I'm gonna give you a quick lesson. Detective 101. The detective asks the questions; the witness answers them. Is it that difficult?"

"That's a question?"

"Was Vito carrying anything?" Hurley barked.

"Jeez, Detective, lighten up. Don't remember, be honest with you. Maybe he had a bottle of beer. Yup. That's right. He had a bottle of beer. Oh, and he had a gun, too."

"What?"

"I'm kidding, Detective. You can't even detect a good joke? All he had was a bottle of beer."

"Thanks, Reddog. There's a trash can down by the playground. Get rid of that shit. I got a phone call to make."

Hurley started to walk away when another question occurred. "Hey, Reddog."

"Yeah?" Reddog, who was following Zinfandel to the playground, said over his shoulder.

"You said another officer asked you questions. Curious—who was it?"

Reddog said, "Didn't get his name. Had an accent."

"Like a Mexican—you know, Hispanic accent?" Hurley was thinking of Velazquez, the only pronounced foreign accent on the force that he could think of.

"Nah," Reddog said. "I know Velazquez. It was more European, like Eastern European. Like, I don't know, like, Romanian? I don't know, be honest with you."

Reddog, despite his quirkiness, would make a credible witness. This placement of a good suspect—Vito, with motive and opportunity—at the scene was all they needed to arrest the man, and Hurley knew it and Keene would know it. He punched Keene's number into his cell.

CHAPTER
32

Detective Keene thought he had an extra ten minutes. He decided to walk the paths of the Eastern Promenade overlooking the waters of Casco Bay, the islands, the fort, and the flotilla of pleasure boats. Freshly oxygenated blood encouraged the brain to escape the constraints of conventional thinking. Keene deplored the inside-the-box/outside-the-box thing, but it was constructive in illustrating his fresh oxygen hypothesis. Strolling the walkways, sucking in the air and appreciating the view, the sounds of summer and people at leisure, and the birds and distant traffic, calmed his mind. He'd used this very spot after the shooting one year ago to meditate and reflect on the necessity but debasement of taking a life. It had been necessary to save others' lives. Protection. Protect and serve. The taker of life, for whatever purpose, is debased. Brought down to a level God, or whatever notion of a higher power there is had never intended for the human animal to achieve. Had there been an alternative? It had happened at the corner of this road less than half a mile away. Had he followed the exacting protocol delineated by policing procedure? Yes, he had—he knew this for sure. It had been a righteous shoot, declared righteous by the internal investigation. But the taking of a man's life? Even though the man in question was trying to kill him? And would kill again. Righteous, yes. Necessary? Probably. Had there been a nonlethal alternative? Maybe.

Keene shared the fresh air with wheeling and needling gulls, other walkers, cyclists, and food trucks. The trucks were a recent phenomenon serving human and avian life alike.

He watched a seabird face off with three crows, ink stains next to the dazzling white gull. The single bird bobbed its head and spread its wings. The confederation of crows shared a purpose. They wanted the morsel of food the gull owned. Keene had read that crows were smart, foraging and hunting in groups using a complex form of communication. Seagulls had gotten some good press as well, being advertised as tool users, dropping a crab from a height to break the shell, risking the capital to increase its value. Not unlike the stock market, it seemed a dicey management of one's resources, exposing one's security to the misbehavior of opportunistic rascals. A thought crossed Keene's mind: He and Melena were due to meet with their investment adviser. Melena seemed eager to discuss their financial positions, for what reason, he knew not. He and Melena. Due to meet...

Predictably, the larger, more well-dressed bird relinquished the morsel to the ragged but aggressive lot and launched itself, leaving the feast to the delighted crows.

Keene walked back to the car and sat behind the wheel. He tapped it, teeth itching with anticipation. This case was twisting his brain: Granda Mack and the Mack brothers and their hatred of Grogan. But motive alone doesn't make a murderer. Vito Troiano hated the butcher, too. Once again, exhibiting motive but nothing more. The real estate angle might provide more, as yet unidentified, subjects with motive, but if Keene couldn't put somebody at the scene, he might be looking down the long lonely road to inconclusiveness.

His cell rang.

Hurley said, "Keene, where are you?"

"The Prom. What's up?"

Hurley said, "We got Vito at the scene. We got Vito at the damned scene."

"Holy shit. Who's the witness? Is he credible?" Keene asked.

"Reddog."

"O'Roark?"

"How many Reddogs you know?" Hurley said.

"Yeah, yeah. Okay. What'd he see?"

"Let's meet at the Tap. Have some lunch."

Lunch?

Keene said, "No, Vito's probably there. Go to the Bricks. I gotta see Sandblaster if this is good info."

"Oh, it's good all right."

There was a pause.

"Oh, shit!" Keene growled.

"What? What?"

"I was supposed to meet Melena at Suki's for lunch at one."

"Uh-oh. You're a little late, dude."

The Charger's clock, an old-fashioned analog job, established beyond the shadow of a doubt that it was fifteen minutes to three. Seriously late. He stepped on the gas. He was fifteen minutes from the restaurant. He thought about telling Melena he thought they'd agreed on three. Stupid. Why would you schedule lunch for three? No, an important meeting had run long or... He'd never lied to her and never would. He called her.

"Hello?"

Keene felt she was distant, her voice quiet, and her demeanor disappointed.

"I'm sorry, baby. I'm so sorry. Are you still there? At the restaurant?"

"No. It only took me about a half hour to realize I'd been stood up. I guess it took you longer to figure it out. I texted three times. You didn't get my message?"

He looked at the icons on the top of his screen. Text messages were waiting for him. "I am so sorry, Melena. I was looking forward to seeing you, having lunch with you."

She said, "Oh well." A pause hung in the air like a foul odor.

Keene had to say something. Some people have the distinct ability to make a pause suck. Melena was one. "So, what did you do this afternoon?" he asked.

"I went out to the animal shelter."

"The animal...? Why?"

"Because the puppies are so cute," she said as if the point was self-evident and she hardly had the patience to tell him. "They made me feel a little better after being stood up by my husband."

"My competition for your affection is puppies?"

"It is now," she said. "And they are way ahead."

Keene thought, *I'm screwed.*

CHAPTER
33

Hurley and Keene met at the Bricks in less than five minutes. Their car doors boomed closed, reverberating through the parking garage.

"This is good. This is great," Keene said, thrilled by the hunt. He had the confidence of a bloodhound.

"Damn right. He may not be dripping with motive, but it's there and we got him outside the scene at the right time, lying to an investigator, and if we can find prints... We got him, we damn well got him." Hurley held the door for Keene.

They hustled to the bowels of the building where Sandblaster would be, either grinding in his office or sweating in the gym. The gym came first and they found him there.

The evidence tech knelt on a bench pumping a dumbbell with a lot of weight on it. He was in a mid-count of a series of reps. After the final one, he guided the weight to the floor.

Sandblaster put a white towel to his face and sat on the bench, his chest heaving.

"What's up, guys?"

"What did you find for fingerprints at the store? In DeLuca's," Keene asked.

"If you're going to use prints to identify suspects, there's like five or ten thousand," Sandblaster said wryly.

Keene said, "No, no; did you complete a survey?"

The ET said, "Does Ironman have a stainless-steel dick? Of course I did."

"We need it ASAP."

"You got a guy for it?" Sandblaster asked. "Only way a survey will work."

"Maybe," Hurley said. "Can we use the Blue Check with your database?"

"Hell yeah," he said.

"Do we need a warrant to get his thumb on the Blue Check?" Hurley asked Keene. The cops had to collect the suspect's thumb print using the

145

tool's pressure-sensitive pad, then the device would access the database for comparisons.

"Yeah, but I think with Reddog's affidavit... Go get one from him right now. I'll find Vito. You got a Blue Check?"

Hurley said, "Charlie's office. I'll get it."

Keene said, "Okay, send an officer to get the affidavit. I'll call Wainwright." Judge Harvey Wainwright was the Department's go-to judge.

As Keene searched his contacts for Wainwright's office number, Hurley made another call. "Eileen? Detective Hurley. Vito there? ... Troiano? ... Yeah, he is? ... Yeah." He tapped off the phone and verified, "Vito is at the Tap."

"Would Eileen tip him off?" Keene asked as Wainwright's phone rang.

"Eileen? Nah. Maybe if Vito paid his bill."

Keene waved Hurley quiet. "Detective Basil Keene, is the judge available?" Then, "I need a warrant... Okay, hang on." He gestured a writing signal to Hurley, who produced a pen and paper. Keene jotted the cell number down.

Wainwright told Keene that the motive alone wasn't probable cause, but the defective alibi attested to by Reddog O'Roark sealed the deal. The warrant would be no problem, but the judge was fishing and wouldn't be available until after six p.m.

Hurley said, "Let's get him away from Sully's. Not inside. I got informants there, you know."

"Yeah, I get it," Keene agreed.

"Good answer. I get a lot of good stuff from there." Hurley, above all other cops, had a distinct network running through Sully's Tap. "So, where?"

"Does he ever go home?" Keene asked.

Hurley said, "I'll call Eileen back and have Vito kicked out for some reason."

Keene said, "She told him to leave last night for not paying."

"Good."

"But will he go home?" Keene asked.

"Probably not."

"We'll grab him on the street," Keene said. "Let's get that affidavit and the warrant."

"I wouldn't mind getting him outside the neighborhood, take him on Congress." The less cop action near Sully's, the better.

"I'll get the warrant at six," Keene said. "Meet back here at eight-thirty, right?"

Hurley redialed. "Eileen, boot him at eight-thirty, no sooner. If he tries to leave earlier, don't let him."

Keene had plenty of work to do before six. The book on Troiano would be started with Keene's initial meeting at Sully's. He entered his notes from that meeting and printed them. The affidavit and a copy of the warrant would be next. Subsequently, his efforts regarding the other suspects would be entered into the digital record, then printed for the hard-copy records. The paperwork took time, and it was six o'clock before he knew it. He roared out of the garage at the Bricks to the judge's office at the courthouse.

Judge Wainwright, red from the sun and possibly alcoholic beverages, was in a jovial mood. He wanted to talk. Keene, on the other hand, needed to think. Best done on the water. However, he had a social obligation to hear the man out. He stayed.

"Scotch?"

Keene waved the offer off. "I still have work to do."

"The warrant? You're apprehending tonight?"

"Yes. Eight-thirty. So, how was the fishing?"

The judge finished pouring two fingers for himself. Then he said, "We caught sun and salt air. That's about it."

Keene thought, *And a buzz.*

"I've been thinking about you, Detective Keene," Wainwright continued. "How are you doing? What is it—a year now since the dust-up?"

"With all respect, sir, I'm not sure I'd call it a dust-up."

"Of course; poor choice of words. But the question remains."

Keene said, "How am I doing? Not sure a man is ever the same after something like that. I guess that's why I wouldn't call it a dust-up." Keene looked into the judge's eyes and recognized a sorrow in them, and he wished he hadn't brought up the bad choice of vocabulary. Wainwright had meant no harm and maybe just the opposite: He sincerely wondered about Keene's state of mind and mood. "I'm doing okay, Judge, and I truly appreciate your asking."

"Sure thing, son." The judge might have been ten years older than Keene, certainly no more. "I—and you, no doubt—wish the words had never escaped your lips."

"I thought Leo and I were off the record. He said we'd never established that. I guess that was true. I was so goddamned frustrated by then. It had been weeks of nonstop harassment."

Keene drove to the marina, punched in the code, walked down to the Whaler and thought about the words that had escaped his lips. He had said to Leo, *Just because the man is black, doesn't mean he's innocent.* Ten words that changed his life. Or at least the trajectory of his career.

He stepped into the boat and started her up, untied and motored out through the fairway among moored boats and boats underway, returning from a day on the water. When he was free of all traffic, he gunned the boat into Casco Bay, the visiting yacht, *Ice Cold*, looming near Clapboard Island. She seemed to rise out of the water and she reflected the setting sun in stripes. He motored around her in a sweeping arc, a bit too fast. His mind raced with the outboard engine. Grogan had been murdered and Keene knew the murderer was a professional. It wasn't Tom Grogan—no motive, no evidence, he was there at the finding moment, but why wouldn't he be?

It hadn't been the Macks. The motive was thin. He and Hurley had struck out on evidence. The brothers had alibis, for what they were worth. Both were seen at the Portside, drinking with friends at the time of Grogan's death.

Now they would look at Vito. If they could get him and put him at the scene, which it sounded like they might, Keene was fairly sure they could make the case, but it niggled at him that the scene seemed professional. The professional angle was a difficult sell to Charlie Riordan. It was a difficult sell to himself. For one thing, the Interim Chief didn't want to hear it. As simple as that. He didn't want to hear it because apprehending a pro was infinitely more difficult than an amateur. An amateur committing a crime— for example, one done in a fit of passion, rage, or jealousy—is rich in clues. Always. That sort of murderer makes many mistakes and leaves behind gobs of evidence. The pro simply does not. But first things first. It was time to have a look at Vito. He had been there. It had to have been Vito, Keene's hunches aside.

Keene slowed the engine and took another turn around the yacht. She was five decks high. At a closer look, the stripes of the reflected sun were created by glass balconies outside the staterooms. It was impossible to be sure, but it seemed there were—six on one side, six on the other—about twelve rooms on each of the three middle decks. Thirty-six rooms plus four on the lowest deck that must be meant for the crew, as there were no balconies, just portholes. A floating hotel more than a yacht. A small cruise ship. Keene looked at his watch. It was eight, the sun would dip below the horizon before he reached the dock. The glass balconies were a flaming orange now, and against the white hull, which appeared salmon pink in the low sun, the ship made a striking display. He slowed and turned around the stern of the *Ice Cold* to head back to South Portland. His revelation to Leo—that they were changing tactics—would have to be explained not only to Charlie but to the rest of his team and, most importantly, to himself. Leo better pay dividends somehow shortly. Keene may have sent the killer a big fat notice: Time to hit the road, Jack. The professional hitman would know not to come back because they were onto him. Keene may have made his job significantly more difficult.

Let's go get Vito, he thought. *Troiano did it; the investigation's over. We start to prepare for trial, and Charlie can concentrate on the Senator's visit, and Melena and I can go sailing.*

He tied off at the dock and climbed from the boat. Many times, he'd done the same thing with the Eastern Prom Sniper's bloody forehead dancing in his mind. He gazed up at the Prom, where it had happened. Leo, the reporter, had been no help to him then. Just the opposite. There had been some dark days for Keene, thinking he might have killed an innocent man. There still were dark days, and darker nights. He knew he had more of the same ahead of him. Innocent or guilty, you don't simply kill a man, remove him from the earth, send his soul to where God intended, and who could know God's schedule? There wasn't a carefree life after that. Not for Keene, anyway.

CHAPTER
34

Eileen turned a cloth around on the bar top accomplishing little. The hurricane-like whorls made her think about swirling tonic and gin and how she could make that happen and how a hurricane worked with the warm water and cool air, all of which made her wonder about Pete's kids. How old they were, boy or girl, things like that. How many kids did Squirrel's Nest have? Had he heard from them? And, as she wondered about Pete vaguely, he walked through the door.

"Hi, Pete. I was just thinking about you."

"Uh-oh," he said and smiled, which was indicated by a rustling of branches in the underbrush of his face. Subsequently, the brambles and leaves hinted that the smile had faded quickly.

"Have you gotten through?"

"Still no word," he said. Eileen poured a beer for him. "And now they say another one is coming that could be worse. Liam was a category three and all the damage was storm surge. My ex's house was pretty far inland. I'm sure they're okay." His assuredness wasn't entirely convincing. "But this next one—?"

"Hear from your ex, Pete?" John sat down next to Pete. Then Paul sauntered in behind him. Paul sat on Pete's other side. Support.

Paul said nothing.

Pete said, "Nope, not yet."

"Man," John, wearing the customary tie, said. "Ei? Bud." The beer was in front of him before he applied the concluding consonant of *Bud*. Another one cooled its heels on the bar in front of Paul. Pete's eyes were locked on the TV.

He said, "I got a text from Verizon saying the cell towers were down, and have patience if you're trying to reach anyone down there."

"Yeah, I got that, too."

Pete interrupted John and said, "Turn that up, Ei."

They listened to the storm warnings for the panhandle of Florida. Melody was going to nail Panama City again, but this time she was going to pack a punch. She was likely to make landfall in the middle of the night, tonight.

The pretty blonde interviewed a man who was tanned and white-haired, and she identified him as Florida's governor.

Blonde: "Cleanup hasn't even begun, and it looks like a more powerful storm is going to hit Panama City dead-on tonight. What are you recommending your fellow Floridians do to prepare, Governor?"

Governor: "We're saying to those who haven't evacuated yet, you should do so right now. Liam was the warm-up act. Get out now."

"They're calling this your Katrina. What differences do you see, if any?"

"Although this is a deadly, dangerous storm, and it will do disastrous damage to infrastructure, we have been successful in evacuating over ninety percent of the people who live in harm's way. The weather bureau has provided us with exceptional intel, and we all feel much better, in that respect, about Melody, the coming storm."

"What do you have to tell folks around the country who have loved ones in the Panhandle?"

"Same thing. We've got most Floridians who were in danger, out of harm's way. Please be patient." The governor looked straight into the camera. "I know this is hard. But please know that there are first responders and National Guard troops ready for search-and-rescue operations. You may not have heard from your loved ones, but that probably is because cell towers down here have been decimated." He paused, then said directly to Pete, "Keep the faith, my friend; keep the faith."

Keene and Hurley got out of Peterson's car. Keene looked at the unmarked Explorer that he had left parked outside Sully's Tap since noon, four or five spaces from the door.

"What the...?" He snatched something off the windshield. "I got a freaking ticket."

Hurley laughed and said that Keene deserved it, taking up a parking space all afternoon. "You should have a card. Official police business. Oh, wait, you do have a card. I believe I made one for you."

"Get in and shut up."

The plan was for Eileen to refuse service to Vito—who had yet to pay his bill—as soon after dark as possible. Eight thirty came and went.

"What's taking so long?" Keene said.

"I don't know." Hurley tapped a number into the phone. "Ei-mack…" He listened to Eileen for a few seconds. Just as Keene was thinking Eileen had given some important information, Hurley said, "I'm sorry, Eileen, I forgot you don't like Ei-mack. … Yup. … Okay. … Sorry. Listen, this is important. Is Troiano still there? … Vito, not Rick … Okay, five minutes." He clicked off. "He's in a big bowling match. It wouldn't be right throwing him out in the middle of it."

"Oh, what the…? *It wouldn't be right.* Is that what you said? This guy may be a cold-blooded murderer and it wouldn't be right to interrupt his match?"

"Yeah," Hurley said, begrudging the point but stubbornly holding onto the validity of his own. "See, he's bowling, man. I mean ya gotta have a sense of decorum. Besides, it would be suspicious for Ei-mack—"

"Eileen."

"For Eileen to toss him, you know?"

They waited.

Keene said, "Your wife out of town?"

Hurley glanced at him sideways.

"Ah, shit, Dennis. I forgot. I shouldn't have…" Keene wasn't stupid. If he stepped in a pile of shit, it didn't take the odor to clue him in.

"That's okay that you ask. Sandra's out of town on a buying trip to Italy, I think. Two weeks, probably." Hurley's soon-to-be ex-wife was a buyer for a shoe manufacturer in Freeport. She, a beautiful and sophisticated woman, the yin to Hurley's yang, traveled extensively, which had worked well for Dennis seeking the comfort of Michaela Mack's bed but not well for the marriage. Keene knew Hurley and his wife were legally married but fully separated.

"Yeah. That's nice. Did you ever go with her? On those trips?"

"Once. To Switzerland. The place was too damn clean."

After a pause, Keene said, "Ah, not sure what you mean by that."

"For example we're at a sidewalk café in Lucerne, and there's a traffic accident right in front of us. No real big deal. But there's glass and fluids and shit all over the place. One driver was bleeding from the forehead. This gang of six guys shows up in a truck. Before we finish our coffee, it's like nothing ever happened. Glass cleaned up. Fluids gone. Wreck towed away. Patient whisked off to some hospital."

"What's wrong with that? Sounds efficient." Keene looked at his watch. It had been about five minutes.

"Too clean. I like dirty. I like chaos. Without chaos, we wouldn't have jobs. Sandra, on the other hand, lives to eliminate chaos. It's a way of life."

The door to Sully's opened and Vito wandered out. He stepped onto the sidewalk like it was an airport people-mover advancing at varying speeds.

"I wonder how he did in his bowling match, all those pins moving around like that," Keene said. "Listen, read him his rights, okay? Be good to have witnesses. I don't want this messed up because he's drunk."

Troiano turned right and walked a few steps and stopped. Keene wanted to honor his promise not to take Vito down in front of Gary Sullivan's business. He knew that police activity was bad for business even with law-abiding clientele. He also knew that some of Gary's best customers didn't fit precisely into the legal definition of law-abiding.

"We'll get him when he turns the corner," Keene said. "We'll disrupt less traffic on Congress Street." Keene and Hurley both knew it was empty reasoning. They wanted to protect Gary, that was all there was to it. "Get Arnaud over in a squad car."

"Are you kidding? Do we need backup? Look at him stumbling on the bricks."

"Not backup, legitimacy. Another witness. I want him to see blue as he's being arrested," Keene said. "Blue car, blue lights, blue uni." He also wanted any random witness to know blue was in charge.

Keene pulled forward another car length. He wasn't sure he could stand the suspense. Troiano wandered another six or eight steps and stopped. He stepped next to the side of a building and whipped it out. As he was taking a leak, a squad car turned onto Washington from Congress.

"Oh, shit," Keene said. "He's gonna get him for indecency. Get out. Flash your badge. Tell the officer to get lost."

Hurley scrambled from the car, but it was too late. The blues flashed a couple of times and the officer chirped his siren. Troiano didn't seem to notice, just continued to relieve himself. Keene waved his arm out the window and watched Hurley approach the squad car, his credentials extended. The blues flashed off; the siren stopped chirping. Troiano was fixated on his tool. Hurley rushed to Keene's door and told him the officer's name was Shannon Scales. "I told her we were involved in a low-speed car chase. She's going around the block and will meet us when we finally get to Congress. If we ever do."

Now Troiano was zipping up and stepping forward to continue his leisurely pace toward Congress Street. He stepped forward. Stopped. Began again. Keene crept ahead another car length. Vito walked like a man on a lawn full of dogshit. Keene rolled forward another car length until he was finally at the intersection. Vito hesitated. Decision time.

"Jesus Christ," Keene said. "He still has no idea we're here."

"I don't think he has any idea *he's* here," Hurley said.

Keene said after a minute, "You ever known him to carry?"

"Nah, he'd blow his balls off," Hurley said.

Officer Scales rolled to a stop at the light. Troiano turned right past the entrance of the Cougar Club. Keene turned right and the patrol car skidded into an angled halt in front of Troiano, hitting the blue lights and the siren. Vito was trapped like a rat. A stripper held a fedora over her breasts as she watched the arrest. Hurley called her name and told her to go back inside.

"Jesus Christ, these girls," he said.

"Vito Troiano," the officer said. "You're under arrest for the murder of Patrick Grogan." She clicked metal cuffs on the inebriated man's wrists.

Keene sidled close to Troiano and said, "We gotcha, Vito."

Troiano said, "Suck me."

With the excitement of the arrest capturing the attention of strippers and bartenders and wait staff and bouncers at the front entrance of the Cougar Club, no one saw a petite woman in a red top and white miniskirt slide behind the building. Silk slipped a camera from her shoulder bag. Putty and a transmitter were in the bag also. She stuck a camera onto the brick wall, under a windowsill, turned the transmitter on, brought up the app, and saw herself standing near the back entrance of the strip joint. One night was a small sample size to get a complete understanding of the closing routine of the club, but it was better than nothing.

She learned the layout of the small parking lot behind the building where she assumed the car of Nurzhan's brother, Yakov, was parked. The hot, sleek sports cars were likely the property of the hot, sleek dancers, the earners in the joint. The dumpy sedans belonged to wait staff and bartenders and the new Ford F250 pickup, black with twenty-two-inch aluminum wheels and black exhaust stacks, had to be his. The camera would tell her for certain. She checked the door. It was unlocked.

When she was sure the camera was performing, she stole back around to the front. The excitement had died, the drunk was gone, the cops had cleared out, and the crowd had filtered back into the club. Silk decided to stay after identifying the exits. She watched the show from the darker recesses of the crowd, where only a waitress would see her. Maybe a dancer or two. Counter to what one would think, familiarity would bestow on her a certain anonymity. Tomorrow night, her presence would be accepted—the same chick; she was here last night—giving her an extra minute to slide in and out.

At the end of the night, she left and watched from the park down the street. The staff left first. She knew many of them by sight. Waitresses, tired and irritable but finally wearing clothes that didn't squeeze their tits and jam their asses, got in the predictable sedans. Most of the dancers took off in their cars, some alone, some not. A couple of sports cars and the F250 stayed in the lot. The music was loud, her ears were ringing, and her eyes were burning from all the different colognes and perfumes. She left. She had what she needed.

CHAPTER
35

Hammers imported from China. Umarov had people in the country sourcing the hammers. Wrenches and screwdrivers as well. Their real purpose was espionage. Umarov's goal was to repurpose forges he owned in Siberia and capture the worldwide market for cheap hardware. An insatiable demand. He was becoming one of the largest manufacturers in Russia. Hardware, clothing, consumable goods. The *Ice Cold* served as a commendable suite of offices.

As the oligarch contemplated the future of his empire, he heard the drone of twin Mercs. He recognized the sound of the *Dominator's* power plant. DeLuca had been given the task of delivering Rhenko's daughter to him all summer long. Umarov would enjoy a pleasant fling with Silakha on the trip to Venezuela.

She would accompany him in Caracas as he negotiated the final terms of the deal. Then, upon completion of the exchange, they would secure the new cargo on board and make a course for Ukraine. All the while, he would clasp Rhenko's surviving daughter to his bosom. Exactly as his supposed ancestor and hero, Genghis Khan, had prescribed.

The elevating Marina deck lifted Silk up, and she took the three sets of stairs. She turned to the so-called Volga pool. Umarov had instructed her to meet him there. She walked across the deck, through the empty lounge. The pool occupied the aft of the deck, beyond the lounge. It was a sunny day. Hot. Pleasure boats nosed around the *Ice Cold*, their owners taking time to ogle and gawk. Silk passed the waitress with an empty tray. The Russian girl asked Silk if she wanted anything. A glass of white wine would be brought to her, and Silk thought about this girl and the captain frolicking in the pool with nothing on their bodies and only one thing on their minds.

"Silk. Pull up a chair," Umarov said.

He was poolside, under an umbrella, wearing a skimpy bathing suit. The effect was less than attractive.

The waitress brought her wine, and Silk realized the poor girl had to look at this ugly flesh all the time. It probably thrilled him. It was not unusual for him to wear nothing while he and Silk discussed business.

Silk thanked the girl and said to Umarov, "It is done."

He fingered his sunglasses down and said, "Clothing is optional."

She wore a short white dress and wished she'd worn jeans. The lecherous old bastard would be trying to look up her skirt. Ach, who cares, let him take an eyeful. That's all he'd get. She got a thrill like those Ukrainian nights skinny-dipping in the lake, if she was honest.

"You heard me?" she said.

"I see, Silk is all business. You need to let your hair down occasionally. Have a little fun." He watched her carefully and said, "Business it is. Yes, I heard you. This is good."

Silk said nothing.

"I'm told we have nearly a full load; we're ready to sail. We sail for Caracas Sunday or Monday, You are coming with us. I told you."

"Yes?" Silk said.

"We will see the Treasury Secretary, among others. Possibly even Maduro. He's under an extreme amount of pressure. Maybe we can help ease that a little bit." Umarov's eyes sparkled behind his blue-tinted glasses.

"I don't like sex," Silk said matter-of-factly.

"I don't mean you would have to sleep with him. Never mind. We probably won't even meet him." He sipped the drink the Russian waitress had brought him. "But if we do, you will be..." The old bastard considered his words. "Friendly and obliging with him."

"I don't know what that means, to be friendly and obliging." She sipped her wine. Silk knew exactly what Umarov meant, but she honestly didn't know how to be friendly and obliging. She knew how to service and survive. That was it.

"Don't worry about it." He seemed disappointed.

"Yes?" Silk said.

"Get your final assignments done, then we go."

My final assignments? He meant Yakov of course. The other? He must be referring to the drunk. But if they were leaving, to never return?

"Yakov?"

"Yes, of course," Umarov said happily. "And the witness."

"Yes." Meaning the drunk.

"When were you going to tell me about the girl?"

She said, "I don't know who you're talking about."

"Don't screw with me. I told you I learn everything. The girl who saw you and Nurzhan. Get her for me. A little American meat won't hurt the stroganoff."

What was he talking about? Now she needed to find the girl from the bike trail.

"Let's get our unfinished business done and sail to the International Line. Then to Venezuela. When we get to Caracas, you'll see. Have you been to Caracas? Have you been to Venezuela?"

She said nothing. She'd never left Europe until she came to America and he knew it.

"Ah. It's lovely."

Silk was surprised. She'd read about filth, squalor, and poverty. Anything but lovely.

As if he read her mind, he said, "It's lovely if you're rich. That's where we come in, Silk. We capitalize the rich. We make the rich wealthy."

CHAPTER
36

Detective Keene hadn't made it into the Bricks before Leo Venti accosted him.

"Do you have the killer of the butcher of Hunger Hill in custody?"

Keene said, "No comment."

The beautiful TV reporter, Aneni Moyé, was tag-teaming with Venti. "Detective Keene, can you tell us why the subject, Vito Troiano, was apprehended in the first place? Was it on a related offense or a coincidental..."

Keene tuned her out because he knew what her question would be.

He simply said, "No comment."

Hurley, Peterson, and Arnaud were already collected in 223 when Keene walked in. Arnaud was convinced this would be the last of the team's assemblies. The three detectives were less sure. The more experienced trio knew that Vito Troiano's arrest was only the beginning of an obstacle course for the team.

"I don't want to drop the other balls we have in the air just yet," Keene said, though he was almost convinced they had the right guy. There was a small voice, though, that said, *Be careful.* Some things had gone too well. Reddog witnessing Vito at the murder scene; Officer Scales happening on the scene when she did; Vito wandering around and ending up on Congress Street; Vito being at Sully's in the first place. It had all come together within the time frame he had hoped. It had been too easy.

A lot of work still had to be done to ensure that the case would end in a conviction. They couldn't let the other leads drop. "Peterson?"

Peterson said, "I called the lawyers yesterday. If it isn't Vito, we gotta take a look at Dominic DeLuca. With Grogan out of the picture, the real estate deal is null and void. Allows Dom to renegotiate, but the deal was pretty sweet for him. It just doesn't make sense. Can't hurt to talk to him, though."

"Okay, do it," Keene said. A common misstep in an investigation was to be convinced by your line of reasoning and blind to all other possibilities. "People, we gotta stay on our other lines. Hurley, you stay on Vito. Blue Check him as soon as the warrant comes through. Last night's warrant didn't cover that."

"What?" Hurley said.

"Wainwright screwed up. He wrote the warrant to arrest, but not to Blue Check."

"But you asked him for both, didn't you?"

"Yeah, I did," Keene said, irritated that Hurley would question that; particularly in front of another detective and an officer. "This is what happens when you hurry a judge at cocktail hour. I should have known better."

"This gonna be a problem?" Hurley asked.

"Well, yeah," Keene said, pissed that his partner of fifteen years had to ask the question. "Troiano's lawyer's going to throw a goddamned fit. He's already on it. Gonna say Vito was drunk when we arrested him. We violated his rights because he was in a compromised state. Didn't under-stand his rights; didn't understand Miranda."

"Even though he exercised those rights and slept in the drunk tank waiting for his lawyer to show up?" Hurley fumed.

"We might have a problem here," Keene said. "We gotta keep looking at other possibilities."

A hubbub of disbelief rose among the collected cops. Keene watched. His people were not accomplishing anything as they complained about the situation. These were constraints they always worked under, and bitching about it was useless.

"Okay, okay," Keene raised his voice, maybe not shouting but closer to a shout than a whisper. "We have a real problem here." The room went quiet. "We may lose Vito; you guys get that?" After a long pause, he went on, "We'll get back to the Macks. I want to talk to Eileen. She's right there in the middle of it."

Hurley said, "Okay, then." His voice sounded dry. "Meanwhile, Arnaud. Who talked to Reddog O'Roark? He said somebody interviewed him. Some plainclothes he didn't know."

Arnaud consulted a file. "O'Roark?" she asked.

"Yeah, O'Roark. Reddog said the cop had some kind of accent but he couldn't pinpoint it."

"He's on the to-be-interviewed list," she said. "We haven't gotten to him."

"Huh. He said he was interviewed. The guy found him in the park, just like I did, with Zinfandel."

"Zinfandel?" Peterson asked.

"It's his Irish setter," Hurley told her as he looked her up and down. "She's a redhead, too."

"Wait. Wait," Keene said. "What are you talking about, an accent?" Keene tapped a pen on the desk.

Hurley said, "Like, Eastern European. Reddog said Romanian but he doesn't know. Coulda been Greek for all he knows."

"Why am I hearing about this now, Hurley? You didn't think this info was germane to the conversation? Could be a setup, could be anything. God. Dammit."

"Sorry, Basil," Hurley said, holding his hands up defensively. "I didn't think so at the time. Who's going to set up Vito?"

"I don't know, Dennis. I'm a detective," Keene said, his eyes drilling into Hurley's. "I'm going to ask that question of somebody who might be able to answer it, not someone else who doesn't know."

"Okay," Peterson said. "Okay, let's move on. This cop had an accent, right? Let's figure out who this guy is and ask him the questions."

Keene appreciated what Peterson was doing, calming things, putting the conversation back on track, but he felt like he was losing control. "Hey, Diane." He put his palms down in a cool-it gesture. He counted to five mentally to keep his shit together. "Diane's right. Let's find out who this guy is. An Eastern European accent. Arnaud, we got any Russians or, like, Chechens, or I don't know what?" Keene stood and walked to the white-boards. It was all he could do to keep from kicking one over.

Arnaud thought. Then, "I don't think so."

Arnaud. He'd worried that she might not be up to the job. Charlie worried about her. Hurley told him outright that she wasn't up to it. She'd screwed up the canvass. A simple job. She'd screwed it up. How could he have missed it? She was a rookie, and she made a costly rookie mistake.

"Could Reddog have gotten it wrong?" Keene was furious. Typical Hurley corner-cutting.

"Nah," Hurley said. "Reddog saw what he saw."

"What the hell does that mean, Hurley?"

Never one to back down, Hurley's voice rose. "It means what it means, Detective. I don't think Reddog is bullshitting us."

Count to five again. Keep control, Basil. An unknown officer. An unknown officer interviewed a witness. Is someone trying to stay ahead of the police? Planting evidence? Or just an officer Keene didn't know? He certainly didn't know them all.

"So, what is this?" Keene asked rhetorically.

Peterson said, "We got another actor."

"Yeah, yeah, yeah," Keene said, thinking.

"Coffin's evidence suggests two guys. This guy is one of them? A fake cop?" Hurley said.

"That would mean Vito's not our guy," Keene suggested. "Arnaud, talk to HR. See if any cops have that kind of Eastern Euro accent. Hurley, go see Reddog. Get more info about this guy. Get a goddamned decent description of the guy." Keene worried he couldn't trust Hurley to do this right. He hadn't felt that way for years. The veteran cop should have already gotten to the bottom of this. This phantom cop who interviewed Reddog should not be a problem at this point in the investigation.

"Peterson, stay on DeLuca. I still think Vito did it. But we gotta make sure he was at the scene. Hurley, lean on Reddog. Lean hard on that bastard for a description and certainty in what he saw Sunday night. If he's screwing with us, I'm putting him in jail. And you can tell him that. He's gonna do time if the sonofabitch is lying to us."

Keene reached into his pocket and fished around, found his pack of Orbit gum, and unwrapped a piece with his hands shaking. He got a piece into his mouth and held the pack up in offer. Peterson took a piece and popped it into that big mouth of hers.

There was a light rap on the door and it opened. Cali Wordsworth poked her head in. "Detective Keene? Chief Riordan needs you right now."

"Now what?" Keene snapped at Cali and immediately wished he hadn't.

His cell rang and he snatched it off the table.

"What?"

It was Sandblaster. "Perfect match on the DNA. Annabella's. Which probably tells us nothing."

"What it tells us is the DNA evidence you collected is bullshit." Keene ended the call.

"The hair belonged to Annabella," Keene said to no one. "Of course it did. She might as well live there." Keene stuffed the Orbit back in his pocket. "Hurley. We need to talk. My office. Cali, give me and Hurley a second."

"Hurley, I needed to know this before we started getting warrants for Vito's arrest," Keene said as he swung the door to his office closed. "This could be a... I don't know what this could be." Keene stopped to think. "First of all, does Riordan know this?"

Hurley said, "Yeah, I told him."

"Okay. Why didn't you tell me?"

Hurley said with an edge in his voice, raised a bit, "I'm tellin' you now."

"I mean, if this guy is a fake cop, he set Vito up. Probably to take the fall. We played right into his hands. Do you think Reddog could be playing us? Think hard about what he told you."

"I've thought it through, Basil. I know Reddog. Straightforward. He's an open book he always says, and it's irritating but true."

"Yeah, I know. This worries me, Dennis. We could've been led by our noses. The thing we needed most was a witness putting Vito at the scene. Then that's exactly what we get. Seemed too easy. It was too damned easy. I've worried about this happening."

Hurley said, "Still could be Vito. There could be some simple explanation."

"Yeah," Keene said. "Could be."

Keene didn't have much faith in the postulate that the sound of hooves is more likely to come from a horse than a zebra. As true as it was, the concept could lead to bad policing, poor investigating, and cutting corners. But the idea had its place in crime solving if judiciously applied. It was Keene's job to determine the usefulness of the application, go after the simple explanation, and bring in the obvious suspect, Vito Troiano, the man who couldn't arrange a party of one without help. Even then, he'd need to send himself an invitation. Keene didn't want to forget that there were zebras out there, and not just on the Serengeti.

CHAPTER
37

"Hat's going on?" Keene asked Cali as they left 223 and mounted the stairs for Riordan's office. In the interest of expedience, Keene used to take the elevator within the building. But since Melena was on his ass regarding his weight, he took the stairs whenever he could.

"Troiano's lawyer is sitting with the Chief and they want to see you." Cali seemed tentative, and Keene again wished he hadn't snapped at her. This was not good. It was one thing for legal counsel to meet the arresting officer, or even the lead detective, but the Chief? And in the Chief's office? Not good.

"Williams? The new Public Defender? I read the name on the file folder."

"Attorney Williams. That's correct."

Keene took an extra stair and sliced a glance at her. She was stone-faced. Riordan's door was closed. Cali knocked, opened the door because Keene was expected, and turned away whispering, "Good luck."

Riordan growled, "C'mon in, Detective Keene. Have you met Natalie Williams?"

Natalie? Natalie Williams? He was sure he had read it as Nat Williams. Keene took in the scene. Riordan, at his desk. An unoccupied chair. The third chair was occupied. By Natalie Williams, the new Public Defender from Dirigo Legal, and she was, possibly, the best-looking woman he'd ever seen to whom he was not married. Even her scowl was gorgeous. *Imagine if she was smiling*, he thought. Her auburn hair turned and twisted in the back and was woven to a peak leaving her neck bare. She was stylish in a dressed-down way, with creased jeans and a cotton polo shirt. She nodded.

"Yeah, well," Riordan said, giving Keene no idea what was happening. "Between calls from the FAA and the Secret Service and the goddamned FBI, I was pleasantly surprised to find Ms. Williams darkening my doorway. However, things aren't going as well as I'd hoped."

"Good morning." Keene nodded at Williams. "What's up? Want to clue me in about what's going on, Chief?"

"Ms. Williams represents Vito Troiano. Have a seat, Basil."

"He's coming with me, Detective. You're holding him without cause," Williams said.

Keene sat and said, "Wait a minute, Counselor. We're waiting on a warrant for a Blue Check on your client."

"No, we're not," Riordan said.

"Sure, we are," Keene said. Then he said less surely, "Aren't we?" He rapped the arms of the leather upholstered chair with his thumbs.

"No," the beautiful attorney said. "You're not. The quote 'defective alibi' end quote doesn't hold up."

Riordan said, "Wainwright refused. Gave us the warrant to arrest. But we have no further cause to hold him."

"All you have is that my client disliked the victim intensely. Which he freely admits. I don't know about your world, Detective, but in mine not everybody gets along wonderfully."

"I understand that," Keene said, brewing up a sour batch of dislike for this woman. "But we have your client at the scene. Enough for the judge to draft a warrant for a Blue Check of the suspect."

"My client was at home with his wife. You say defective alibi; I say, defective witness."

"She's right," Riordan said. "The fucking judge refused this morning. Excuse me, Ms. Williams."

"I've heard worse."

I bet you have, Keene thought, then said, "He said, last night, the confluence of evidence, if not the preponderance, particularly 'suspect at scene,' was enough."

"We don't live in a police state, Detective. Should I be afraid for my client? I hear there are some trigger-happy cops on the force."

Keene almost shot from his chair, but he held himself back. She seemed to have caught herself, cut herself off, and Charlie was as red as an Irishman can get—which is damned red. Keene seethed, boiling inside but arranged on the surface.

Williams took a breath and said, "I'm merely saying my client should be allowed to go anywhere he pleases, anytime he pleases. Now he pleases to go home." She stood abruptly and wouldn't look at Keene. She seemed aware that she'd committed a faux pas. Or, Keene thought, had she not blundered at all? Was she setting him up? Seeing how far he could be pushed?

Keene voiced, for the first time, what had been troubling him since Hurley reported his meeting with Reddog O'Roark. "Ms. Williams, we have reason to believe your client is in danger—you should be afraid for his safety."

Williams interrupted, "I've heard that one before, Detective Keene."

"Maybe you have, maybe you haven't," Keene retorted, his voice rising. This woman seemed determined to get under his skin. "We believe a man impersonating an officer interviewed one of our witnesses. Maybe manipulated the witness."

"The witness who saw Troiano near the scene, Ms. Williams," Riordan interjected, and at that point, Keene was glad Riordan had been filled in by Hurley. "A fake officer may be the real threat."

"I'm sorry, I'm not buying it. My client walks with me. We will consider action against the Department."

"Do you understand what I'm trying to tell you?"

The attorney whipped around with the fiery eyes of every woman ever subjected to "man-splaining." She said, "I'm not sure *you* understand, Mr. Keene." Keene did not miss her use of *Mr.* instead of *Detective.* "My client has been wrongly accused and held without court order or arrest. I understand perfectly well what's going on. You have a high-profile murder on your hands, and you have no suspects." She made a show of smoothing her clothing, which was already perfectly in place. "And I expect you to never question my grasp of the facts again."

Vito had been held with a court order, but without the warrant for a Blue Check, the order was expiring.

"Ms. Williams, I suggest you advise your client not to leave the state of Maine. That's a court order I can get all day long and will have—" Keene looked at his watch. He damned his luck and said, "After lunch." Jesus, he had wanted to say *in five minutes.*

The attorney said, "Vito Troiano isn't going anywhere because, despite your extra-constitutional eagerness to suggest otherwise, he's innocent of the charges." Then she said over her shoulder to Riordan, "I can see myself out. I'm going to have to get to know this place anyway."

"Ms. Williams," Keene said quickly. "I'm not screwing around. I think your client could be in danger. A witness was interviewed about your client by an individual impersonating an officer. That is not good. That is not good. I think we should keep Vito in protective custody, but I suppose you won't go for that. At least tell him to be careful. Please."

Williams considered Keene's suggestion.

"Gentlemen, I'm a firm believer in the Constitution. The Fifth Amendment gives my client the right to unfettered travel, a liberty of which Vito can't be deprived without due process of the law. An act of Congress, literally. I'll recommend he stay in the state, but Vito's not a big traveler anyway."

"Detective Keene is concerned for his safety, Ms. Williams." Riordan took a handful of M&Ms. "He's not concerned that he's a flight risk."

"Thanks for your concern. Vito's a free man. Can go anywhere he pleases. He's innocent, Detective."

She looked Keene in the eye, and despite himself, he believed her. She left without another word. Keene thought about what she'd said for a second, then rushed the door.

"Ms. Williams." He caught her before she got on the elevator. "The media are going to say we have the suspect. If Vito didn't do it, the killer wants to think we still have him. If you can avoid the media, that might keep Vito out of further danger. Understand?" Realizing how that had come out, he added, "I'm sorry, I know you understand."

"Yeah, I do. Mum's the word."

In Riordan's office for damage control, Keene closed the door and dropped into his chair. Too angry to speak, he gnawed on his fist.

Riordan said, "Wainwright screwed us. I know you, Keene. You usually cover your ass. He screwed us up."

"Yeah. Jesus Christ. I knew something like this was going to happen. I could just feel it. It was too easy."

Riordan said, "Does the force have a uniformed officer with a pronounced foreign accent?"

"Yeah, what's his name, new guy? Hispanic guy...Velazquez," Keene said.

"Oh, yeah, yeah. But, any Eastern European or whatever?"

"Nope, nothing like that," Keene said. "I mean, no one I know. I got Arnaud down at HR."

Riordan wiped his forehead. "I don't know that HR can even tell her that. Without a damn warrant."

"Are you serious?"

"I don't know," Riordan said, deflated. "Seems like everything is designed to make our job harder. 'Course, if HR can say that there *isn't* such an officer...that might be all we need."

"If HR says no, we don't have a guy like that, then we got a real problem. Someone impersonating an officer," Keene said. "But why?"

"Yeah," Riordan said. "Why would someone want to frame Vito?"

Keene said nothing.

"Convenience," Riordan said. "Vito takes the fall."

"Which means someone else has the intelligence and the balls to impersonate an officer," Keene said.

"Who? Tom Grogan?"

"Nah," Keene said. "I still don't like him for this. Grogan didn't do it. Motive is paper thin. Besides, O'Roark knows him."

"The Macks?"

Keene said, "Chief, we're getting ahead of ourselves. Could be as simple as Arnaud losing the handle on her canvass job."

"Yeah? Like Reddog don't know the difference between Mexican and Russian? Could be as simple as Vito Troiano isn't safe outside of custody, too. That's not good."

"No shit," Keene said. "Can we put someone on him?"

"I can't get the money for that. Overtime without a solid reason." Then Riordan said, "Reddog's a drinker, right?"

"I don't think he sees little green men and flying elephants."

"How 'bout seeing Vito Troiano where Vito Troiano ain't?"

"For now, we have a credible witness telling us what he saw. Everything points to Troiano. Arnaud's going to tell us: New officer from Wherethefuckistan; forgot about him; forgot to put O'Roark's name on the list. Whatever. We still could get Vito for this. We still might get his prints inside the store and go from there. Don't worry, we got this one." Keene was far from convinced.

There was a tick of quiet between the men. Then Riordan changed the subject, "Pretty good-looking, huh?"

Keene said, "Williams? Yeah, until she opened her mouth."

"Cut the shit, man, she's hot," Riordan said.

"Yeah, but I wouldn't mind if I never saw her again."

"You're gonna see plenty of her. She's the newest PD in Portland." He paused. "Look, she's new, she's only got half the story on the shooting. She doesn't know it was a righteous shoot, Basil."

"Or won't admit it." *Like the rest of them*, he thought. "I gotta go to work."

"What's next?"

Keene said, "If I don't get anything on Vito, we'll interview the creditors that Patrick Grogan left high and dry. Peterson is on the financial end of this. I got Hurley and Arnaud getting to the bottom of this phantom cop."

"Anything there?" Riordan asked hopefully.

"That's an empty bottle."

"That's what I like about you, Keene, always an optimist. Glass half-full guy."

"Yeah, I'm not half-full or half-empty. I'm a detective. I want to know what happened to the missing half."

"Yeah, yeah. But wrap this up. Watch Vito. I'm not as convinced as Lucretia Deville, that he won't run."

"Why the FAA?"

Riordan said, "What?"

Keene said, "You said you'd been talking to the FAA. What's the FAA got to do with the Senator's visit?"

"Oh, Christ," Riordan said as he pressed his hands around his face like he had an aching head, aching from his chin to his balding pate. "Long story." He was interrupted by the phone. "What do you have, Cali?" He listened. "Aw, Jesus." He put his hand over the phone and said to Keene quietly, as if someone was listening in, "The Chief Surgeon of Maine Med. I'm gonna be a while." He dismissed Keene with a wave, and Keene overheard Riordan mangle the man's name, a Pakistani doctor, and then, "Thanks for calling back. We gotta talk about the Senator."

Keene left Riordan's office wondering about the irony of things. The Senator had spent a good deal of time on the campaign trail discussing the possibility of defunding the police. Keene guessed that meant the police would be strapped in all policing other than protecting visiting dignitaries. He was sure there would be funding for that.

CHAPTER
38

Silk was sure the woman hadn't seen her outside the bakery across the street. The woman was the detective who'd been working with the two male detectives on the case. One of them, Keene, was the tall one. Silk had spied on them from various places over the last couple of days. She had watched from the Cougar Club as the two men arrested the drunk for the murder of Grogan. As she continued to observe from across the street, the shorter cop drove in and finally Keene arrived in his old American car that made a lot of noise. Silk imagined the three discussing the drunk and his role in the murder. The drunk would tell them about her. Had he already told his story about a cat-burglar type perched at the front door of the variety store only minutes before the death of the butcher?

At the garage, many other cops came and went in their blue Explorers. An ambulance rocketed out. Then a car arrived that was, like the tall cop's car, different—an older Volvo. She pressed the pause button on the phone screen and scrutinized the driver, an attractive auburn-haired woman. Silk watched from the outside table at the bakery. The tiny camera was affixed to the edge of the rounded frame of a basket-weave, wrought-iron tabletop. The device was perfectly hidden, and the view was a direct shot of the parking garage entrance of the police station. Silk knew all the vehicles in play now. Keene's green Dodge Charger, the red Toyota Supra that his partner drove, and the Ford Explorer that the red-headed detective drove. She decided to watch for that Volvo, too. The fact that they arrived within minutes of each other told her the Volvo was part of the deal, involved somehow. Or not, but better to watch and be wrong than otherwise.

Silk went into the Polish bakery and bought a kolache. She gazed at the phone. She finished the pastry at the table and decided to wander the neighborhood. It was neither an exclusively retail neighborhood nor a particularly industrial area, and it wasn't residential, but there were buildings with all three usages scattered among them. Small shops or light industrial businesses on the first floor had apartments above. Silk wandered among the uninviting shops, one place sold quilts and another pottery. The goods were uninteresting to her because she was fixated on her phone.

Nothing happened. She lifted a ceramic pot and replaced it, then a serving dish and then another piece of pottery. After more than an hour of killing time—monitoring her phone, pretending to be interested in junk, choking down pastries that were hardly more appetizing than raw potatoes—the Volvo emerged. Silk used her phone to snap a still. Holy shit, the passenger seat was occupied by the drunk. Silk rushed to her rental car, started it up, and moved out onto the street, nearly mowing down a pedestrian. Roads are for cars. Sidewalks for pedestrians. This thing had happened before and it almost had again. She had to brake hard to avoid another one of these idiots, and she lost the Volvo. It would be ironic if she went to jail for vehicular homicide.

That night Silk hid in the shadows. It was nearly midnight, and a few people had left the bar but not the drunk. She guessed he was celebrating his close call with the law and subsequent escape. Be careful what you wish for. Girl went to bar. She waited. Silk was a patient girl. This was a dark street, which suited her. Darkness was good to her and always had been. When she was younger, it served her fetish for arousing strangers. For nearly two years, it had cloaked her vocation, a career conducted entirely in the dark. Now the dark hid her and her true intentions.

She was within walking distance of the water, Back Bay in one direction and the docks in the other. Either side, it didn't matter; she would take the drunk with the tweed fisherman's cap to the docks or the bay. Use her feminine mystique that had worked well with the butcher. Make it one down and one to go. Plus, the girl. Can't forget about the girl.

As she thought about the girl and how to maneuver her to the boat, the door opened and there he was. The drunk, tweed cap and all. Once again, unsure of his footing.

She followed him. Just as the night before, he stumbled down Washington Avenue to the end and turned right toward his apartment building. This night he made it past the Cougar Club. No cops out of the blue to bring him down. He pissed once and she felt like taking him right there. She stayed about fifty yards behind him. They were on their way to the docks. He was unaware of his surroundings, a condition one should never allow oneself to be in. A condition Silk was well suited to take advantage of.

He turned left, leading Silk down the hill. They turned right on Commercial Street and Silk caught up with him. She wore a black top that was tight and cut to just above her navel; even a drunk would see a lot of her.

"Whoa," Vito drawled when he saw her. "Jesus."

She took his hand. It was rough and scaly. But she held onto the repulsive man.

"Come." She turned her back to him, pulling him down the length of the dock.

"Okay," Vito said. "What do you want? I don't have any money."

"I am lost." She wasn't going to like this, but it had to be done. Some consistencies and textures bothered Silk. The nerve endings in her fingers and body and legs and arms were hypersensitive. She had to ignore it to do her job. She'd always had to ignore it. On the streets of Kiev, men had pawed her with disgusting hands and she'd endured it. She could do this again. As long as she was in charge, she could endure the feeling of someone else's hands on her. There were times when not servicing a customer, she'd endured sex and been surprised by a lovely feeling, an explosion. Almost impossible to get there, but a feeling would overcome her like the sensation of being folded into a silken flower. But this drunk gave her shivers and the feeling of spiders running all over her body, but she had to do it. Convincing a drunken fool that she wanted to have sex with him might be the most difficult part of the job. If she could kill a man, she could pretend to want him.

She stood facing him. Reached up as if to kiss him. He was disgusting.

She maneuvered him to the end of the dock. "I am on cruise ship. Out here, maybe? You help?"

He stammered and stumbled.

Silk turned his face to her. "I give you a little kiss for thanking you, yes?" She pulled a condom from her bag. She made a show of opening it and putting it in her mouth as though she had an oral method of applying it. Which she did.

Vito was surprised and delighted. She took his face in both hands and he leaned into her. Silk opened her mouth and he opened his. She kissed him and took a deep nasal breath. She had a piece of cellophane in her hand. Their lips met, and she blew into the condom still in her mouth as she covered his nostrils with the cellophane. Alarmed, Vito sucked in his breath, the worst thing he might have done. The membrane perfectly melded inside his oral cavity, blocking the nasal cavity as well. The device didn't need to be inflated any longer; it was a perfect membrane. He succumbed even more quickly than the butcher had. An effect of alcohol, maybe. She left the condom in place until she knew the drunk was dead. She was delighted the kiss of death had worked well. Seduction of the victim was the key. If she had to kill the girl, or any woman, for that matter, seduction would be trickier. But not impossible, and if anyone could do it, Silk could. She looked forward to trying. The creosote smell of the docks was foul. It turned her stomach.

Back at the parking lot of the Cougar Club, Silk checked the F250. The passenger door was unlocked. She tucked her handgun in the side pocket of the door, then walked through the parking lot to the back door of the club and inside like she owned the place. She wore her black yoga pants and the abbreviated black top.

"Ah, excuse me," a guy who might have been a bartender said over the music. "We're closed."

Silk said, "No shit," and walked past him like the only attention he needed was watering once a week.

Nurzhan's brother, Yakov, sat in a chair on the stage, his legs spread, a nude girl's face buried in his jeans. He was stretched out, snorting something from a small mirror. A second nude dancer was wound around the stripper's pole above him. Impressively, her conventional down side was up. She was sniffing a line with a rolled-up bill. From the same mirror, at the same time as Nurzhan's brother. Silk walked to the side of the stage and wondered about the logistics of the operation currently being performed on the stage.

"Party's over," Silk said.

The upside-down girl said, "Whoa, nice outfit, girl. I love it."

Silk glared at her and said, "Get lost."

The other naked girl straightened and cautiously started to leave.

"Hey!" Yakov hollered. Then to the girls, as though they were dogs, he said, "Stay."

The two women stood on the stage as if they were auditioning for a nude performance and were waiting to be told what to do next.

In measured tones, Silk said, "Get out of here," and the girls scattered. Silk told Yakov to get up and walk with her. He zipped up, ambled to the back of the stage, and disappeared behind the curtain. The bartender had left with the girls.

Yakov reappeared and said, "Why I come with you?"

She grabbed him by the balls and squeezed hard, and he dropped to his knees.

"Because I say? Yes?"

He regained his feet and followed her out the back door, subdued in the way only a man whose balls have just been squeezed by a small but attractive Russian girl could move. They walked into the parking lot.

"You are girl who works with Nurzhan."

"Sure," she said. "Okay. We go see him."

"Where is he? Haven't seen him since night butcher was killed."

"He tells me to come to get you." Silk pointed at the F250 and said, "Yours?"

He nodded and she said, "I thought so. Take me for ride now to see Nurzhan."

She got in the passenger side, which involved a bit of a hike for her, and he got in behind the wheel. The likeness to his brother was amazing.

"Name is Silk, yes?"

"Yes."

He started the truck and it roared to life, then idled down and ran quietly. He said, "You want try out to be dancer? I put in a word for you."

She said, "Let me think about it. Okay. I thought. No."

"Nurzhan usually call or text daily. What happened?"

"He's okay," she lied.

"Where do we go?"

In one smooth motion, Silk found the Tokarev with a sound suppressor threaded onto its muzzle in the molded pocket where she'd left it earlier. She said, "Nowhere," and pulled the trigger. The hollow-point killed the man instantly and left no exit wound. She pulled the big bouncer's body toward her and down, invisible to passersby. The dancers would assume he had left with the crazy bitch in black. She turned the truck's ignition off and would climb down out of the truck, but not quite yet. When the girls came out to their hot sleek sports cars—they needed time to get dressed—Silk would be gone.

She was making progress. Now that the drunk and her accomplices were out of the way, her final task was to get the girl. Why Umarov wanted the girl, she didn't know, but give the man what he wants. Umarov wanted American cash and booze and cigarettes. That's what she gave him. If it was a girl from Portland he desired, then Silk would get her for him. Why he wanted her was immaterial.

CHAPTER
39

Riordan's door closed as Keene approached. He knuckled it and heard a voice, not Riordan's, tell him to wait. He stood at the door, frozen.

Keene was getting pissed. His people had screwed up. They were back on track, but Hurley had screwed up the Reddog deal. The canvass hadn't gone as smoothly as it should have. That was his mistake, putting Arnaud on the detail in the first place. Peterson, well-meaning no doubt, had overstepped her position in the Troiano meeting. Now, someone unknown to him was telling him to wait outside Charlie's door like a kid with detention waiting for the principal.

"C'mon in, Basil," Riordan said. "You two met?"

Keene looked at the owner of the voice that had told him to wait outside. It was the short guy, his head freshly shaved, his beard freshly cropped, his ears propped forward as if by some unseen toothpick. He wore dress pants, charcoal with a tan chalk-line; handsome trousers, Keene thought, and a short-sleeved white shirt, crisply pressed, with a red silk tie spilling like blood from his neck.

"No," Keene said and did not offer to introduce himself.

The short guy said nothing.

Riordan said, "Say hello to Agent Philips Harding, Special Agent in Charge. Financial Crimes Enforcement Network."

Harding stuck out his hand without getting out of his chair. He still said nothing.

"Philips?" Keene said after a brief shake of the agent's hand. "Like, more than one Philip?"

"FinCEN," the agent said as if that explained everything. His voice was an octave lower than Keene expected such a small guy to have.

Riordan said, "Agent Harding is on special assignment on the Grogan case."

"You mean my case," Keene said.

"My case now, Keene," the little man with the low voice said.

"That's a funny story, Philips." Keene allowed the *s* to linger.

Riordan said to Harding, "Detective Keene deserves an explanation."

"I agree," Harding said.

"I'm all ears," Keene said, a dig at the man with satellite-dish ears. He sat down heavily in the third chair in the room. He'd been spending too much time in that chair lately. Not enough time running down leads.

"We believe," Harding started, "the murder you're looking at is related to an ongoing FinCEN investigation. We've been following a suspect for a long time, named Umarov. Fyodor Umarov. Drugs, prostitution and porn, gambling, and now probably wholesale money laundering."

"I'm looking for a murderer, not a small-time hood," Keene said.

"There is nothing small-time about this guy, Detective. If I may continue?"

Keene wanted to say *No, you can't continue* and stick the little man's head out the window and watch a gust of wind catch an ear and twist his head off. He looked at Riordan, who said, "You gotta hear this, Basil."

The agent said, "We're investigating something called a parallel economy. Venezuela, Iran, even North Korea have markets in cash. Have you ever wondered how the favored classes in these countries have goods—expensive goods—lots of very expensive things...personal effects, clothing, cars?"

At the risk of sounding intellectually incurious, Keene said, "No, but go on."

"They have nice things because they buy western currency and goods. It's a complete economy—only for the privileged few—backed by some desirable resource. Oil. Political power. Manpower. Even perceived moral or religious authority."

"But what about countries with no resources? Like North Korea?"

"Every country has some sort of resource to trade. North Korea has a three-and-a-half-million-man army with the largest special ops force in the world. North Korea is the region's rent-a-cop business. So, the ruling class can have nice things."

"You said that. What's this got to do with us?" Keene asked.

"We're in Portland because we're interested in the boat that came in at the beginning of the summer."

"The *Ice Cold*?" Keene asked.

"Yes," Harding said. "Owned by Fyodor Umarov."

"Your guy," Keene said.

Harding continued, "Our theory: He harvests currency from bunches of small, cash-oriented businesses in tourist towns up and down the coast. Beach towns, harborside villages, lake communities. He buys—legitimately—kiosks and hotdog stands and arcades and collects the cash. Siphons it out of the country illegally and trades it to, our best guess is Iran, for oil."

"Or Persian carpets," Keene said.

"Yes," Harding said. "Perhaps." The guy seemed to lack a sense of humor.

Riordan said, "I'm not kidding, Keene. This is a good lead in a case that's been going nowhere."

"Okay, fine. Umarov killed the butcher. How does this help him launder money?" Keene was legitimately perplexed. He watched the FinCEN agent bite back on frustration, but Keene wanted to understand this. "I know what you're saying, I think, but I don't understand how this fits in."

Harding started again. "We think Fyodor Umarov wants to leverage the currency-rich economy of vacation spots into even bigger cash machines. Many apartment dwellers and owners are known to deal in cash. Apartment houses are Umarov's next money machine. His genius is legitimacy."

Keene said, "You have to nail the *Ice Cold* en route to Tehran. Then you've got Umarov. But that's the only way you'll get him."

"We could get him on illegal foreign transfers of US cash, but that would only be a speed bump for him. We want to stop this, shut it down."

"Fascinating, but I do have a murder to solve, and you still haven't told me how this all relates."

"Real estate. I think he wanted Grogan's business and property, and Grogan wouldn't sell to him."

Keene said, "That's something we've been looking at, the real estate deal DeLuca made. It was DeLuca's property to sell, not Grogan's. This is what's bothering us."

Harding said, "We need you to help us figure this out. The names Grogan and DeLuca both came up in certain chatter. Who killed Grogan may be a key to something big. Something bigger than you realize."

"Let's think about this," Keene said. "Umarov is trying to buy the Hill, is what you're saying. DeLuca sells his property but not to the Russian. Maybe the guy tried to buy it and DeLuca said no?"

"If so," Harding put in, "DeLuca's lucky to be alive. Umarov isn't a man you say no to."

Keene said, "But his brother-in-law is the dead guy, and he had to sign off on DeLuca's deal that cut Umarov out. Fyodor says sorry, but this deal is no good, and snuffs Grogan. Kills him. Has him killed."

Riordan said for Harding's benefit, "That's a thing Keene was interested in early on in the investigation." Chalk one up for our man.

Keene explained, "Looked too clean. Like the scene had been manipulated. Like a pro."

"Yeah, well, we can't get Umarov with financials, but I think you and your Detective Peterson are onto something. I just want to get him on anything and follow the money," Harding said.

Looking over tented fingers at the agent, Keene said, "Umarov has Grogan killed so that the pending deal falls through. The deal he wanted in the first place. DeLuca has to make a different deal. A deal with Umarov. Peterson's been all around this without hitting the bullseye. This could be a thing."

"We gotta find the pro," Riordan said, referring to the suspected killer, "to connect this to Umarov. Otherwise, this isn't a thing."

"Vito," Keene said. "He was in that neighborhood. Possible witness."

"I'd say we gotta keep an eye on Tom Grogan," Riordan said.

"Can you spare a uniform and a car?" Keene asked.

"I gotta go in front of the Council for approval of extra-budget expenses. It's in the charter, a provision for Interim Chiefs. Plus, we're stretched pretty thin through the Senator's visit."

"I think we need a guy."

"Me," Agent Harding interrupted Keene. "I'll do it." A little goodwill for Interim Chief of Police Charlie Riordan.

Keene was never happy with outsiders participating in an investigation unless chosen specifically for a unique skill: A doctor with a useful specialization or an arms specialist. He was particularly put off by an individual who unctuously insinuated himself into Keene's program. Like Harding, for example. Detective Keene was very unhappy with the way things were going. But Riordan seemed to welcome the assistance.

CHAPTER
40

Portland was once called a fishing town with a drinking problem. It was now referred to as a drinking town with a fishing problem. Tourists came to drink and eat and stay in town and were averse to the stink and noise of diesel engines at four a.m. when the few leftover fishermen untied and roared out of port.

The crime scene was at the end of a dock, which made it tough to manage. The fishermen were loading and offloading their boats. Dockside also hosted the SV *Maria del Mar*, a fifty-eight-foot sailboat that catered to tourists interested in a sailing trip around Casco Bay. A screen, placed by the techs, blocked the body—and the technicians' gruesome work—from the view of the families boarding the sloop.

Hurley wore his Hunger Hill cap and blue golf shirt. He was at the scene when Basil Keene arrived.

"Positive ID?" Keene asked.

"It's Vito. No doubt," Hurley said.

"Means of death?"

"Drowning maybe. No injuries that we can see."

"Son of a bitch. Son of a bitch. I knew something like this..."

"Guess Vito didn't do it," Hurley said experimentally. "Grogan, that is."

"Yeah, guess not. What time was the discovery?" He fished out his pack of gum. "Gum?"

"Nah." Hurley waved away the offer. "One thirty this afternoon. High tide."

"So," Keene said, popping a piece of Orbit Winter Mint into his mouth, "low tide was one thirty or two this morning?"

"Yeah, something like that."

Keene said, "So we can guess at the time of death being sometime after one thirty or two a.m.?"

"All we can do is figure he drowned on the incoming tide because here the body is at high tide."

"We? Peterson?" And as he asked, Peterson joined them.

"Guess Vito didn't do it," she said in greeting.

"Or did," Keene said. "Couldn't live with the consequences."

She said, "Okay, but I think we're looking at a setup."

Keene said, "Who found the body?"

Hurley nodded his head toward a man wearing a T-shirt and rubber boots that covered his jeans below the knee. "That guy," he said. "Gerry Cyr."

The man Hurley referred to was well under six feet and bone skinny.

"Did he fish the body out of the water himself? Or did he get help?"

"No need," Diane Peterson answered. "That guy is strong as dirt. Doesn't look it, but he's been hauling traps all his life." She hand-fanned her face.

"Gum?" Keene offered.

"Nah."

Keene slipped the pack of gum back into his pocket, which was sticky and smelled a little wintergreen-y itself. "We have no idea when he was killed."

"*If* he was killed," Peterson said.

"Big Sis can give us a better idea, but he's been dead a few hours," Hurley said. "Crabs were already at him." The body would be transported within the hour, once the crime scene technicians were done on the dock.

Keene said, "What do we think? Is the Eastern European back on the playing field? Covering his tracks? Or unrelated?"

Peterson said, "He's our best lead."

"We gotta find this Euro guy," Keene said.

"The question is," Peterson said, "is he following us, or are we following him?"

"What do you mean?" Hurley asked.

She said, "We grab Vito, let him go. Vito's dead. Did our guy already know about Vito? Or did he act after we showed Vito to him?"

Keene said, "I think he gave us Vito. Then we spit Vito back and he did him. He's watching us. Who's he gonna go after next?"

"There was at least one other person who we know for certain was out that night." Peterson waved at her sweating face.

"You mean Tom Grogan?" Hurley said.

Peterson said, "Okay, two. Besides Grogan. I ran the East End bike trail Monday morning. I do almost every morning."

Keene said, "Okay, go on."

"There was new graffiti. Graffiti that wasn't there the day before," Peterson said.

"You think the graffiti guy was there the night before?" Hurley said.

She said, "I know he was."

Keene said, "If he was there Sunday night, he could be in trouble."

Hurley said, "He might be, if our guy thinks he saw him."

"Or our *guys*, plural," Keene said

"What makes you two think the suspect or suspects are men? And the artist isn't necessarily a dude either, is he? She?"

Both men looked at Peterson without an answer. Stumped.

Peterson said, "Lighten up guys. I'm just busting your balls."

"Jesus," Keene said. "I thought I was going to be brought up before the Commission of Equal Opportunity for Crime and Criminals."

"Listen," Hurley said. "Seriously. We gotta make this artist. Nobody knows who he is."

"Or she," Peterson said.

Keene said, "Is this true? Nobody knows this artist? And what makes us think it's always the same person?"

"Same signature," Diane said.

"So then, we do know who he is. What's the problem here?"

"The signature is a plus sign followed by a question mark followed by a minus sign."

"Huh," Keene said. "Like, plus equals minus."

"Yeah," Diane said. "Or more is less."

Hurley said, "It doesn't matter what it means, does it? What it means to us is we have no idea who the artist is."

Keene: "Hurley, ask the street."

Hurley: "I will, but they won't talk."

Peterson: "Why not?"

"Don't forget, spraying graffiti is an illegal activity," Keene said.

"Huh." Hurley waved at his face with his hat.

"We'll put Arnaud down there," Keene said.

Peterson pulled at the collar of her shirt as if getting some sticky air under it would help cool her down and said, "Novel idea."

"Will Charlie go for the overtime?" Hurley asked.

Keene said, "With this political rally coming up, I doubt it. You know that for him to spend anything outside the budget, being Interim Chief, he has to run it up the flagpole at a City Council meeting? I'll talk to him. I'll get him to approve. Somehow. Shift the expense into next month or something. This is important."

The three detectives stood quietly for a moment, then Hurley said, "We need to interview Gary Sullivan and, while we're at it, Eileen Mack. Did Vito leave alone last night?"

"Was Vito even there last night?" Peterson said.

"Good question. It's kind of a given, but the question needs to be asked," Keene said. "I'll take care of that. I'll head down there right now. Either of you find Eileen kind of cool, like, aloof?"

Peterson laughed and said, "Maybe to you. I think she's a sweetheart. Must be a *you thing,* Detective. You think maybe she's afraid you're going to bust her for being underage?"

Keene said, "I gotta get out of this heat."

"I thought you liked the heat," Hurley said.

"I do. Because I have AC in my car."

Before he entered the coolness of the Explorer, he asked about Mrs. Troiano and the answer was yes, she'd been given a next-of-kin visit and informed of her husband's death.

CHAPTER
41

Keene woke to the jangling of the alarm clock and Melena clomped it off. She walked around the end of the bed and used the bathroom.

He sat up and waited for her.

"Good morning," he said with a certain hesitancy in his voice.

"Yes," she said, "it is."

Keene had gotten home late the night before. He hadn't called. Or even texted. "Look, I'm sorry I didn't call last night," he said.

"Why?" she said.

"Well," the hesitancy back in his voice, "I guess I should have let you know everything was okay."

"You should have if you could have."

"I could have found a way, I guess."

"Look," Melena said. "You've got a job to do. You do it. I certainly don't want to get in the way. How's it going anyway?"

"Hold it. You're stonewalling me. Yeah, I have a job to do. The reason I do it, though, is you. I couldn't do my job—or any other job, for that matter—without you. I couldn't do anything without you. Do you understand? My life would be, like, not worth it without you. I'm sorry I'm wrapped up in this case."

"Don't apologize if you don't mean it..." She took time to arrange her thoughts. When Melena was a less confident English speaker, she started a process of organizing what she wanted to say in Spanish and self-translating. She continued the organizational method even as her fluency in English had become nearly perfect. It worked to her benefit. "Don't ever apologize for being you. Basil Keene was the present and the future I chose twenty years ago. The arc of life I accepted back then. I knew what I was getting into." She leaned over and kissed him and got back in bed and said, "Go. You can't be late."

He kissed her back and said with a clarity he hadn't felt in the last few days, "I love you."

She said, "Me too. Bye-bye."

When he started the Charger, the police radio, the rover, came to life and the instant static of a mic check splashed into the speakers, and then a call came in about a dead body.

"Washington Ave," the voice continued. "Back lot of the Cougar Club. Victim is in a pickup truck. The cab, that is."

"602," a disembodied voice identified his unit number. "Is the location secure?"

"Affirmative, 602. We cleared and secured the area."

Keene took the Washington Avenue exit. The Cougar Club was about a mile from there.

He fingered the mic, "601 here. I'll be there in five minutes."

"Ten-four," and the radio clicked off.

Keene pulled the Charger into a scene that was already buzzing with activity. A red Supra pulled in a minute behind him.

"Who is it?" Hurley said by way of greeting.

"We think it's the bouncer at the Club. The manager arrived to open up. Found him. Called us. ID'ed him."

"The big Russian?" Hurley asked as they walked to the truck.

"You know him? Have a look."

"Yeah," Hurley said as he peered into the F250. "That's him."

"Did he have enemies?"

Hurley said he wasn't well-liked.

"Vito and now the bouncer. Both of them might have been on the street the night of the murder," Keene said. "Verify that with the manager, okay? We thought about the graffiti guy but never this guy. It makes sense, though. Doesn't it?"

A black Nissan Maxima pulled in. Agent Philips Harding stood and said hello to the officers and Hurley and Keene.

"I'm surprised Enterprise doesn't supply a magnetic sign advertising the rental agency's phone number," Hurley said.

"That obvious?" Harding said.

"What do you need here?" Keene said brusquely.

"My interest was sparked by the national origins of the guy. Think about it, Keene."

Keene's cell rang.

"Detective Keene? This is Dr. Coffin. I have some interesting information on the Troiano pathology. Do you want to take it over the phone?"

"What do you have?"

"I found acidosis in the blood once again. Just like the Grogan autopsy. Very similar."

"Doesn't drowning deprive the lungs of oxygen and therefore have the same result?" Keene asked.

"Yes, of course, Mr. Holmes. Very good. Very smart of you. But what did I *not* find in this so-called drowning victim?"

"I don't know, Doctor. Um, water in the lungs? I don't know. Help me out here."

"You're exactly right, Holmes. He drowned without ingesting water; they used to call it a dry drowning, but there is no such thing."

"He was already dead," Keene said confirming his suspicion.

"He was already dead, yes. Correct again, Sherlock."

"The acidosis suggests he was asphyxiated before entering the water."

"Bingo!" the irritating doctor screeched in Keene's ear. "You've got another murder on your hands, Detective. Charlie is going to be ecstatic to hear this news. I'm glad I don't have to give it to him. Good day, Detective." She clicked off.

Keene's phone rang again. Leo.

The detective said, "Keene."

"Another body. Connected?" the reporter asked.

"Who is this?" Keene knew who it was. "Can't say it's connected. We don't have anything yet, Leo. The only thing I got that might—I say *might*, Leo, with a capital M—connect this is the bouncer worked Sunday night. At least we think so. Haven't confirmed, but he woulda been on the street Sunday if he was working."

"So, this is the same perp. You're pretty sure of it?"

"What did I just say? We're not sure of anything."

"Same MO? Acidosis in the blood?"

Leo couldn't know about acidosis in Vito's blood. Keene refused to confirm the reporter's suspicion.

"I have no idea what you're talking about, Leo. Jesus. Besides, it's too early to have any pathology at this point. I can tell you it's not the same MO. At all. I would say that this situation looks less contrived. Messier than the others. Maybe no planning. This might be something else entirely," he said. "It probably is something else. You can quote sources close to the investigation if you want."

"I don't believe you," Leo said. "I think you're hiding something. I think that's three now. Anybody that was out and about the night of the murder. You know there was a body found in the marsh near OOB?"

"Old Orchard Beach is outside my jurisdiction. Why?"

"You'll see," Leo said and hung up.

———— •••• ————

Keene drove to the Bricks and ducked in. He climbed to the second floor. His able-bodied backside having been reestablished as shipshape; he found the engagement with the stairs agreeable. The door to conference room 223 was cocked open. Arnaud was there.

First, he checked on Riordans's office. Charlie was on the phone, held up a finger.

When he clicked off, he said, "We got another stiff on the Hill? Back of the Cougar?"

"Yeah," Keene said. "There's an employee parking lot back there. The bouncer. Guy named Yakov Iskakov. At least that's what his license says. Found behind the wheel of his pickup. Tox is going to be complicated. First responders said he had a pharmacy up his nose."

"Overdose?"

"He OD'ed on lead," Keene said.

"What the... Do we think this is connected to Grogan? What was T.O.D.?" Riordan asked.

"We don't have an official time, but the manager left around two and the guy was still very much alive at that time. With two naked girls and piles of white powder."

"Who called it in?"

"That guy, the manager, opening up this morning," Keene said.

"We know who was still there when he left?"

"We're calling everybody who was on the clock at the Club last night. Calling other girls, too. Michaela says some party girls like to stop in after hours, whether they worked or not. For a little moonlighting." Keene pushed a pad of yellow-lined paper across the desk. "We're moving on this thing like it's related to Grogan and Vito."

Riordan held out a jar of peanut M&Ms. They looked good that morning. Keene dug in and said, "If we find out it isn't related, okay. But two suspicious deaths, victims known to frequent establishments within a block of Grogan's murder, couple days apart? Both victims are possible witnesses to the initial murder? I'm considering them related. You see what's going on, right?"

Riordan said, "Yeah. Someone's cleaning the fish guts off the deck. Vito sees the shooter. Bouncer sees the shooter. We need to know who else saw the guy. What are you telling Leo?"

"Not the same MO," Keene said. "Doubtful they're related. That's it. He doesn't buy it. Look, I gotta get to my guys. We got a couple things to talk about."

"Wait," Riordan said. "The name of this guy? Something Russian?"

"Yeah, Yakov Iskakov."

"Iskakov?" Riordan asked how it was spelled.

"I don't know."

"Old Orchard Beach cops found a body. Identity? Nurzhan Iskakov."

"No way." Keene thought about the name. "That goddamned Leo. He knew all along, but he wouldn't tell me. That's interesting in so many ways."

Riordan said, "I ain't no linguist, but I'm guessing Eastern European with all the k's and o's and v's."

There was a knock at the door. As it opened, Harding walked in. He wore a blue silk tie on a white shirt. He was the last person Keene wanted to see. No, next to last. Leo Venti brought up the rear. Between Harding and Venti, they could mess up a search party for Mount Washington.

Harding walked into the office like it was his. He acknowledged Keene and greeted Riordan. He wiped his forehead as if he'd been laboring over something. He sat and weaved his fingers behind his head, his bent arms making Keene think of a hammerhead shark.

"Another Iskakov," Harding said. "It's no coincidence that we're looking at Umarov, and Russians are dropping dead in the streets of Portland, do you think, Detective Keene?"

The son of a bitch was questioning Keene's investigation, Keene's capability. Keene left the office.

CHAPTER
42

Pete and his squirrel's nest walked into Sully's and said, "Gimme a Bud, Ei." He hiked up onto a stool with Paul and John right behind him.

"You sound chipper. Did you hear anything?" Eileen asked.

Pete said, "They got out. Between the storms. Got a lot of wind damage during Liam. Lost power so they split. I don't understand why she waited so long, but everybody's okay."

"Where are they?" Paul asked. He sat and ordered a Bud.

"Her mother's house. She can't stand her mother, and the kids don't like her much either. I told her to come stay with me."

John said, "I thought you hated your ex." He held the Bud up and toasted the safety of Pete's family. He loosened his tie.

Pete downed his beer and asked for another. "Well, *hate's* a strong word. Besides, disparate times call for disparate measures. I'll take one for the team. I'm just relieved they're all safe."

"*Desperate*," Eileen muttered under her breath as she drew another one for Squirrel's Nest.

Detective Keene watched these three guys—the regulars at Sully's Tap—celebrate a personal victory as he moved to the bar from the door. Then he thought he heard the blonde news anchor on TV say something about the President.

"Eileen, did you hear what they just said on the news?"

"Hello to you, too. Thanks, it's nice to see you as well. I'm fine, thanks. Yes, it is a beautiful day. The news? The President's going down to Panama City to survey the damage. Lotta good that'll do. Cripe sake, he'll just be in the way."

"No shit," one of the three guys said. "When?"

Eileen turned the volume up.

The blonde on TV said, "The President will visit tomorrow after today's flyover. He said the devastation was obvious from the air. In Raleigh, at a campaign event, the opposing Presidential candidate expressed his concern and said he was sending the Vice-Presidential candidate to survey the damage tomorrow as well."

"Holy shit," Keene said. "Hope she can make it back for Saturday."

"Why? You a fan?" John asked.

"No. Charlie Riordan has been putting in a lot of work preparing for her visit."

Paul said, "Elvis's next gig was scheduled for Portland, Maine."

"I don't even have the slightest idea what you're talking about," Eileen said, and then to John she said, "But I usually don't."

Sully's Tap was a dark environment until Harding walked through the door. The outside light started to wane again as the FinCEN agent said hello to Keene. Then he said, "You wanted to see me?" He motioned with a head wag for Keene to follow him to a table. Keene carried his beer with him.

They took a table near the bowling machine. The smell of burnt cheese and stale beer and cleaning products mingled into the singular smell of Sully's.

Eileen brought two coasters, one that said Heineken, a high-end product that might never have been served at Sully's, and another circle that read O'Doul's, an alcohol-free product that had never been served and never would be served at the bar. She asked the smaller man what he'd like. Keene absent-mindedly set his beer glass next to the coaster.

"Scotch," Harding said.

Keene watched for it. He was ready. He waited. It shouldn't be too long. There it was. Eileen's pretty hazel eyes rolled back in her head. She was hardly able to deal with the stupidity of the FinCEN agent's order.

She said, "Like, I've got scotch behind the bar? Just scotch? No brand. Plain old scotch? Just plain old frigging scotch. That's what I have behind my bar. Scotch."

Harding said, "Glenfiddich?"

"Jesus," she said with more eye-rolling. "I thought FBI guys were smart. You said Chivas Regal, right? Neat? Rocks? What?"

"Rocks and I'm FinCEN," Harding said.

"Gesundheit," Eileen said. "What is a FinCEN agent anyway?"

"An FBI agent with an accounting degree; in case things don't work out with the Bureau."

Before Eileen left to get Harding some scotch, she centered Keene's glass on the coaster with a glare at the detective.

Harding said to Keene, "What's on your mind?"

"You mentioned Venezuela in Charlie's office," Keene started as Eileen left.

"Yes," Harding said. "I used it as an example. The Chavez government worked with a parallel system."

"Okay," Keene interrupted. "Okay. Stop right there because this is where your theory falls apart. Or, might come together elegantly, as they say."

"Meaning?"

"Well, let me ask you this. How does the Venezuelan government buy dollars or euros? You said every country has something to sell. The obvious answer must be oil, right? They're paying for this parallel economy, funding it?"

"Capitalizing it," Harding interjected. After all, he was a finance genius.

"Yeah, okay, capitalizing it. With something. Now, Iran pumps oil but can sell directly to the Russians and the Chinese. Who needs Umarov to facilitate this? Venezuela, on the other hand, can't even pump the oil reserves that they have. So, nothing to see here, folks. A classic misdirection."

"You did some research. Interesting."

"But take this in a different direction. Forget about Iran. That's the misdirection. Umarov wants you to look toward Iran. This is where the elegance comes in."

"Yes? Give it to me." Harding was getting interested now.

"Let's look back at Venezuela. They're easy to ignore. They've got nothing.'" Keene sipped his beer. "Harding, my wife is Cuban. She and her family escaped Castro's dictatorship twenty years ago. Venezuela is pretty similar today to Castro's Cuba then. The two countries have nothing. Venezuela's oil fields and refineries have dried up through mismanagement and corruption. Cuba never had anything other than tourism and sugarcane, and Castro destroyed both by alienating western democracies, his biggest customers. Cuba clung to its only renewable resource, its young people. That's why Melena had to escape. Sneak out in the dark of night, you know?"

"Okay," Harding said tentatively. He was interested. "So put this together for me."

Keene did and Harding realized that the detective, smarter than he'd given him credit for, might have stumbled onto the truth. If Keene was right, that explained where all the cash was going. If Keene was right, now they knew what Umarov was doing. It was all about Venezuela, not Iran. That's how they lost the trail, they were looking in the wrong direction. Keene was onto something.

"This has nothing to do with Iran. This is the connection we've been looking for," Harding said. "Human trafficking."

"Human trafficking." Keene nodded.

Now, Keene knew, the FinCEN agent would do everything in his power to prevent Keene from arresting Umarov for Grogan's murder. Sometimes it paid to have powerful enemies. As long as you kept them close. Sun Tzu was a philosopher Keene admired, and he had coined the friends and enemies juxtapositional advice, not the other notable warlord, Michael Corleone, who was often cited for the quote. Keene was convinced that the Federal Government would bring its full power to bear on Keene's quiet little murder case. But if Keene played his hand well and kept his little, ear-intensive FinCEN enemy close, he would walk away with his suspect, Fyodor Umarov and a piece of the Federal action as well.

———— ◆•• ————

Officer Terry Arnaud tossed her gun belt to the couch. She undid the buttons of her short-sleeved shirt and let it fall open. Her undershirt was wet from a sweltering days' worth of perspiration. She didn't do well with heat. But it was about to break according to the Weather Channel. A front was moving into Portland, the remnants of the first hurricane, Liam. The hot Gulf air would move in with rain and wind followed by cooler air pouring in from Canada. The weather report was ambiguous about the second hurricane, Melody. Maybe the next day. More heat and stickiness.

Arnaud opened the window in her living room and the other in the kitchen. She'd listened to air conditioners hum all day, and the one across the alley from her kitchen was the worst. It sounded like a wasp with a bullhorn. She had an AC unit in her bedroom but resisted turning it on. The electric bill skyrocketed when she used it, and she wasn't making a fortune working for the Portland Police Department.

The second-year police officer lowered the blinds in her bedroom and peeled off her undershirt. She tossed it in the hamper and waved her hands around. There was a fresh undershirt in the top drawer, and she pulled it out in case she was going out again. Keene hadn't committed, but she felt sure they'd work on the graffiti artist that night. The small fan ticked her finger when she turned it on. Maybe an Italian sandwich from across the street for dinner. For sure she wouldn't cook tonight. Arnaud was a good self-taught cook, and it would be a nice thing to invite someone to her apartment sometime. Someone to cook for. Wasn't happening soon, though. There were a few things Arnaud was good at—her job, marksmanship, and she was a strong swimmer—but making friends and simply socializing was not on the short list of strengths.

Her cell phone rang.

"Hello?" she said as if she wasn't sure what a telephone was.

"Officer Arnaud?"

"Yes?"

"Keene here. Let's get started on the stakeout. I'll authorize overtime for you."

"Of course," she said.

"Take an unmarked at about eight. Take it down to the railroad embankment and watch from around the curve. You know the place? I want to get the graffiti artist in the act. That'll give us a reason to bring him in and talk to him."

Arnaud arrived at the parking lot in diminishing light. She parked the unmarked car in a line of other automobiles. She decided if she parked with a view of the wall, the vehicle would stand out. How the artist arrived was unknown. Through the parking lot? Did he drive and use the parking lot himself? She left the car and tucked herself behind the abutment. This was too easy. A streetlight provided a cone of light that shone on the wall of graffiti. The work of art was shaping up to be some kind of scene with a lobster figure emerging from a cyclone or a vortex. It was kind of creepy, like a Godzilla figure. The scent of the still ocean permeated the muggy air. A mosquito attacked. Maybe this wasn't so easy. She waved at the bug and saw nothing. The bike trail remained empty as the sky darkened. The bay lapped the rocks behind her and the late commuter traffic hummed overhead. Bugs started to swarm. Arnaud waved, then heard a soft clink.

A slight figure emerged, slung a backpack off his shoulder, and waved his—her—hair from under her hood. Pink hair. Cotton-candy pink. Arnaud waited for the girl to pull a can from the backpack and shake it vigorously. She applied paint to the wall in a dramatic up-and-down gesture. There was a certain gratification in watching the artist work, forms taking shape, the unrecognizable becoming perceptible. She made long sweeps of paint and other shorter ones. As the artist with pink hair swept and dashed the picture, the work of art resolved itself more and more into something less creepy and more... heroic, Arnaud thought. Yes, of course, a heroic shellfish.

The cop watched Eileen Mack, whom Arnaud would have known as the bartender at Sully's Tap if she'd ever joined her fellow cops. Eileen stopped and stepped back to critique her work. She crooked her arm and considered her painting. Arnaud felt she had enough evidence to bring the artist in, which was Keene's objective.

"Put the can down," Arnaud said as she left the shadow of the bridge abutment.

"Jesus, cripe sake, you scared me, Officer," Eileen said as she followed orders. The artist put the cap on the can and placed it in her backpack as she held her other arm in a hands-up gesture.

"You're coming with me," Arnaud said.

"I'm sorry, I'm sorry. Is graffiti illegal? I didn't know it was illegal," Eileen lied. "I think people like it. I'm sorry, cripe sake, I'm sorry."

"Lighten up. I'm not arresting you, yet. Okay? Detective Keene has some questions," Arnaud stated, hoping that would put her charge at ease.

"Keene? I don't think he likes me. Any of those other guys wouldn't mind me doing this. That darn Keene. He never liked me. Why is he arresting me?"

Arnaud was afraid the girl was going to cry. She couldn't have that. "No, no, don't worry."

"Should I have a lawyer?" Eileen asked.

Despite herself, Arnaud laughed. "I don't think you have to worry about being arrested. I was instructed to bring you in. There might be some other things you have to worry about." She wasn't sure how much she should say. The truth was, she didn't know what was in Keene's mind, but she was sure the girl wasn't guilty of any real crime.

Then Arnaud put out a call to Keene. "I have the suspect."

CHAPTER
43

At nine o'clock Keene walked around the curve and saw Arnaud with Eileen Mack.

"Officer," Keene said in greeting. Then, "Eileen, what are you doing here?"

"Do I need a lawyer?"

The lateness of the hour dulled the synapses and pathways from one part of Keene's brain to another. The reality of the situation became clear the way a boat materializes in fog—first a hint, then a possibility, then an undeniable reality.

"So, Eileen," Keene said slowly, "you've been painting some concrete down here. I had no idea you were so talented."

"I take the fifth. I want a lawyer. Nothing I say can—I mean nothing you say, you know?"

"Eileen, you are not in trouble with the police, okay?"

"So, I can leave?"

"Before you do, we're worried you may be in some danger. Were you painting Sunday night? The night Grogan was killed?"

"No." She thought a moment then said, "Yes." After another moment of deliberation she said, "It depends."

"Depends on what?"

Eileen said, "It depends on if graffiti is illegal or not. If it is, then no. If it isn't, then yes."

"What we want to know is if you saw anybody or anything that night that you'd characterize as out of the ordinary. Did you see any person or persons you'd say acted unusual in any way?"

"Um, like, how do you mean? I didn't see anybody shoot Grogan. Or anybody painting graffiti. Or did we establish it's legal?"

"Eileen, Eileen, enough with the goddamned graffiti."

"Jeez, Detective. Sorry for looking out for my own best interests. Cripe sake."

Keene ground his teeth. "We need to know if you saw anybody after nine-thirty. Were you even on the path at that time?"

"Yes."

"Which question? Were you here, or did you see anyone?"

"Both. I was here and I saw a couple of people. Big guy and a petite woman. She was cute."

"Holy shit. Hold up. I want Hurley and Peterson to hear this. Come with me to Sully's."

Eileen turned to her left. Keene turned in the other direction.

"It's right up there." She pointed up the hill behind the painted concrete.

"My car's over here." Keene pointed away from the painting. "Let's go, I have other things to discuss with you."

"But where I saw them is right up there. Detective Keene, bartending is the only way I can make money. Cripe sake, if you take that away from me, I'll have to stay with my father forever, and he's not a great guy and can be kind of mean and the apartment smells like fish when he's working and smells like him when he isn't. Don't take this away from me. It's the only thing I've ever had that's my own."

"Whoa, whoa, slow down, Eileen." Now he felt horrible. Why did she have to say that last sentence? The only thing she'd ever had that was her own. He was sure that was true. The Francis Macks had nothing. Eileen had zilch because of the bad decisions the old man had made. "I have no desire to keep anybody from working. That's not what I'm talking about."

"What *are* you talking about?"

He held the car door for her, and she said, "I can open my door. Unless you have some kind of secret code or something." She changed subjects. "You know people like the graffiti. They call me the Portland Tagger, and it's not against the law."

Keene said, "Well, in fact, it is against the law, but that's not the point."

"I thought you said it wasn't. Jeez, you are a confusing man, Detective Keene. What kind of name is Basil? Sounds like an ingredient."

"I think you know graffiti is illegal," Keene said.

"What? What are you saying? Like I'm guilty or something? Cripe sake. I want a lawyer."

"No, that's not what I'm saying." He pulled away from the commuter lot. "Despite your legal opinion, graffiti is against the law, but that has nothing to do with what I want to talk to you about. I'm not interested in how old you are. I simply want to ask what you know about these people you saw."

"Do you think they killed Grogan? They seemed like nice people. I mean, I guess. More like lovers than killers."

The detectives looked surprised to see Keene and Eileen come through the door of Sully's with Arnaud right behind them.

Keene asked Gary for a root beer; Arnaud ordered a glass of ginger ale, and Eileen said beer. Gary glared at her. Eileen changed her order to water.

"Food coloring?" Gary asked.

Keene said, "Food what?"

"Never mind," Eileen said.

Keene said, "Hurley. Peterson. Meet the Portland Tagger."

"No way," Hurley said.

Peterson said with her famous smile wider than usual, "Eileen? Really? You are too cool."

Eileen broke into a grin with an aw-shucks tilt of her head.

Keene said, "Arnaud caught her in the act. The illegal activity that it is." And he glared at Eileen who glared back at him.

"Cut the shit," Gary said. "Are you serious?"

"We need a table," Keene said. "We got some things to talk about."

They found a table in the back room. Keene said to Eileen once everybody had settled, "Were you painting Sunday?"

She looked around the table skeptically. "Well..." She didn't speak further. The four cops waited.

Keene broke the silence, "Christ, Eileen, we're not going to bust you. What did you see Sunday?"

She seemed to consider options, options that Keene couldn't possibly discern. Finally, a dam broke, and she began chattering like a loose fan belt. She told them of the couple in black, the petite woman and the large guy. That she'd seen them well enough to pick out of a line-up. Maybe. Definitely the guy. Big man. She gave the exact time and circumstances of the sighting. She told them that she'd seen the guy on the bike trail. She'd climbed the path and then seen the woman on Romasco Lane just as the woman entered the path. That path was hers, Eileen's, she said. She said that she'd been scrambling up and down that path since she was just a little girl.

Then—when she first saw the woman—she heard the sirens, exactly fifteen minutes after Grogan's death was called in. At least, she was pretty sure.

"Two people," Hurley said. "Had to have been them. They saw you?"

"Of course."

Peterson said, "Did they know you were painting?"

"What do you mean?"

Peterson said, "If they were looking for you, and they knew you were the Tagger, they'd look for you on the path."

"No. They have no idea I'm the Tagger. You guys didn't even know."

Arnaud nodded and said the PPD only discovered it because they'd looked.

"Meaning?" Hurley asked.

Arnaud answered, "Well, if they had a suspicion, they might case the graffiti wall, too."

"They must be desperate to find her. They must have their suspicions," Peterson said.

Keene, who had been quiet, finally said, "Why haven't they been there and grabbed her before?"

"I haven't been down there since Sunday," Eileen said.

Peterson said, "And they didn't take her tonight because of Arnaud."

A pause followed, a break in the action.

"Bait," Arnaud said. One word. That was all.

"That's a good idea, Arnaud," Hurley said. Then, as if he knew Keene was predisposed to rejecting the concept, he said, "Maybe you don't want to hear it, Basil, but..."

Keene said, "It's not a good idea. It's a dangerous idea. We can do this another way."

Something passed between Keene and Hurley that Arnaud and Peterson didn't understand. Eileen didn't get cops in general, but she sure didn't get the weird atmosphere that had suddenly settled on the table.

Peterson said, "And to try it after dark and down there on the bike trail where we can't have enough people, with enough control, without tipping them off... You're right Keene, it's a bad idea."

Keene mulled it over. The idea had its merits, but Peterson was right... he was right. It could be dangerous. It would be dangerous. He said, "We should never use a civilian like that."

Hurley hesitated. He cleared his throat. Then, "The guy, the truck driver. Palmer? It wasn't a complete loss."

"His name was Parker. I don't ever want to put a civilian in that position," Keene said. "We're here, first and foremost, to protect. Right?" Keene made his argument directly to Hurley. "We put Parker in danger. I didn't like it and you know what happened. I don't want to drop another citizen into a crazy dangerous position. Or a cop into that kind of situation."

To Peterson, Hurley said, "You weren't here. You were still in Indy."

"Just before you," Keene confirmed.

Hurley started, "We put a tactical vest on Palmer."

"Parker," Peterson reminded Hurley.

"Parker," Keene said and continued. "We ran his truck across Tukey's Bridge for three nights. It was the fourth night."

He gripped his glass like he wanted to crush it.

"The Eastern Prom Sniper worked at sundown," Keene continued. "He'd shot and killed three truck drivers, each killing resulting in a spectacular crash over the side of the bridge. We think he got his rocks off watching it."

Peterson said, "Yeah, I remember reading about it. It was a reign of terror up here."

"It sure was," Hurley said. "And we were getting our asses kicked till Keene came up with a great idea."

"Not that great. Almost got an innocent guy killed." And, he thought, for a hot second, I thought I'd killed an innocent guy. But not innocent after all.

"But didn't," Hurley insisted.

Keene's phone rang. He stood and said, "Excuse me. Gotta take this." He walked away.

Hurley took up the story quietly. "We geared up this guy Parker and waited for EPS, the sniper. We knew we had him. Knew the vehicle. It was him, no question except he'd had a new wrap done on the vehicle. The unadorned silver Ford Transit now had a bunch of bubbles and the name of the company, 'Something Mobile Wash' or something like that. Keene shoots the guy. Head shot. One round. But there's no gun, no rifle in the van coupled with the fact the van has a significantly different appearance.

We knew it was the van, but try telling that to the press. Leo Venti went nuts throwing Keene under the bus. It was guaranteed the suspect was the killer, but without the evidence, we were out of the game. Top it all off, the guy was African American. Leo ran with it. Made a big BLM deal of it."

Keene returned. "Yeah," he said. "Leo did a great job of making me feel like I'd killed an innocent guy. Not before he duped me into saying...I can't believe I said it, but he got it on his phone: 'Just because the man is black doesn't mean he's innocent.' I was toast. Still am."

"Then finally," Hurley said, "when we found the murder weapon hidden in the van, you think Leo cleared everything up? Apologized?"

"I'd only drawn down on a suspect a handful of times in my entire career, and suddenly I'm a killer. That's hard enough. To think for all that time that I killed an innocent guy. Maybe because I'm a damn racist."

Peterson said, "I thought there was no rifle in the van."

"The guy had built an ingenious hidey-hole in the floor of the van. Investigators didn't find it for three weeks."

The table was quiet. It seemed all of Sully's Tap was listening in. Keene continued, "Killing a man changes your life. You're never the same once you're a killer. You're not the same person."

"Yeah," Peterson said. "Our weapons trainer in Indy talked about that. It's a club. One you don't want to join. I've never discharged in the line of duty." She looked at Hurley. "You?"

"Nope. Never. Basil, you're no racist."

Keene said, "Yeah, yeah. But probably sixty percent of Portland citizens think I am."

"No," Eileen said, surprising them all. "No, they don't. I live here. That guy was a terrorist. I can tell you, Hunger Hill doesn't think you did anything wrong."

Peterson said, "Sounds like a righteous shoot to me."

"It was," Keene said. "But it ain't like TV. I killed a guy and I still feel terrible about it. Even though it was the right thing and all that. But I'll never get the reputation back."

There was a pause in the conversation. They all knew they had to move on but also knew the moment needed some breathing room.

Eventually, Hurley broke the silence. "What about using Eileen to draw the guy out?"

"If we can control things…" Keene started, "so there's no chance she gets hurt."

Arnaud said,. "We feed Leo. Identity of the artist; that she works here at Sully's, and that she was painting the night of the Grogan murder. Leo will help us. He owes you," she said to Keene.

They huddled quietly and Arnaud filled them in.

Hurley said, "If it's someone from the Hill, it won't work. For one thing, they'll know us.

"They're not from the Hill," Eileen said. "I woulda recognized them."

"Keene." Harding approached the group of cops. "Charlie said you'd be down here. Maybe I can help?"

"Harding. Meet Detective Peterson, and you know Eileen." Harding had met Hurley and Arnaud. "Harding's gonna help with the plan."

"You have one?" Harding asked.

"Yeah," Arnaud said. "We have one."

The plan required Leo's help. Keene stepped outside the noisy bar to call the reporter. Harding went to the bar.

Peterson asked Arnaud for some privacy. "Maybe stand at the bar for a minute. Just a minute." Arnaud said she'd use the restroom. Peterson watched her leave then said to Hurley, "That's quite a story. Is he okay? To have your back?"

Without hesitation, not even a moment, Hurley said, "I'd trust him with my life. With Michaela's life. With my unborn children's lives."

"How did he handle it? You know, other than beating himself up."

"It messed him up. He took six months off. Every time at the range, he said he saw the guy's face instead of the targets. For a while, he couldn't shoot. At all. That messed him up even worse because Basil Keene is one hell of a shot. He put three shots in one hole once. Made a second hole and put the fifth shot in that one. These were timed trials."

"Did he see a therapist?"

"Yeah. Worked hard with her. He worked on his car and did some writing. Short stories or something the therapist suggested he do. The worst part is it's going to follow him around. The City Council refuses to recommend him for a promotion. He's back, though. We have nothing to worry about from him in the field."

Arnaud returned to the table.

"Leo? It's Keene." And Keene explained the idea to the reporter on the other end of the line.

Venti listened to Keene, then said, "No problemo."

The following morning, a headline story would feature the unmasking of the graffiti artist, a bartender at Sully's, the bar down the street from the scene of the Butcher of Hunger Hill's infamous murder. Leo would slide into the body of the story that the pink-haired bartender's hours were typically noon to 6:00 p.m., and that day was unlikely to be an exception.

CHAPTER
44

As Keene watched her, Eileen rummaged in her bag for something, acting exactly like an innocent bartender after her shift. Keene guessed Eileen was curious to see all the fuss. A glance or two would not have been a deal-breaker, but Eileen was one step better than that. She lifted her phone from the bag. A natural thing to do. She hooked her hair behind her ear, and tucked the cell there. Listened. Maybe to a voice mail. She stepped away from the door and headed home just like any other day.

As Keene had watched, Eileen had listened to Michaela's message explaining that she was not at home and to please leave a message.

"Hey, Michaela, it's Ei. Call you later." Eileen hung up, swung her pink hair, and started her walk home. If anyone was watching, they would see a girl interested in not much more than her social life. She sauntered away from the bar, a confident young woman. She felt Keene's eyes on her. She walked toward Congress. The difference between a policeman and a tourist was as obvious as one seagull among a flock of pigeons. The policemen were the cops trying to look like tourists; the tourists were the tourists who looked like tourists, the natural-looking guys and women who weren't *pretending* to be tourists. She liked all the cops that hung out at Sully's. Even Keene. But they were horrible actors. Like that guy with the Sox hat and aviator glasses. *Sox hat* or *aviator glasses*, she thought. *Not both. Cripe sake.*

She turned left on Congress. She felt Peterson behind her one minute, not the next. The detective, Eileen's fave, had peeled off. She didn't know Peterson had stopped and kept a sharp eye on Eileen's progress. Arnaud picked her up at the Cougar. They walked together, the cop just behind her, two dude cops pressed around her.

"Excuse me," a woman said haltingly. "You help me please?"

Eileen thought, *Cripe sake*, but said, "Sure, how can I help you?"

The blonde woman held the map the tourist board published. "Is... no..." the small woman said something to herself in a foreign language. She continued, "Is this where the museum is?" She planted her index finger on the icon indicating the Observatory. "Yes?" She looked deeply into Eileen's eyes and said again, "Yes?" She held the map close to Eileen, close enough that Eileen was uncomfortable.

"Museum?"

"Yes. Arts Museum?" the woman said. Eileen pointed at the map and in the direction of the museum. The petite blonde walked in the opposite direction, toward the Observatory, and Eileen presumed she wanted to see the attraction on Hunger Hill first.

"Weird," she said and thought about how closely the woman had looked at her.

Eileen didn't know that three detectives and several more plain-clothes cops had focused sharply on Eileen and this blonde woman and hadn't relaxed until the woman left. If one of them had followed the blonde, it would have been apparent that the woman was not interested in the Observatory. The woman shook her black hair from beneath a blonde wig and scrunched her natural hair into a loose ponytail. The follower would have seen the woman step out of taffeta shorts in favor of tight spandex running shorts. The woman slipped from her tank top; she was wearing a spandex running bra underneath. She rolled everything quickly and fit each article into her fanny pack. Then she took off at a fast run along Quebec Street to Montreal and finally back to Romasco, where she saw Eileen mount the steps of an apartment building. Thanks to the news-feed story Umarov had sent her, the stunning stupidity of the cops, and her cunning, she now had the address that the news-feed article had left out for obvious reasons. It was the last bit of information Silk needed.

She ran back along Montreal to her car, got behind the wheel soaked in sweat, and drove back to Eileen's address. Waiting, she was eager because it was her, the girl on the path, the artist. It had been dark Sunday night, but she knew those eyes. The cops had led Silk directly to Eileen who, in turn, led Silk directly to Eileen's house. All she had to do was wait.

Wait until Eileen stepped out into the anonymity of the city and its dark places. Silk had simply to scoop her up, take her to Umarov, and dump her in the ocean when the boss was done with her.

Eileen picked up on the first ring. "Hello?" she said tentatively. She usually answered with something like she was Eileen and she was ready when you were.

"You okay?" Keene asked.

"Sure, why?"

"You're in for the night, right?"

"I guess so," Eileen said, leaving Keene less than fully confident.

"I meant to say that you *are* in for the night."

Eileen said nothing.

"We have Officer Scales at your door for the night. You saw her?"

"Yup."

"Is your dad there?"

"Yeah, he's here. We're all good, Detective."

"Okay. We're at Sully's having a post-mortem about tonight. We'll figure out what to do next."

Keene clicked off and asked Gary for some root beer.

Hurley said, "Let's grab that table." Arnaud and Peterson joined him and Keene there. Hurley asked Peterson, as if it were her turn to watch the FinCEN agent, "Where's Harding?"

"I don't know why you're asking me, but he had a conference call to attend."

"What do you think?" Keene asked the group.

Peterson said, "I don't think the killer or killers read the news feeds or newspapers. That's all."

"Yeah," Hurley and Keene said at the same time.

Keene's phone vibrated. "It's Leo. Yeah?" he barked at the reporter.

Venti said, "No go? Not even a bite?"

"Nah; sorry to say it, but our guy isn't a reader."

"Wanna try again?" Venti asked.

"We're talking about it right now. I'll get back to you." At the last minute before clicking off, he said, "Thanks, Leo." He bumped the phone to the table.

"Leo's offering to try again," Keene said.

"Can't do the same article. That'd look fishy," Hurley said.

Arnaud said from the bubble at the back of her throat, "Wouldn't look fishy if the guys never read it in the first place."

"It would look bad to the public, though." Peterson had a nervous tic Keene had only noticed recently. She double tapped the top of her phone. She did that now. "We have to keep that in mind."

Arnaud asked, "What did Eileen say? Is she staying in tonight?"

"Yeah," Keene said optimistically. "She's in and her dad is home. Plus, Officer Scales is in a cruiser for the night in front of the apartment."

Hurley said, "Okay, Ei's buttoned up pretty good."

Keene said, "Let's go home; get some sleep; come back tomorrow with fresh ideas about where to go next."

"Yeah," Hurley agreed. "We have got to bring this to an end. Peterson's right—we're beginning to look bad."

Arnaud said, "Another possibility that we haven't mentioned is these two may not be looking for the graffiti artist at all. That's a big assumption on our part."

"That's true," Keene said. "The assumptions are that they read and are even interested in Eileen at all."

"I'd say it's very likely both assumptions are invalid," Peterson said.

Keene said, "I agree. Let's wrap this up unless there's anything else." He looked around the table and said, "Let's go."

CHAPTER
45

At least the air moved. It was hot air, but it moved. For the last week, it had lain like a blanket over the city, a hot, moist blanket. Heavy, not moving. The Weather Channel, the only non-sports channel Pete, Paul, and John tolerated, had been following the second hurricane, Melody, watching her bear down on the Northeast. After ripping through the Gulf states, the storm had assumed a track with Boston and Portland squarely in her sights. Now the air was moving, hot and humid but moving.

It was an atmosphere that made Eileen want to be outside. She was convinced she had nothing to worry about; the couple she had seen were not killers. Eileen went to her bedroom to retrieve her backpack. If it wasn't raining—even if it was misting—she could work. She had ideas. She had been painting in the style of old-fashioned wish-you-were-here postcards and now she was going to paint a video play button, a circle around a white triangle, and a white cursor arrow. A slight move of the mouse and all hell would break loose with the menacing crustacean.

Eileen hadn't exactly told Keene she would stay in. Hadn't mentioned that the cellar window led away from the cruiser out front, and the cop would never see her make her way to the path. It hadn't been a lie that her father was in the apartment. She never said whether he was awake or not. She ran down the cellar stairs, out through the window, along the alley, and down to the root-bound path. The ambiance of the approaching hurricane enveloped her. She came to an immediate standstill, dropped her pack, and threw her arms up, soaking it all in.

She had to get to her work. Pink hair flipping in the wind, she slipped and slid down the path to the bike trail and then to the wall on the left. The waves churned, the high tide building with the incoming surge. The wind hummed as it swirled under and over the bridge. Combined with the slosh and rattle of the surf, the aura was invigorating. More than that: inspiring.

She shook the silver paint can, nearly new, and stopped. She could finish this tonight.

The woman with black hair appeared on the dramatic stage the storm provided. Mist swirling as on a stage with an abundance of dry ice—perhaps *The Hound of the Baskervilles*, or *Hamlet*. The woman's hair flew behind her, a witchy suggestion of madness. Before last Sunday night, Eileen hadn't seen anyone on the trail in all the nights she'd worked on the wall. She peered over her shoulder and then looked back at her work. Her concentration was broken. She stepped back, looking half at her work and half at the woman. The woman was attractive. She wore all black. Eileen knew she was the same woman she'd seen last Sunday night. The same woman, in a skin-tight black outfit like last Sunday. She held a gun in her right hand hanging by her hip, ready but not pointed at Eileen.

"Didn't recognize me today? 'Where is art museum?' Blonde wig."

"That was you," Eileen said, understanding a previously unformed thought.

Eileen's feet were wet. The storm surge had sent spume and tidal wash onto the trail.

"Yeah. Me." Silk lifted the gun and casually pointed it at Eileen.

Eileen dropped her can of silver spray paint.

When Keene got home, he was exhausted and pissed.

Melena greeted him with a drink and said, "Hola, mi amor. You look tired. Cómo está?" She was psychic, knowing when he was tired and displeased, and she knew that hearing her speak Spanish was comforting to him.

"I am tired. I was sure we were going to get this guy tonight. I was convinced. We did everything right. We had all the people in the right places."

"Okay, but relax now." She used a soft voice and took his hand. "Está bien. We'll get him."

"Yeah," Keene said. "It's just that we put an innocent girl at risk for nothing in the end."

"Is she okay, though?"

Keene said, "Yeah, she's fine."

"Let's do a steak on the grill."

They took out a steak that Melena had in a Cuban marinade: cumin, oregano, lime juice. Keene started the grill. Melena hugged him from behind.

"You'll get this guy, Basil. You always do." She hugged him tighter, then let him go. She knew where he was at that moment and knew to allow him his space.

He was exhausted. When he got this way, profoundly tired, his mind carried him along to a place he didn't want to go. A policeman lives in a place no one else would care to. He exists somewhere among violence and injustice and abuse, and he is expected to be the peacemaker. The cop is required to be a referee, a judge, and a negotiator. He should never be an executioner. When Keene felt this way, when he went to this place, he had to manipulate this mind-set, which starts out self-destructive. It becomes an internal debate that always goes back to the EPS. The sniper. What steps could he have taken to avoid killing the suspect, a man who deserved his day in court, not five minutes in front of a firing squad? This argument raged within him during those weeks while he still thought he had killed an innocent man. The rage had threatened to engulf him. The therapist had convinced him to turn it into something positive. First, create a personal protocol to exhaust all solutions before resorting to violence. This was Policing 101, of course. But *turn it into personal policy*, the therapist had said, and suggested he work with others in the same place. He had the support of the Union and the Department and would visit policemen around New England wrestling with the same difficulties. It was a work in progress.

"Basil?" Melena said. "Are you okay? I think I lost you for a minute."

"I'm fine. I was just thinking, I wish I shared your confidence about getting the guy." He turned to Melena. She was cutting vegetables. He kissed her on the top of her head.

He grilled the meat and they ate. He helped clean up and thought about all the manhours they had wasted watching Eileen walk home.

He brushed his teeth and slumped into bed. He was dead tired and, counterintuitively, that often meant he would not sleep. He lay on the cool sheets in the air-conditioned bedroom. It wasn't a hundred degrees, but Melena conceded and allowed him to turn on the AC. He turned out the lights and started thinking. What had they done wrong? Wasted the manhours, is what they'd done wrong. All they did was watch her walk home, never attracting the attention of the killer. He bolted upright. They watched her go home. Of course. As did the killer. But Officer Scales was there. There was no problem. Unless...

"Shit," he said. No problem unless Eileen escaped to the bike trail. There was no officer stationed there.

Melena, still washing and readying for bed, said, "What?"

Hurley let himself into Michaela's apartment. He needed some rest. The failure that afternoon had sucked the energy out of him. He was tired. He was angry. He was worried. This couldn't go on. If they couldn't bait the killer in, how were they going to get him? Was he going to kill again and make a mistake the next time? Was that going to be the way this would go? One more time? Or maybe two? Or three? When would this end?

...With Eileen?

He looked into the bedroom.

"Hi, Honey," Michaela said. She was in bed looking at her phone.

"Hey, sweet. How are ya?"

"Better than you. Eileen called me. Told me all about it. Rough day?"

"Not a great day." He lay on the bed next to her. Kissed her.

"You smell great," he said.

"Thank you." She kissed him back.

"Did you say Ei called you?"

"Yeah. She's so cute. I love her."

"Yeah, me too," Hurley said, not quite matching Michaela's enthusiasm. "What did she say that was so cute?"

"She was talking about these ideas she's had for the graffiti. You know, Dennis, I had no idea she was the Tagger."

"Me either. So, what did she say about the graffiti?"

"She thinks she's going to finish it tonight."

Hurley's head came off the pillow. "When was this?"

Michaela said, "I got off the phone with her just before you got home."

As he called Keene, the wind stripped his Hunger Hill cap from his head. It cartwheeled away and he didn't even think about chasing it.

Keene answered, "Yeah?"

Hurley told him what he suspected, that Eileen was on her way to paint.

Keene said, "I'm on my way. She's probably on the bike trail. But so's our guy. You got a rover in the Supra?"

"No. Just use the phone."

Keene tried Eileen's cell.

"Good morning, afternoon, or evening. Say some words." *Beep.*

He called Officer Arnaud. "You in your squad car?"

She said she was.

He said, "Okay. I'll be there in a minute. If necessary, approach very carefully. She's probably being watched. By a killer. Hurley doesn't have a rover. We need to call him on his cell." He gave her the number.

"Where's Peterson?"

Keene said, "She's my next call."

"Going to the bike trail?" Hurley asked.

"Yeah," Keene said.

"Me too. Where are you?" Hurley asked.

"Just crossing the bridge." Keene passed the place where the truck drivers had been shot by the EPS. "We led him right to her, where he waited for her to show up. On the bike trail, though. Not Romasco. Keene smacked the wheel with his open hand. He craned his neck trying to see over the guard-rail. He could see Eileen's work, but he couldn't see Eileen. Or anybody else, for that matter.

Keene: "I'm just off the bridge."

Hurley: "I'm on Washington."

"Okay. Go to the top of Romasco. You know the path down the embankment?"

"I grew up here," Hurley said.

Keene exited the interstate and caught the green light at the bottom of the ramp.

Keene said, "I'm on Marginal. If he has a car, that's where it'll be. We'll pincer in on him. Be careful, Hurley. This guy's dangerous."

A dark sedan passed Keene going in the opposite direction. The car roared by.

"Yeah. Got it." Hurley clicked off.

Keene touched the rover and said, "Arnaud, a dark sedan went by me on Marginal. Got on the highway going north. Maybe two women. Get on that car."

"Got it."

"Pull that car over. Be careful, Arnaud. Be very careful."

Hurley had pulled to the side of Romasco as he dropped his phone. He had a view of the intersection of Marginal Way and the Arterial. He saw Keene's Charger turning from Marginal into the commuter lot and a dark sedan at the same time entering the interstate, northbound. The detective eased his door open and left it ajar. He walked noiselessly to the path down the embankment that led to the paved East End bike trail. He imagined Keene doing the same not too far below him. They would come toward the suspect from both sides, the ocean on the third side, the wall on the fourth.

Arnaud saw the dark sedan, the only northbound vehicle in sight. If the driver took the next exit, Arnaud would follow and call the Falmouth Police for backup. They would make the arrest, as it was their jurisdiction. But the car continued straight, past the Depot Road exit. It picked up speed.

Hurley slipped and skittered down the path. He stopped before landing on the bike trail and listened. Nothing.

Keene called Peterson and told her to meet them at the bike trail.

"Where's Harding?"

"Right here," Peterson said, "We're finishing a late dinner at the Olive Garden next to his hotel." Keene had known he could count on Peterson.

"Lights and siren; get here ASAP."

He pulled into the commuter parking lot and discovered it empty. He met Hurley in front of the brightly painted scene of a lobster attacking like a Godzilla/Tasmanian Devil.

"Did you see anybody, anything?"

"Nothing," Hurley said, "except a dark sedan."

"She's in that car. A woman was driving. I'm sure of it."

Arnaud's voice on the police radio interrupted him. She was chasing a dark sedan north on I-95 at high speed.

Keene said to Hurley, "Get in."

CHAPTER
46

The dark sedan hit a hundred miles an hour and then topped it. Officer Arnaud thought to use the radio to ask for down-road help but chose not to. She simply maintained speed and followed the Malibu. The Chevy's brake lights shone red suddenly and the car rounded an exit. Arnaud followed.

The exit had been blasted out of a rock formation and was blind around the circle. When she arrived at the top of the ramp the Malibu was gone. She had a fifty-fifty chance of left or right and guessed left, toward the water. She drove to Route One and turned left, reasoning that the Malibu had gone north on the highway; perhaps the driver would continue north.

Arnaud's shot-in-the-dark guess was rewarded. She saw a flash of red on a curve. Then gone. She followed. She didn't know these roads—she had grown up on the southern side of Casco Bay, Cape Elizabeth.

Arnaud hadn't had a visual for over five minutes, but they were on a peninsula with only one road down. She navigated the cruiser slowly along this stretch, watching each side of the road carefully. Nothing. During the day, she might have seen dust hanging in the air, but the dark gave her no such clue.

She saw nothing until she saw something. A security gate had been crashed through. Busted and bent pieces of steel and splintered planks lay on the ground. She slammed the brakes and backed up, calling for reinforcements. Cumberland and Yarmouth cops responded, only minutes away, they said.

The storm was picking up. Pine trees leaned from the wind in waves. Loud snaps of breaking branches punctuated the roar of the wind.

Arnaud's training emphasized the personal safety of the officer if there was no imminent danger to a citizen. But there was. Eileen Mack was in a life-threatening situation. Arnaud barreled ahead toward a poorly defended position. This was exactly what she had signed up for.

The *Ice Cold* would be underway in less than thirty minutes, she'd been told when she called the captain. She would be on it and steaming for the International Line.

"Don't do something stupid," she said to Eileen. "My job is, I kill people."

"Where are we going?" Eileen asked, challenging, not resigned.

"Boat ride."

They stood in the driveway of a big house, a beautiful seaside home. Silk turned the knob. It was locked. She pushed a button and knocked on the door insistently.

"What the hell?" Dom DeLuca said as he opened the door. The oak slab door was blown from his hold and slammed into an interior wall.

"Let's go. Take us to *Ice Cold*."

"Jesus Christ, Silk. You can't just show up and make demands."

"I can," she interrupted and stuck her gun in his gut.

"All right then, let's go. What are you doing with her?"

Silk was in no mood for talking. She pushed Eileen forward and DeLuca grabbed keys from a hook on the wall. As they ran down the lawn toward the dock, DeLuca said, "This is a very bad idea. The chop alone will sink us."

The rear tires spit river-rounded pea gravel as Arnaud ate up the yards of DeLuca's driveway. She rounded a last curve and found the blue Malibu, doors open and empty. Arnaud swung her door open and drew her weapon. She scanned the scene. Darkness. She clicked the barrel-mounted LED light on. They were new, these light-emitting diodes. Four flood diodes, 2400 lumens, light up your world. Arnaud's world consisted of an empty yard and DeLuca's house, dark but conspicuously opulent. Half-round stone steps led to the door. The door itself, big enough that two people could enter side by side, was wide open.

Arnaud thought about the help that was on its way. Then she thought about Eileen. She entered and cleared the large rooms to the left and right. The huge foyer was lit by sconces, and more light came from the next room in. The wind was blowing into the house and rain was starting to spit.

"Police! I'm armed. Drop your weapon and make yourself known to me. I can and will use deadly force if necessary."

There was no response. She cleared the next room to the left. The kitchen. She knew the better decision was to wait for the Yarmouth police but...Eileen. A door was open from the kitchen to the outside, and the wind had it pinned against the outside wall. She pushed against the wind through the doorway, heard the rumble of an engine come to life, and, in the light of her flashlight, saw a boat leaving the dock with three people on board several hundred yards from her current position.

She keyed the rover radio and said, "I lost them. They're on DeLuca's boat, a Grady-White. Twenty-four-footer, I think." Arnaud had grown up around boats.

Peterson came back, "What direction?"

"Only one direction here. They're headed out the river." But Arnaud knew where they were going after that. She had a hunch about Detective Keene's reaction. She wouldn't get to South Portland in time to get on Keene's boat, but she could be there for the return. If there was one. "Detective Keene, I think there were two women in that car."

FinCEN agent Harding said, holding the open mic, "The *Ice Cold*. That's Umarov's boat." Keene hit the brakes hard. Hurley expected the airbags to deploy, then remembered the car was a '68.

"Sometimes the fastest route isn't the straightest line." Keene ripped through an official-use-only cross-median lane. He hit the Kojak light and the siren and the gas. He knew the car was designed to do 130 mph. He hit it.

Hurley said, "Two women? Gotta be Eileen. But the other woman? She said there was a couple."

"Yeah," Keene said. "Gotta be Eileen." He had the accelerator pinned to the floor.

Keene grabbed a backpack from the trunk of the Charger as he and Hurley arrived at the South Portland marina. Extra mags if needed. Extra weapon. He verified that his partner had a gun. Three minutes later, Peterson and Harding leapt from their vehicle and ran the length of the dock to the Boston Whaler. They jumped onto the boat and Keene gunned the engine. The

Whaler was up to it despite the chop. The pitch of the chop was greater than the freeboard of the Whaler, but the boat was built for these conditions.

The *Dominator* cleared the mouth of the river, and DeLuca turned to the southwest, making for the channel between Sand Island and Littlejohn. He sliced through the channel at nearly all-out speed.

Silk said, "This boat won't go faster?"

"Like I said on the river, you have to be careful of obstacles under the water. Especially at night and in weather like this. We're going way too fast as it is."

DeLuca wove between the two islands and got to the *Ice Cold* sooner than he'd thought they might. They arrived without radio warning. A blinding spotlight lit them up, and the captain, using an electronic bullhorn, called in Russian, "Announce yourselves."

Silk cried out above the wind.

The captain sent two of his sailors down to the boarding deck to help. DeLuca eased the Grady-White to the deck and tossed a line to one of the seamen. He fastened the pitching boat while the other sailor helped Eileen and Silk to the deck and Dom busied himself tying off the stern of the boat. When he was finished, he stood and looked at the business end of Silk's 7.65 mil handgun.

She said, "Thanks for the ride," and shot him in the forehead. He stood up straight as if at attention, then keeled over backward, into the cold water of his beloved Casco Bay. He went under and resurfaced, a floating corpse. Silk commanded the sailors to cut the boat loose and it was gone in an instant in front of the wind.

She and Eileen and the sailors rose with the hydraulic boarding deck. The sailors scattered; the ocean becoming rougher, the captain had ordered them back to the bridge. Silk kept Eileen within arm's length of the end of her Tokarev 33.

The *Ice Cold* pulled at her anchor at the back side of Clapboard Island. The tidal energy worked against the energy of the incoming swells, the side effect of the storm churning powerfully off the coast of Maine. The swells rolled in like giant barrels as the tide swept out. These contradicting influences resulted in serious chop. The wind created whitecaps and spray.

The constant slapping of the Whaler's hull at speed gave way to pitching and falling. Keene drew the throttle back. He didn't understand what was happening on the Grady-White as he watched it drift away from the rising boarding float. He maneuvered his overloaded Whaler in next to the *Ice Cold*'s stern. The hydraulic boarding deck was gone, eight feet above them. Keene was looking at its underside as, invisible to him, Silk and Eileen ran from the portable deck to the lounge and beyond.

Keene needed to get aboard that ship. But the inaccessible deck was a wall's height above them. He heard the telltale sound of a chain in motion at the bow of the yacht. Her anchor was being raised.

"Can you run this boat?" he yelled at Hurley, ignoring Peterson and Harding.

"Yes," Hurley hollered back.

"You're on!" Keene said and put the Whaler in gear. He grabbed his pack, hung it on one shoulder, and left the wheel to Hurley. Hurley motored to the bow of the *Ice Cold*, and as the anchor broke the surface, Keene grabbed a chain link the size of his fist. He crooked a foot in a fluke of the anchor and rode the big piece of iron like an old-fashioned man-lift.

Keene hollered, "I'll see you at the loading deck. It'll be tricky because we're underway." The building wind carried Keene's words to Hurley, Peterson, and Harding as they swung away. They returned to the stern of the *Ice Cold* in a couple of seconds as the larger boat gained speed and shot past the Whaler. Hurley turned in behind the yacht and kept pace with her. The effect of the churning props was contrary to what Hurley had guessed. Their opposition to one another flattened the surface of the otherwise choppy water. They rode like that for a while, all wondering what was happening to Keene somewhere above.

———— •••• ————

The electric windlass made the ride smooth, delightful if not for the gale winds, the sheets of rain, and the fact that, because of him, a girl's life was in danger. Keene rode the anchor eight feet and reached the rail where the chain disappeared through the hull. This was the tricky part. This was the part where he trusted in the notion that good triumphs over the opposite, and that there wouldn't be a bunch of guys with .45s trained on him as he jumped onto the boat. He kept his footing as the chain links rattled through the hull side. He flipped his pack over the rail, gained a handhold on the rail, and pulled his foot from the anchor fluke as it came to rest. He hauled himself up and over the rail, landed on the teak decking, and found it empty except for the backpack. He reached to his belt and drew his Glock 19, put the pack on and secured it with a buckle at his sternum. There was a sailor's passage, as narrow as the average sailor, down the seaward side of the ship. He considered the consequence of meeting another person along the length of this walkway. Only one of them would survive. He took the walk with his carry gun ready.

The wind and the water passing eight feet below him covered any noise he made. He had to move: The faster the *Ice Cold* went, the harder it would be for the rest of them to climb onto the boarding deck from the Whaler. He walked quickly along the side of the ship, came to an open deck, and pressed his back against the wall. He turned carefully and realized he was in a lounge. It was empty. He saw a pool, and beyond that, the loading deck. The surface of the swimming pool shivered and chopped as the ship pitched and yawed in the wind. There was a hydraulic control unit on an open console facing the seaward side of the *Ice Cold*.

Keene looked at the deck above. It featured, as expected, another observation deck. Empty as well. He rushed back to the console and figured out how to send the hydraulic deck down. He peered over the stern and saw Hurley right there keeping pace with the yacht. Hurley made a goofy salute as Keene hit the down control.

"Go!" he yelled. Peterson clambered over the bow. She reached and caught the deck and dropped to her knees safely. Harding scrambled over the bow, too. Hurley found a cleat and fastened the Whaler at the bow. The yacht towed the boat like a dinghy. Hurley got a handhold on the deck and was half on when the Whaler slipped away from under him. His legs dropped and slapped against the stern only inches above the churning water, and he lost his grip and dangled by one hand until Peterson grabbed his other forearm. She held on, the muscles in her arms and back strained to their limits. Harding latched onto Hurley and, making a chain, Keene grabbed Harding's collar. They hauled Hurley on board like a tuna. The ship rolled and he rolled with it. It rolled back and Hurley stumbled as he tried to stand.

"We're in Hussey Sound," Keene said. "It's a bitch through here even when it's calm."

CHAPTER
47

Silk and Eileen approached the bridge. Silk shouted her identity to the captain, requesting he not shoot her or Eileen.

He turned and when he saw Eileen, he said, "Who is this?"

Silk said nothing.

Silk knew little about ships, but as the captain pushed a stainless-steel control forward, the thing she knew for certain was they were moving forward. He had a small wheel in front of him, the size of a car's steering wheel.

"We're going?"

"Umarov says yes," the captain said. "We go to Caracas. I say not a good idea, is a goddamned hurricane."

"Where is Umarov?"

"Cabin," he said, pointing up to Umarov's cabin above the bridge.

"Good. Tell him I'm here."

The captain picked up a wired phone set that rang directly into Umarov's cabin. He never removed his eagle-like eyes from the ocean. She listened to him tell the boss that Silk and another girl were on board and at the bridge with him.

"He wants to see you."

The climb up the steep stairs was awkward for the two women, as the sea was pitching and rolling.

"This is her?" Umarov asked Silk. "What's your name?" he asked Eileen.

Eileen wasn't up on the international protocols regarding a conversation between the kidnapper and the hostage. She said nothing while Silk answered for her.

"Were you followed?" Umarov asked Silk.

"Yes. Captain pulled the boarding deck before they reached us, though."

"Are you sure?"

"Yes."

Umarov picked up his end of the wired phone line and said, "Did you operate the lift from the deck or the bridge?"

"I lifted from here," the captain said.

"So, you didn't see the deck as it lifted?"

"No."

"You idiot, you just gave them a ride to the first deck. You didn't think this possible?"

"I don't think they are on board, sir," the captain said.

Umarov said, "I think we should act like they are. Let me know when we pass the International Line."

International waters existed approximately twelve miles off the shore. This was sometimes called the continental line. Umarov and the captain knew that crossing this theoretical line would strip the Portland Police Department of jurisdictional authority if they had managed to board the *Ice Cold*. What they didn't know was that in New England, the line was drawn from West Quoddy Head Light in Maine to Race Point Light on Cape Cod, sometimes inside the twelve-mile mark and sometimes outside. The other anomaly of New England waters was that Melody, the hurricane, sat near that twelve-mile line churning the piss out of those waters, international or not, at that very moment.

The three detectives and Harding huddled in the lounge, backs against the forward wall. Each carried a weapon, muzzle up, trigger finger flat against the gun above the trigger cage.

"We'll pair up and each pair take a deck, one at a time," Keene said. He looked at Harding. "You can use that thing?"

"I did FBI weapons training. I'm a pretty good shot."

Keene gave Harding a quick nod. "We'll meet at the top of these stairs. This is a search and rescue mission, now. Clear each room. Left to right. Stern to bow. That's back to front, Peterson."

Hurley and Keene worked together. Keene looked down the dimly lit space, like a hotel hallway. Mood lighting. See-you-in-the-morning lighting. There were only two doors where Keene had expected four. There was one on each side, numbered 14 on the port, the left, and 15 on the starboard. A door at the end was marked "No Entry" with the universal red circle-back-slash sign. Keene guessed the door led to the engine room.

At the first berth, numbered 14, Hurley backed against the wall at the hinge side of the door, Keene the opposite. Hurley flicked on the chassis-mounted light on his weapon as Keene kicked the door open. They pivoted into the room together and swept their firearms, fingers on triggers; the room was clear. Keene had hardly drawn his weapon since the shooting. His range work had come around to nearly normal. But he hadn't sighted on a human since the shooter at the Eastern Prom park—the Eastern Prom Sniper. The barrel-mounted floodlights exposed beds. Too many beds—some assembled, and other mattresses and frames leaning against the walls. As if some other rooms had been cleared out. Keene counted eight beds in this room. They discovered a second door, a second room. These rooms were suites. The detectives cleared the second room in much the same way. They found six more twin-size beds. All fourteen beds were for singles, little more than cots. Not the luxury one might have expected. As if for the crew.

Keene's mouth was dry, his hands wet.

Hurley said, "Okay, partner?"

"Fine."

They cleared the suite numbered fifteen and found the same setup, the outer room with some small beds and an inner room with some more.

"A lot of beds in each," Keene tried to clear his throat.

"Yeah," Hurley said. "Maybe they cleared out the other rooms for something. Weird."

Keene said, "Maybe." They needed to find out what Peterson was discovering.

Simultaneously, Peterson and Harding had been doing the same on deck number two. They discovered six suites, not the twelve single rooms Keene had predicted. The four cops met at the staircase.

Peterson said, "Six suites. All clear except for the locked door at the end. Engine room, I think. Funny thing."

Keene interrupted. "Did you find a couple of extra beds?"

"A couple? Yeah, right. A couple dozen extra. Each suite has a bunch of single beds in it."

Keene said to Hurley, "Blows the cleared room theory. Probably six more suites on the next deck."

They crept up the next staircase. Like the first, gritted rubber strips were nailed to teak treads.

Keene was wrong again. They climbed to the third deck and found four suites, an exercise room, and a media room with a vast wide-screen TV.

"You guys take five and six; we'll take three and four."

Keene kicked in the door of Suite Three first. The outer room was empty of people, full of boxes. Boxes upon boxes, like a clothing warehouse. No longer surprised by anything in these berths, he whispered, "Clear," as Hurley passed him for the interior door.

"Holy shit," Hurley said.

Keene caught up with his partner and peered into the room, their shoulders touching.

"Jesus," he said as he and Hurley estimated how much Kentucky bourbon was stuffed into the inner room, devoid of anything but cases of liquor. They crossed quickly to Suite Four and found an identical setup, the inner room full of wholesale cartons of jeans and sneakers and jackets and dresses and resort wear.

"Suite Five looks like a warehouse of cigarettes and Six is full of cash," Peterson said when they met.

Harding said, "There must be hundreds of millions in currency. Dollars and euros. He's been at work on the Adriatic and the Black Sea like we thought. Interesting thing is that it's all denominations. This is parallel economy stuff, Keene. These are the fuels that make it work."

At the rear of the third deck, they found observational windows into the pool, the surface of which was one deck up. A wide staircase swept up and to the stern, leading to the pool. Even though the stairs were wide enough for a half dozen people to ascend side by side, the three detectives and the agent pinned their backs against the walls with their guns extended, fingers inside the trigger cages. Even so, they stumbled as they climbed. The ship was pitching hard in all directions. They climbed, the pool and a lounge and dining hall in front of them. A mirror of the aft part of the first deck. They turned to see a hall between Suites One and Two. They searched the two suites and found them empty but furnished more conventionally. The rooms were bigger. The hall between them led to a door at the forward end. The detectives and Agent Harding had cleared all four decks in less than ten minutes.

Peterson said quietly, "Anybody notice these doors are all locked from the outside?"

"Yeah," Hurley whispered. "I kinda get the ones with merch and cash, but what's up with the rest?"

"Reluctant guests?" Keene whispered.

"There are no guests," Harding said.

Peterson said, "This boat gives me the creeps."

"Future guests," Keene said. "Seems like, soon there might be a couple hundred people on this boat who don't necessarily want to go on a cruise." Then he said to no one in particular, "This is too easy. Why haven't we seen anybody?"

"A ship this size with modern electronic gear requires a minimal crew," Harding said. "Three or four men."

"But why've we gotten no resistance at all?" The door at the end of the hall was unlocked and had a sign that Harding misinterpreted as "Observation Deck" since they'd all assumed the bridge would be on the top deck. Keene inched it open and peered around the door and found himself looking across 30 feet of the deck at the bridge.

A shot whanged off the wall a foot in front of Hurley, the gunman probably as surprised as they were. Keene's neurons fired up, his hands and feet thrumming with the fuel of adrenaline. His heart beat faster and his hands went clammy. The shooter ran for the cover of an exhaust funnel. Peterson fired and hit him in mid-stride. Keene and Hurley marveled at the shot, Peterson having executed it from a moving deck. The wounded sailor stumbled to the deck and when he came to rest, his gun was propped in a shooter's position on his hip, his body straddling the passageway. He pulled the trigger. The shot was high and wide. He had his left hand on the gun resting on the fulcrum of his hip. He shot down the length of his body, Keene looking over the man's feet, a foreshortened perspective. The recoil kept the man from being able to fire off a second shot with any accuracy. Hurley, on the other side of the bulkhead, took a shot at the guy, center mass. He clipped the man's left shoulder. The sailor's gun spilled away from him and skittered across the deck.

The injured man presented a tactical problem. Keene couldn't leave Hurley or Peterson to stand guard. He couldn't leave the man unattended. He couldn't kill him in a legal sense or a moral sense. He wondered, could he if he needed to? Emotionally? Was this what the Council worried about? He jammed those thoughts back into the barrel they tried to leak out of. What he knew he could do was reach for the gun on the deck and toss it overboard.

He had nothing to go on other than Harding's guess that four or five men were running the ship. He knew the woman and Eileen were on board. He guessed the mysterious Umarov was, too. Six or seven combatants and a hostage? One down?

"Cover me," he said to Peterson and Hurley, both good marksmen. He crawled onto the deck using the sailor's prone body as cover. The firearm was another six feet away. He slipped behind the sailor inch by inch across the teak deck. Peterson poured a steady stream of lead at the bridge. Hurley covered behind their position. Keene slid his arm forward, beyond the sailor's head. A bullet buzzed his arm. Closer than comfortable, it had come from the direction of the bridge. The downed sailor seemed to have lost consciousness. Keene considered slipping back to cover. *An unconscious sailor can't reach that gun. He can do little harm. A sailor faking a catatonic state, on the other hand, knows how to screw up a picnic.*

Hurley covered the stairs that led to the deck above the bridge. Nothing came from there. He alternated his fire—stairs, bridge door, stairs, bridge door. He also looked for sniper fire from the top of the bridge. He spied the barrel of a gun protruding from a window on the port side. He fired a shot that broke glass over the barrel and it receded. Keene snaked his body farther out, farther into a dangerous place. Keene latched onto the gun and scaled it sidearm over the side. The bridge returned fire at Peterson and Hurley with no real consequences. As Keene returned to the protection of the staircase, even as he was behind the sailor, a teak splinter seared into his face, less than a half inch below his right eye. The odds of the sliver jumping over the sailor's body and into Keene's face were astronomical, but he didn't have time for the calculation.

Then the game changed for the worse. Semiautomatic gunfire is one thing. Automatic fire is a whole different ball game. It commenced from the deck above the bridge. The top deck covered the bridge housing and appeared to extend beyond it toward the bow. Most of the features of this deck, the pool and lounge, and the dining area, were open to the air. However, a fifth deck provided private quarters, Keene guessed. Umarov's quarters probably, Umarov who was armed with an AK-47 and zipping open the bulkhead like it was made of aluminum foil.

CHAPTER
48

Silk held the Tokarev on Umarov. "Drop it. Kick it away." Silk referred to the AK-47. Umarov did so.

Silk, her feet spread for balance on the pitching floor, told Umarov to sit, her gun trained on him, her other arm wrapped around Eileen's neck.

"You," he spat, "are telling *me* to sit?"

"Sit down."

"Who do you think you're talking to, Silk?" Umarov said with the tone of a father putting an impolite child back in her place.

Silk's hostage, Eileen, was docile, her feet moving in place to retain balance. Silk didn't need to tie her up. Instead, she simply pointed the gun at Umarov's forehead.

"That's precisely the right question, Fyodor. I know exactly who I'm talking to."

"Okay?" Gunfire cracked below as Umarov sounded genuinely puzzled. "Do you know who *you're* talking to?"

Umarov hesitated a second then laughed unaffectedly, an authentic laugh. "This is what this is about? Who I am? Who you are?" He sat casually.

Silk said nothing. She feared she was losing control of the situation. Don't ask a question you don't already know the answer to. This pertained to lawyers and to killers wanting to teach their prey a lesson before the final lights-out.

Umarov's laugh was no longer genuine but was a performance meant to infer that she'd been defeated.

"I think you need to understand who I am, Silk—Silakha Rhenko. I ordered your father and, sadly, the rest of your family burned out of their hole like irradicating rats. That was me. Arkady, no friend of your father's, as it turns out, reported to me that you had escaped. Naked as the day you were born, as I heard it."

"Shut up." Silk pounded the Tokarev 33 on the table.

"When we were done with Arkady, Silk, I'm sure you figured out why he didn't come home from the convenience store."

"How do you know all this?" Silk interjected.

"Arkady was my agent, Silakha. You don't understand this?"

"Stop!" Silk pounded the table again. She didn't want to hear this. She only wanted to kill this man. But he was filling in all the blanks. She should hear it, then kill him.

"When your landlord dumped you in Kharkiv, I watched you. I hear you give a good blow job for less than fifty kopeks."

"Fuck you."

"I lost you in Kiev for about a month. But my people found you. The lesbian? I own her. I hired you in Odesa. You had no idea. Did you know I owned the casino where you started selling cigarettes and drinks?"

She said nothing. Her mouth was dry, her eyes were on fire.

He said, "I guess not, then."

"So..." she said. She licked her lips as if they were glued. "So, you made this happen. Why?"

"You are my project, Silakha. Do you know what Genghis Khan said? To paraphrase, he said: Kill your enemy and screw his women, particularly his daughter. Oh, and I promised my mother, on her deathbed, that I would do something good. She feared for my soul. So, I decided to help you. One stone, two birds on a lovely cruise to Caracas."

"And what will you do in Caracas?" Silk asked.

He explained his economic project that featured the contraband in the staterooms below. "We will trade our goods and cash for Venezuela's most valuable resource, beautiful women. I keep Venezuela's ruling class's micro economy fueled, and they stock my business enterprise with fresh talent. Eileen, would you like to be a porn star?" He asked it in the way he might ask a little girl if she wanted a pony.

The boat lurched hard to the left and Silk staggered.

"Tell me one thing. Be honest." She implored Umarov to answer this one question. If she was to live, she needed to know. If she was ever to sleep again, she must know the answer. If death was her destiny, she needed to understand whether her only lover, Arkady, had loved her or simply used her to get to her family. "Did Arkady set the fire?"

He laughed. It was a rolling laugh, building and self-perpetuating, gaining momentum because the answer must be self-evident and funny.

"I should kill you right now!" Silk cried. "Did Arkady set the fire?" She screamed above the noise of the wind and the sea and the gunfire and something occurred that didn't often happen to Silk. Tears ran down her face.

Umarov just laughed until Silk shot a hole through the roof.

Then the door crashed open and Umarov started to say something, and Silk shot the sailor coming through the door dead, the bullet entering his throat and exiting the back of his head.

"Ah, shit," Umarov said. Silk realized his performance had been to stall, waiting for this guy to show up. All his laughter and abuse of her had been tactics and procedures.

Eileen threw her arms over her head as Silk stood from the crouch she'd taken when the sailor burst in. Umarov leapt from the chair. He stumbled as the yacht pitched and yawed heavily in the opposite direction. Silk did too. He made a move toward the AK-47 but staggered with the heave of the deck. Silk staggered and the gun slid across the floor toward them. She was steadier than he and kicked the weapon away.

"Did he?" she cried. The question had become all-important. She wanted to know the answer more than anything else. She'd devoted three years of her life to killing Umarov but decided to wait until he gave her the answer. "Did Arkady start the fire? Did he kill my family?" Then she would kill him.

They stumbled together and unwillingly embraced. He squeezed her hard. She couldn't breathe and her skin screamed in pain. She pushed against him, tried to wriggle from his arms. She still had the Tokarev 33, her finger outside the trigger cage. A wave threw the boat and they went down, now in a mad scramble on the floor, and she tried to get away from his embrace. Her finger slipped into the cage and the gun went off at his forehead. The bullet entered his frontal lobe and made a mess of his ice-blue-framed glasses.

Silakha Rhenko screamed at Fyodor Umarov, "Did Arkady kill my family? Did he? *Did he?*" But she had killed Fyodor Umarov, who was the only man who knew who had set the fire in the compound that night. He was the man who knew whether Arkady had killed Silk's entire family to become her lover and now she had to leave his ship not knowing.

She pushed Eileen to climb down a ladder to the observation pulpit of the third deck and then into the hallway. Eileen was thrust into Suite 3 with crates of bourbon. The door clicked closed.

———◆◆◆———

Arnaud, using lights and siren, made it to the Bricks in twenty minutes. She had called for a police boat.

A night dispatcher met her on the first floor. "Go to Maine State Pier. They're leaving, you might catch them." The dispatcher referred to the police boat that was shoving off in five minutes.

Arnaud spun around for the pier, which was no more than a half mile away.

———◆◆◆———

As Eileen had been pushed along the passageway, she had noticed that some of the doors had swung open in the pitching of the storm. Silk had pushed her through the door marked Three and slammed it closed. Eileen heard a click. She tried it. Locked. She pounded on it, but of course, Silk didn't open it. She gazed around. There was a light switch. She flicked it on and looked across the room. Drapes decorated the entire wall. She stumbled across the room as the ship pitched under her feet, pulled against them, drew the floor-to-ceiling curtains open. The wall was all glass, and she saw the ocean running from the ship like a machine that was out of control. She pulled the sliding glass door open, and the wind nearly knocked her backward. She forced herself onto a balcony twenty feet long by six feet wide. She looked over the railing. Twenty-four feet to the choppy, cold water. The space was cantilevered over the ocean. Eileen had nowhere to go.

Silk knew the crew consisted of three sailors, the captain, and Umarov. Umarov and a sailor were dead, and she'd seen another one down on the deck, probably dead. She had learned that the Russian girl, the captain's girl, worked on the boat but lived ashore. It was down to Silk and the captain and the third sailor against however many men the police had on the boat— at least the four she'd seen. She was at the bottom of the sweeping stairs and peered up to the bulkhead that framed them. She was behind the three men and the woman. Silk fired and the black man wheeled around and fell, hit in the back of the shoulder. She scrambled for cover behind the outside wall of Suite Three. She thought she'd evened the playing field, or at least the number of contestants.

Harding went down. None of the detectives knew what had happened. They hadn't heard a shot from the direction below decks. Harding corrected that notion. He had been hit in the shoulder and the pain was excruciating. Hurley turned and covered behind them. Peterson continued her firefight with the bridge until she realized there was no return fire.

Harding said, "I can move." He got to his feet. "I'm okay."

Keene said, "Keep it up, Diane. Hurley's got our back."

As Keene said so, Hurley fired a volley at a movement.

"Cover me, I'm gonna take him around the side here. Then follow us. I got eight mags in here," Keene said, referring to his backpack. He gave Peterson four and Hurley two. He hadn't fired a shot. "Harding. You go ahead of me." Harding scooched way down and pushed himself along the outside of the bulkhead. The walk was narrow, not big enough for more than two. Keene knew Harding was pushing himself through intense pain.

They made it behind the bulkhead. Keene turned back with the bridge in sight. He hollered to Peterson, "Go!" And he finally fired his pistol. A barrage. He emptied the Department-issued 17-round mag. At empty space. Not at a human. Out of the corner of his eye, he saw Hurley go too. He'd been counting on Hurley's fire, but he was too busy with the bridge and thinking about the AK-47 above to think much about it. He was far too busy to think about his emotional reaction to discharging his gun in the line of duty.

Peterson slid feet-first to safety like a base runner into third. The two detectives ran to the back of the bulkhead and found Hurley and Harding there. They huddled.

"Goddamned Harding!" Hurley hollered. "Love ya, man!" To Keene he said, "Covered me all the way. Bad shoulder and all."

They hadn't seen any more crew. They were counting on Harding's intelligence about the crew of a ship this size, they had the woman to worry about. She had outflanked them. Where was she now, and where was Eileen?

"We gotta get up there," Hurley said.

"We gotta clear that cabin first," Keene said. "Eileen might be up there. Or on the bridge. This is gonna be tricky. Let's get Harding below. Into a cabin."

"You're kidding, right?" Peterson said as she field-dressed his wound. "He just saved Hurley's ass."

"How are you doing, though?" Keene asked Harding. "Honestly."

"I'm okay, honestly."

"How's the wound look?"

Peterson said, "Not bad. It's not bleeding terribly." Then she said to Keene, "How *you* doing?"

"Okay," Keene said. "You two get my back as I cross the deck for the stairs to that fifth deck. Hurley, you stay with me. He can't get a bead with the AK from there. I'll go in; Hurley goes in with me. Peterson, Harding, cover our backs. I see FinCEN taught their agents how to use a handgun as well as a calculator."

"Hey, Keene," Hurley said. "Nothing from that AK in a while."

"You think he's incapacitated?"

"Or out of ammo."

"We can't be too careful."

The wind howled. The rain fell in sheets. The *Ice Cold* was sailing directly into the influence of Melody, directly into the intensifying storm that was about to up its game to a category three hurricane.

Eileen took a few steps away from the door. She ran a shoulder into it ineffectively. She backed up and leveled a kick at it, but she wasn't going to break the mahogany door. A bottle. She could swing it like a bat. She pulled a bottle from a crate and smacked it. The bottle shattered into a hundred pieces. Mr. Sullivan would have killed her. All that good bourbon. A million little pieces of glass did her no good.

Hurley said, "Who else have we got? A guy or two on the bridge and the stateroom up top. And the woman, behind us."

Keene said, "I wonder what's going on in that stateroom. When you have the high ground, the only place you can't see…"

"Is under your feet," Hurley continued.

"Go," Keene said.

Peterson fired the better part of a mag at the bridge and the stateroom above it while Hurley ran. He ran with his arms extended and he pumped rounds at the bridge with a second look above it.

Peterson said, "Go," and Keene ran. Keene had his gun pointed at the bridge, but there was no action from there. He had a feeling no one was home. Hurley made it behind the fresh air funnel. Keene leap-frogged him to the bulkhead of the bridge and kept firing but received no return fire. He peered around the bulkhead and said, "Hands up."

The captain was alone. He had brown hair threaded with gray like rusting iron. His beard was curly and grayer than his hair, and he had fierce eyes. He sat in the command-post chair, hands on the wheel with the calm of command.

"Hands off the wheel."

"I'm not armed. I think in this sea I keep hands on wheel," the captain said, his English more than adequate. The floor pitched up and down.

"Yeah," Keene said. "Good idea."

"I am only crew." The captain nodded to the other chair where a sailor sat having bled to death. "Others dead, I think. Just me."

"Who else is on board?"

"Is Umarov. Is Silk and her girl."

"Who's Silk?"

"Is girl who you want to kill. Yes?"

Keene said, "Well, when you put it that way it sounds a little extreme, but yes, one could make an argument. Does she have a hostage?"

"Yes. Pink hair."

"Where's Umarov?"

The captain pointed nonchalantly at the ceiling. He said, "Upstairs. Maybe dead. I don't hear nothing up there."

The Russian adjusted the wheel. He said, "Is very rough. I tell Umarov we not go to Caracas. He says yes, is okay to go. I think no but don't say it."

"I think you're right. We need to get turned around."

"Not until International Line. Maybe fifteen minutes."

Keene said, "Yeah? And what do we do then?"

The police boat shoved off just as Arnaud reached it. Charlie Riordan handed her a tactical vest and she strapped it on over her uniform. Then he handed her a life vest, and at risk of disappearing in all the foam, she strapped it on, too.

"What are you doing here," she asked. "Sir," she added.

He wore tactical gear under a shirt and tie with a life vest over it all. "Those are three of my best people, and Washington would be pissed if I lost one of theirs. I can't sit at my desk and wait to hear how it turns out."

The skipper hit a siren and a blue flashing strobe at the same time.

Eileen slipped a second bottle of bourbon from the case. She thumped it against another bottle with a controlled motion and it broke. She took the broken bottle by the neck and began running the jagged edge that smelled of lovely whiskey up and down against the wooden door, up and down resulting in splinters and sawdust but nowhere close to sawing through the wood.

She sat on a crate of booze and thought. The balcony. She had seen that the suite next door was open into the hall unless Silk had locked it. She went to the head of the balcony, leaned over the rail, and then bent to her right to explore her options. The other balcony was right there, but because it was cantilevered like the balcony she was on, she would have to swing out over the open water that churned like a food mixer twenty or more feet below. Being light, the wind threatened to blow her over the side. She ducked into the lee and caught her breath. Then she looked again. She got a break. There were a series of bars that seemed to serve as steps, like ladder rungs, for the crew to service the ship somehow, painting or cleaning. If she could get her hand around the highest rung that she could reach, she might be able to swing the rest of herself around and onto the other balcony.

She needed to stand as high as she could to clear the rail of Suite Four's sun deck. She brought four cases of bourbon out to the deck. The gale blew hard but steady. She leaned into it as she stacked the four crates. The top one was dislodged by the wind and crashed to the floor, bottles breaking inside the box. She shoved it aside. Her hair whipped into her eyes. Salt was splashing from the sea, and she didn't know which was stinging her eyes more. She stacked the remaining three crates snugly against the railing and tested them. The top crate was far too unstable for her to trust. Two crates were the maximum. She reached and a gust hit her broadside and she wheeled her arms to regain balance. Rain sheeted with the gale. Eileen was as wet as if she'd taken a shower. She reached again and nearly fell. She hopped down deciding the crates were a bad idea.

CHAPTER
49

The absolute best boat operator in the business couldn't do more than run a parallel course alongside the *Ice Cold* in the conditions outside Casco Bay that night. Portland's police boat skipper did just that, and Riordan took the bullhorn when the ship was briefly visible on the starboard side. He could barely see a Boston Whaler tied to the stern of the ship.

"This is the Portland Police Department. Give up control of your ship. All hands on deck. Now."

"Charlie," the skipper lifted his voice, "I don't think that was effective. I can't stay with this ship in these conditions."

Eileen decided her best option was to grab onto the rung closest at hand and climb. Then she could swing and drop onto Suite Four's sun deck. This was not a good idea for someone afraid of heights, a phobia Eileen harbored, truth be known. But she had to get away from that crazy bitch, Silk. The only way was to monkey-bar her way onto that other balcony. Before she lost her nerve, she ran onto the deck, reached around for a rung, and was suddenly hanging twenty-four feet above the roiling Atlantic in hurricane winds and sheets of rain. The rung was slick in her hands. She pulled her legs up and her foot found another rung. She held tight and ignored the fear that tried to cripple her.

The human animal responds in two ways to its various phobias—heights, water, enclosed spaces. The first response might be surrendering to the fear, balling into a fetal position or dropping and sinking. Eileen was an animal prone to the second response. She fought. She held onto the slippery rungs but wasn't ready to move a foot or a hand. However, if she didn't, she'd be blown off the side of the ship like a bug from a windshield. She moved a foot up one rung. That wasn't bad. The hell it wasn't; it nearly scared her to death. She moved a hand. She was one rung higher. She looked farther to her right. Her destination balcony was right there; she merely had to convince herself to let go with her feet and swing. In a gale. From the side of a boat. So, she did. She removed her feet and swung far enough to clear the railing of Suite Four. She let go and slid safely onto the sun deck, which currently didn't live up to its name. It felt like a million bucks to Eileen though, solid under her feet. She lay on the deck, looking at the sky, getting her breath back, and had a word with God. *Thanks, Dude*, she prayed.

She jumped to her feet, which slid on the wet deck and she caught herself, then ran through the cabin, pushed the door open, and scrambled into the hallway. Into Silk's grasp.

"Drop your gun!" Harding yelled.

Silk whirled around with Eileen hugged like a dance partner.

"I will kill her," Silk said calmly. "Drop *your* gun," she said with an ironic twist. "Kick the gun. I thought I already killed you."

Hurley shouted at Keene still at the bridge, "The woman is down below. I'm going after her. Cover me."

Keene wheeled toward the top deck and began firing. There was no return fire. Peterson was firing sparingly at the top deck as well.

"The captain's got his hands full steering the ship," Keene said to Hurley. "Look for Umarov and the woman. I think she has Eileen."

"Where's Harding?" Hurley hollered at Peterson.

Peterson ejected a mag and put in her last one. "Harding went down below. Hasn't come back. It's deadly quiet up there," she said motioning to the stateroom above the bridge. "I think Umarov's dead."

"The woman's down there," Hurley said.

"Whoa, whoa. Stop. Back up." She nodded her head toward the back of the ship. They both knew about the back ladders. "Get behind her. I'll keep her busy from here."

Hurley ran for the rear access, took the ladder down, and waited for Peterson to get in place in front. She took the last step down.

Silk saw her and tightened her grip on Eileen.

"Look," Peterson said. "Speak English? Let her go. She's done nothing. We can figure this out. What do you need?"

"Need? International Line is all."

"What do you mean? What's your name?"

Silk wouldn't fall for that. No names.

"I need to be out of this country. Beyond International Line. You can't stop this now."

Peterson said, "No, you're home free. We are twelve miles out. Just let me have the girl."

Eileen squirmed lower in Silk's grasp.

"Hey," Silk said to Eileen. "Don't be stupid."

Eileen dropped her left side slightly then drove upward as if she was on springs. Her right shoulder moved like a machine, jacking the woman's gun hand away from Eileen's head. The gun went off. The bullet whistled by Hurley's head, uncomfortably close, but Peterson saw the compromised position and dove for the woman's gun. As she did, the woman fired a second shot and the bullet caught Peterson above the knee, but she got her hands on the gun and wrestled it away from Silk. Hurley, moving at the same instant, smothered the woman and Eileen. Peterson rolled to her back in agony, her arms wrapped around her wounded knee.

Keene thought he heard a scream. He left the captain on the bridge with an unspoken agreement that the unarmed man had a vested interest in the safety of the ship, as did Keene himself. Keene ran forward, down the wide stairs to the end of the hall. The woman was under Hurley. Harding had Eileen by the shoulders. Peterson was hurt. Keene fingered his mic. "Officer down; officer down!" Instantly, he heard the wash of helicopter blades—Coast Guard, he thought. Other operators were at work. Charlie Riordan was making things happen. But in these rolling swells and these gale-force winds, the helicopter was useless to Peterson. Or at least it would be a difficult maneuver to load the patient. Getting her on the police boat seemed a much better option. He dropped to a knee.

"My leg is on fire," Peterson said to Keene.

"Okay. There's a lot of blood." He looked around the scene. Hurley had the small woman in cuffs. Eileen was okay, none the worse.

"I'm feeling a little lightheaded," Peterson said.

"Oh, shit. A lot of blood loss." Keene whipped his belt off and tightened it around Peterson's leg. He knew the chopper could life-flight her directly to the hospital. Above the knee meant the base of the femoral artery might have been hit. If not the femoral, then several smaller arteries at the knee that bleed nearly as badly. The police boat would have an EMT and supplies on board. Getting Peterson onto the boat would be a hairy maneuver itself. They were nearly twelve miles from shore and there would be nothing quick about the voyage. No. It had to be the helicopter. The Coast Guard chopper would have some supplies, too, including a better tourniquet. He fingered his mic and asked for a little advice.

The Coast Guard told him they had already dropped a rescue basket including rubber tubing to stop the bleeding. How many personnel were available to secure the patient? The police boat hadn't been able to tie up to the *Ice Cold*, the swells were too much. Keene had Hurley, Harding, and Eileen to work with.

Hurley cuffed the dark-haired woman to the railing of the sweeping staircase.

Keene said, "Eileen, you and Harding go to the fourth deck and secure the rescue basket. It's probably swinging pretty hard. It'll take a lot of muscle to control it, but you gotta do it."

"Got it," they said in unison.

"Hurley, we gotta get Peterson up these stairs. She's lost a lot of blood."

Keene could not wait any longer. They had to move. They worked out how to carry Peterson. Keene would get under her shoulders and Hurley would carry her from the knees. They realized the impossibility of that when the radio sounded.

"Keene, it's Charlie. Eileen and Harding are unclipping the basket. They'll bring it below-decks to you. Load Peterson into it like a litter and carry her that way."

"Roger that."

Hurley said, "He's right. We should wait."

"Every second she loses blood, Hurley. We gotta..." Keene honestly didn't know what to do. Hurley was right, of course.

Hurley said again, "We need to wait."

Keene said, "Yeah. We'll carry her up in the basket. Better to keep her heart level with or below the wound."

Eileen and Harding brought the rescue basket down the stairs.

Eileen took Peterson's head. The ship pitched and dropped from beneath them. Eileen fell forward, nearly crashing into Peterson.

"Diane, can you hear me?" Hurley asked.

She nodded lethargically while Keene removed his belt from her leg. He took the new rubber tourniquet from the Coast Guard litter and expertly tied it above the wound. The bleeding slowed.

Hurley said, "Diane, I won the coin toss, so I decided to take your butt 'cause it's so cute." He slid his hands under her. Keene carefully took her knees, and Harding secured her feet.

Keene counted to three. They lifted and moved her to the basket, then carried her slowly up the wide staircase. The fourth deck was awash with swirling downdraft from the helicopter. The harness was spinning. The rain came in sheets. Keene grabbed the reinforced carabiner clip and secured it to each latch at the ends of the basket. As the *Ice Cold* lifted on a swell then dropped, the harness pulled taut then slackened again and again. There was a turnbuckle above the carabiner about the size of a large coffee mug.

"Jesus!" Keene groaned to no one in particular. "Is this gonna hold?"

Eileen yelled, "They do this all the time, Detective."

"Yeah, yeah. Okay," and he gave a thumbs-up to the Coast Guard officer hanging halfway out of the chopper.

They waited for a swell to drop, the harness became taut, and the chopper lifted. Peterson rose past them as the rescue basket began turning in the wash of the chopper's blades with the wind contravening the wash. Keene and Hurley had to twist to avoid being struck by the rising litter. The basket began to spin counterclockwise like a propeller. Keene knew the spinning was out of control and couldn't imagine how to stop it. The turnbuckle that attached the cable to the basket was designed with a universal joint that allowed the freedom for the spin, probably expedient at most times, but it was disastrous on board the *Ice Cold* in the middle of a hurricane. The more the blade-wash of the aircraft countered the blow of the storm, the more the basket, with Diane in it, spun. The chopper pilot lowered the basket into the lee—in essence, the wind shadow created by the bridge. The spinning slowed.

"They can't hoist her on board with the basket spinning like that," Hurley said.

Keene just watched. He couldn't say a thing that would help.

The chopper lifted and lowered the basket a couple of times, and the device spun in and out of control. The minute the basket rose above the level of the ship's bridge, it began spinning again, and the closer it was to the ship's deck, the slower it spun. The pilot took the chopper as low as he dared, but with the ship bucking like a bull, he could get no closer. The possibility of a quick lift seemed out of the question.

They tried again. They hauled the basket up, and the spinning started immediately and was instantly out of control, much too fast. The chopper lowered the basket again trying to get Peterson out of the wash, trying to slow the litter, but it continued.

Riordan said on the radio, "What's going on? We can't see what's happening. Why's it taking so long?"

He sounded on the verge of hysteria, and Keene thought charitably, *How could he not be?* Keene fingered his mic. "The basket started spinning. They gotta get it back in control. The wind is working against the blade wash, and the litter just spins." He thought of Diane in there. Spinning. Out of control. Aw, Jesus. He said, "She's lost a lot of blood."

"Cripe sake," Eileen said. "They gotta get going." She thought about the spinning and that it was simply a matter of opposing forces, how the atmospheric low pressure of the hurricane was being influenced by the concurrent down pressure created by the helicopter's blades. Just the right pair of vectors to set the rescue basket spinning. She'd been reading up on the physics of spinning and energy, and if her theories were right, if she could summon the correct psychic energy, she might be able to stop that goddamned basket. With her mind. She concentrated. Her mind was strong, the strongest part of her body. Eileen could make this work. Inside the mysterious cavern of her brain, she knew she had the energy.

Keene couldn't take it, without anything to do or add, no way to help. He looked at Hurley gazing upward, powerless, his shirttails flying in the breeze, his hair blown straight away from his scalp; Harding the same minus the hair. Keene glanced at Eileen and was struck. Her eyes were closed and she looked serene, almost blissful, amid the rest who were embattled by the storm and circumstances.

Keene believed in physics and order, and he believed that most human observations have a simple explanation. We understand why the sun rises and sets and why the seasons change more or less quarterly. Weather is weather. We get it. However, he would go to his grave believing that what happened next was real, and, though inexplicable, he observed it and would report it to whoever would listen.

Eileen's pink hair lay down on her shoulders as still and undisturbed as if she was standing inside Sully's. It seemed as if the wind wasn't blowing at all, as if nature wasn't throwing a tantrum. She stood still among the others on the deck of the yacht, the rest staggering and bracing against the hurricane. Clothing slapped around them, at once plastered against their bodies and then flying away. She, however, smiled, her face serene and her T-shirt fluttering as if in a mild breeze. Suddenly, she opened her eyes and stared directly at Keene, her eyes clear and sparkling. Then she looked at the basket which was suspended just above them and wordlessly told Keene to gaze at the litter as well. He didn't know how he understood her direction, but he did. Keene was nearly overcome by a feeling of good, an ebullience that was out of place, and he no longer staggered. He felt a heavy arc of air holding him in place. Even in the maelstrom, the pressure flowed from Eileen to the rescue basket to him. Just then, the chopper crew lifted the litter tentatively through the trough of inexplicably calm air, through the blade wash, despite the blade wash. At last, the crew had control over the rescue basket, and they hoisted Diane quickly away from Eileen and Keene. The detective and the pink-haired girl watched the litter rise and saw the Coast Guard crewman secure the basket under the chopper as the pilot hit the throttle. The aircraft sped toward shore, nose down, props tilted forward, basket secure. Keene caught Eileen's eyes and, as she and the detective staggered again like the rest, she gave him a double thumbs-up and she hollered into the wind. Keene couldn't hear her, but he didn't have to read lips to know what she had yelled.

"They got her!" Keene shouted into the wind.

Later there would be debate about what happened. Many would agree with the pilot of the chopper, who was a reasonable man, a man of science. He would claim the eye of the hurricane passed directly through the scene. For an instant everything calmed, there could be no other explanation. Other weather watchers would observe that the eye had slipped by forty miles to the south and an hour earlier, and that it was a large eye that calmed the scene for well over fifteen minutes. Keene knew. Eileen knew. The power of the mind is awesome.

CHAPTER
50

B asil Keene started for the bridge. The swells had grown to mountains. The *Ice Cold* climbed one side as Keene lurched forward. At the peak of the wave, the ship suddenly leveled and Keene made a run for it. Then the ship dived and surfed the back side of the wave and Keene lost his balance and slammed to the deck. He considered making the last twenty feet on his hands and knees, but the ship was moving uphill again and he staggered the last few feet to the bridge. He found the captain, still sitting, hands on the wheel, the electronic chart on the monitor. He looked around at Keene and stared at him wordlessly.

Keene peered at the monitor and said, "You're going to turn the ship around, captain." He leveled his gun and said, "Now." It was the first time he'd been required to point a gun at a human since he'd shot the killer on the Eastern Prom. He felt fine. No problem whatsoever.

"You won't shoot me," the captain said. "Is twelve miles. International waters. You'd be tried for murder in an international court. I will not turn the boat around."

"We're right here," Keene said and indicated a point on the chart that was just beyond twelve miles from shore. He pointed to Quoddy Head on the chart, then moved the cursor with the mouse and scrolled out. The Massachusetts coast came into view. He pointed to Race Point on Cape Cod. "This is the accepted International Line, captain." The imaginary line drawn between the two points was very real in international maritime law. "My jurisdiction ends there. You're under arrest."

Keene cuffed the captain, who made him aware of another practical problem: how to navigate back to Casco Bay without his expertise in guiding this ship.

Keene looked at the anemometer. The wind was blowing out of the northeast, meaning the hurricane was beyond them, but they were sailing directly into her. Melody's severe effects were hitting the ship hard. The wind was blowing a sustained 35 knots. It gusted to 60 while Keene monitored the instrument. The wave height reached thirty feet. The ocean was a hot mess.

"Charlie, it's Keene. I gotta turn this bitch around. These waves are going to..." He wasn't entirely sure how to handle this sort of wave. "They're gonna make this tricky. I can do it, I think. But I can't bring her into the harbor. I don't know what she draws. I wouldn't know how to drive her, you know? Get the pilot out here."

A pilot service exists to bring ships into the pilots' home ports. Tankers, cruise ships, and freighters, even naval vessels, rely on the local pilot to navigate the tricky waters of their home harbor. Portland is no different. The transfer of the pilot from a launch to the ship in calm waters is fine and well-practiced, but under these conditions, in the swells of a passing hurricane, virtually impossible.

"Keene, the pilot says he can take the ship if you get her into the mouth of the harbor. He says to get her to Junk of Pork and he can take over. You know where that is?"

"I'll get her there," Keene said. "The navigational instruments seem state-of-the-art. There's an electronic chart. Once I get her turned around, I can navigate there." The problem, he thought, is getting her turned around and remaining upright in the bathtub. The reassurance in his voice had been as much for himself as for Riordan.

He maintained the set course up the wall of the immediate swell. When he reached the crest, he turned a tick to the port side. He navigated the face of the wave to the trough like a surfboard, at an angle, then shifted the bow again to the left. He climbed the next wave at an angle and did the same on the peak and the same in the trough. After several of these graded turns, the *Ice Cold* was nearly parallel with the waves, broadside to their pounding, which he recognized as the moment of truth. Gravity defeats buoyancy at a specific point on any ship. It's called the degree of roll, and Keene had seen its disastrous effects in a Coast Guard safety course. He was in a trough and chose the next crest to expose the ship to the waves and its potential final roll. The ship climbed at a drastic, dangerous angle, then he turned the wheel hard. The water below the boat surged against the keel and grabbed it, twisting the ship to list hard toward the weather. The water was trying to spin the *Ice Cold* like a log in a stream.

Keene turned the wheel hard to the port, as far as she'd go. He leaned into it even though common sense told him that more effort on the helm would have no more effect. The entire ship leaned dangerously to starboard, and she side-slipped down the back of the wave. Keene had neglected to calculate the energy profile of a wave. As the ship rolled, he thought of a curling breaker that surfers search the world for. The energy on the windward side is predictably greater than on the leeward side, resulting in the cascading curl. As the *Ice Cold* was fully ninety degrees to the wave, she was in tremendous peril. The starboard window of the bridge plunged into the cold water of the Atlantic as it rose to meet the ship in the following wave.

The yacht was nearly on her side. Rolling, rolling too far, too close to her degree of roll. The ship's buoyancy pushed against gravity, trying to right the ship as gravity tried to sink her. As the competing forces met, something had to give. The windows on the bridge bulged. Gravity needed just one break in the ship's design, and Keene knew if the windows blew it would be all over. They would go down.

He tried to spin the wheel back to starboard and turn the bow back toward the wind, perhaps his last chance to save her. He experimentally turned the wheel in the opposite direction and discovered the rudder had no purchase. There is green water, white water, and black. They were in white water, the rudder effectively out of water, the surf was breaking and full of air. He needed green, water with integrity. Black was not an option. Black meant you were underwater. Sinking.

The captain slid across the floor of the bridge, out of control with his hands cuffed behind him. His skull smashed into the starboard wall of the bridge.

"Uncuff me, you fool!" he screamed above the noise of the roaring wind and the waves crashing green over the side. "Straighten the wheel and reverse the engines!"

Keene knew he couldn't let go of the wheel to uncuff the man, but he followed the captain's other orders. The ship backed into the powerful energy of the wave, the bow turned one more degree to port, the upside of the wave. This angled the broadside of the ship away from the damaging energy of the windward side of the swell, away from the rolling influence of the sea, and the ship flattened temporarily. He clicked around with the wheel; each degree of turn brought him farther away from the dangerous degree of roll. Finally, Keene had the *Ice Cold* climbing and surfing toward home. They weren't entirely out of danger, as rogue waves had been known to catch a surfing boat and drive her nose-first into the sea, the offended ship either popping back like a cork or turtling and sinking straightaway.

The captain said, "You did good job. Now, uncuff me." When Keene hesitated, the captain said, "I'm not going to try to turn her around." He held his cuffs in front of him.

Keene uncuffed him and said, "Don't try anything. You're still under arrest."

"I don't understand how you didn't capsize us. Amazing."

Junk of Pork was a fancifully named deserted rocky island at the outer limit of Casco Bay. The Russian said, "We make for Junk of Pork, yes? This is bearing you make?"

"Yeah," Keene said. Keene steered the ship toward the island with the police boat accompanying her, and the wave height had diminished to six feet. Flat, in a relative sense.

He turned the ship's radio to the frequency the pilots used. He raised them and gave them their position. Fifteen minutes later, a small boat would pull alongside the *Ice Cold* and sound a signal and call Keene. But first, Keene had some unfinished business.

"Take the helm," he said to the captain. "Don't do anything stupid. Make two-hundred-sixty degrees."

"Da," the seaman said.

Keene pulled his service weapon and stole across the deck looking toward the stateroom above the bridge. He kept his back against the wall and sidled like that to the ladder to Umarov's cabin. He climbed quickly and quietly. He ducked below the window. The door was unlocked. He turned the handle and pushed the door. Nothing.

"Umarov? Portland PD."

Nothing.

"I'm coming in. Drop your weapon."

With each moment, Keene was surer that the man was dead. He allowed the door to swing open all the way, and there was still nothing from inside the cabin. Keene pushed his back against the door and finally turned his body inward. The oligarch and his brains occupied the same space only in a marginal sense. The human trafficking bastard was dead.

Keene walked back to the bridge, sure now that there were no more threats on the ship. He stepped into the wheelhouse. The captain was maintaining the course Keene had established for Junk of Pork. He put his hand to his cheek feeling for a hot itch below his right eye. He discovered the splinter he'd forgotten. His hand came away, pink with watery blood.

The radio came to life. "There is a rope ladder they stow under the rail next to the power plant door on the first deck," the pilot said. "I brought her in when they first arrived. Is there any crew left?"

"The captain."

The pilot said, "Can he help? Or is he being detained?"

Keene said, "We can get the ladder to you without his help." As Keene said this, he handcuffed the Russian again.

The moon, no longer shrouded by Melody's remnants, shone and the swells had moderated. Keene didn't know if it was the lee of the shore or Melody's declining influence as she pushed farther out to sea, but he was happy to have a steadier ship underfoot.

"Hurley, where's Eileen?"

Hurley said, "Right behind me. She found that the workout machines were anchored down. We all held onto them for our lives."

"Literally," Eileen said as she came out of the stair's bulkhead with Harding.

Harding said, "I've never been through anything like that."

"None of us have, partner," Hurley reminded him. "What the heck happened?"

"I don't need to tell you that the farther out we got, the worse the weather got. Turning the ship around was a precarious maneuver. We almost lost her. Where's the woman, Silk?"

"She's cuffed to a workout machine," Hurley said.

"Keene?" Charlie Riordan called on the radio. "We're coming aboard."

"Any word on Peterson?" Keene asked immediately.

"They tell us it was a rough ride. She's in surgery. I don't know anything else. It wasn't life-threatening until..." Riordan trailed off.

"Is it life-threatening now?" Keene barked.

"I don't know, Basil. One thing at a time."

The police boat was at the rope ladder by now, and Keene and Hurley met Arnaud on the first deck. She was halfway up the ladder. Keene gave her a hand over the rail.

"Take custody of the woman; she's cuffed to a workout machine in there." He pointed to the gym. "Her name's Silk Something."

Hurley handed the cuffs key to Arnaud.

"Silk? Okay," Arnaud said dully from the bubble at the back of her throat. Then, "We lost you out there. We had to turn around. I thought you guys were goners."

"So did I," Keene said.

"You did?" Harding said.

"Hey, you gotta get down to the police boat," Keene said. "Get fixed up."

"Where's Umarov? I need to see him. This," he nodded to his shoulder, "is nothing. Not like it's a sucking chest wound."

Arnaud led Silk through the passageway.

Harding asked Silk, "Where's Umarov? Is he dead?"

Silk said nothing.

Keene said, "You want to make sure? Because I guarantee you a man separated from his brains like Umarov is, is sincerely dead."

Sandblaster hopped over the rail and said, "Be careful. This is my crime scene. You guys probably already corrupted it touching everything in sight. Am I right?"

"Yeah, yeah. We've already touched the stateroom doors. We're just going to take a walk through and make sure we touch everything." Keene said to Harding and Hurley, "Let's go."

Harding pulled something from a pocket, his badge wallet. He flipped it open and said to Sandblaster, "Hang on, Mr. Sanblasio. This is a federal investigation."

So much for keeping your enemies close, Keene thought.

Eileen said, "I'm coming."

Keene said in measured tones, "No, you're not, you're climbing down to the police boat."

"Cripe sake, Detective. I just wanna see what I might have been in for."

"When we get back from Umarov's stateroom, you can join us below. I don't want you to see that shit."

"Detective, I watched it happen," she said.

Keene took her by the shoulder gently and said, "I'll need a statement." Then he said, "Are you okay? Are you good?"

"Just a little wet," she said.

Harding knelt by the body as a new beat of helicopter rotors approached. "I can't believe I'm looking at him. We've been chasing him like a ghost in the wind."

"Literally," Hurley said.

The two men looked at him.

Self-consciously he said, "You know, the wind part?"

"Yeah," Keene said. "Let's let Sandblaster have a go at him."

"No," a clipped voice from behind said. "He's ours." Three men entered the cabin and told the rest to get out. "We'll take it from here, Harding. Good work."

"What the—? Who are you?" Keene asked, his voice drowned by chopper wash.

The biggest of the three men escorted Hurley and Keene out. Not one of them answered Keene's question.

Harding said to the Feds, "I'm going to check the rest of the ship." He left with Hurley and Keene. When they had gotten beyond the beat of the rotors, Harding said, "Sorry, guys. But, you know, orders are orders."

Keene thought Harding sounded sheepish, and of course, he'd never liked the little man.

Eileen joined them and they went from room to room, the detectives reviewing what they'd already seen now in greater detail. There was a total of one hundred and twenty beds in fourteen rooms, Suites One through Fifteen. No Suite Thirteen. *Sailors*, Keene thought, *superstitious lot.* They found and secured an uncounted amount of cash in Suite Six. Counting it would not be an easy chore. The currency was well used and in denominations of hundreds and smaller. Let the Feds have at it. They found jeans and bourbon and cigarettes in other rooms. There were cameras mounted at the underwater observation windows for the pools. There were other cameras mounted in various positions in Umarov's suite. It appeared some filming was to start during the journey back from Caracas.

Harding said, "All the makings of a parallel economy. American goods and US cash."

"The captain verified that Caracas was Umarov's destination," Keene said.

"Yes," Harding said. "You were right, Basil."

"You can call me Detective Keene," the detective said curtly.

After a brief pause, Harding continued, "Umarov provided Venezuela with the economic necessities for the privileged few while Maduro traded away the one renewable resource he still controlled—the youth. Young women in this case."

Eileen said, "That's exactly what he said. He also said he was going to make me a porn star."

"He was buying women?" Hurley asked. "He was a human trafficker?"

"We've seen this out of some of the Eastern European countries. Girls are kidnapped and never seen again."

"The sex trade," Harding said. "Prostitution. Porn. Who knows what else?"

"Cripe sake, that could have been me."

A uniformed cop came up the stairs to the third deck and asked where the second subject was.

"Cuffed on the bridge with the pilot," Keene said. "I'll come with you."

"I'm going to the police boat," Harding said. "This thing is getting sore."

Keene and the uniform went to the bridge. Keene secured the captain for the cop to take into custody. He stood next to the pilot, watching the bow cut the water that he and Melena sailed frequently. He watched Ram Island pass on the starboard side. There were many times on the *Ventosa* when he'd had to observe the rules of navigation. The smaller vessel concedes the right-of-way to a larger ship like the *Ice Cold*, and Keene would wonder: *Who would own such a ship? What personality type needs such a toy?* Portland Head Light, one of the most photographed scenes in America, splashed by on the port side. House Island on the starboard.

The pilot said, "The captain told me what you did out there. Sounds like you saved this ship."

Keene thought for a moment and said, "I couldn't have done it without him."

"He said that, too. But he said it was a rare guy who could have pulled it off. Like you were a natural or something."

"I don't know," Keene muttered and thought how he and Melena had considered vacationing out among the offshore islands this week because of the fish-kill and he shivered. "I'm just glad I wasn't out here in my boat."

"Yeah, well an experienced blue-water captain was impressed with your handling of this ship under pretty challenging conditions," the pilot said. He pulled back the throttle and feathered the rudder and turned the wheel. He brought the ship to a virtual standstill. Then he dropped the anchor. They were a few hundred yards to the northeast of the island fort, Fort Gorges. "A launch will be out for you guys. Wild ride, eh, Detective?"

"Yeah," Keene said. "Wild ride."

CHAPTER
51

Squirrel's-nest Pete sat at the bar and said, "Hey, Eileen, what'd you do last night?"

"Nothing; you?"

"Hey, Ei," John said, taking a seat and loosening the ever-present tie. "Bud." But there was a dripping bottle already in front of him. "What did you do last night?"

Eileen was popping a Bud for Paul as he took his seat, and she said to John, "Nothing; you?"

Paul said, "Hey, Ei, do anything last night?"

Eileen said to herself, *Is this a joke?*

John said, "We heard all about it. Are you okay?"

"Yeah," she said. "I'm okay."

"Kinda surprised you're in tonight." The squirrel's nest crackled when Pete spoke.

"Gary told me to take the night off, but I figured, why? You know? Besides, I need the money."

Basil Keene watched Melena kneel in the bow while the *Ventosa*'s teak deck shimmered and the stays vibrated and the engine's cooling water splattered into the bay. He stood at the wheel casting a sharp eye around the anchorage, and he nudged the throttle. As the boat inched forward Keene saw Melena slip the pickup buoy under the pulpit rail and hold it by its flagged wand, allowing the line to stretch out and out. She played the mooring rope until she knew when to toss the float; they had done this often as a team and Keene knew her exact timing. They worked the boat without conversation.

He watched his wife of twenty years step the length of the boat back to the cockpit to join him. How smart he was to have married her.

"Cocktail?" she asked. A question that didn't require an answer.

The diesel turned its lazy rpms and pushed the *Ventosa* across the bay that bore no resemblance to the sea of a few nights earlier.

Melena went below and he heard the snap-fizz of tonic. He steered the boat around the last of the moored boats in the harbor and pushed the throttle forward. The slapping of water on *Ventosa*'s bow felt like worry being washed away and problems being shed like dead skin. It was a later start than they had wanted, but the good news was, the high tides and the swells of the storm had flushed the rotting fish out to sea, and the Keenes' new vacation plan included this first night in Cundy's Harbor, a leisurely three-hour sail. He planned to take the *Ventosa* just beyond Clapboard Island and then raise the sails.

Melena rose from the galley with a board of hors d'oeuvres and a tray of cocktails. She set it all on the folding table Keene had fashioned out of mahogany a few winters earlier. After all was secured, she handed him a gin and tonic and lifted hers and said, "To vacation. Finally."

He said, "To us," and they both took a healthy drink. "Vacation. Late but not never."

Melena said, "It's four already. How did it get so late so soon? It's already four before it's noon. Oh my, how the time has flewn." She giggled at herself and said, "Dr. Seuss. It's something like that."

They laughed together; she'd always made him laugh. They drank and she pointed out the osprey nest that she always pointed out and said she thought she saw a white head poke out, which was also what she always said.

Keene said, "I saw Diane at the Bricks. She's feeling much better. She looks good, all things considered." And she had smelled great, like melon or cucumber or maybe a salad of both. "She lost a lot of weight."

"She didn't have it to lose. Did Harding offer her the job?"

Harding had told Peterson when they had dinner at the Olive Garden that she had the skill set to join him at the Financial Crimes Enforcement Network. He had the authority to offer her a job.

"Yeah, he offered. She declined. Said she wants to stay in Portland. Likes the 'vibe.'"

After a moment she said, "How's Charlie?"

"Pulling his hair out." Keene steered the *Ventosa* around the tip of Clapboard and into the channel the tankers navigated to exit through Hussey's Sound.

Then Keene said, "Charlie told me the Senator rescheduled a Portland visit for next month."

"Aw, poor Charlie."

"He'll get through it. He already has most of the work done. I'm pretty sure with all that's happened, if he can manage the Senator's visit, they'll give him the Chief's job."

Keene asked Melena to take the helm and steer into the wind. The lines clacked against the aluminum mast until he took the main halyard and raised the sail, flapping lazily in the light breeze. When it was almost fully up, he wrapped the winch three times and raised it the rest of the way using the winch handle until the leading edge was taut as a drum at the mast.

"Okay," he said, looking back at his wife. "You can fall off." She was already turning the bow away from the wind which filled the sail and the *Ventosa* gained way. Keene adjusted the sail to optimize its efficiency. He sat and squeezed a tube of Vitamin E cream on his finger and massaged the scar below his right eye. Dr. Flint recommended the cream to minimize the scarring. Keene had refrained from calling him Dr. Skin Flint because the doc was still a dick.

Melena killed the engine. There's no such thing as silence on a sailboat; something always makes noise. When there is wind, the stays that support the mast hum. When there's no wind, the halyards slap. Water spanks the hull while under way and raps rhythmically in the night. But the moment the engine stops and the wind takes over and the boat races along influenced by the vectors of physics alone, there is a momentary illusion of complete and utter silence and neither of the Keenes wanted to break the spell. They sailed in the relative hush, content with their wordless and soundless conversation. Melena steered past the theoretical point where the *Ice Cold* had pulled at her anchor for most of the summer. The Feds had towed the yacht from Casco Bay to waters unknown. Melena fell farther off the wind and made a course for the northern reaches of Casco Bay.

"It's horrible to think of Eileen disappearing into Umarov's world, isn't it?" Melena said after a long while. "It gives me shivers." Melena lifted her drink from the built-in holder near the wheel and wrapped her hands around it.

"Eileen turns eighteen in a couple of weeks. Gary's gonna have a party for her." Keene sipped his cocktail. "There's something I wanted to talk to you about."

"Yeah?"

"She—Eileen—wants to go to college. Her parents. Well, her father, Francis, doesn't have a pot to piss in. I was thinking maybe we could help her out. Maybe?"

"Sounds important to you."

"She's a special kid. She's...she's something else." There was something about Eileen that Keene would always be in awe of. Was she the daughter he and Melena never had? "Yeah, something special."

Melena didn't respond right away.

Keene attended to the jib that was rolled in on the roller-reef, a mechanism not unlike a window shade. He loosened the windward line and allowed the sail to pay out with the wind and fill.

Melena said, "Yes. Maybe she could do some work for us or something."

Work? Keene thought. *What kind of work?* He decided to change the conversation.

"Harding told Charlie that Silk is talking."

Melena said, "Will she be tried for killing Grogan and Troiano?"

"Eventually. She killed DeLuca, too. Eileen watched her do it. But the Feds get her first."

"Why?"

"Just the way it is. This time. But she'll have to answer for as many as five killings eventually." He was convinced she had done Grogan and Troiano, but all the evidence at this point was circumstantial. Not good enough for a jury. He was sure she had killed the Iskakov brothers. But again, he had a lot of work to do before making the case for those two. He wrapped the jib sheet around the winch. "We got her dead certain on DeLuca. Another drink?"

Melena said, "Sure, but I'm just having sparkling water. With a lime."

Keene returned with the drinks. "She told Harding that the cop impersonator was Yakov Iskakov. She said he killed his brother, too, Nurzhan, who she was close to. Maybe in love with. Harding doesn't believe her on that one. Why would Yakov kill Nurzhan?"

"Maybe it was a love triangle. Both brothers were in love with her. How romantic."

"Yeah, right. Who knows? When I get back, I'll lead that investigation. We want to take her down, but it's going to be a lot of work."

"When do you take the sergeant's exam again?"

Keene thought a bit before he said, "A thing like the other night, a near-death experience, makes you think. Hurley's moving in with Michaela; doesn't want to lose her. Eileen's gonna go to college. Diane's going to settle down in Portland. I don't know if I'll take the exam after all. Wouldn't have made a difference out there getting the *Ice Cold* back. It isn't that important to me right now. I know I can do the job." He always had; he'd simply needed the opportunity to prove that he could handle it on his terms.

They drank quietly, and after a while, Melena voiced a declarative sentence that, despite its self-evidence, was meant to be said: "We're on vacation." She threw her head back to catch the longer rays of the end-of-day sun.

They continued toward Cundy's Harbor, cruising outside Great Chebeague Island. They had a lot of open water through which to sail quietly. Melena sipped her water and Keene drank his G&T. The wind was coming out of the southeast the way it does in the summer on Casco Bay. Melena wondered if now would be a good time to break her news. Or should she tell him in the middle of the vacation? Or the end? It was *their* news, she needed to share it immediately. But how? She'd never been in this position. She had alluded to the change in their family makeup earlier. He hadn't taken the bait. What kind of work could Eileen do for them? Baby-sitting, of course.

She said, "Basil?"

"Yeah?"

"Don't you think it's a good thing for a kid to grow up with a dog?"

ACKNOWLEDGMENTS

In the truest sense of the word, I must acknowledge the greatest gift from my parents, which was to bring me up in a reading household, among a thoughtful family who had articulate discussions on many subjects. There is no greater gift. My mother was a reader and my father, a storyteller. I am an author.

Many thanks are due to many without whom *Hunger Hill* would not have been possible. Thanks to my early readers, Linda Gifford, Gilly Hitchcock, Tina Turgelsky, Jean Driscoll, and the insightful John Wells. Thanks to my wife, Cynthia Baker, who read this book over and over and offered astute advice and even wants to read it again. Thanks to our many friends who have supported me in my progress on this book and other projects through the years. Thank you immensely to my talented friend Elise Bolduc, who created the exquisite cover for the book, putting to rest the admonition against judging a book by its outward appearance. Special thanks are due to Gwen and Celine Baker, who have put up with Dad's incessant yacking about the book. The book, the book, always with the book!

Picasso said artists are thieves—a quote he stole from a guy named C.E.M. Joad—and I must acknowledge all the great, excellent, and mediocre writers I've stolen from over the years. Simply by reading. I hope easy access to digital media encourages authors to write and readers to read. I trust the media won't have the opposite effect of scuttling the written word. Here's to the continued success of the traditionally printed book.

ABOUT THE AUTHOR

Philip C. Baker is a graduate of Colby College. He has traveled to five continents and driven over a million miles. He managed a drill rig in Nevada, prospecting for gold. He searched for precious minerals in California, Arizona, New Mexico, and Utah. He has sold sporting goods and wheels and snow-and-ice management products in New England. He grew up in Falmouth, Maine, sailing on Casco Bay and enjoying the land where it meets the sea. He now lives in southern Maine with his family and two rescued beagles who find great sport in growling at blowing leaves, barking at squirrels, and, of course, baying at the moon.